"THERE'S BEEN A

Charley froze. All t

evaporate in an instant. She didn't have to ask what "another one" meant.

And it sent a chill through her heart.

The voice on the other end of the receiver belonged to assistant director George Kelly's secretary. The woman was calling on his behalf to inform the special agents assigned to the serial killer task force that another victim had been claimed by the monster who was laying siege to the southland.

Charley pushed back her hair from her forehead. *Damn it, anyway.* "When?"

"They found the body this morning. It's believed she was killed sometime yesterday. Kelly wants to hold a meeting as soon as possible."

Yesterday. Sunday. The same day her sister had been killed. The same day all the victims had been killed. She was beginning to hate Sundays.

Dear Reader,

It's hard to believe that the Signature Select program is one year old—with seventy-two books already published by top Harlequin and Silhouette authors.

What an exciting and varied lineup we have in the year ahead! In the first quarter of the year, the Signature Spotlight program offers three very different reading experiences. Popular author Marie Ferrarella, well-known for her warm family-centered romances, has gone in quite a different direction to write a story that has been "haunting her" for years. Please check out *Sundays Are for Murder* in January. Hop aboard a Caribbean cruise with Joanne Rock in *The Pleasure Trip* in February, and don't miss a trademark romantic suspense from Debra Webb, *Vows of Silence*, in March.

Our collections in the first quarter of the year explore a variety of contemporary themes. Our Valentine's collection—*Write It Up!*— homes in on the trend of alternative dating in three stories by Elizabeth Bevarly, Tracy Kelleher and Mary Leo. February is awards season, and Barbara Bretton, Isabel Sharpe and Emilie Rose join the fun and glamour in *And the Envelope, Please*.... And in March, Leslie Kelly, Heather MacAllister and Cindi Myers have penned novellas about women desperate enough to go to *Bootcamp* to learn how *not* to scare men away!

Three original sagas also come your way in the first quarter of this year. Silhouette author Gina Wilkins spins off her popular FAMILY FOUND miniseries in *Wealth Beyond Riches*. Janice Kay Johnson has written a powerful story of a tortured past in *Dead Wrong*, which is connected to her PATTON'S DAUGHTERS Superromance miniseries, and Kathleen O'Brien gives a haunting story of mysterious murder in *Quiet as the Grave*.

And don't forget there is original bonus material in every single Signature Select book to give you the inside scoop on the creative process of your favorite authors! We hope you enjoy all our new offerings!

Marsha Zinberg

Marsha Zinberg
Executive Editor
The Signature Select Program

SPOTLIGHT

MARIE
FERRARELLA

Sundays Are
for Murder

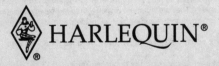

HARLEQUIN®

TORONTO • NEW YORK • LONDON
AMSTERDAM • PARIS • SYDNEY • HAMBURG
STOCKHOLM • ATHENS • TOKYO • MILAN • MADRID
PRAGUE • WARSAW • BUDAPEST • AUCKLAND

ISBN 0-373-83687-2

SUNDAYS ARE FOR MURDER

www.eHarlequin.com

Printed in U.S.A.

Dear Reader,

You know how you sometimes get a song, or more often, a lyric, stuck in your head and it follows you around for hours, sometimes days, teasing you, haunting you, giving you no peace? Well, that's how it was with *Sundays Are for Murder*. It began as a kernel of an idea, just a hint, and it refused to leave me alone. It begged for development and when I had no time to devote to it, it would just sit back, popping up to haunt me whenever I had a couple of moments to rub together. Unlike bits and pieces of an idea that usually fade when I try to remember them, this story wouldn't go away. It was there every December, my usual "downtime" when I try to catch up on the rest of my life, decorate a ten-foot tree and search for new recipes to try out on my unsuspecting family for Christmas. It became the white elephant in the room, except that no one could see it but me (in that respect, I suppose it was more like Harvey, the six-foot rabbit only James Stewart could see in the movie of the same name). Yes, I've been carrying the story around that long. So, finally, through the grace of Patience Smith, my beloved editor, Marsha Zinberg, executive editor in charge of miracles, and the powers that be, here's the story that wouldn't go away. I hope you find it entertaining (at least there'll be one less place at the table for Christmas this year).

I wish you love,

Marie Ferrarella

To Patience Smith & Patricia Smith
(no relation except for wonderfulness),
for always believing in this,
and to Marsha Zinberg, who let me do it.
You all have my greatest affection.

PROLOGUE

IT WAS TIME.

He could feel it in the air, taste it on his tongue. Every fiber of his body told him that it was time, that it was Sunday. He knew without looking at the calendar, without hearing the thud of the Sunday paper as it landed on his rickety doorstep.

Because only on Sundays did the feeling come.

And it made his palms sweat, his fingers tingle, his loins tighten in anticipation. The need was getting too large to manage.

It was time again.

Sunday was his time to kill. Because only with death did salvation come.

It had to be quick. Before it was too late.

Each Sunday, the feeling grew until close to exploding within his veins. He was just the instrument.

He looked at his reflection and smiled. No one would ever suspect. No one would ever keep him from his work. He looked so kind, so harmless. There was a time when he had been all that. Oh, he hadn't looked like the reflection in the mirror—that had taken time and talent and patience to achieve. But he'd *been* kind, harmless. Eager even. Eager to do the right thing, to be loved.

But all that was before.

Before the betrayal.

Before the need to purge and purify had begun. Before the deaths.

Before he had discovered that he liked it, the feeling of dispensing everlasting redemption. Because it was up to him to make it right. His father had seen to that. It was because of his father that the calling had come to him. The calling to set troubled souls free.

The calling came now.

He took a deep breath and began the ritual.

Because Sundays were for murder. And redemption.

CHAPTER ONE

STACY PEMBROKE WAS angry. Very angry at being shoved into second place.

Second place meant runner-up. Nobody ever remembered who came in second in anything. Second place was an insult. And lately, it was a position she was becoming all too familiar with. A position she had been forced to occupy much too often in the last few weeks. Maybe even the last few months if she was being honest with herself.

It was time for Robert to make up his damn mind.

"I don't need this kind of grief," she shouted into the telephone receiver, which she held in a death grip. She was squeezing so hard, if the receiver had had a pulse, it would have been erased by now. "Just who the hell do you think you are, canceling on me at the last minute this way? You think I have nothing better to do than sit around, *waiting* for you to show up on my door?"

The fact that she didn't have anything better to do didn't change her indignation. It was the principle of the whole thing. Robert was taking her for granted, something she had sworn would *never* happen to her. And if by some chance it did happen to her, she'd promised herself to take drastic measures. Like castrating the bastard who was guilty of the crime.

"I'll make it up to you, baby, honest I will."

Stacy fumed. He was whispering. Keeping his voice low so that *she* wouldn't hear him. That harpy of a wife he supposedly hated. If she listened very closely, Stacy could almost hear Robert sweating. He had to be fidgeting, the way he did when he was caught in a lie.

Good. She hoped his damn blood pressure went through the roof, killing him. He deserved it. Nobody treated her like day-old trash and got away with it. For two cents, she'd pay a call to his precious Emily, tell her what her husband had been up to all those nights he'd told her he was working to provide a better future for them.

As she toyed with the thought, her full, freshly made-up lips peeled back into a smile. It would serve him right if she did just that.

"I am through rearranging my life for you, Robert." And she meant it. She was through serving up her heart only to have it carved into small, bite-size pieces. "Now you're obviously not going to leave that frozen Popsicle of a wife—"

On the other end of the line, Robert Pullman drew in a shallow breath. She could hear it. God, but he was a mouse. "I told you, the kids—"

"The kids. The kids. The kids!" Stacy shouted into the receiver, her face turning red, a stark contrast to her ash-blond hair and her all but alabaster skin. It was an effort for her to keep her temper from really breaking free. Her nerves were frayed and strained. These days, she reached the boiling point at lightning speed. But if she finally let go, she knew that she ran the imminent danger of falling completely apart.

If that was going to happen, it would be because

of someone who was a hell of a better catch than Robert Pullman.

But her dwindling opinion of him didn't stop her from verbally assaulting her lover for his transgression. "Don't you think that I want kids of my own?"

Frustration throbbed in his voice. "Stacy, I know. Look, I don't have much time to talk. Emily thinks I'm in the garage, working on a project."

Emily. She'd have thought by now that Emily Pullman, along with her bratty kids, would have been a thing of the past. Hadn't Robert promised her as much? When he couldn't make Christmas last year because he had to take his family on a trip to Lake Tahoe, he'd promised her that this year, they would be ringing in the New Year together. Well, it didn't look as if he was capable of ringing in a Sunday night, much less the New Year.

And she was sick of it.

"I hope to hell that it's a noose to hang yourself with!"

"Honey," Robert pleaded as loudly as a whisper would allow. "I know you're mad—"

"Mad?" Stacy scoffed. "Mad? I am way past mad, Robert. I rounded the corner at 'furious' a long time ago. But you know what? I just don't care anymore."

"You don't mean that."

"The hell I don't. You've stood me up for the last time. I'm having a cleansing bonfire tonight. I'm going to burn all the things you gave me—and the clothes you left here," she added as the idea took on breadth and form. She knew how particular Robert was about his clothing, how everything had to be hung up just so. Well, she was going to take extra pleasure in stomping on all of it before she sent the articles to their final resting place. "As far as I'm concerned, you are just an unfortunate chapter of my life and I'm closing that chapter, Robert—"

"Stacy, please," he begged, "don't you think I'd rather be there with you?"

"If you wanted to be here, you would be here," she retorted flatly. "I'm not the sharpest knife in the drawer, Robert, but even a dull knife can cut once in a while. This is my once in a while, Robert. This is my time to cut bait and run. So I'm cutting you off at the knees. Go back to your ice queen—"

"Stacy—" Robert began, only to stop as another voice echoed in the background, calling him. A female voice. "In a minute," he responded irritably.

Stacy's fingers tightened so hard around the receiver, it was in danger of snapping. She'd been such a jerk, such a hopeless, stupid, stupid jerk. But that was all going to be behind her very soon.

"Go, Robert. Your wife's calling," she ordered him coldly.

"No, Stacy, I want—"

She cut him off before he could get any further. "It's not about what you want, Robert. It's about what I want for a change."

With that, Stacy slammed the receiver back into its cradle.

Her tears began immediately. Tears of anger, of remorse and, most plentifully, of regret. Barrels of regret. Not for coming in between a husband and his wife, or even a father and his children. Regret that she had spent the past three years of her life, three of the most youthful-looking years at her disposal, sneaking around with a married man. In the beginning, she had been incredibly naive. Thrilled at the fleeting moments of attention he could spare her. Thrilled to have caught his eye to begin with. And he had been generous. Incredibly generous. Before Robert, there had only been costume jewelry. Now there were diamond earrings and gold bracelets.

Diamonds and gold. How the hell could she have sold herself so short? What was wrong with her, anyway?

Stacy stopped to look at herself in the oval hall mirror. What she saw was a still-gorgeous blonde in a filmy negligee. But for how much longer? God, she deserved better than to stand there, waiting for crumbs while Robert's wife got to eat at the banquet table, devouring whole portions.

"Okay," she addressed the woman in the mirror. "Okay, so we start over. We stay strong and we start over." She said it over and over again, until she felt as if she meant it.

What would help, she thought, would be getting rid of every single shred of evidence that Robert had ever *been* in her life. She took a deep breath. It would be like a caterpillar shedding its cocoon.

"There's still a butterfly in there," she promised herself. "A butterfly that's going to do hell of a lot better than Robert Pullman when she's through." It amounted to a declaration of independence. She was through with that lying cheat. That she was the one who had made him such didn't trouble her in the least.

Crossing back to the bedroom, she went straight to the closet and began to pull Robert's garments off their hangers. Stacy made a point of stomping on each item she took out, grinding her heel into the fabric.

She'd just yanked off his sweater, the black one she loved so much on him, when she heard the doorbell ringing. Her revelry froze.

Robert.

He didn't live that far away from here. Only a few blocks. But there was always traffic to reckon with. Still. He must have gone through all the red lights to get here this fast.

A smug expression slipped over her lips. She *knew* he couldn't stay away. Knew he wanted her. But she wasn't won over that easily. Stacy intended on making him crawl for his supper. Or for his pleasure.

Maybe she'd take him back, maybe she wouldn't, but whatever way she was going to play this, she was determined that he was going to beg.

Confidence filled her veins. She checked herself over in the mirror, ran her fingers through her storm of ash-blond hair, then subtly adjusted the negligee she'd put on when she'd thought he was coming over. Left on her own, she slept in the T-shirt that her first lover had left behind when he walked out on her. She'd spent the past eight years hating him.

Ready to knock him dead, Stacy made her way to the front door, the negligee she'd bought for Robert flapping in her wake as she moved.

"There's nothing you can say to make me change my mind," she announced, flipping the two locks the super-intendent had recently placed on her door. "Because I—"

The second she yanked open the front door, she froze, stunned. Instead of the rugged physique of her lover, she was looking at a tall, thin, nervous-looking young man. He looked anywhere between his late twenties and early forties. He had the type of face that was impossible to place, although he did look vaguely familiar. But then, she waited on so many people during the course of the evening at Robert's restaurant, it was hard to remember a select number, much less everyone.

"Oh." Impatient, disappointed, Stacy gripped the doorknob. "Who are you?"

The man was dressed completely in brown. Brown shoes, brown slacks, brown pullover. He seemed to almost fade into the hallway. He cleared his throat before answering, as if he wasn't accustomed to speaking to anyone but himself. One of those nerd types who invented things the world suddenly couldn't do without, Stacy thought. She wondered if he'd done anything of importance and if he was worth a lot of money. Certainly he didn't dress that way. But then, rich nerds never did.

"Jason, ma'am. Jason Parnell," he added after a beat. "I'm sorry to bother you, but I live just down the hall." Turning, he pointed vaguely toward the long hallway. "And my phone went out." Brown eyes looked into hers, imploring. "I was wondering if I could use yours to call the phone company."

She remained where she was, her hand still on the doorknob, ready to slam it shut. "It's Sunday."

He bobbed his head. "Yes, it is. But their customer service line is opened twenty-four/seven. You have to go through several menus, but you wind up with a live person eventually. I've been through this before," he added sheepishly. "Um, I knocked on some of the other doors." He turned again, nodding at the various apartment doors, behind which all sorts of lives were being led. "But you're the only one who answered."

"Look, I'm expecting someone—"

"I'll be quick," he promised. "My mother lives with me and she's not well. That phone is her only lifeline when I'm at work. If I leave tomorrow morning and the phone's down, she'll be helpless."

He looked pathetic, she thought. Exactly what she would have thought a man past the age of twenty and living with his mother would look like. She didn't remember seeing him in the building before, but then, he was one of those people she wouldn't have noticed unless he was lying on the pavement next to her feet.

She supposed there was something to be said about a man who cared that much about his mother. At least he was better than a dirty, rotten, cheating husband who used his wife as an alibi every time he didn't want to bother coming over.

"Your mother, huh?"

"Yes, ma'am." His head bobbed again, like a subservient creature. "She's eighty-five and in a wheelchair."

"All right, all right, you're breaking my heart." With a sigh, Stacy opened the door and stepped back. "Come on in. But make it quick," she added.

Turning away, she didn't see the smile that curved her neighbor's lips.

"As quick as I can. I promise."

CHAPTER TWO

THE INSTANT the apartment door slammed shut behind her, Charlotte Dow tossed down the dog leash and began stripping off her dripping clothes.

Taking this as a signal that a new game was afoot, her sixty-seven-pound jogging companion stopped shaking herself off and watering everything in sight. Instead, the German shepherd leaped up in front of her to catch one of the flying garments. Only sharp reflexes on Charley's part kept mistress and pet from tangling together and falling on the floor.

"Dakota, if you ever hope to see another table scrap, you'd better get your hairy little butt out of my way. Now. I'm running late," Charley said.

Ears down, a mournful look aimed directly at Charley's heart, the German shepherd retreated to her favorite sunken-in spot on the worn gray sofa, still dragging her leash with her.

Charley could all but hear the violins playing in the background. She frowned. Great, more guilt, just what she needed.

Hopping first on one foot, then the other, Charley yanked off her running shoes. She needed new ones, she noted. The heels were beginning to wear.

She heard Dakota sigh. "I know, I know, it's my own

fault. I should have remembered you don't like running in the rain, not unless it's after a cat."

Which was exactly what had appeared on the greenbelt that ran just behind her apartment complex. A golden-colored ball of fur had materialized to taunt Dakota before turning tail and flying down off the path.

In her eagerness to give chase, Dakota had nearly sent Charley sprawling into the freshly formed mud created by an unexpected shower on the city. Who knew it was going to rain? Certainly not the weatherman.

Charley rotated her right shoulder. She had no doubts that her efforts to hang on to the dog had lengthened her right arm by an inch, possibly two. The dog was far from a puppy, so why did she still feel she could chase after cats and catch them?

For the same reason you're always chasing after the bad guys, hell-bent to bring them all in, even with the odds against you.

Like dog, like master.

Charley tossed off the last of her wet clothes, grabbed the pile and hurried into the bathroom. Habit had her grabbing both her cell phone and the wireless phone that was perched on the table against the wall two steps shy of the entrance.

She was an FBI special agent attached to the Santa Ana field office. That meant on duty or off, she was on call twenty-four/seven. That meant everywhere, including the bathroom.

Charley closed the door behind her and set both phones on the window ledge in the shower stall before she slipped in. After angling the showerhead, she turned on the faucet. Warm water turned to hot almost immediately. Steam formed, embracing her, leaving its imprint in the form of tears along the light blue tiles.

It would have taken Charley no effort at all to remain there for the next hour, just letting the heat penetrate, melting the tension from her body. But there was no room for indulgence this morning. Her alarm clock had failed in its effort to rouse her. When she finally had woken up, thanks to Dakota's cold nose pressed up against her spine, Charley had taken one glance at the clock and hit the ground running.

She was forty-five minutes behind schedule.

Another person would have foregone the four-mile jog that began each morning. But Charley was all about dedication and routine. Come six o'clock, she was out there, pounding along the thin ribbon of asphalt that threaded its way from one end of the greenbelt to the other. Rain or shine. Only the call of duty arriving in the middle of the night interfered with her schedule.

Charley shampooed her long blond hair while humming the chorus from the Rodgers and Hammerstein song, "I'm Gonna Wash That Man Right Outa My Hair." There was no man to wash out, not from her hair or her life, but she liked the song. She'd always taken comfort in the familiar.

Not like her twin sister. Cristine had always been the risk-taker, the one who was willing to rush off into the unknown. The one who hadn't needed the familiar or the comforting. Charley had been the one who took things slow and easy.

And she'd been the one who'd survived.

Not now.

Charley shook thoughts of her sister away. Had to be

the dank weather penetrating her soul. She liked the sunshine better.

She'd just started to work the lather out of her hair when the phone rang. The chimes identified it to be her cell, not the landline. The sound worked its way through the running water, through her humming.

Never a dull moment.

With a sigh, Charley wiped her eyes with her fingertips, shut the water and brought the cell phone down to her ear.

"Dow."

"There's been another one."

Charley froze. All the warmth within the stall seemed to instantly evaporate. She didn't have to ask another one what, she knew.

And it sent a chill through her heart.

The voice on the other end of the receiver belonged to Assistant Director George Kelly's secretary, Alice Sullivan. The woman was calling on his behalf to inform the special agents assigned to the serial-killer task force that another victim had been claimed by the monster who was laying siege to the Southland.

Charley pushed back her wet hair from her forehead. *Damn it, anyway.* "When?"

"A.D. Kelly said they found the body this morning. He believes she was killed sometime yesterday. He wants to hold a meeting as soon as possible."

Yesterday. Sunday. The same day her sister had been killed. The same day all the victims had been killed. She was beginning to hate Sundays.

But maybe this time there'd be something they could work with, something that would help them finally catch this bastard.

"Tell him I'm on my way." Charley looked at her free hand. There were traces of foam on it. "Just got to get the soap out of my hair."

"You're in the shower?"

Charley could hear the apology hovering in Alice's throat, ready to leap out. She'd never met anyone so ready to apologize for absolutely everything. Given half a chance, Alice would have apologized that February only had twenty-eight days instead of thirty.

She cut the other woman off quickly. "We've all got to be somewhere, Alice. I'll see you in a few minutes."

Traffic allowing, Charley added silently as she pressed the off button.

With the speed of someone accustomed to living her life on the run, Charley rinsed the stiffening shampoo from her hair and toweled herself dry, all within two minutes of ending her conversation with Alice.

Wrapped in the damp towel, she opened the bathroom door and promptly tripped over Dakota, who had stretched herself before the threshold like a living, furry obstacle course. Charley braced herself against the doorjamb at the last moment.

"Dog, this is not the morning to test me. We'll play when I get home, okay?"

As if giving her tentative approval to the bargain, Dakota trotted after Charley as she dashed into her small, untidy bedroom. Her next mission was to find something suitable to wear that wasn't badly in need of a visit to the laundry room. Not the easiest of missions.

Charley settled on a dark blue skirt and light blue pullover, both of which she yanked over her body. She grabbed her gray jacket, slipped on a pair of high heels, then went for the hardware.

First, the weapon she wore tucked into the back of her waistband, then the small one that this morning was strapped to her thigh rather than her ankle. No matter how much of a hurry Charley was in, this part of her ritual was precise, methodical. Slow. The fate of Dakota's next meal depended on it. If she was careless, if she hurried, there might be no one to give the dog her evening meal. And Dakota had been through enough in her lifetime. She had been Cris's dog first and the transition, after her sister's murder, had been a difficult one for both her and the animal.

Dakota followed her to the door, emitting a mournful noise that sounded very much like a whistling wind.

"Don't start," Charley warned.

She glanced toward the dog's water and food bowls. Both were full. The teenager she paid to walk Dakota in the afternoon would be by at two o'clock. The dog was taken care of.

Time was short. Charley knew she should already be in her car. Still, she paused for half a second to squat down beside the German shepherd and give the animal a hug. She loved the contrary beast. They had something in common. They both missed Cris.

"I'll be back," she promised. "And then we'll laugh, we'll cry, and one of us will get a big treat."

Squaring her shoulders, Charley rose. It was time to leave the shelter of her small apartment and take down the bad guys.

The realization that they might very well be waiting to take her down never escaped her.

TRAFFIC WAS UNUSUALLY sluggish this morning, doubling the fifteen-minute trip from her apartment to the Federal Building where the Bureau field office was

housed. The annoying deejays on the radio did nothing
to lessen the tension that rode along with her in her four-
year-old Honda. She kept switching back and forth
between three stations with no luck. None played a
song she liked.

Would they catch him this time?

Would the bastard who had cut short the lives of
eleven unsuspecting women finally trip up and leave a
clue behind so that they could put him out of everyone
else's misery?

She wished she could believe that he would, but her
customary optimism was in short supply this morning.
Maybe it was the rain that was responsible for her less-
than-cheery outlook. It had been raining the night she
had come back from the part-time job she'd taken only
to find her sister dead in the off-campus apartment they
shared. Cris, it turned out later, had been the Sunday
Killer's first victim.

Or, at least, his first known victim, she amended.
Who knew if there had been others? Just like who knew
why it had been Cris and not she who had been the
victim.

Maybe the killer had made a mistake. Maybe Cris
was supposed to live and she was the one who was
supposed to have died.

Don't go there, Charley. It's not going to help.

She could feel her nerves jangling, beginning to fray.
If she let them unravel, she wouldn't be of use to
anyone, not her sister, not to the latest victim. Not even
to herself. Unraveling was selfish and indulgent, and she
didn't have time for that. Solving this case was all that
mattered. She owed it to Cris.

Charley's hands tightened on the wheel.

THE ROAD OPENED UP just as she took a turn for the cluster of modern buildings that made up the Civic Center in the heart of Santa Ana. In the middle, standing slightly taller than the rest, was the Federal Building.

Turning on her blinker, she merged to the right.

A car sped by her, cutting her off, splashing water all over her windshield and hopelessly obscuring her view for the length of a very long heartbeat.

"Bastard," she muttered. The second her wipers cleared the windshield for her, she saw the offending vehicle's D.C. plates. A tourist. It figured. Obviously the man behind the wheel had no idea how to handle slick roads out here.

She laughed shortly to herself. Californians barely remembered how to do it themselves from one rainy season to another.

As she drove into the bowels of the underground parking structure, she had a feeling it was going to be a very long day.

Dakota was not going to be happy with her when she finally got home.

CHAPTER THREE

AS A KID, Nickolas Brannigan never much cared for Mondays.

Mondays always meant regimentation. They meant getting back to the real world, whatever that might be. And First Mondays were the worst. They meant being thrown headlong into yet another new situation. Finding himself in yet another new location, with new names to remember, new faces to commit to memory.

And once there, those names remembered, those faces committed, they were immediately scheduled for future erasure, because as soon as his father's new orders came through, he and his family packed up, headed for another army camp, another part of the country or the world. With more faces, more names waiting for him.

One would have thought that with eighteen years of this under his belt, he could get through another First Monday with his eyes closed.

Maybe if his eyes were closed, it would be better.

But his eyes were wide-open, taking in every new thing. His need to observe and evaluate always made him feel like a duck in the desert, searching for an oasis. Or at least a decent puddle.

Not that anyone ever noticed he felt this way. He

wouldn't let them notice. Nick prided himself on his ability to hide his true feelings. People called him outgoing, even charming, without ever getting to know the real Nick Brannigan at all. They got to know the outer facade, the man he had to be.

So here he was, facing yet another First Monday. This time he was doing it three thousand miles away from the dot on the map that he had come to call home. Washington, D.C., where most of his family had settled down.

Even his wanderlust father. Retired Army Colonel Harlan Brannigan had decided to face the sunset of his life—though he never referred to it as that—as a teacher of all things. Much to his mother's relief, the family had finally come together to set down roots.

Until the Bureau had seen fit to transfer him to the other side of the country. A spot had suddenly opened up in the California Santa Ana field office and they needed an experienced man to fill it. He could have refused the assignment but you couldn't say no to the Bureau and expect to advance in the ranks. And he wanted to go far.

Now if he could only bring himself to unpack his things. He'd been living with moving-van boxes for companions these past few days. The boxes had arrived at his Bureau-chosen apartment at roughly the same time he had. Even his father would have approved of the Bureau's efficiency.

For this First Monday, Nick was set to report in at nine-thirty. A phone call from someone identifying herself as Alice Sullivan from A.D. Kelly's office had changed that. Because he was a transfer, he needed to check in and get official clearance before he saw his new boss. Fun and games were to begin an hour and a half earlier than expected. Eight o'clock in the morning was not his favorite time.

Negotiating the unfamiliar streets in the rain only intensified the feeling of dread he couldn't quite hide from himself, even if he did manage to keep it from the public at large. But then, if he hadn't managed to get his persona in place at twenty-nine, he might as well have handed in all the marbles and gone home.

A horn blared behind him and he realized that he'd inadvertently cut someone off as he made his turn into the Civic Center.

He'd been told that no one used their horns out here in Orange County. That kind of quick-to-flare temper was something reserved for drivers in metropolitan areas, most notoriously in New York City. Although he had to admit that drivers in the Washington, D.C., area were by no means slouches in that department.

He glanced in his rearview mirror, but couldn't make out who had been at the wheel of the car now behind him. Hopefully some forgiving soul. He'd heard it was the season for road rage out here in normally sunny California.

Searching for a parking structure, Nick admitted that he missed Washington. More than that, he missed his family, his mother, his brother, his sister and her brood. Hell, he even missed his old man.

Nick smiled to himself. Never thought he'd own up to that.

But he and his father were finally making some headway, finally seeing each other as people. It had been a long time in coming. Harlan Brannigan didn't know how to relate to children. God knows the man was hardly around long enough to get the hang of it. But now that he and Jeff and Ashley were all grown, things were different.

Nick blew out a breath as he traveled into the underground parking structure. And now it was going to have to be different without him. At least for a while.

Spoils of war.

The ironic phrase had his mouth curving ever so slightly as he found a parking space and got out of his car. The clichéd phrase would have made his father proud.

PROCESSING WENT a great deal faster than Nick had anticipated. Within the hour he found himself on the seventh floor, standing before the A.D.'s office, looking at a woman who gave every appearance of having been lifted out of some 1940s farce and mercilessly transplanted into the twenty-first century.

It was hard to pin an age to Alice Sullivan, but she looked young. Possibly under thirty, although he couldn't be sure. Definitely not in her forties, even though she dressed like a schoolmarm. She wore wire-rimmed glasses perched on her sharp nose. She was thin, with light blond hair pulled back from her face into a tight knot at the nape of her neck. Her conservative clothes seemed designed to hide her. She definitely had body-image issues, Nick mused. With a shy smile, she stood up to bring him into the A.D.'s office. Nick found himself feeling sorry for her. Despite her position, she made him think of a lost waif.

"He's looking forward to meeting you, Special Agent Brannigan." Her voice, high-pitched and reedy, was only a little higher than it had been over the telephone this morning.

She managed to knock on the A.D.'s door while standing behind him. When a deep voice from within ordered, "Come in," Alice turned the doorknob, then stepped back in order to allow Nick access to the inner office. She gave the impression of fading into the background.

In contrast to his secretary, Assistant Director George Kelly was larger than life. His face was florid and when he rose from behind his desk, he was on eye level with Nick's six-foot-three-inch frame. But while Nick was athletic, Kelly's days in that department were long over. Broad shouldered and heavyset, Kelly carried his mass strictly thanks to his wife's extraordinary cooking.

The man's handshake was firm, hardy. He looked at Nick from head to foot, his eyes passing over him evenly like a giant scanner.

"Get yourself squared away downstairs, Special Agent Brannigan?" were his first words of greeting.

"Just finished."

The nod of approval was short, as if the assistant director were stifling a sneeze that hadn't dared to come out. "Good. Then we can get right to it."

Nick hadn't been briefed by anyone from his old office as to the reason for his transfer other than someone had taken early retirement in the field office.

"'It,' sir?"

"You're part of the task force," Kelly announced without preamble, then realized that he'd gotten ahead of himself. "You've probably heard that we have ourselves a serial killer on the loose."

Nick inclined his head. He thought of the newspaper he'd read on the flight over. The story had been buried on page twenty-three of the first section, but it had caught his attention.

"I heard something about it," he said vaguely. Seven years with the Bureau had taught him never to give away anything unless pinned down and asked.

Kelly merely nodded his head. His thinning red hair was fading, evolving into the color of unripened strawberries. The florescent lighting managed to find all the sparser areas and reflect off them. Nick tried not to notice and kept his eyes on the A.D.'s flushed round face.

His new superior made no effort at more of an explanation. Instead, he rounded his desk and headed for the door.

"Come with me. You need to meet the others."

BILL CHAN WIPED AWAY traces of the raspberry jelly that had oozed out of his doughnut. His latest conquest worked at a bakery three blocks away from the building and he made a point of stopping there each morning for a double sugar hit. Abby's lips were almost as sweet as the jelly was. He tossed the napkin into his basket just as Charley hurried in.

Turning, he gave her an appreciative look. Her navy skirt hugged curves he was the first to appreciate. "Hey Charley, you got legs this morning."

Charley dropped her purse into her bottom desk drawer, then shoved it closed with her foot. "I've got legs every morning."

Bill leaned back in his chair, deliberately eyeing her. "Yeah, but they're not usually out in plain view."

Not to be left out, Sam Daniels, Bill's partner and the other man in the room, added his two cents. "And a very nice view it is, too."

The relationship Charley had with the two partners was one deeply rooted in friendship and mutual respect. Which was why the hazing was generally good-natured, and at times relentless.

She grinned, leaning her face in close to the older man's. "Behave. Especially you, Daniels, or I'll call your wife and tell her you're trying to kick up your heels where you shouldn't."

In reply, Sam drained the last of his coffee and set down his less-than-sanitary mug.

"Seriously Charley, how come you've never gotten married, or at least heavily involved?" Sam asked.

She shrugged, deadpanning. "Just lucky, I guess."

Placing himself in her path as she went to get her own mug of coffee, Bill raised and lowered his dark eyebrows. "I'm just the man you've been waiting for."

She laughed shortly, moving around him. "In your dreams, Billy-boy."

Bill sighed, covering his heart.

Charley poured inky-black coffee into a mug whose interior was only slightly lighter. "Anyone got any details yet?"

Sam shook his head. "We're all sitting tight, waiting on the A.D."

She sighed. The nature of the game. Hurry up and wait. "Might as well get some paperwork done," she murmured half to herself.

At the coffeemaker for her second hit of caffeine in less than ten minutes, Charley felt her attention divert to the noise in the doorway. She turned around as the A.D. entered with someone she didn't recognize. A very tall, good-looking someone.

A witness, she wondered hopefully.

THE ASSISTANT DIRECTOR brought Nick into a room that was not much larger than Kelly's had been. The main difference was that four desks had been crammed into the room. Lining the walls were bulletin boards perched above aging file cabinets. Photographs of the Sunday Killer's victims ran across the boards. Each bright, young face had a column of facts directly beneath it.

Nick felt the energy in the room mingled with a sense of futility.

There were three people in front of him, two men and a woman. One less than the number of desks. Nick wondered who the fourth desk belonged to.

And had a feeling he knew.

"That's Special Agent Bill Chan," Kelly said as he nodded toward the young Asian in a designer suit. In response, Bill smiled broadly at him. Not standing on ceremony, he crossed the room and extended his hand in welcome.

"Over there's Special Agent Sam Daniels," Kelly continued.

Prematurely middle-aged, Sam looked as comfortable as Bill was dapper. His clothes gave the appearance of being chosen for ease rather than for style. They might have even been slept in.

The man nodded in his direction, choosing to look him over from a distance. Sam's body language was deceptively lax. Nick had a feeling that was how the man operated and that not much got by the older veteran. Sam's thick mustache effectively covered his lips, hiding his expression.

Nick moved over toward him and shook his hand.

"And this," Kelly said, nodding at the remaining person in the room, "is Special Agent Charlotte Dow."

The woman moved toward him like fog encroaching the moors, telegraphing an inherent sexuality with every step. Her eyes washed over him. Nick felt something stir in his gut. He would have had to be dead not to have felt it.

"I'd say it was nice to meet you," she said in a voice that made him think of whiskey being poured into a glass, neat, "but the assistant director hasn't given us your name yet."

Her eyes were an intense Florida ocean blue. "I can give my own name," he said.

She cocked her head. "And that is?"

"Nick Brannigan."

Kelly stepped into the arena. "Your new partner, Charley."

It took everything Charley had not to let her mouth drop open.

CHAPTER FOUR

THE NEXT MOMENT, Charley regained the use of her brain. "New partner?" she echoed, staring at the assistant director. "What do you mean, new partner?"

A.D. Kelly kept a tolerant expression on his face. "Temple's gone, Dow," he reminded her evenly. "He's not coming back. Get used to it. Only *I* don't have to be partnered with anyone. You do. Brannigan's your new partner. Get used to that, too."

That settled, Kelly turned to the four main people who headed up the task force formed expressly to apprehend the Sunday Killer. The nickname had come about inhouse, because the killer seemed only to strike on the seventh day of the week.

"Our boy's newest victim was Stacy Pembroke. Like the others, she's young, single. This one was a food server at La Boheme."

"That new trendy place on the Pacific Coast Highway in Newport Beach?" Bill asked. "Dinner for two over there's at least a hundred dollars, without drinks."

"Out of my league," Sam commented.

"One and the same," Kelly confirmed. "Her boss found the body after she didn't come in to work last night."

Charley was still chewing on the bombshell that Kelly had thrown her. She'd been secretly nurturing the hope that Ben Temple would change his mind and return to work, despite what he'd told her. To know that he wasn't going to be part of her everyday life was going to take some getting used to.

But her current state of unrest didn't prevent her from listening to what the assistant director had to say.

She raised her hand now, stopping him before he continued. "Wait a minute, the owner of the restaurant came to her place when she didn't show up for work?"

"That's what the report said," Kelly confirmed.

Charley shook her head. "That doesn't sound very kosher to me." She looked at Kelly, a hint of a smile playing on her lips. "You wouldn't come looking for one of us if we didn't show up."

"Not unless Pembroke and her boss had some kind of personal relationship going," Nick interjected.

Standing beside Charley, Bill leaned toward her and whispered, "And the new guy scores a point."

Not with me, Charley thought. It would take more than a no-brainer guess before she gave the new man any points.

"That's what the detectives on the scene thought," Kelly told them.

"Detectives?" Charley echoed. "What have they got to do with it?"

"The latest victim lived in Tustin. The police who were called in thought it was just another homicide. One of the detectives noticed that the M.O. was the same as the other serial cases we've been working on so he called us. The investigation didn't go any further. Nobody questioned the owner."

"What's the owner's name?" Charley asked.

Kelly checked the report he'd been handed. "Robert Pullman."

Charley made a notation in her worn notepad, taking care not to rip off the tattered cover. "Is the crime scene still intact?"

Kelly shrugged his wide shoulders in suppressed frustration. "It's been walked over by the patrolmen who responded to the call and then the detectives they called in. I'm told that Pullman lost it when he saw the body. He threw up."

"Terrific. Hope they didn't preserve that," Sam muttered.

"The body's in the morgue," Kelly volunteered. "Here's the address to the apartment." He handed it to Charley.

Charley glanced at the location. Tustin was a nice little city. Murders weren't par for the course. *I hope you slipped up, you bastard. I hope, this one time, you slipped up.*

Ignoring the man that Kelly had brought in to be her new partner, Charley turned toward Sam and Bill. She held out the report that Kelly had given her. "You guys want to take the body or the crime scene?"

Except for Nick, everyone in the room knew how Charley felt about viewing dead bodies. Given a choice, she would just as soon work the case without seeing the victim. It wasn't that she had a queasy stomach, but viewing the Sunday Killer's victims vividly reminded her of the moment she'd walked into the apartment to find her sister lying on the sofa. Strangled.

But despite the fact that she had managed to get herself placed in charge of the task force before the details of her sister's murder caused the case to be connected to the Sunday Killer, Charley went the extra mile when it came to fair. She didn't believe in playing favorites, even if that "favorite" was her.

Especially if it was her.

Sam held up his hand. "We'll take the body, Charley," he said, speaking for himself and Bill. "You can deal with whatever the boys in blue stomped over." And then he stopped abruptly, an uneasy expression descending over his craggy face as his glance shifted to the newest member of their team. Some people were touchy about family and he'd just been less than tactful. "Your old man didn't walk the beat, did he?"

Nick smiled and shook his head. "Retired army colonel."

Sam pretended to breathe a sigh of relief. "Okay then. Cops tend to tread with a heavy foot. Half the time, they don't know what they're dealing with."

"Not like us," Charley commented drily.

Nick glanced at her to see if she was being sarcastic, but her expression told him nothing. Except that she avoided looking his way. He wondered if he had a prima donna on his hands. He'd never worked with a woman before, but he knew a couple of agents who had. One was currently involved in divorce proceedings.

Charley turned her attention toward Kelly. "Is there anything else, A.D. Kelly?"

"Yeah." Kelly paused for a beat. "Catch this son of a bitch for me, Dow," he said with feeling. "I want him so bad I can taste it."

Charley looked over at the posted photographs of the serial killer's victims. Eleven women who had not been allowed to live up to the promise of their lives. Stacy Pembroke would be the twelfth victim.

"Get in line," Charley replied solemnly. The next moment, she shook off her mood. Looking at Bill and Sam, she said, "We'll meet back here."

"You got it," Sam agreed.

As she began to walk toward the door, she glanced over her shoulder at her new partner, trying to contain her resentment that he was now in the position that Ben had once held.

"I'll drive." It wasn't an offer, it was a statement.

"Whatever rings your chimes, Special Agent Dow," Nick answered.

Charley stopped. "Was that supposed to be amusing, Special Agent Brannigan?"

"That was supposed to be an answer, Special Agent Dow."

This was turning out to be one of his more memorable First Mondays, Nick thought, not altogether certain he was happy about it. He figured there were two ways he could play this. He could either take offense or laugh it off. The latter seemed to be the better way to go.

His new partner said nothing as she led the way to the bank of elevator cars.

THEY RODE DOWN in the elevator and made their way through the basement of the parking structure without any further exchange of words. The silence accompanied them as they got into her vehicle. It continued as Charley started up her Honda.

Nick kept his peace until after she'd pulled out of the structure and was on the road. The rain was still coming down in a fine, annoying mist. It coated the windshield just enough to demand intermittent swipes from the windshield wipers.

"Want to fill me in?" he finally said.

She'd retreated into the same thoughts she always had when dealing with one of the Sunday Killer's victims. Had the death been quick? Had the woman suffered? Had Cris suffered those last few moments of her life? What had gone on in her mind during that time? Had she known she was facing death, or was it just too improbable a situation to comprehend?

Charley realized the new man had asked her a question and waited for an answer. Belatedly, she replayed his words in her head.

"About?" she asked, taking a right turn.

Nick banked down a wave of impatience. Would it get any better or did he need to pass some magical test to prove himself to this woman?

"The serial killer," he said evenly, then added with a smile, "although feel free to fill me in about anything else you might want to throw in."

You're not being fair to him.

It was Ben's voice, not her own, that she heard in her head. Ben, her teacher, her mentor, her surrogate father. No, more than a father, she thought. Her own father had never treated her with the kindness and understanding that Ben Temple did. And she was going to miss Ben. Miss having him by her side, teaching her things even at this stage of her career. She knew it was better for Ben to finally take the retirement that the Bureau had been waving before him. As for her, she'd always hoped the day would never come.

She spared Nick a glance. Man has a profile like Mount Rushmore. "It's going to take me some time to adjust."

He looked at her. "To…?"

She could have easily made it through the yellow light, but for once she eased back on the gas pedal, slowing down enough so that the light slipped into red before she was at the crosswalk. She looked at the man beside her.

"You."

Nick wasn't sure if he was supposed to take offense at that or not. "Most people don't find me that difficult to get along with."

The man was young, good-looking and in excellent shape. His jacket hugged his muscles. Probably had to have his jackets altered to fit, she mused.

"I liked my old partner," she informed him flatly.

He slipped in through the opening she'd offered. "What happened to him?"

The light turned green, and she pushed down on the accelerator.

"He took a bullet. One meant for me." Her heart had stopped in that one minute. Curbing fury and fear, she'd fired at the gunman, mortally wounding him. The time between when she'd placed the call and the ambulance's arrival seemed interminable. She'd stopped the flow of Ben's blood with her shirt and her hands. Charley glanced at the new man's face. It annoyed her that she couldn't read his expression. "Don't worry, that's not part of the requirement. I don't expect you to do the same."

"Is your ex-partner—"

"Dead? No, thank God. But he took his retirement straight out of the hospital. Said he was too old to walk into dark rooms with his gun drawn." Charley bit back a sigh. "Ben Temple was a great partner."

"I'll try to live up to that."

"Don't. You'll fail."

He was too much his father's son not to rise to a challenge when one was issued.

"Don't count on it, Special Agent Dow. Want to tell me what you know about this serial killer we're after?"

All he knew was what he'd read in the paper. He'd done that with half an eye, never thinking he'd be assigned to this particular force. Now he wished he'd paid more attention, even though half of it was undoubtedly media hype.

"What I know about the serial killer," she repeated. "I know that he's a son of a bitch, no slur intended on female dogs everywhere. I know he rips families apart. That he probably watches his victims, getting their routines down pat before he strikes. I know I want to pin his hands and feet down and vivisect him."

Something in her voice commanded his attention. "You sound like you really hate this guy."

"I do. I should," she added. "He killed my sister."

CHAPTER FIVE

IT TOOK NICK a minute to process what she'd just said. He thought his new partner was either pulling his leg or speaking figuratively. But the woman's profile was rigid. If she was kidding, Special Agent Charlotte Dow held the world's record for a deadpan.

"You're serious," he said.

"Yes."

"Hold it. Back up a minute," he said. "Isn't that considered a conflict of interest?"

On the team less than an hour and already the new guy was pointing out protocol to her. She couldn't say she was exactly warming up to him. Charley spared him one cutting glance. "If it doesn't bother the A.D., I don't see why it should bother you."

He'd just been put in his place. Nick felt his even temper become a little less even. His new partner obviously had a stick pushed up in regions that did not entertain the rays of the morning sun. But if what she'd just said about her sister was true, he supposed she could be afforded a little slack.

And, he reminded himself, he was the new kid on the block. That meant he had to go along with things, had to roll with the punches until he got the lay of the land and could block the blows.

"I only meant…" His voice trailed off.

Squeaking through a left turn and plowing through a particularly large puddle that shot plumes of water out on either side of the front of the vehicle, Charley sighed. She was being waspish. What was worse, she was taking it out on the new guy.

She spared him another glance. The man didn't look any the worse for her sharp tongue, she'd give him that. "Sorry. I didn't mean to snap your head off. I'm a little testy this morning."

Brannigan pretended to wipe his brow. "Well, that's certainly a relief. I'd hate to think you were like this every day."

Nick knew he'd just taken a gamble. It was one of those lines that could go either way. It could make her laugh or climb up on her high horse and read him the riot act about affording her respect. He was hoping for the former and held his breath until there was some kind of response.

After a beat, a hint of a smile made an appearance on her lips.

"Fortunately for you, I'm a pussycat most of the time. And, to answer your question about conflict of interest—not that I have to," she told him pointedly, "neither A.D. Kelly nor I realized that there was a tie-in until certain data was fed into the Bureau's in-house database program. By that time I was already on the task force." Her smile widened slightly. "And I'm not without my charm."

"Where did you leave it today?"

The remark had just slipped out. He decided to leave it there. He'd never been comfortable pretending to be something he wasn't and what he wasn't was someone who allowed a person to walk all over him. As a kid, it had earned him more than one black eye and more than a few disciplinary sessions administered by his father, sometimes months after the fact because the Colonel was away so much.

Special Agent Dow's expression was unfathomable. "Good one," she said with no emotion. "You're entitled to one zinger."

"A day?"

A sea of red taillights lined up in front of her vehicle. By all indications, there'd been an accident up ahead. The police had shut off the stoplights and were directing traffic, none of which was presently moving. Stuck, Charley took the opportunity to turn toward the new man.

"Ever," she informed him crisply. "And that was it. I'm afraid you've used up your three wishes, Aladdin."

He wondered if that was an example of her sense of humor, or if he'd just been put on notice. Rather than make a guess, Nick decided to shift the conversation. "So what was it?"

They were moving again. Good thing. Her leg felt as if it was cramping up. "What was what?"

"The certain 'thing' which made you realize your sister—"

"Cris," Charley supplied.

"Cris," he repeated, "was the serial killer's first victim?"

That was taking something for granted and she wasn't altogether sure they could, given the nature of their killer. "Alleged first victim," she corrected.

Nick stopped, slightly annoyed at the second interruption. "Don't you let someone get a question out without interjecting footnotes?"

"If that someone gets it right, no," she answered
simply. And then, because she didn't really feel like
butting heads this morning, entertaining though it might
be, she decided to explain why she'd just corrected him.
"Call it a gut feeling, but I don't think we have found
all of the victims. It's a big country, Special Agent Brannigan. There might be graves in places we haven't even
thought to look. As of now, we know of three states
where the Sunday Killer has struck. They were all California natives, but he obviously targeted them and
followed them out of state. Given that, there might be
more victims that, for one reason or another, we don't
know about yet." She frowned. "There's no real
common thread to link the women or give us a reason
why he chose them and not some other women to kill."

Traffic was picking up again, and she shifted in her
seat. "The only thing the victims have in common is the
way they died."

Charley detailed the similarities that connected the
deaths to one another. "He kills on a Sunday. Always.
He doesn't abuse them sexually. No penetration in any
manner, no clothes even moved out of place. Every
body is found in what could be described as a ladylike
pose. The killer strangles them with his bare hands.
That means, through the magic of science, we have an
approximate idea of how big a man he is—"

"Unless he has freakishly large hands," Nick interjected. When she shot him a look, he tagged on, "Sorry,
the footnote thing is catching."

Charley made no comment. She didn't know if she'd
been partnered with a wiseass or someone whose dry
sense of humor she was going to like. For the time
being, she continued. "The women are under forty and

are all reasonably attractive. That is, they were before he branded them."

This was the first he'd heard of any disfigurement. "Branded them?"

Charley moved the windshield wipers to the last position. They began to slide back and forth across the glass in double time, maintaining clear visibility for half a cycle.

"It might have something to do with Sundays," she guessed. "Maybe the killer's some kind of religious fanatic—we haven't determined that yet. But he lightly carves a tiny cross in the middle of all his victims' foreheads."

"A cross," he repeated. A vision of Rasputin from an old Russian history textbook materialized in his mind. A mad monk, or someone in that vein. Nick shrugged. "Maybe the killer thinks he's saving them somehow."

"Saving them from what?" Charley demanded. "From breathing?" She shook her head, dismissing the notion. "Your theory might hold water if these women were all prostitutes, or each in her own way had committed some kind of heinous crime, but as far as we can see, the victims are just a group of average middle-class women. We've got a waitress—" she referred to the latest victim "—a supermarket checker, a teacher, a would-be actress, an insurance clerk, an airline stewardess, a bank teller, a private in the army, a girl who worked in a stationery store, a nurse, a paralegal and a grad student." The last was her sister. "Nothing out of the ordinary. Nothing to tie them together. They didn't belong to the same club, see the same doctor, like the same movies."

Charley pressed her lips together. She could taste her

frustration rising like bile in her throat. There were days she was hopeful and days, like today, when she thought they were never going to get Cris's killer. Maybe it was the rain, she reasoned. The rain always made her think of Cris. And that she'd lost half of her soul.

"They didn't even have the same things in their medicine cabinets," she said in frustration. Every angle had been checked and rechecked. But obviously, they were going to have to check again.

"And yet there has to be some kind of link," Nick pointed out, saying out loud what she was thinking. "At least in the killer's mind."

"Which could be totally psychotic and delusional. For all we know, he thinks he sees the same person over and over again when he kills his victims."

And when he saw Cris, did the killer think he was seeing her instead? Charley wondered. It was something that continued to haunt her. She and Cris had been identical, right down to the tiny white crescent birthmark on their left hips. There'd been times when their own mother hadn't been able to tell them apart. It was their personalities, not their features that enabled people to distinguish between them. Asleep, which was the way the killer had found Cris, they could easily be mistaken for each other.

No, you're not going to do this to yourself, Charley silently insisted. Getting bogged down in endless self-questioning wasn't going to get Cris's killer. Wasn't going to find him before he could kill another girl.

She stepped on the gas and made the light before it turned red. Barely.

"You always drive like that?" Nick asked.

"Like what?"

"Like you're running a race with the traffic light to see who makes it to the finish line first."

"I don't like to dawdle."

"No, but some of us might want to live to see our thirtieth birthday."

She raised her eyes to his as she turned into a parking lot. "Then you picked the wrong profession, Special Agent Brannigan. You want a long life expectancy, become an insurance investigator."

As she pulled into the first available spot, rain began to fall as if someone had upended a barrel. Pausing only to pull up the hood of her jacket, Charley got out of the vehicle. She waited for her partner to emerge on his side before she hit the security button.

Nick turned up his collar. Not that it did much to protect him from the rain. He glanced in her direction as he made a run for the apartment building.

"No umbrella?"

She hated having to carry anything. Everything she felt she needed was stuffed into one small shoulder bag she resented having to drag along. An umbrella would have been too much.

"Too inconvenient. Besides, haven't you heard? It never rains in California."

Reaching the doorway, he turned his collar down again and wiped the rain from his hair with his hand. "Isn't the rest of that line 'but it pours?'"

Throwing open the door that led into the building's foyer, she looked over her shoulder. A spark of mild interest rose within her. "An oldies fan?"

He'd never cared for labels, preferring to go from one thing to another. "My taste's eccentric. I like most music. Helps while the time away."

Stacy Pembroke's apartment was on the first floor, in the rear of the building. Since she was the only one of them who knew that, Charley led the way. "Time hang heavily on your hands, Special Agent Brannigan?"

He kept pace with her in the narrow hallway, refusing to follow her like an underpaid servant. "It did when I was a kid, sitting between my brother and sister in the back seat of my father's station wagon, traveling from Texas to New Jersey."

She made the connection instantly. "Army brat?"

"Army." Nick allowed part of her label. "But I was never a brat." His mouth curved slightly. "Just ask my mother."

"Maybe I will."

The moment Charley walked across the apartment threshold, she sobered. Someone had died here, had the life squeezed out of her by the hands that belonged to a maniac. No matter what that woman's offenses might have been, the victim deserved some sort of dignity.

Just like Cris had deserved.

CHAPTER SIX

A SINGLE LINE of yellow tape separated the apartment from its brethren. That, and the aura of death.

Only one man was stationed inside the confines of the late Stacy Pembroke's one-bedroom apartment. The man was shifting his weight from foot to foot like a bird marooned on a tiny slab of ice, floating down a river and nervously trying to decide which foot would keep him steadiest.

From his short-cropped haircut to his crisp white shirt down to his neatly pressed brown trousers, the man reeked of newness. Not new to the scene like Brannigan, but new altogether. New to the Bureau. New to the sharp reality of murder. He had the smell of someone who had just graduated from the academy and had drawn the Santa Ana office as his first assignment.

Because he was thin, he appeared taller than he was. And nervous. Throwing off his restlessness, the special agent came to attention the moment she and Brannigan walked into the small, tastefully furnished apartment.

In a beat, he was going to go for his weapon, Charley thought. She judged that he was more likely to shoot his own foot than get a bead on either one of them.

Something made her doubt that the man behind her had ever been that nervous, that raw. Brannigan exuded confidence with every move he made.

Charley raised her hand, as if she was gentling an overanxious poodle that fancied himself a guard dog. "Relax, newbie. I'm Special Agent Dow, this is Special Agent Brannigan. We're on the task force that's investigating this murder."

To back up her claim, Charley withdrew her wallet and showed the young man her ID. His eyes moved from line to line, then looked at her photograph carefully before stepping back. Only then did relief relax his features.

"Newbie," the man repeated, digesting the term. A tinge of color rose up on his cheeks. He had the kind of face that would always be boyish. "Does it show?"

"Only when we look," Charley told him. "Don't worry about it. Even God had a first day. What's your name?"

"Jack Andrews, ma'am."

Nick noted that Charley winced ever so slightly at the polite salutation. His sister hated to be addressed that way. It made her feel old, she'd confided. Probably did the same for Dow.

"Special Agent Dow will do, Special Agent Andrews," Charley addressed the younger man. And then she surprised Nick as well as the new recruit by smiling and adding, "If we solve this case, you get to call me Charley."

The look on Jack Andrews's face said that he would never presume to call her by anything so familiar.

Nick turned to look at her, puzzled. "Charley? How did you get Charley out of Charlotte?"

But even as he asked, Nick decided that the nickname probably suited her a great deal better than the name she'd been given at birth. Charlottes did not carry concealed weapons or relentlessly pursue serial killers. They served tea to their friends at a country club and made sure they stayed out of the sun so that their fair complexions wouldn't freckle.

"I didn't. My sister did." For a precious moment, she allowed herself to remember when she'd felt a part of something greater than just herself, and yet was very much an extension of who and what she was. "Cris couldn't wrap her tongue around the name 'Charlotte' when we were little. All she could get out was 'Charley.'" Her mouth curved as she raised one shoulder in a careless shrug. "I like that name better. 'Charlotte' belongs to a woman on a verandah who has vapors. Like my father's mother."

Whom, judging by that slight frown, she didn't much care for, Nick thought. "Let me guess, you're named after her."

Charley snorted. "See if you can put that finely honed guessing talent to work here." And then she turned toward the newly minted special agent. "Did the police leave us any information?"

Obviously happy to be of some use, Jack rattled off the particulars of the discovery. Nothing new.

"Any of the neighbors hear anything suspicious?"

Jack shook his head. "They haven't been canvassed yet."

She didn't hold out much hope, but all ground had to be covered. And sometimes they got lucky. "Why don't you nose around, see what you can find out?" she suggested.

The words were no sooner out of her mouth than Jack vanished from the apartment, eager to do her bidding.

Nick watched him leave, amused. Chronologically, probably only five years separated him from Andrews, but he couldn't recall ever being that young. "Well, you made him feel useful."

"It's a gift." She stopped when she saw that Nick was heading for the door. She hadn't meant for both agents to canvass the neighbors. "Are you planning on going with him?"

Nick stopped just shy of the door. If she thought that he was going to clear every move with her before he made it, this partnership wasn't going to work out.

"No. Just wanted to check something out." Crouching, he carefully examined the lock on the door and the area around it. "No sign of forced entry." He rose again. "Looks like she knew her killer."

"Maybe." This was a first-floor apartment. Which meant there was possible access through one of the windows. But they all appeared to be locked from the inside from what she could see. "Or maybe she just opened the door."

Where he came from, people were a lot more cautious. "To a stranger?"

Charley smiled. "Why not? Had an aunt once. She opened the door to anyone who knocked or rang. Thought it rude not to."

"She get mugged?" he guessed.

"Not so far." She didn't add that she'd finally persuaded the woman to put a chain on her door so she could open her door and still have a semblance of protection in place.

According to the police report, Stacy Pembroke's body had been found in the living room. Nick walked into the bedroom. "You want to come here and look at this?"

"Can't wait," Charley murmured under her breath.

She stepped away from the small desk and walked into the bedroom.

Nick was squatting over a pile of men's clothing that had been unceremoniously dumped in the middle of the room. He lifted the jacket that was on top of the heap and examined it.

"Forty-two tall." He closed the jacket and replaced it on the pile, then rose to his feet again. "You know, maybe we're dealing with a jilted lover." He threw a theory out for her to mull over. "Maybe to draw suspicion away from himself, Mr. Forty-two Tall killed her and staged it to look like the Sunday Killer."

But Charley shook her head. "According to the preliminary findings, the victim had a tiny cross carved on her forehead. That's a detail we never released to the press."

He looked at her. Maybe the woman wasn't quite as sharp as she seemed to believe she was.

"And you think that kept it a secret?" Nick laughed shortly, shaking his head. People talked. Even those with good intentions. It was the nature of the beast. "How many people have been involved in the Sunday Killer case since the beginning? Twenty?" he asked, then doubled the figure. "Forty?" It was still a conservative estimate. If they counted all the peripheral people involved, including forensics, that brought the count up to over a hundred. "Think about it. There have been M.E.s and civilians who've stumbled across the bodies. Not to mention the family members who had to bury the killer's victims. You honestly think no one said anything about that little branding fetish the killer's got? You think that nobody had a few too many while sharing some quality time with his buddies or his best girl and let that little spine-chilling detail slip without realizing it?"

He had a point. But she had another one. "Okay, maybe that happened. Maybe more than once. But what are the odds that they'd let that slip within the earshot of the possibly ticked-off lover who belongs to that pile of clothes on the floor?"

Nick believed in picking his fights and this one didn't seem to be important enough to do battle over. So he shrugged and continued working his way through the otherwise neat blue-and-white bedroom. "Guess you've got a point."

She hadn't finished with the living room. Turning on her heel, she went back. "I always have a point, Special Agent Brannigan."

Opening up a bureau, Nick discovered the dead woman's underwear drawer. The garments seemed rather pricey for a woman living on a waitress's salary. He assumed they were gifts from Mr. Forty-two Tall.

"You know," he called out to her, "with all these special agents floating around, the label tends to lose some of its specialness, don't you agree? How about you just call me Brannigan. Or Nick if that's too much of a mouthful."

"I'll take that under advisement, Special Agent," Charley promised.

Nick leaned over to get a better view of the other room and her. He couldn't make out if she was smiling, but he thought he detected as much in her voice.

One step at a time, Nicky, one step at a time, he counseled silently.

The bottom drawer had negligees and the scent of expensive perfume. He paused a moment to inhale and appreciate, then another moment to mourn the waste of a human being before he gingerly rifled through the soft, filmy garments. And found a prize. A small four-by-six beige leather-bound book.

He took it out and thumbed through it. Delicate handwriting marked every page.

"Found a diary," he announced, holding it aloft.

"I'll see your diary and raise you an address book." Crossing back to him, she displayed the volume she'd unearthed in the desk. "Maybe by reading that and calling some of the people in here, we can reconstruct her week."

"Week? Don't you mean day?"

Charley shook her head. "I always say what I mean," she informed him crisply.

He was feeling her out, she thought. Circling her and looking for a weakness like a new buck entering an established herd. She was accustomed to doing things her own way. Ben had been a mentor and a guide, but he'd always given her her own lead. Early on, he had told her to trust her instincts and then he'd proved it by showing her that *he* trusted them. She had a strong hunch that Brannigan just wanted to be leader of the pack.

Not gonna work that way, Special Agent.

"This bastard stalks them. One of the victims' brothers came forward and told us that his sister had confided to him that she thought she was losing her mind because she felt someone was watching her all the time. I don't doubt that she was right. The Sunday Killer follows them around, gets their routines down, then waits for just the right moment to take them out."

"As long as it's on a Sunday."

"As long as it's on a Sunday," she echoed.

"But why?"

There was frustration in Charley's voice as she said,

"That is the million-dollar question, Special Agent Brannigan. We get the answer to that, maybe we can get the son of a bitch."

A noise in the other room told her that the rookie had returned. She crossed back to the living room. Brannigan was right behind her.

Jack looked eager to share what he'd managed to discover. "One of the neighbors on the floor said she thought she heard yelling coming from this apartment around noon yesterday."

"What kind of yelling?" Nick asked. "Screams for help? An argument?"

Jack shook his head. "She just said yelling. But she said it was a man. And she thought it was the TV. You know, one of those daytime cable channel crime series that's always being rerun. The woman said she was just about to go knock on Stacy Pembroke's door when the yelling stopped."

Nick exchanged looks with Charley. "Bad luck for Stacy," he commented.

"Yeah," Charley agreed sadly—if something as heinous as what had transpired in this apartment could be described with such sanitary words.

CHAPTER SEVEN

CHARLEY PUSHED the key into the lock. Turning it took effort. She felt bushed, really bushed. Worn-out from the inside clear to the outside.

This was probably the way someone with their foot caught in a stirrup felt after they'd been dragged for three miles by a wild horse. Going around in wide, fruitless, unproductive circles always did that to her.

With a sigh almost as big as she was, Charley pushed down on the door handle and walked into her apartment. She was instantly greeted by Dakota, who moments earlier, if the warm spot that met her feet when she kicked off her shoes was any indication, had been lying on the floor directly in front of the door.

Tail wagging like a metronome on caffeine, the German shepherd ran back and forth as if she couldn't make up her mind what to do or where to go first.

Charley laughed softly. "You and me both, Dakota."

The dog returned to angle her head beneath her mistress's hand. It was almost as if the animal was petting her instead of the other way around. Charley smiled to herself. Dakota had her trained well.

She could barely place one foot in front of the other and make her way to the living room where the sofa beckoned to her. Sinking into the cushion was like sinking into an old friend. The slightly worn gray up-holstery embraced her.

A beat later, Dakota joined her.

Charley closed her eyes, petting the animal again. She'd long since given up trying to keep the dog off the furniture. The sofa was her favorite spot. But Dakota listened to her most of the time, which was more than she could say for the rest of the world.

After a moment, Charley forced herself to open her eyes again. It was either that or fall asleep sitting up. Turning in Dakota's direction, she noticed that the telephone on the table beside the sofa was rhythmically blinking at her like a red-eyed, menstruating Cyclops.

Three quick blinks, then a long one. That meant three calls.

Charley frowned.

She didn't have to listen to the messages. Experience told her who had called. *He* must have heard it on the news, she thought grimly. She had to psych herself up before she tackled returning the calls.

Better yet, she needed to hear a friendly voice first. Charley picked up the cordless receiver and pressed a single button on the keypad, the one connecting her to the only person she could turn to at a moment like this.

It took several rings before she heard the phone being picked up. The moment she heard the deep, rumbly voice honed by years of devoted Scotch-and-soda imbibing, she smiled.

"Hello?"

Charley didn't bother with a greeting. She didn't need to. Slipping into a conversation with Ben Temple was as easy as breathing.

"They gave me a new partner today." She couldn't help making it sound like an accusation.

She heard the voice on the other end chuckle. "About time."

She could envision Ben leaning back in that chair he always favored, the one his late wife had begged him to get rid of. Worn, shapeless and faded in a multitude of places, the once-hunter-green recliner matched nothing in the house except for Ben. "I kept hoping you'd change your mind and come back."

The shoulder that had caught the bullet still hurt when he moved it a certain way. It probably always would. At sixty-three, he didn't heal the way he had at twenty.

"If I do, it's going to be to sit behind a desk and puzzle things out, Charley. Don't forget, I'm not the man I used to be."

She knew Ben was only baiting her, but she hated it anyway. "You will always be the man you used to be."

Ben chuckled again, clearly warmed by her loyalty. Childless, he thought of Charley as the daughter he would have liked to have had if Ruth could have had children. "Saying it doesn't make it so, kid. Saddest thing in the world to watch is a player who doesn't know when to leave the field."

"Just because a pitcher loses his arm doesn't mean he can't be used for another position in the game." She was only half kidding even though she knew that Ben had made up his mind. Had known it even when she'd gone to the hospital to visit him right after his operation. Ben's disability leave had swiftly taken on signs of a more permanent nature. "You wouldn't have to leap over any tall buildings in a single bound. I could do that for you."

"Charley—"

"I know, I know." She tried to sound upbeat, but the truth was, she missed him. He'd been gone only six weeks and she'd visited him as often as she could, but she missed him. Missed seeing his rumpled, lived-in face looking at her from across their desks every day. "But you can't like just sitting around the house, doing nothing. I know you better than that, Ben."

"I'm not sitting around, getting bored," he protested good-naturedly. "I signed up for a night class. I'm finally learning Spanish the way you always kept telling me to. And I've got twenty-eight years of TV programs and books to catch up on. Got a whole bunch of tapes and DVDs," he added to back up his claim. "So give me a few years to get bored. I've earned it, kid."

"I know you have."

He heard the sadness in her voice and felt the prick of nostalgia. But that part of his life was behind him now, just as being part of a marriage was behind him. "So, tell me. How's this new guy working out for you?"

Dakota had moved her chin onto her lap. Charley began to stroke the dog's head. It soothed her. "He's not you."

Humor echoed in his tone. "Ugly, huh?" When his former partner didn't immediately respond, Ben knew what that meant. He'd intended his gibe as a joke, but he'd managed to stumble on a little bit of truth in the process. "Not so ugly, I take it."

Charley paused before answering. She wanted to be fair. Special Agent Nick Brannigan might have struck her as being a lot of things, none of which she particularly liked, but ugly was not one of them.

"No," she finally allowed, "not so ugly."

What she didn't say spoke volumes to Ben. He'd

tried to pair her off with one of his nephews once, but it hadn't gone too well. That didn't change his opinion that Charley needed someone in her life. Someone to go home to. Or with.

"So tell me about him," he coaxed.

"Not much to tell." She tried to remember what Alice had told her when the woman had stopped by her desk that afternoon. The A.D.'s secretary had managed to just catch her in between trips out of the office. She and Brannigan had canvassed the entire neighborhood, spoken to a good portion of the people listed in Stacy Pembroke's address book and met with a very broken up Robert Pullman at his restaurant. The man spent most of the interview fighting tears even as he attempted to deny that he and Stacy had been romantically involved. "His name's Nick Brannigan. He's just transferred from Washington, D.C. Been with the Bureau for about as long as I have. Maybe longer."

Ben picked up on the obvious. "Then you must have trained together."

It gave her pause. For some reason, she hadn't thought of that. She tried to recall the people in her class at Quantico. As best she could remember, Brannigan's face hadn't been among them. "Not that I recall. And I'm pretty sure I would have remembered him."

Ben had spent five years learning to pick up subtle nuances in her voice. "Are you butting heads with him yet?"

"I never butt heads."

Ben laughed. "Yeah, you do. With everything and everyone who gets in your way." His tone grew a little more serious. He worried about her. "You don't have me around to smooth things out anymore, Charley. You're going to have to mind your *p*s and *q*s."

She loved his quaint sayings. "*P*s and *q*s I can mind, Ben. It's orders from people when they're clearly wrong that I've got trouble with."

"Try not to have trouble with them," Ben advised. And then he paused before saying, "I hear he's surfaced again."

Ben had been on the task force with her. She'd only taken over as primary after he went on disability. "Yeah. He's crawled out of the woodwork. But this time we're going to get him, Ben."

He knew what it meant to her. "Just don't get hurt doing it."

Charley smiled. She liked her independence, liked having no restrictions except the rules of the Bureau. But she had to admit she liked to know that someone worried about her.

"I'll do my best." Call waiting sent a pulse through the receiver. She was tempted to ignore it, just as she was ignoring the blinking answering machine. But eventually, she was going to have to face him. It might as well be now. "Ben, I'm getting another call."

"Maybe it's your new partner."

They both knew it wasn't. She'd told Ben all about her father. About how Cristine had always been his favorite and how he hadn't forgiven her for not being there that night to save her sister. Charley was certain her father blamed her as much as he blamed the man who had strangled Cristine.

"I doubt that."

"Ask this Nick out for a drink, Charley," Ben advised. "Get to know him. Your partner's all that stands between you and the crazies."

She knew that. The message had never been brought home as clearly as the day Ben had shielded her with his own body. She wished it had been her to catch the bullet. Then Ben would still be on the job. "They don't make them like you anymore."

"You never know."

The line beeped again. She knew the more her father had to call, the more agitated he became. "I've gotta go, Ben. Talk to you later."

"Anytime, kid," he told her.

"Thanks."

She knew he meant it. Knew that she could call on him at any hour of the day or night and he would be there for her. During the time they had worked together, Ben Temple had not only been her partner, but her best friend and her surrogate father as well. A surrogate father who had been better than the one she'd been given at birth, Charley mused as she pressed the button on the telephone that would connect her to the incoming call.

The smile on her lips faded the moment she did. Despite her best efforts to remain calm, Charley could feel her shoulders bracing even before she heard her father's voice. "Hello?"

"Where the hell have you been?"

Nice to hear from you, too, Dad. "Out fighting crime, Dad."

"Why didn't you return my calls?"

"I told you, I was out, working." *And I wish I was out there now, so I could miss this one.* "I didn't get them."

Christopher Dow had never been known for his good humor or his patience. He displayed none now toward his remaining daughter. "You've got one of those remote things to get your messages, don't you?"

She was twenty-eight years old and had been on her own for almost the past ten years. Why did he always insist on treating her like a little girl who'd misbehaved? "I didn't have time to access them, Dad. I've been pretty busy today."

She heard her father make an indistinguishable guttural sound. "That son of a bitch struck again."

"Yes, I know."

"You going to get him this time?" It was almost an accusation.

Charley worked her lower lip with her teeth. She stroked Dakota harder. "I'm going to do my best."

"Your best hasn't been good enough yet," he reminded her coldly.

She closed her eyes. "Yes, I know."

"He killed your sister. You can't let him go free."

"I don't intend to, Dad."

"So what are you doing about it?"

She felt even more weary than she had when she'd walked in through the door. Talking to her father always drained her. "It's an ongoing case, Dad. I can't talk about it."

Anger filled his voice. "I'm your father."

"And I'm a federal agent. There are rules. I've got a call coming in, Dad. I have to go." She disconnected before he had a chance to protest. Leaving the receiver on the sofa, Charley leaned her head against Dakota and forced herself to think about nothing.

CHAPTER EIGHT

WHILE JUGGLING his pizza box, Nick managed to insert his key into the lock. Because the key was new and the lock was not, there was an awkward dance between the two, a moment of inflexibility before the tumbler finally gave way and turned, allowing him into his newly rented garden apartment.

His palm had grown uncomfortably warm where it was making contact with the bottom of the pizza box. The small mom-and-pop store directly behind his apartment complex took pride in serving their food hot. Very hot. He was going to have to curb his hunger if he didn't want to burn the hell out of the roof of his mouth, Nick thought.

He closed the door with his shoulder, then flipped the lock. This stretch of Santa Ana, where he'd chosen to live, was away from the high-crime area that marked the center of the old city. Located across the street from Costa Mesa and South Coast Plaza, touted to be the largest shopping mall west of the Mississippi, the area was almost safe enough for him to leave his door unlocked during the day.

Almost being the operative word, Nick mused as he slid the box holding his dinner onto the tiny table in his breakfast nook. *Nook* was a perfect word to describe the area. *Nook* could also aptly describe just about every part of the apartment. There was a nook where his sofa and TV set resided, a nook for his bed and battered bureau.

Maneuvering between the nooks was a challenge because, in addition to the furniture, the moving company had delivered a myriad of boxes. Within the boxes was the product of his twenty-nine years on earth. The boxes had been here, largely untampered with, for the past six days. He didn't see a grand opening in any of their near futures.

Nick paused to remove his holster and weapon and place them on the table beside the pizza. He'd then crossed to the refrigerator and took out a can of soda.

You'd think that someone who'd moved and lived in six different states before his fifteenth birthday would be able to unpack everything and get things in their rightful place in a reasonable amount of time. The trouble was, every other time he'd moved, and this included when he'd gone to his own bachelor digs in D.C., his mother and his sister were the ones who did the unpacking for him because he just never got around to it.

It wasn't his strong point. He knew how to work a case, had a knack for mining the hidden nuggets that could eventually lead to solving it. The gift his mother and sister possessed was that they knew how to make order out of chaos. Something he definitely was *not* good at.

Popping the lid on the can, he shrugged. There was no sense in unpacking what he didn't immediately need. And, since dinner tonight had come courtesy of Salvatore and Selena's Pizzeria, he didn't need to unearth anything. Certainly not plates or utensils. The pizza represented the ultimate in finger food. He always drank his soda right out of the can, so no need to dirty a glass.

Taking a long sip from his soda, Nick rotated his shoulders before picking up a slice of pizza. Man, he was tired.

His body hadn't adjusted to the time difference yet. His internal clock was still on East Coast time. It was ten o'clock in the evening back in D.C. right now and, although he'd never been one of those souls who turned in early, the day he'd spent with his new partner, coupled with the time difference, had all but wiped him out.

Catching a serial-killer case his first time up at bat in the new office threw him headfirst into the deep end of the pool.

He was going to have to find a gym and get himself back into shape. Special Agent Charley Dow struck him as a long-distance swimmer. He didn't want her showing him up. His pride wouldn't allow it. Not that he had anything against working with a woman. But there was just something about this woman that forbade him to look bad.

There was no doubt in his mind that Dow had a chip on her shoulder. Whether she had something against him in particular or men in general he didn't know, but it made things difficult. He had the feeling that she was waiting for him to screw up somehow. He was going to have to stay on his toes, not let down his guard. And he was going to have to learn how to get along with her, at least for a while. It wouldn't look right asking for a transfer his first week on the job. Especially since he wanted in on this case.

He'd gone alone to the morgue to see about Stacy Pembroke. The M.E. was in the middle of his evaluation. Stacy Pembroke was only twenty-five. Ashley's age. Hell, under different circumstances, that could have been Ashley on the table.

The Sunday Killer's victims were all someone's sister, someone's daughter. The bastard had to be stopped and put away if not put down. And he wanted to be there when it happened.

That meant staying partnered with Dow.

He thought of Gerald, the partner he had before coming out west. Gerald and he had hit a rhythm. So much so that they didn't even have to talk much. They each seemed to know what the other guy was thinking. He doubted he'd get to that level with Dow. If today was any indication, he had no idea where her mind was going.

Thinking the slice had had enough time to cool off, Nick took a bite. He chewed slowly, evaluating the flavors that came to meet his tongue.

As far as pizzas went, he had to admit that this sampling wasn't bad. But Salvatore and Selena didn't hold a candle to the pizzas he'd had in New York City. Cheese there tended to be one long, continuous strand from first bite to last. Sloppy, sure, but tasty as hell. A love affair with the palate.

He couldn't help wondering how else California would fail to measure up.

Nick went over and turned the TV on, switching to the all-news cable channel he'd discovered earlier in the week. He adjusted the volume, then sat down on the freshly cleaned beige rug.

The blond, perfectly made-up woman behind the news desk looked grim as she announced: "The top story in the Southland tonight is a grisly one. The serial killer has claimed another victim. Stacy Pembroke was discovered early this morning by a friend who was concerned when the twenty-five-year-old restaurant hostess failed to appear at work last night. This makes the young woman the twelfth victim in six years. Our reporters tried to get a statement from the family."

Nick cringed. Why was there always some reporter looking for a sound bite of attention, willing to shove a microphone into the face of a grieving soul? He reached for the remote to change the channel.

The doorbell rang.

Nick swallowed a curse. "Wouldn't you know it? Murphy's law."

Leaning back, he could just about see around the boxes to make out the front door from his position on the floor. He took another bite, debating whether or not to ignore whoever was at the door or answer it.

Most likely some kid was selling something. He'd already been subjected to that on his first day here and wound up buying wrapping paper he didn't need in support of some elementary school he'd never heard of. He'd chalked it up to forging good community relations.

But he wasn't in the mood for wrapping paper. Or interruptions for that matter.

Whoever was at the door rang again. Apparently they weren't about to give up easily. Persistent, he thought darkly. Which immediately brought his new partner to mind.

Maybe that was Dow at the door. He frowned, taking another bite of his dinner as the woman on the cable channel faded into a commercial.

Likely as not, Dow had probably thought of something after he'd left the office and was here to bust his manhood. He hadn't told her where he lived, but he had no doubts that she had ways of finding out.

With a sigh, Nick got up, leaving the TV on. He thought of putting his pizza slice back in the box before answering the door, but hunger proved to be greater than his desire for neatness.

After pausing to wipe his fingers on a napkin, Nick opened the door.

No one was there.

He should have remained where he was, he thought. About to retreat, he glanced down at the mat the complex superintendent had given him as a "welcome to Sunflower Creek Apartments" gift.

The body of a small, brown rabbit had been placed right in the middle of it. The rabbit's throat had been slit.

CHAPTER NINE

NICK REACTED instantly, ducking back into the apartment. He grabbed his sheathed weapon from the table.

When he crossed the threshold, stepping just outside of his apartment, his movements were precise as if in slow motion. No one needed to remind him of the value of caution. One misstep could cost him his life, or at the very least, turn him into a target.

There was no one in the immediate vicinity.

Gun cocked, he scanned from left to right, then out into the parking lot that faced the door of his first-floor garden apartment.

Nothing.

The rain had receded to a fine mist. Just annoying enough to keep evening strollers from venturing out of their dry apartments. The streetlights were on. Nick squinted, trying to make out a solitary figure hiding within one of the carports. There was no one. Whoever had rung his doorbell was as fleet as the rabbit they'd left on his doormat had once been.

A noise caught his attention. In the distance he thought he heard the sound of a car pulling away. But that could have just as easily been one of the complex's residents going out for the evening. It made no sense to attempt to give chase. Especially when he'd only heard the vehicle, not seen it. He had no idea what direction the driver had taken.

Nick lowered his weapon. His adrenaline was another matter.

Pity wafted through him as he looked down at the dead animal on his doorstep. There was no blood, so it had been killed somewhere else and then transported here. He hoped the animal hadn't been tortured. Something told him that it hadn't been, that killing the rabbit wasn't the object. Leaving a message was.

Though a good three thousand miles separated him from his old life, Nick had an uneasy feeling he knew exactly who'd left the dead rabbit on his doorstep.

How the hell had he known where to find him? Granted, Nick's transfer to the West Coast wasn't a secret. His superiors knew and his family. But the information wasn't exactly posted on the Internet.

Apparently Sean Dixon had hidden talents he didn't know about. The thought did not fill him with joy.

Shaking his head, Nick went back into his apartment to fetch a plastic grocery bag and a pair of plastic gloves. The rabbit was evidence. Nick carefully slipped the animal inside the plastic bag, then tied off the top, making a secure knot.

The rabbit was going to have to spend the night in his refrigerator, he thought grimly. Luckily, it was pretty much empty, except for a few cans of soda and three bottles of beer.

He deposited the rabbit on top of the lettuce crisper. Under the circumstances, it seemed an appropriate temporary resting place.

That done, he crossed back to the table and glanced

at the pizza still in the box. For a split second, his stomach threatened to cohabitate with his windpipe.

A man had to keep up his strength, he argued silently. His not eating wasn't going to matter to the deceased rabbit. With far less enthusiasm than he'd experienced only minutes earlier, Nick picked up another slice of pizza and returned to the living room. The program he had switched on had finished a round of commercials.

Nick sat down in front of the set.

THE FORENSIC LABS used by FBI special agents were located in the basement of the Federal Building that the Bureau occupied. The A.D.'s secretary, Alice something-or-other, had mentioned it to him yesterday in an effort to give him a thumbnail sketch of the area. At the time her description hadn't been important to him, but he was glad now that he'd paid attention to the woman, even though she had a voice guaranteed to put insomniacs to sleep.

Nick stepped off the elevator. As the doors closed behind him, he became conscious of the stillness. The office was quieter than a tomb. He wondered if anyone was in so early.

Only one way to find out, he thought.

The overhead fluorescent lights seemed to be using up their last wattage of energy. The hallway appeared almost unnaturally dim, enhancing the emptiness. It was just before eight o'clock.

Nick could hear the sound made by his shoes as his soles made contact with the floor. Upstairs, rugs throughout the area muffled the sound of approach. In the basement, the acoustics seemed almost incredibly amplified.

The floor covering here appeared to be some kind of man-made tile. The pattern was speckled and monotonous. He hoped that didn't say something about the nature of the work being done in this area.

Not knowing exactly where he was going, Nick made his way down the winding corridor until he came across an open door. As he looked into the room, he saw a tall, thin male technician in a white lab coat.

Headphones on his head, the technician seemed to be in his own little world as he sat on a stool next to a long counter that ran half the length of the room. Holding a large eyedropper, the man was depositing a single drop of liquid into each of the test tubes lined up in front of him.

Nick walked into the room and attempted to place himself where the lab technician would be able to see him. The name tag just over his breast pocket identified him as one Hank Garcia. Caught up in his work, Hank Garcia continued humming and dispensing drops of opaque liquid, completely oblivious to Nick's entrance.

Trying again, Nick leaned over until he was directly in Hank's line of vision.

Startled, Hank drew in a quick breath. Putting the eyedropper down, he took off his headphones, sliding them down around his neck. The headphones hung there like an incomplete necklace, audible music coming from both earpieces. Hank looked at him, suspicion and annoyance washing over his face.

"Hey man, don't sneak up on me like that."

Nick nodded toward the dangling earphones. "Listening to music at that level will make you deaf."

The next moment, he wondered how his father's voice had managed to emerge from his mouth. That was the kind of caution his father had been guilty of voicing. He'd always viewed it as the Colonel's constant attempts to curtail his freedom and control him.

"Hey, Snakepit's gotta be heard loud in order to be appreciated," Hank protested. And then he frowned slightly. "Should you be down here?"

Shifting the bag with its carcass to his other hand, Nick fished out his wallet and held it up for the tech's benefit.

"Special Agent Nick Brannigan," Nick introduced himself. Tucking his wallet back into his pocket, Nick placed the plastic grocery bag on the counter. He nodded at it. "What can you tell me about this?"

Hank leaned over and took apart the bag's knot. Very carefully, he exposed what was inside. If he was surprised to find the dead rabbit, he didn't show it. Nick got the impression that the young tech viewed surprises as uncool. The only indication that Hank found the bag's contents less than appealing was the slight flaring of his nostrils.

Hank replaced the sides of the bag and looked at his visitor. "Right off the top of my head, I'd say it's dead."

"Brilliant deduction," Nick replied drily. "What else can you tell me?"

A shade of confusion highlighted the young face. "Like?"

Good question, Nick thought. He didn't really know what he was looking for, except he was pretty certain you couldn't get prints off fur. But there might be traces of other things, things that might turn his suspicions into certainties.

He left it open to interpretation. Garcia was the forensic tech, not him. "Anything."

Hank pressed his lips into a tight line. "That's going to take some time. I'm a little backed up here." And then

Hank laughed under his breath. "But then, I'm always a little backed up here. How fast do you need this?"

That was easy. Yesterday. "As fast as you can get it to me."

Cocking his head, Hank took another peek at the grocery bag's contents. His brows knit together, as if he was trying to connect invisible dots in his head. "This part of a case you're working?"

Nick didn't believe in lying. Stretching the truth, however, was something else. He knew that, as a rule, the Bureau frowned on using its facilities for personal matters. But then, he argued, maybe he was wrong about the rabbit's origin. Maybe it was a message from the serial killer. It was a well-known theory that most serial killers started out killing small animals.

But the Sunday Killer wasn't just starting out.

"In a manner of speaking," Nick said.

"In other words," Hank said knowingly, "you'd like to keep this just between us."

Nick nodded. "I'd appreciate that." He paused, then added honestly, "I'd consider it a favor."

When Hank smiled, he looked more like a mischievous boy than a young man who had graduated from Polytech with honors.

"Never know when that might come in handy," he murmured. "Okay, Special Agent Brannigan, I'll see what I can do."

"Thanks." His mission accomplished, Nick began to leave.

Hank called out, stopping him. "If I find anything, where can I reach you?"

"Seventh floor," Nick told him. "I'm on the Sunday Killer's task force."

Hank looked duly impressed. The next moment, he retreated to his task and his earphones. Nick noted that he hadn't bothered to adjust the volume level.

CHAPTER TEN

TO MAKE UP FOR HER later-than-usual entrance the day before, Charley came to work the following morning approximately forty-five minutes earlier than her customary starting time. No one would have said anything about the missing minutes, but doing this evened out some inner balance sheet she kept in her head.

Besides, she wanted some time to herself to think about the case. She found the atmosphere at work more conducive to steady and constructive thought. Home provided too many distractions. And home was where her father called her, wanting to be kept abreast of her progress. As if she could somehow magically bring the case to a close if she just applied herself enough.

At least, that seemed to be her father's opinion. She'd told him that he couldn't call her at the office, saying it was against company rules. Her father had no idea she owned a cell phone. If he did, she'd really have no peace. But, mercifully, her father wasn't one to keep up with the times so she was safe for now.

Time had stopped for Christopher Dow and for his wife the night Cris was murdered. The only difference being, of the two, her father had continued to function. To get up each morning and go to work, to put the sorrow that haunted his soul on hold until he returned home at night.

There were times, when she visited, that she'd catch her father looking at her and she knew what he was thinking. Why hadn't she been the one? Why hadn't she been the one to have stayed home that night when the killer had struck? Then she would be dead and Cris would still be alive. It was no secret that Cris had always been his favorite. As far back as she could remember, Cris had gotten their father's attention. Cris had been able to make him smile. It was as if she and her older brother, David, didn't even exist.

Her mother had played no such favorites. But her mother had been utterly devastated by Cris's murder. Within six months, she had fallen completely apart, withdrawing into herself where the world couldn't get at her. These days, her mother resided in a psychiatric hospital. Part of every paycheck she earned went to pay for the facility. Her father couldn't handle the burden on his own and she couldn't bear the idea of her mother living in a state institution.

She hadn't gone to visit her mother in several days. Maybe she'd swing by tonight on her way home, Charley thought as she got off the elevator. Not that her mother knew one way or another whether or not she came by. Claire Dow just sat in her chair, staring off into space, existing somewhere in a place devoid of pain. Charley supposed that somewhere in her heart she nursed the hope that if she could catch the killer, if she could bring Cris's murderer to justice, her mother would come back from her dark place.

It made her try twice as hard. Gave her twice the stake.

At eight o'clock in the morning, the seventh floor was still rather empty and quiet. Even though Charley liked the energy generated by agents going at full throttle, she had to admit a fondness for the aura of tranquillity that embraced the various offices before the day began.

The task force's room was located in the middle of the floor. Walking in, an extra-tall container of ordinary black coffee in her hand, Charley had fully expected to find herself alone for at least half an hour, if not more. Both Bill and Sam usually arrived at the start of the workday, sometimes a little later if Sam's new baby had kept him and his wife up, or Bill had had a particularly adventurous and exhausting night with his date of the month. The various other people attached to the task force trickled in around the same time.

Aside from A.D. Kelly and, on occasion, his secretary, Charley was the only one who came in early on a regular basis.

So it went without saying that she was surprised to see her new partner at his desk, absorbed in his computer screen.

So much for solitude.

Charley put her container on her desk. "Playing solitaire?"

He'd been aware of her entrance. It was soundless, but she wore a scent that lightly rode the air currents, announcing her presence. He found the perfume appealing, even if the woman's personality really wasn't.

Nick glanced up at her for a moment before looking back at the screen. "Going over the evidence."

She pried the lid off her container, tossing it into

the empty wastepaper basket beneath her desk. "Very commendable."

He couldn't make out if she was being sarcastic and couldn't decide if she irritated him or just intrigued him. She was damn attractive, but that didn't tip the scales one way or another. He'd always been a personality man. Except for once, when he'd miscalculated.

"I was going for practical," he told her. On the Internet, he was scrolling through old newspaper stories about the serial killer. "A fresh set of eyes, that kind of thing."

So, he was a go-getter, despite his easy manner. Or was he only interested in brownie points? It wouldn't have taken much for him to find out that the A.D. came in early most mornings. "And what did your 'fresh set of eyes' come up with?"

The stories he'd read were just a rehashing of the data he'd already familiarized himself with. "Nothing new," he admitted. And then he raised his eyes to hers. "So far."

Her lips twisted in a patient smile. Because she had to get along with him, she gave her new partner the benefit of the doubt. "Hope springs eternal."

Charley dropped her purse into its usual hiding place, the bottom drawer of her desk, then pushed it closed again with her foot. Picking up her coffee container, she made her way over to the back wall. To the photographs of the dead women impatiently waiting for closure.

The photograph of her sister drew her to that side the way it always did. Cris was smiling, captured in a moment of pure joy. She remembered when the photograph was taken. Cris has just hinted that there might be someone special in her life. Charley had known by the way her sister talked that she was in love.

Cris never got the chance to introduce her to him. She was killed the following Sunday.

Charley stifled a sigh. She felt that same leap inside her throat, that same tightening of her stomach. It occurred each time she found herself standing here looking at Cris. Wondering for what amounted to the thousandth time if her sister had actually been the serial killer's intended victim, or if he had made a mistake. If he'd actually intended on killing her and had gotten the wrong twin.

And just like all the other times, frustration overtook her, because she had no way of knowing the answer.

Not until she had the serial killer in front of her.

"I don't know how I missed that."

Her partner's voice penetrated her thoughts, bringing her back to the present. She turned, a surge of hope surfacing. Had Brannigan actually found something, the clue that was continuing to elude them? As sure as one day followed the other, she was confident there had to be one. It was there, probably out in plain sight, taunting them.

"Missed what?"

Instead of calling her over and pointing to something he'd found on the screen, Brannigan had abandoned his desk and was making his way over toward her.

He indicated her sister's photograph. "That she looked like you."

She felt deflated. It was all she could do not to snap at him for having raised her hopes, however unintentionally.

When this case is over, I'm taking a very long vacation.

"That's because all blondes tend to look alike," she answered sarcastically, "or so I'm told."

"By who?" he asked mildly. "A jealous brunette?"

The response had caught her off guard. Charley laughed. "If you're trying to get on my good side—"

Nick raised a brow. "Yes?"

A clever put-down rose to her lips. Charley shrugged, letting it die unspoken. She'd resolved to be less hard-nosed when it came to dealing with Nick Brannigan. To try to make the best of the situation and sheathe her resentment. It wasn't his fault that Ben had retired.

So she smiled and said, "I'd say you made a nice start."

Nick moved until he could see both Charley and her late sister's photograph at the same time. The girl in the photograph looked as if she didn't have a care in the world. The woman he was partnered with seemed to be shouldering the weight of that same world. The difference had thrown him.

"Damn, she does look like you."

The smile on her lips turned sad. "She should. She was my twin. Older by two minutes."

"You or her?"

"Her. We were identical twins." *And I miss her every day. Miss her as much as Dad does.* "You couldn't see the difference between us," she told him. "You had to be there for it."

Nick's dark eyes narrowed slightly in confusion. "Meaning?"

"Meaning Cris was the one who was always full of life. Full of energy." And she had been content to hang back in Cris's shadow.

"I've only been around you for a day, but you don't exactly strike me as a slacker."

No, she wasn't. Now she went full steam ahead—until she dropped. "That came after Cris was murdered. I felt I owed it to her. Kind of like living for two," she murmured, taking another sip from her container, her eyes on the photograph.

"Is that why you joined the Bureau?"

"Part of it." The biggest part, she thought. If Cris hadn't died, she probably would have gone on to join the local police force. To keep things on a small scale instead of joining a national organization. "I was always interested in criminology, in getting the bad guys." She wasn't aware of the sigh until it escaped. "Just never thought it was going to feel so personal."

Charley stopped abruptly and looked at the man at her side. She had no idea why she hadn't realized it before, but the new guy had a definite sexy aura about him. Was that going to be a problem? Did he have a need to charm every woman he came across? If he thought that applied to her, he'd picked the wrong woman.

"Are you pumping me, Special Agent Brannigan?"

His expression was unreadable. She didn't know if he was being sarcastic or genuine. "Wouldn't dream of it. Just making conversation with my new partner."

She studied him for a moment over the rim of her swiftly cooling container of coffee. "You'd rather be working with a man, wouldn't you?"

The question had come out of the blue. As far as he knew, he'd done nothing to give her that impression. Maybe she was speaking from experience. "All things being equal, I just want to work with a good agent. Male, female or pollywog, doesn't matter to me."

His response amused her. "The recruitment for pollywogs is drastically down this year," she deadpanned. "Something about a height requirement."

Nick matched her, tone for tone. To anyone listening, they could have been engaged in a serious conversation. "Oh really? I would have thought it might have something to do with the fact that they have trouble hitting the mark on the target range."

She nodded, this time using the container to hide the smile that was curving her mouth. "No opposable thumbs."

"No hands to put them on," he countered.

"That, too." She lowered the container. The smile remained. "Maybe we'll get along after all, Special Agent Brannigan."

It would go a long way to making things easier. "Then maybe you'll call me Nick."

"Maybe," Charley allowed as she returned to her desk. She added, "We'll see," and then got to work.

CHAPTER ELEVEN

THE MOMENT Robert Pullman saw them enter his restaurant and head straight toward him, he looked uncomfortable. Rounding the reservations desk, he waved to one of the hostesses, indicating that she should take his place.

It was obvious that the handsome owner didn't want them to be overheard.

"We have a few questions we'd like to ask you, Mr. Pullman," Charley told the man.

The restaurant owner stood about six-two, and right now every inch of him seemed to sweat.

"Of course. Anything I can do to help," he murmured. "If we could just go into my office."

"Your office is fine," Charley agreed obligingly.

As she followed Pullman to the rear of the restaurant, she was aware of the fact that her new partner wasn't trying to take over the interview. She appreciated that. At the same time she couldn't help wondering why. In her experience, men Brannigan's age usually engaged in some sort of jockeying for position. So far, he hadn't. She didn't know whether to relax or remain on her guard. He could be counting on her relaxing that guard.

Only time would tell, she supposed.

The moment the door was closed, she appraised Pullman. *Mr. Forty-two Tall,* she thought. She was willing to bet a month's salary that the clothes in Stacy Pembroke's bedroom belonged to him.

"What size are you, Mr. Pullman?" she asked mildly.

Pullman seemed in danger of swallowing his own tongue. "Excuse me?"

"What size are you?" Charley repeated. "Specifically in jackets." Charley glanced over toward her left where Nick was standing. "I'd guess a forty-two tall." She turned her head toward Nick. "How about you, Special Agent Brannigan?"

Nick backed her up. "That would be my guess."

Pullman's intake of breath was audible. It told them everything they needed to know.

"We found clothes in Stacy Pembroke's bedroom, Mr. Pullman," Charley told the man. "Men's clothes."

"Piled up on the floor," Nick interjected in a low-key voice. "Like she was dumping someone."

Charley straightened slightly. The look in Pullman's eyes was that of a cornered animal. "That wouldn't have been you, would it, Mr. Pullman?"

"Was Stacy dumping you?" Nick pressed.

Pullman looked nervously from one FBI agent to another. She was willing to wager that ordinarily Pullman was probably a smooth operator. But the layers were being peeled away, leaving a frightened man beneath. A frightened, married man who didn't want his wife to know about his affair. Graying at the temples and more than twenty years Stacy's senior, Pullman had probably seen the young waitress as a fantasy come true.

"No!" he cried with emphasis, then realized what he had just admitted to. "I mean—" Desperate, he appealed to Nick in an apparent man-to-man play for sympathy.

"Look, if my wife finds out that I was having an affair, she's going to leave me."

"I think, right at this moment, having your wife walk out on you might be the least of your problems," Nick said.

Pullman's brown eyes grew huge as the words registered. "You think I did this?" His head almost swiveled as he glanced from one agent to the other. His voice fairly squeaked. "You think that I killed Stacy?"

Charley exchanged looks with Nick before answering. "The thought did cross our minds."

"No. Hell no." Pullman's voice rose with each word of denial. "I can't even kill a roach. Ask anyone." He pointed wildly toward the outer room. "I get one of the busboys to stomp on it."

"So who did you get to stomp on Stacy?" Charley asked, moving in a little closer to the man.

Pullman squirmed. "It's not like that."

Quietly Nick had moved to his other side. "Tell me what it is like, Mr. Pullman," he urged evenly.

"Stacy was fun. She made me feel young again. The way I hadn't felt in years."

Same old story, Charley thought. Older man needing affirmation, younger woman needing trinkets. But she wanted Pullman to spell it out for them. "And what did you make her feel like, Mr. Pullman?"

Pullman gave a helpless shrug of his shoulders. "I don't know. I—I gave her things."

The owner looked from one to the other again uncertainly. Was he trying to guess if he'd given the right answer? Charley wondered. Was this the guilt of a cheating husband they were witnessing, or of a murderer? Everybody was a suspect. Until they had their man.

"Like promises?" Nick guessed.

"No," Pullman cried.

Charley was quick to push the advantage. If Pullman was going to be pressured into telling the truth, it would be now. "Maybe you promised to marry her and she found out you were lying."

"No!"

Charley continued as if the man hadn't made the protest. "Stacy threatened to tell your wife about the two of you. You saw your business going south, losing everything you'd worked for. You tried to talk Stacy out of it, she refused. You lost your head. You grabbed her by the throat and squeezed, trying to get her to say she wouldn't ruin your life. You squeezed a little too hard." Charley lifted a shoulder casually. "These things happen."

"No, no." Panic was rising in Pullman's voice. "That's insane." He was visibly shaking now. Charley raised her eyes to Nick. Her partner kept a solemn expression in place as he listened to the restaurant owner. "Look, I never laid a hand on her. *Ever,*" he emphasized. "I really liked her. A lot. I wouldn't have hurt her. I swear," he repeated, his eyes pleading with them to believe him.

"You were the last one she talked to. We checked the phone records," Charley interjected before the man could protest.

The breath Pullman released was shaky. He was a man on a tightrope, knowing he couldn't remain in place but afraid of falling if he took a step. "I did call her on Sunday. But it was to tell her that I couldn't make it. She got really angry at me and hung up. It was the last time I talked to her."

The significance of his own words seemed to penetrate. Pullman pressed his lips together, struggling with tears. The tears won. They slid down his cheeks. He brushed them away angrily.

"The last time," he repeated in a voice choked with emotion. He looked directly at Charlie and added, "I swear."

"You swear a lot, Mr. Pullman." A tolerant sigh escaped her lips. After a beat, Charley nodded. "All right, Mr. Pullman. That's all for now. We'll be in touch."

THEY LEFT HIM standing in his office, visibly shaken. Not by the threat of incarceration, Nick thought, but because the death of his mistress had finally registered.

Walking out of the building, Nick automatically held the door open for his partner. He was mildly surprised that Charley didn't say something about being able to get her own door. Maybe she wasn't all that militant after all.

"You believe him?" she asked as they approached her vehicle.

Nick didn't have to think about it. He'd formed an opinion during the questioning.

"Yeah, I do." Then, because he knew she wanted reasons, he added, "Pullman really looks broken up about the girl's murder."

After deactivating the security alarm, Charley opened the white Honda's door and got in behind the wheel. "Could just be acting."

After getting in on the passenger side, Nick buckled up. "I don't think so."

Instead of starting the car, she turned to him, curious. The beginning of a working relationship was like a dance with a stranger. You had to feel him out, make sure you didn't wind up with flat, crushed feet. "And you base this on what, gut instinct?"

Nick shrugged. "For lack of a better word, yes."

Key in the ignition, Charley started the car. She kept her profile to him so he wouldn't notice her amused smile. "How often has your gut been right?"

"More than not." He shifted in his seat as she peeled out. The woman had an Indianapolis 500 complex, but he was determined not to show her that her driving rattled him. "Besides, aren't we operating under the assumption that the girl was murdered by the Sunday Killer?"

She glanced in her rearview mirror. Traffic was almost nonexistent. Just the way she liked it. She opened up a little more. "Just ruling out a copycat murder."

"I thought the tiny cross on her forehead did that," he reminded her.

For the most part, he was right. But she liked to cover all contingencies, just in case. "Just crossing my *t*s and dotting my *i*s."

He knew law-enforcement agents who needed only a hint before they ran with something. She was more meticulous than he would have thought.

"You always so thorough?"

"Always," she answered with finality. "If you want a case that'll stand up in court, you have to make sure you don't leave anything for the other side to pick up on."

"Makes sense," Nick allowed. "So we're back to looking for the Sunday Killer."

"Yeah." And she wanted the man so bad she could taste it. She realized that she was holding on to the wheel with enough strength that her knuckles were turning white. With effort, she forced herself to relax her grip. "Let's hope forensics has come up with something for us. Fibers, hairs, something."

The people in the crime-scene-investigation department had taken an incredible number of items from the scene. Undoubtedly, most would lead them to a dead end.

Nick glanced at her rigid profile. The case meant a lot to her. Considering her connection, he didn't wonder. "You feeling lucky?"

Charley stared straight ahead as she drove. She hadn't felt lucky in a long, long time. "No."

"Me, neither." He sank back in his seat, crossing his arms before him. He figured whatever luck he had was being used up right now, as he sat here, watching the scenery whiz by. So far, the woman hadn't crashed them. "Let's hope anyway."

NATASHYA KOVAL WAS bent over her work when they entered the lab twenty minutes later. She glanced in their direction, then smiled.

"Found a hair." She held up a hand, forestalling any comment from either of them. "Before you get all excited, it's a cat hair."

Nick thought back to their examination of the apartment. "The victim didn't have any cats."

Another piece of the puzzle, Charley thought, however minor. She was grateful. "Which means that the killer does."

"Or has friends that do," Nick said.

But Charley shook her head. "I don't see this person as having friends."

They had differing opinions on the profile, Nick surmised. "Maybe our boy's not a weirdo twenty-four/seven," he countered. "Ted Bundy was thought to be a friendly guy. And the guy who confessed to being the BTK killer had a prominent place in society. Was even the president of his church group. This guy doesn't have to be the type to sit and talk to his wallpaper, working himself up until he's ready to kill again. Besides, until just lately, it's been a long time in between victims for him. In the meantime, the guy has had to earn a living in order to eat, has had to interact with people—"

"Just because he works with people doesn't mean he has to be friends with them," she pointed out. "And most people don't bring their cats to work."

Nick wasn't ready to let the point drop. "Ever hear of transfer, Special Agent?"

She sighed. This wasn't getting them anywhere; it was only serving to amuse the lab tech. "I'll keep an open mind."

"Nice to hear," Nick commented.

They had begun to leave when Natashya called after him. "By the way, Special Agent Brannigan." Nick turned around, waiting. "Hank wanted me to tell you something if I saw you."

"I'll just—"

Before he had a chance to cut her off and say he'd swing by Garcia's station, Natashya gave him the message, in front of Charley. Exactly what he hadn't wanted.

"He said the report on the rabbit is ready. And that you might be interested to know that the rabbit was pregnant."

The enigmatic message caught Charley's attention immediately. Just as he knew it would. She stopped and glared at her new partner. "You get a rabbit into trouble, Special Agent Brannigan?"

Instead of laughing her question off, he shrugged carelessly as he continued walking out the door. "In a manner of speaking, I guess I probably did."

CHAPTER TWELVE

HE WAS STRIDING ahead of her. Charley quickened her pace, caught him by the arm and refused to let go until he turned to her.

"Okay, you're not going anywhere until you explain that one," Charley informed him tersely. Her question to him about the rabbit's plight had been a joke. His response apparently hadn't been.

Nick didn't want to discuss it. He wished the technician had kept his mouth shut.

"Just something I need to look into."

"Regarding the case?"

Nick stretched the truth. And credibility. "Possibly."

"And possibly not," Charley concluded. The way she said it let Nick know on which side of "not" she thought it stood.

He had too much on his mind to play games. "Look, Special Agent Dow, if you want to put me on report with A.D. Kelly—"

Charley stared at him, puzzled. "Why would I want to do that?"

Nick threw up his hands. Depending on policy enforcement here, she had the ammunition to get another partner. "For abusing the facilities."

Her expression told him that she didn't quite see it that way, nor did she want to play it like that.

"I just heard a 'possibly,'" she informed him lightly. "That's good enough for me—if you tell me just how a pregnant rabbit figures in your life."

Not wanting the conversation to carry throughout the entire floor, Nick ducked into an alcove. Charley went right along with him. "That's what I was trying to find out."

The alcove, she realized, was just a fraction too small. And she was standing more than a fraction too close to Brannigan. She moved back as far as she could, creating a whisper of a space between them. She found the need for air urgent and immediate.

"I need a little more information than that," she told him. "Did you find one on your doorstep?"

"Yes."

Her eyes widened at the response. "I was just kidding." Charley turned the situation over in her head. "You're new to the neighborhood, aren't you?"

"Yes." He gave the answer guardedly, not knowing where she was headed with this.

"Maybe the rabbit was intended for someone else. The tenant who lived in the apartment before you," Charley suggested. "Or maybe someone got their apartments mixed up."

"Could be," he allowed in a voice that said he didn't really buy into either theory.

Charley was quick to pick up his tone. "But you don't think so."

Nick had never cared for being questioned, second-guessed or probed. "Trying to get into my head, Special Agent Dow?"

"Wouldn't have to, if you volunteered a little."

Nick shrugged, looking over her head. Hoping she'd

get the message without his having to tell her to butt out. "Nothing to volunteer yet."

To his surprise, she caught him by the lapels and forced him to look at her. "Partners are supposed to have each other's backs, Brannigan. I can't cover your back if I don't know what to expect."

She had beautiful eyes, he thought suddenly. Eyes that went right through a man, clear to his spine.

Nick mentally pulled himself back. Those weren't the kind of reactions a man had about his partner. Not if he intended to remain part of a successful team. "It's just a hunch."

She released his lapels but made no effort to step out of his way. If he wanted to get out of the alcove, he was going to have to physically move her. Or give her an answer she accepted.

"What kind of a hunch?"

He shrugged. "Maybe I'm being paranoid." It was meant to get her to back away.

It failed. Charley rolled along with the comment. "Just because you're paranoid doesn't mean they're not out to get you."

She wasn't going to back off until she had what she wanted, he thought in exasperation. "It's a long story, Special Agent Dow."

Charley smiled sweetly. "Fine, I love long stories. We're due for a lunch break. You can entertain me."

He gave her a long, significant look. One that went along the length of her before it returned to rest on her eyes. "Telling stories is not the way I usually entertain a lady."

It took Charley a second to recover, and do it without swallowing. Not that she could. Her mouth had suddenly turned bone-dry. She was aware that the terms of their future partnership depended on her not showing her reaction. She liked to think that when the chips were down she could bluff her way out of anything.

"Think of it as broadening your repertoire," she instructed flippantly.

With reluctance, he agreed to give her at least a partial explanation over lunch. After he got the report.

NICK STOPPED BY the lab to get the report from Hank. Not that there was much to add to what he'd already been told. The rabbit had been pregnant when it died.

But that was enough. It told Nick everything he needed to know.

He muttered his thanks and left. There was no point in saying anything about the fact that Garcia was less tight-lipped than he would have liked. At least he'd gotten to the rabbit quickly.

"You okay?" Charley asked when he came out of the glass-enclosed lab.

"Let's go eat," Nick said.

The fact that he didn't answer the question was not lost on Charley.

SHE TOOK HIM to a nearby taco restaurant, one she frequented. When it came to placing his order, Nick told her to pick for him, then added that he'd never had anything on the menu so he was going to have to trust her. She'd looked at him as if he'd just admitted to hopping the ten-fifteen shuttle from Mars, then ordered two beef-and-cheese burritos.

"I can't believe you've never had a burrito," she said when they received their order several minutes later.

"Missed that in my education," he responded.

Charley waited until he'd taken a second bite, then asked, "Well, what do you think?"

He enjoyed it. As far as fast food went, this was preferable to a hot dog. "It's a theme and variation on a crepe."

As good an assessment as any, Charley thought. She also estimated that she'd given him enough time to frame the answer she was waiting for. Unwrapping her own burrito, she looked at him before digging in. "Okay, so much for the gourmet portion of our program. You were going to entertain me with a story."

Nick regretted not lying to her. He wasn't comfortable with lies, but he wasn't exactly comfortable with the truth in this case, either. It wasn't that he felt guilty. He couldn't have played his hand any other way. But he did have regrets about how things had ended up.

He shrugged and gave it one more try. "Not much to tell."

The hell there wasn't, she thought. "It went from a long story to a summary? All right, give me whatever you want to give me. But give me something." Their eyes met and she added, "We're partners."

"Right, the bonding thing," he muttered, taking another bite. He slid the paper that was wrapped around the burrito down further. "Can't we just make a slit in our thumbs and mingle our blood?"

He wasn't wiggling out of it that easily. This was something that was eating away at him, and might have some maniac camping out on Brannigan's doorstep. She needed to know what she was up against if she was going to be there for him.

"Talk," Charley ordered. Her expression grew serious. "Are you in some kind of trouble, Brannigan?"

She headed him off, in case he was going to offer a flippant remark. "And before you staunchly deny it, most people don't open their door to find dead rabbits lying on their doorstep, not unless there's something else going on in their lives."

He frowned, lowering his eyes to his meal. "It's personal."

"So am I. Stop stalling, Brannigan," she insisted. This wasn't something she was going to back away from. It was in her nature to get involved. Not to merely test the waters but to jump in with both feet. For better or worse, the man was her partner and if that was going to work, trust had to be involved. He had to give her his. And then maybe she'd give him hers.

The slightest hint of humor surfaced around his mouth. "Anyone ever tell you that you're a pushy broad, Special Agent Dow?"

Her mouth curved. "Part of my charm. Talk," she repeated.

He took a long breath, then finally said, "There was this woman back in D.C."

When he paused, she pushed. If she had to crawl down his throat with forceps to get this story out, one piece at a time, she was determined to get it. "Yes?"

"Her name was Linda." He tried not to remember her face. Tried not to remember anything at all. He just wanted this behind him, although he was beginning to doubt that it ever would be. "Linda Dixon." He studied the paper cup that held his soda. "She was a little intense, but we had a good time. At first."

"And then?" Charley prodded.

"And then she began closing in on me. Talking

about marriage, kids, rocking chairs side by side on the porch—"

Guaranteed to send most men running for the hills, Charley thought. "All the things a man wants to hear."

"Maybe," he countered, surprising her. "From the right person."

She looked at him with interest. The man was deeper than she thought. It wasn't hard to make the next guess. "But she wasn't the right person."

"No, she wasn't. When she got too intense, I tried to break it off. That's when she really got weird on me, threatening to kill herself if I left." Nick took a breath, retiring what was left of his burrito. He'd lost his appetite. "Turned out she was pregnant."

Charley sat perfectly still. "What did you do?" she asked quietly.

He sighed. "I didn't marry her, which was what she wanted."

Nick checked to see if there was any condemnation in Charley's eyes. Women tended to stick together in his experience, even when they didn't know each other. Something about a sisterhood.

The look on Charley's face encouraged him to continue. "I offered to help support the baby, pay her hospital bills, that kind of thing." He tried to ignore the helpless feeling his words stirred up.

"What did she say?"

"A lot of things. Hysterical mostly. I thought she'd calm down eventually." Which was stupid of him, given Linda's nature. He should have seen it coming, but he didn't. He never thought Linda would go through with it. Never thought Linda would kill herself. The only women he really knew thoroughly were his mother and his sister. Neither one of them would have killed themselves. They would have persevered.

"But she didn't," Charley guessed.

"No, she didn't." He took a breath. "She killed herself. She left a note, saying it was my fault. That if I couldn't love her, she was better off dead."

Her compassion was immediate. Nick wasn't just reciting something that had happened in his past. This had affected him a great deal, and continued to. She was tempted to cover his hand with hers. But there were boundaries to respect, so she refrained.

"You know it's not your fault," she said firmly.

"Yeah, I know." But there was little conviction in his voice.

She pushed the conversation forward, not wanting him to dwell on what couldn't be changed. "Do you have any idea who might have left that rabbit?"

"She had an older brother. Sean. He said a few things, made a few threats. But that's all I thought they were. Threats brought out by grief. I didn't think he'd track me down cross-country." Nick shrugged, dismissing the whole thing because there was nothing he could do about it at the moment. "If it's him."

She studied him for a moment. "Do you have anyone else in your past who would send you a dead pregnant rabbit?"

He laughed drily. "No."

Charley paused, trying to gauge how he would receive her next suggestion. "Maybe you should file a report with—"

"No," he said adamantly. If this was Sean, he wanted to give the man every opportunity to back off. Sean had already suffered enough. "He's just blowing off steam."

"And if he's not?"

"Then I'll handle it," he told her curtly.

Her eyes met his. She didn't agree with his decision, but it was his call to make. "Make sure you do. I wouldn't want to have to get another new partner so soon. The department might think I'm jinxed," she quipped.

They sat in silence for a few minutes, with nothing but the noise of the cars passing outside on the street filling the emptiness.

Charley took it for as long as she could. And then she asked, "How did you feel?"

He looked at her uncertainly. "About finding a dead rabbit on my doorstep?"

"No, when she killed herself." She was about to refer to the woman as his girlfriend but stopped herself in time. She had a feeling he wouldn't have appreciated the label.

"I thought it was a waste." He paused. "And guilty. Because I thought there might have been something I could have done to stop her."

She'd felt that way once, too. About her mother. But she'd learned otherwise. "Sometimes, no matter how hard you try, you can't reach someone else. All you can do is watch them go spiraling down."

He raised his eyes to hers. "You say that as if you had a front-row seat."

Charley thought about denying it, then shrugged. There was no point in that. "I did."

Curiosity got the better of him. "Your turn."

Not today. Charley tossed the empty wrapper onto the tray they'd shared. "Lunch is over."

He rose when she rose, picking up the tray. "We still have the rest of the day."

"To work," she pointed out.

Nick deposited the tray on top of a stack by the door, then followed her out. "I bared my soul."

"No, you didn't. You just took off your shirt, Brannigan. I'm sure there's a lot more to your soul than that."

He followed her to the car, which was parked at the curb. A grin played along his lips. "Now it's your turn to take off your shirt."

She laughed before she got in. "In your dreams, Special Agent Brannigan. In your dreams."

CHAPTER THIRTEEN

CHARLEY STOOD before the array of photographs on the wall, lost in thought. There were times when she almost felt the victims were calling to her, asking her for closure. For justice.

Or maybe that was just her own need to solve the case weighing so heavily on her. Her need to finally, after six years, lay her sister's spirit to rest. And maybe in solving the crime, she would find out if Cris had been the intended victim. Or if Cris was dead because she was in the wrong place at the wrong time and the killer had meant to kill her instead of her twin.

Some nights the question came screaming at her. But she had no answer, no one to give her an answer.

Except for the killer.

Even if her father were suddenly to stop harassing her to catch Cris's killer, she knew she would doggedly continue with the search. Because she knew she would never have any peace until she found the truth.

Right now, doggedly determined or not, she wasn't getting anywhere.

It had been over a week since the last murder had been committed. A week filled with leads that led nowhere. A week filled with several hundred phone calls that had to be answered, logged in and investigated. Neighbors and coworkers had been interviewed without a single clue being found. Their computer expert had pulled up Stacy Pembroke's e-mail while an electronics tech had followed up on her cell-phone calls.

Nothing.

Stacy Pembroke's murder turned out to be like all the other Sunday murders that had occurred prior to hers. No one had seen anything. And, except for cat hairs which may or may not have been connected to the killer, not so much as a single loose thread or fiber had been left behind as a clue. Only the killer's M.O. told them that the murder had been committed by the same person.

But there had to be something, Charley thought. Something that was probably staring them in the face, daring them to make the connection.

She dragged a hand through her hair, fanning out the long, blond strands.

It was driving her crazy.

"So what do we know?" she said out loud, more to the dead women on the wall than to anyone else in the room.

Sam looked up from the file folder he was reviewing. For the fifth time. "That the killer is damn lucky," he muttered.

Charley turned around to look at the agent. "Besides that."

"The victims were all young, single." Bill came up to stand beside her and look at the photographs. "Other than that, none of the women seemed to have very much in common."

Charley frowned. He was right. There wasn't a club, a religion, a favorite grocery store, a hair color to tie them all together. They were all white, but that could have been a coincidence rather than a pattern.

"There has to be something, something that sets our killer off. Why these women?" she asked. "Why not something else?" *Why Cris and not me?*

"Well," Sam said slowly, leaving his desk to join them too. "Opportunity's the first thing that comes to mind."

"But they weren't just in his line of vision. The killer didn't drag them off the street in the middle of the night," Nick pointed out. "More than half were killed in their homes. That means he seeks them out. Follows them. He does select them. What makes them so special?"

"Or unlucky," Bill commented.

"Brannigan's right," Charley said. "There's *got* to be a common thread. Maybe they were all adopted. Maybe they were all born at the same hospital. Maybe they all once lived in the same neighborhood, attended the same school—"

"But then how do the two out-of-state murders fit in?" Bill asked.

Sam's thin shoulders rose and fell in an inevitable shrug. Jack Andrews, their newly assigned recruit, merely kept silent, as if afraid of saying the wrong thing. Satisfied just to listen and learn.

"People move," Nick ventured. The others looked at him. "They don't always stay in the same place. Hell, I lost count how many times we moved when I was a kid."

"Exactly. People move," Charley echoed.

Stowing away the piece of information her partner had just volunteered, she gained momentum as she spoke. This was more like it. This gave her something to do, something to investigate. Much better than just sitting around, mentally going around in narrowing circles.

Excited, she began to pace, looking at each of the four men closest to her and addressing her words to the rest of the room as well. Sullivan had given her a team of ten more to help with the canvassing.

"We need to compile an in-depth history on each one of these women. Go back over their lives with a fine-tooth comb. I want to know who their teachers were, who their friends were. Maybe someone they all knew in common is behind this. If we get a handle on that, on whatever ties them together, we might be able to get to the next woman before our killer does."

Behind her, Nick nodded. "It's worth a shot," he agreed.

Charley turned to look at him. She wondered if the man thought she needed his validation. About to say something, she changed her mind and let it drop. She was being touchy again. That's what came of fielding calls from her father and then dropping by to see her mother.

She'd stopped by at the psychiatric hospital after work last night. To talk. To tell her mother how the case was going and what she was doing. Ordinarily, an open investigation wasn't allowed to be a topic of conversation, but it wasn't as if her mother was going to sell the story to the tabloids. There were times she didn't think her mother heard anything at all.

Other times, she told herself that she did. That her mother did hear her even though she stared off into the air vacantly, giving no indication that she even knew there was someone in the room with her.

Every once in a while, Charley could swear that she saw a glimmer, a spark. Something that told her her mother was only a short distance away. A distance that could be bridged if only she could find the right words. If only she could tell her that Cris's murder had finally been avenged.

That was her ultimate goal.

"Okay, now that it's met with everyone's approval," Charley said, slanting a look in Nick's direction, "let's get cracking." She indicated the photographs. In each one, the woman was smiling. Somehow, that made the loss of life even worse. "We have twelve victims. Dividing them up, that gives us two apiece with two left over." Before anyone else could comment about that, she added, "I'll take the extras."

"Never doubted it for a minute," Sam quipped. His eye caught Nick's. "In case you haven't figured it out yet, our Charley is an overachiever."

"Yeah." Nick nodded, his eyes meeting hers. "I figured it out."

"Good, I like 'em quick," Charley responded. Her smile was almost wicked when she added, "Makes the team move faster."

"Any preference as to which ones we take?" Sam asked, nodding at the array.

"No, but I'll handle my sister."

"Maybe a fresh pair of eyes on that might be more productive."

She looked at Nick, surprised at the suggestion he made. A suggestion she might have made herself had the matter not been so close to home. "In the interest of time, I should be the one to do it. I already know who her friends were, what teachers she had."

Nick remained firm. "You might have missed something."

It was the wrong thing to say. "Missed something? Brannigan, before I was part of this task force, before I was part of the FBI, I went over and over the events leading up to Cris's murder. It's branded into my brain—"

Her voice began to rise, but it was cut down. Not by Nick, or any of the others in the room, but by A.D. Kelly. He was yelling. Not at any of them, but at the woman whose desk was directly before his door.

The woman in the long navy skirt and pearl-pink long-sleeved blouse who stood all but trembling before the man as he made his displeasure known to her and anyone else within earshot of his loud, booming voice.

"Damn it, Alice, when I ask for a report to be on my desk by ten, I want it there by ten. Not eleven, not ten-thirty, not even ten-oh-five. Ten. Do I make myself clear, or do you need it in writing?"

"Clear, sir," Alice mumbled, her eyes downcast.

Charley, followed by the others, walked out into the hall to see the two standing there. The A.D. was holding a black bound set of papers in his hand. His ruddy complexion was a deep scarlet. Alice was looking down at the tips of her highly polished black shoes. In flats, she was almost as tall as the man bellowing at her.

Charley felt sorry for her.

Kelly was all but breathing fire. He had been under a great deal of pressure, both about this case and several others he was overseeing. He had no right side to stay on these days. "I don't need the director to chew me out because you're not competent."

As always when she was nervous, Alice's long, thin fingers fluttered about her throat and cheeks. "I'm sorry, sir." She raised her head to timidly look at him. "It's just that I—"

Kelly cut her off. "I don't want excuses, I want an assurance that it'll never happen again."

Alice was quick to give him what he demanded. "No, never."

His glare was malevolent. Charley couldn't remember ever seeing Kelly this angry. It was rumored that he didn't care for the secretary that had been assigned to him, that he had wanted a younger woman more in keeping with his fast pace. But inner structure and promotions had placed Alice in her present position almost four years ago, and Kelly had no say in the matter. Which irked him to no end.

Still he threatened the woman. "Because you can be replaced."

Charley thought that Alice looked close to tears. The woman pushed her glasses up her sharp nose. "Yes, sir."

"Easily," he shouted.

"Yes, sir."

Charley lost no time in crossing to the woman the moment the assistant director retreated to his office, slamming the door in his wake. For a second, she thought the glass would shatter.

"Are you okay?"

Alice's lips spasmodically formed a smile that disappeared in the next second. "Not really." Her fingers fluttered about her hair, patting in place what didn't need patting.

Not a strand would have come loose even in a hurricane, Charley thought. The secretary clearly had stock in a hairspray company.

With effort, Alice flashed a quick, grateful smile, which remained for a moment. "But I will be. I just need a moment to pull myself together."

"What set him off?" Charley wanted to know.

"It was my fault." Alice quickly took the blame. "I came in with a report he thought he already had. He was looking through his papers, thinking he'd misplaced it. When he saw me holding it, he became livid."

A.D. Kelly was not known for his neatness. It made Charley think of her brother. David was the last word in disorganized. At least he had been before he'd joined the Marines. The corps had taught him order, both of his possessions and of his mind.

She missed David, she thought.

"He'll get over it," Charley assured the older woman. Because Alice looked unsteady, Charley hesitated. "Want to catch some lunch?"

Gratitude flowered over Alice's pale face. "Oh, I'd love to."

Charley thought of the new direction the case had taken. She really didn't have time to go out for a full-blown lunch break and leave the others to do the work. But she couldn't renege now, not when she'd been the one to make the offer.

Someday, she promised herself, she was going to learn not to be so impulsive. Not to lead with her heart. "Fine, grab your coat and let's go."

Nick watched the two women leave. From what little he could see, the two had nothing in common. Charley was a dynamo and Kelly's secretary was a throwback to the middle of the last century. Seeing them together just didn't gel.

"Now, there's an unlikely pair," he commented to Sam.

Sam nodded. Nick noted that there was a fond smile on the man's lips as he referred to Charley. "Charley's got a soft spot for underdogs."

Underdogs. It was as apt a description as any for the secretary, Nick thought. With a shrug, he returned to his desk. There were two women's lives he needed to acquaint himself with. Another woman's life might very well depend on it.

CHAPTER FOURTEEN

"YOU DON'T HAVE to do this," Alice protested even as they were being shown to their seats within the cozy Italian restaurant.

There were sixteen tables in all, with a small, fully stocked bar in the rear, crammed next to the tiny single restroom facility. Behind the bar was a kitchen where elbows rubbed against one another and the activity never stopped. To Charley's knowledge, there was never more than one table empty at a time. It was her favorite place to eat.

"Do what?" Charley asked mildly. Depositing her purse on the floor, she looked at Alice. The menu was before her on the table, but Charley knew the selections by heart.

"Go out to lunch with me." Alice shifted in her seat. "I mean, I know how busy you are, with the case and everything." The smile on her lips seemed forced. "I'm really all right."

Just being with the secretary brought out all sorts of protective feelings, Charley thought. She couldn't help feeling sorry for Alice. And annoyed with the A.D.

"Nobody has the right to make someone else feel small," Charley told her with feeling.

Loyal, Alice seemed unwilling to blame the man

who had gone from white to purple voicing his displeasure with her. "A.D. Kelly was right. I should have had the report to him at ten."

It didn't seem like Alice to be late, Charley thought. But she kept her question to herself until after the waiter had come to take their orders. When she requested veal parmesan, Alice echoed her choice.

"Why didn't you?" Charley asked as the waiter withdrew.

Alice drew in a breath and then let it out again slowly, as if bracing herself for an ordeal. "I was late getting in this morning. There was an accident on the freeway—"

"See, not your fault. Extenuating circumstances." She offered Alice a thick slice of bread from the basket the waiter had brought, then watched in amusement as the woman pondered her selection before making it. Each slice was of equal thickness. "He should have let you explain."

Alice's thin shoulders rose and fell quickly. "The A.D. has a great deal on his mind."

Charley couldn't help wondering if Alice's backbone had been excised. Why else would she defend boorish behavior so far away from Kelly's earshot? It was just the two of them, and fifteen tables of strangers. No one to carry the tale back to the Bureau.

"That's no excuse," Charley pointed out. "I'm sure you have a lot on your mind, too."

This time, the smile was genuine. And rather sweet, Charley thought.

"Not really," Alice told her. "My life is very simple. I come to work, and at the end of the day, I go home and feed my cat. Nothing else."

That sounded chillingly like her own life, Charley

thought, except that she had a dog instead of a cat. But in her case, there was a reason for the simplicity. Work took up most of her hours because there was so much of it. She felt she was always behind. Alice, on the other hand, kept regular hours, which left her evenings free.

Because her work involved so many questions, Charley never thought to back off when any occurred to her. Like now. "Don't you belong to any clubs? Go to the movies with friends?" She watched Alice's face as she reviewed a few alternatives to spending evenings alone.

FBI special agent, heal thyself, a small voice in her head mocked.

Alice moved her head from side to side in response to each question. "No." She looked down at the silverware, carefully placing the forks side by side, to the right of the water glass. Sparse brown lashes swept along the swell of her cheeks. "I don't make friends very easily."

There'd been a time, right after Cris's death, when all she'd wanted to do was crawl into a hole and die. It had taken a great deal of willpower to venture out again. She was the first to acknowledge how difficult that was. And how necessary.

"Maybe you should force yourself to get out more," she suggested kindly. "Make it a challenge."

The waiter arrived with their salads. Alice politely turned down his offer for extra cheese, then changed her mind when Charley accepted.

"My life's challenged enough just getting through the day." Alice addressed the words to the salad the moment the waiter left.

The woman brought new meaning to the term *pain-*

fully shy, Charley thought. "Do you have any family living close by?" She saw Alice's thin shoulders grow rigid beneath the pink satin material.

"I don't have any family living at all," she said quietly.

Charley felt as if she'd just trespassed on sacred ground with combat boots. "My father died when I was twenty, my mother shortly thereafter." Alice stabbed at the lettuce that was eluding her. "I'm an only child."

"Oh, I'm sorry." Because she looked like someone who might find solace in spiritual comfort, Charley made another suggestions. "Maybe a pastor, then—"

Alice looked up sharply from her half-eaten salad. "I don't believe in pastors."

It was the first conviction Charley had ever heard in the woman's voice.

"They're just a bunch of false prophets, leading people astray for their own gratification."

Charley wondered if Alice was referring to the recent scandal that had been in the newspapers. It had involved charges of abuse that were lodged against a former, once very respected, clergyman. The fall from grace was admittedly a long one. The splash into the mire sometimes sent mud flying on those who didn't deserve it.

"They're not all like that," Charley told her. "There was this priest when I was younger—" She noted that Alice was looking at her with interest, as if the woman's opinion was tied to whatever she would hear next. "He helped me through a very rocky time."

"How?" Alice pressed.

He saved me from going off the deep end, Charley thought. But that was something she wasn't willing to share with a woman who was a relative stranger to her. So she gave her a general overview.

"Talked to me, mostly. Told me I couldn't control everything." Father Scanlon had negated what her own father had said to her—that she was to blame for what had happened to Cris.

"Could he?"

The question had come out of nowhere. Focusing, Charley didn't understand what Alice was asking her. "Excuse me?"

"Could he control everything? The priest. Did he think he could control everything himself?"

What an odd question, Charley thought. "No, he didn't pretend to. Why would he?"

Alice's fingers fluttered in the air, as if physically clearing away the question. The pink splotches on her cheeks testified that she'd suddenly realized that she was being intrusive and was embarrassed at her own behavior.

Her eyes seemed to be everywhere, like tiny brown marbles, uncertain where to land. "I'm sorry. I didn't mean to pry—"

The word "pry" struck a chord. Alice was undoubtedly thinking that she and the priest had more than a meeting of the minds. The idea made her smile.

"There's nothing to pry about, trust me. Father Scanlon was about sixty-five or so at the time and very kind, very patient." She paused. Alice continued to look flustered. Charley decided to tell her a little more. "He was there for me when my sister was killed."

It was a moment before understanding came into Alice's eyes. "By the serial killer." It wasn't really a question.

"Right."

She supposed it was common knowledge on the floor. Perhaps even further than that, although so far, the news media hadn't gotten a whiff of it. Charley prayed that they never would. The last thing she wanted was people shoving microphones in her face, asking her nonsensical questions about her feelings. Questions she had trouble answering for herself, much less a stranger whose umbilical cord was tied to a news camera. The media would have a field day with the fact that the sister of the serial killer's first victim was heading up the task force attempting to apprehend him.

"Are you any closer to catching him? The serial killer, I mean," Alice asked suddenly.

Charley looked at her. As if she realized she'd asked something she shouldn't, Alice's hand fluttered to the collar of her blouse. The fabric rose up to practically her chin. The only skin Alice ever exposed, beyond her face, were her hands. Her skirts, long and shapeless, came down to her calves, meeting dark stockings. To the observant eye, Alice Sullivan was cocooning herself from the world at large. She made Charley think of someone's maiden aunt, the kind who used to check under her bed each night to make sure no one was hiding there.

"I'm sorry," Alice stammered. "It's an ongoing inves- tigation, I know. You can't talk about it. It's just that some- times I get so nervous at night when I walk into my house."

"Nervous?" Charley asked.

As if on cue, the waiter arrived with their main course. Alice pressed her lips together, waiting until they were alone again.

She leaned over the table. "About the serial killer.

Nervous that he might be lurking somewhere about, waiting to pounce on me." She cleared her throat. "I'm not pretty, like the others, I know, but I am a blonde and most of his victims were blondes...."

"Carry some Mace," Charley suggested. She knew she should make some denial about Alice's remark that she wasn't pretty, but she addressed the more important issue first. "And if you're really afraid, I could teach you some self-defense moves."

Alice offered her another grateful smile. "Thank you, but I'm just not the athletic type."

"No athletics," Charley promised. "Just a simple matter of using the attacker's own weight against him. It's really pretty simple."

"Thank you, but no." And then something like a giggle escaped her lips as she leaned forward and confided, "Although I might be tempted to try if that new man offered to show me." More color rose to her cheeks.

"New man?" Charley repeated. Her fork stopped in midair. "You mean Special Agent Brannigan?"

The woman needed to wet her feet, not dive into the deep end of the pool without her water wings on, Charley thought. If she had a guess, she'd say that Brannigan's type was sleek and sexy, neither of which described the woman sitting opposite her.

Alice nodded, then quickly said, "Oh, I know I'm not his type." She looked back down at her plate. "I'm not any man's type."

Part of the problem, Charley theorized, was the way Alice presented herself. She dressed as if she had stepped out of a movie filmed in the late fifties.

"If you feel that way," she said casually, trying hard

to find the right words so Alice's feelings wouldn't be hurt, "you might want to look into getting a makeover. New clothes, a new hairstyle, they'd do a lot to change how you see yourself." She saw a strange look entering the woman's eyes. Hurt? Quickly Charley continued, "And if you feel better about yourself, it'll show and catch someone's eye. Maybe not Brannigan's," she qualified. "He's a little thick," she added to spare Alice's feelings, "but someone of quality."

Alice put down her fork and looked at her for a long moment. "You're a very nice person, Charlotte."

No one called her Charlotte except her father. Not even her mother had called her that when she was well. "Charlotte" referred to someone she wasn't. It was hard for Charley not to shift uncomfortably, but she managed.

"I try," Charley answered.

Just then, the restaurant owner approached to make his usual inquiry about the food and quality of the service. Charley welcomed the respite.

CHAPTER FIFTEEN

"WHERE'S BRANNIGAN?"

The special agent hadn't been at his desk when she'd returned from lunch with Alice. That had been over fifteen minutes ago, more than enough time for the man to have gone to the men's room and come back. Unless he wasn't coming back.

Charley looked from Sam to Bill to Jack, waiting for an answer she had a feeling she wasn't going to like.

"Probably still at the campus," Bill volunteered.

News to her, Charley thought. "What campus?"

"Brannigan said he was going to UCI to nose around, see what he could find out," Bill said.

That didn't make any sense. "UCI?" she repeated, wondering if the man had gotten the name wrong. But when he made no attempt to correct himself, she asked, "Why? Stacy Pembroke wasn't a student."

Jack all but faded into the background. Bill exchanged uneasy looks with Sam. Being the older one of the team, Sam took the bullet for him. "No, but your sister was."

Her sister? What did Cris have to do with it? He wasn't supposed to be reviewing Cris's investigation. That was her domain.

Charley opened her mouth, then shut it. Losing her

temper in front of the people she worked with was never a good idea. Besides, Sam, Bill and Jack weren't responsible for the sudden flare of anger she felt. That honor belonged exclusively to Special Agent Pain-in-the-butt Brannigan.

Not wasting a single word on any of the three men, Charley marched off to the ladies' room, the only place in the immediate vicinity that could offer any kind of privacy. She stormed in, generating enough of a warning for anyone who might be inside to run for cover. But there appeared to be no one in the bathroom. Still, she looked under each stall to double-check.

Satisfied that she was alone, Charley whipped out her cell phone and pressed the single number on the keypad that would connect her to her partner.

Nick's deep voice came on after four rings. Her impatience was close to going over the edge, but she gave him the benefit of the doubt. Kind of.

"Brannigan."

Her patience snapped like a sun-baked twig that had been tossed into a roaring forest fire. "What the hell are you doing?"

"My job," he answered simply. Then, on the outside chance that he might have gotten her voice confused with someone else's, he asked, "Charley?"

For a second, it stopped her in her tracks. He hadn't addressed her by her first name before. Why that seemed to make this whole thing more personal, she didn't know, but it did.

She distanced herself from the feeling. Distanced herself from everything except the idea of strangling her new partner and then mounting his head on the wall. Envisioning the end result gave her a momentary surge of pleasure.

"No, it's the tooth fairy. What are you doing?" she repeated heatedly.

There was momentary static. She thought she was going to lose the connection, but then she heard him say, "Talking to people who might have known your sister. Did you know that one of the people she went to school with currently works as an adjunct professor in the drama department?"

After Cris's murder, she had moved out of the room they'd shared and divorced herself from everyone at the school.

"No," she told him coldly, "I lost touch with those people."

"Apparently." She had no idea what he meant by that. But before she could ask, he told her, "I'm standing in front of the Bren Center. I think maybe you should meet me here."

She'd assumed that he would be returning to the office, not suggesting she join him. The man had nerve. "And why is that?"

"Because the report that was made on the investigation into your sister's death never mentioned anyone questioning Lorenzo DeLuca. He's still on the faculty."

The name was vaguely familiar. And then she remembered. Lorenzo DeLuca was one of the professors in the drama department while they were attending the university. Cris had pointed him out to her once outside of the student center, saying she thought he was a hunk. The man had been poetically handsome in a brooding, Lord Byron kind of way. Cris had a weakness for that type.

"Why would they question DeLuca?" Charley asked.

126 SUNDAYS ARE FOR MURDER

"Because he was your sister's married lover at the time of her death."

What a difference a moment can make. One moment ago, she was trying to bank down annoyance. Now she felt as if she'd somehow managed to walk directly in front of a wrecking ball and had received a direct hit.

It took her a moment to find her tongue. "I'll be right there."

She hardly remembered shutting the phone and hurrying out of the ladies' room.

IT HAD TO BE a mistake.

The phrase kept repeating in her brain like the refrain of an old song, the rest of whose lyrics had long since been forgotten.

It had to be a mistake.

Yes, Cris had been the flamboyant one. Yes, she'd dated a number of guys. God knows how many, because she'd long since lost count of her sister's boyfriends. But each of them had been students. And more importantly, they'd all been single.

There was only one conclusion—the so-called witness Brannigan had dug up was either lying or repeating something that he'd heard thirdhand.

In either case, there was a mistake. Cris would have *never* gone out with a married man, much less had an affair with one. No matter how cute she thought he was. Cris just wasn't like that. Neither of them were.

It took her several minutes to find a parking space in the three-tiered structure adjacent to the large entertainment center where Brannigan had told her to meet him. When she and Cris had attended the university, this structure had been the only lot that afforded students ample parking. All the other lots on the sprawling campus were usually full by the time the first class rolled around. Obviously, that was no longer the case. The lot was as crammed as the others.

Walking down from the third floor contributed to her already testy mood.

Nick was waiting for her by the parking attendant's booth.

"It's a mistake," she told him tersely as she strode toward him.

"What is?"

"My sister never dated DeLuca. She wouldn't have gone out with a married man," she insisted.

Nick thought he saw a glimmer of hurt in his partner's eyes. Or maybe that was just the sun.

"Apparently she did," he told her simply. Nick beckoned for her to follow him into the building where he'd left the adjunct professor. "And it gives your sister something in common with our latest victim."

"What? Sleeping with a man who's committing adultery?" Charley snapped. Her voice echoed back to her. "Allegedly sleeping with a man who's committing adultery," she qualified. "My sister wouldn't do that."

Just inside the hall, Nick stopped and looked at her. "Hey, nobody's judging anyone here. Things happen, even to good people with high morals." Her expression told him that she wasn't budging from her stand. "Most people don't wake up one morning and say, 'Wouldn't having an affair with a married man be fun?'"

"Thank you, Dr. Phil, but you're wrong. And whoever you talked to is wrong. Cris told me everything." They had that kind of special bond that only sisters, only twins could have. She knew Cris inside and out and vice versa. "My sister wouldn't have kept something like that from me."

Nick looked at her for a long moment. Listening to the facts earlier, he'd come to a different conclusion. "I think she would have."

Charley curled her fingers into her palms, feeling a very urgent desire to make a connection with the edge of his handsome cleft chin. "Oh you do, do you? Why?"

The answer was self-evident. "Just look at your reaction. Maybe she didn't want to experience that firsthand. You admired her, didn't you?"

Several students entered through the front, then circumvented them as they walked into the inner hallway. She hardly noticed them. Charley stared at Brannigan. "How did you—?"

"I read the report. The police detectives on the scene interviewed you," he reminded her.

That was like another lifetime ago. She remembered the two detectives on the case. The one who'd talked to her had kind eyes. He'd been especially gentle with her mother. And put up with her father's sharp tongue without losing his temper. His name had been Gilroy. Detective John Gilroy. She'd been so disappointed in him when he failed to solve the case.

Charley sighed. "Yes, I admired her."

"Maybe your sister didn't want to risk losing that until she knew where this extramarital fling with the good professor was heading."

What he said made sense, but Charley just couldn't wrap her mind around the concept of her sister knowingly engaged in something that had the potential of breaking up someone's home.

"She just wouldn't…"

But even as she uttered the protest, Charley's conviction slipped a little. In frustration, she told him why she was being so adamant.

"When we were kids, my father had one of those extramarital flings that you just bandied about so lightly. We saw what it did to our mother. It damn near killed her," she told him before he could ask. "Cris wouldn't knowingly be a party to something like that."

She saw compassion enter Nick's eyes.

"Theory and practice are two very different things. She might not have wanted to hurt anyone, but she couldn't help what was happening. Sometimes people get involved without meaning to."

The way he said it, Charley couldn't help wondering if Brannigan was speaking from experience.

Nick held the inner door open for her. "Why don't you talk to her friend and then make up your mind?"

Charley made no further protest, because she was no longer sure.

And because, right now, she hated Nick Brannigan for shaking up the foundations of her carefully reconstructed world.

CHAPTER SIXTEEN

"I HATE HIM, Ben. I really hate the guy."

Charley paced around her former partner's small second-floor apartment, feeling restless and not a little caged. The size of the room had nothing to do with it. The feelings ricocheting through her were responsible for constructing her prison.

It angered her and added to her frustration that she was helpless to do anything about the circumstances.

Damn Brannigan anyway.

Because she wasn't completely ready to be alone with her thoughts, she had come here, to Ben, instead of going home. Ben was the only one she trusted.

Trust. Now there was an expendable word.

Her entire picture of Cris had been thrown out of focus. Apparently her sister wasn't the person she'd thought she was. She'd always credited Cris with such high standards. And now...

She didn't know what was worse, that Cris had had an affair with a married man, or that she'd kept that affair a secret from her. On top of everything else, Charley felt betrayed. It shook up everything she thought she'd believed. Every time she thought she had a bead on who and what she was, someone came along to shake up the picture. She wouldn't feel so confused if it hadn't been for Brannigan.

It was easy to blame the man for everything, but she was an FBI agent. She had to look at the truth first, her own feelings about the matter second.

Not always the easiest thing.

Unchanneled energy pulsed through Charley as she continued to pace. Turning sharply, she narrowly avoided colliding with the end of the bookcase that housed Ben's late wife's Hummel collection.

She slanted a glance toward Ben to see if he noticed. He had. Being Ben, he hadn't said anything. Her father would have been reading her the riot act before she was within a foot of the bookcase, telling her to be more careful.

She needed to get a hold of herself.

The interview with her sister's friend, a former boyfriend named Michael Matthews, who was now teaching part-time at the university while going for his Ph.D., had been far from satisfying. Because it had been convincing. She came away from the interview believing that her sister had had the affair. That Cris was still in the affair the night she was killed.

It wasn't the most pleasant pill to swallow.

Charley was grateful that she and Brannigan had come in separate cars, and that she could be alone with her thoughts on the way back to the Federal Building. The way she felt, she couldn't have been held responsible for what she might have said to Brannigan. Silence was a great deal preferable.

For the most part, she maintained it for the rest of the day, going over the other details in Cris's folder, then comparing them to the details in the two folders she'd selected. One of the two women was having an affair with a married man. Just the way they believed that

Stacy Pembroke was having one with her employer. The coincidence was too much to ignore.

Above everything else, Charley considered herself a good FBI agent. But she was having a hell of a time dealing with this curve she'd been thrown.

She wished she'd never laid eyes on Brannigan. Turning, she looked at Ben, who had calmly taken his seat at the small table for two in his kitchen.

"Brannigan is cocky, arrogant, pushy. He doesn't listen—"

"Sounds very, very familiar," Ben said, his round face consumed by an amused, knowing smile. He lifted his mug and took a sip.

Charley blew out a breath. She wasn't in the mood to be teased. Not even by Ben. "Stop kidding."

His eyes crinkled as he watched her wear a path in his rug. "I'm not."

"I listened to you," she pointed out. Working with him, once she hit a rhythm, she'd absorbed everything the man had to teach her.

Ben knew that he remembered things a little differently than she did. "Only when I made you." He nodded at the steaming mug of tea he'd poured for her. "Sit down and have your tea before it gets cold."

"Tea," she repeated with a sneer. "You're a grown man, Ben. You shouldn't be making tea. You need a hobby," she told him. But she did as he instructed. She sat down and drew the mug closer to her, wrapping her hands around it.

Ben's brown eyes looked straight into her soul. Because she cared for him, Charley didn't flinch. Instead, she waited for him to say something.

"I don't think you're angry at Brannigan," he said.

Charley snorted, looking away. She brought the mug to her lips. Instead of drinking, she let the steam hit her, wishing it could do something about the clouds she felt inside. "And here I thought you were a perceptive man."

"I am," he told her simply. Twenty-eight years on the job had given him some insight. Working with Charley had provided the rest. "You're angry with Cris."

Well, that was a no-brainer, she thought. "Of course I'm angry with Cris. She's dead and I can't yell at her." She struggled to keep her voice down, not wanting to take her feelings out on the person she considered her best friend. She hadn't had one since Cris died. "I can't ask her why she never told me about DeLuca." She felt like hell inside. And it was going to take time to make peace with this. A long time.

"This was a whole part of her life, Ben. According to her old boyfriend, Cris and the horny professor were an item for six months. Six months," she repeated with emphasis, shaking her head at her own blindness. "And I never even had a clue. How dense is that?"

"Not dense at all if she was hiding it," Ben contradicted. "Wives hide it from their husbands, husbands hide it from their wives. Why not one sister from another? You didn't expect her to do something like that, especially after your father stepped out on your mother, so why would you be looking for any signs that she was having an affair?"

"Not looking," Charley conceded. "But this was right under my nose. And it was my sister. My *sister,* Ben. Not some stranger. My twin sister. Why didn't I know? Why didn't I sense it?" She paused to collect herself. To make him understand her frustration. "The night she was killed, just before the M.E. estimated that Cris died,

I felt this sudden wave of unbelievable fear. I was sitting in the science library, reading some mind-numbing textbook. There were maybe five, six people around in the whole place. And all of a sudden, for no reason whatsoever, I was scared. Right down to the bone. More scared than I'd ever been in my entire life. And I knew it had to be Cris. That there was something wrong. I *sensed* it."

As she spoke, she could almost see the events transpiring before her. Her throat tightened as she recited them.

"I ran two red lights driving back to the off-campus apartment we shared. I remember thinking there should have been a cop around. I knew I needed a cop. That Cris needed a cop. When I got to the apartment, it was too late. She'd been strangled."

Charley blinked back tears. Without a word, Ben took a napkin from the pile in the middle of the table and pushed it toward her. She took it. Instead of drying her eyes, she shredded it as she spoke.

"My point is, if I could feel her fear so vividly that night, why couldn't I feel her love before? If she was in love with DeLuca, why couldn't I have felt something that tipped me off?" Finished, she pressed her lips together, the same question still haunting her. "Why couldn't she have trusted me?"

Ben gave her the same answer that Nick had. "Because she loved you and sometimes we hide things from the people we love."

Charley sighed, drawing together the strips of napkin she'd created and pushing them into a pile. She supposed what Ben said was as good an explanation as any.

The upshot was that she couldn't waste any more

time feeling sorry for herself. Feeling hurt. It wouldn't help solve the case.

But what Nick had stumbled across might. At least, it would help. "The cocky bastard found a clue."

Ben nodded. "Sounds like he's not quite as much a waste of space as you indicate."

"No," she agreed reluctantly, "he's not."

Ben rose. "In the mood for some pot roast? I made way too much and I'm going to have to throw it out if you don't have any."

She was on her feet, ready to help. Wanting to lose herself in some mindless chore, if only for a little while. "Sounds good. Can I have some for Dakota?"

"Would I forget my favorite canine?" Ben chuckled as he walked toward the Crock-Pot on the counter.

IF LOOKS COULD KILL, Nick figured he would have been dead twice over by now. She hadn't said anything, but the daggers Charley Dow had shot in his direction after they'd finished talking to Michael Matthews, and later at the office when they hooked up again, would have left at least several mortal wounds on his person had they been real.

His mouth twisted in a half smile. Lucky for him that her weapon had remained holstered throughout the day.

Must be rough, thinking you knew someone, then finding out that they had a big secret they'd been keeping from you.

He still hadn't gotten a handle on his partner. She struck him as more than competent, and he found her more than mildly attractive, but he still wasn't sure if they could mesh well. She'd hit the nail on the head the first day, although he'd told her otherwise. But if he'd had a choice, he would have preferred having a man as a partner. He's never worked with a woman before. Romanced them, yes, enjoyed their company, yes, but he'd never thought of them in terms of life and death.

And partners had your life in their hands.

He didn't like being responsible for a woman. Even as he thought it, he knew she would have gone upside his head for that one, informing him tersely that she could take care of herself and that the only one he was responsible for was himself. Still, he had trouble thinking of Charley Dow as strictly an FBI agent.

She had too many curves for him to be impartial.

He was home. The trip from the Bureau to his apartment complex was a blur.

After parking his vehicle in his carport space, Nick got out and crossed to his apartment door. As he approached it, he looked around cautiously. Nothing appeared out of the ordinary. There was no sign of the man he was fairly certain had left the slaughtered rabbit on his doorstep. Sean Dixon.

He'd already called a friend back in D.C. and had him check out Dixon's whereabouts. Just as he'd suspected, the man had pulled up stakes. No one knew where. Linda's brother hadn't left a forwarding address with the post office when he'd moved. But tracking Dixon's credit card activity had told him that the man had purchased a ticket to John Wayne Airport. One way. That was less than five miles away from where he was.

Since purchasing the plane ticket, no activity on his credit card had been reported. That wasn't necessarily a good sign. As he remembered it, Dixon had once been sent up on two counts of identity theft. Which meant that the man knew how to avail himself of someone else's ID. And someone else's credit cards.

Which in turn meant that he was going to have to remain alert.

Nick shook his head. Problems did pile up, didn't they? He had a partner who kept him on his toes and busted parts of his anatomy he would have preferred leaving untouched, and a psycho with a criminal record possibly stalking him. And that didn't even begin to cover the case he was supposed to be working on.

"Ain't life grand?" he said aloud as he put his key into the lock.

Inside his apartment, the phone was ringing. The smile faded from his lips.

CHAPTER SEVENTEEN

NICK PUSHED his door closed behind him, listening for the click that told him the lock was in place. He strode over to the telephone and jerked up the receiver.

"Hello?" Anticipating who was on the other end made his tone less than friendly.

"You're going to be sorry."

He was right. It was Sean. Nick could feel the anger soaring through his veins, throbbing at his temples.

"Listen, you low-life scum—"

There was a click on the other end of the line. Nick found himself addressing no one.

Just like all the other times.

Since the rabbit had turned up on his doorstep, he'd received at least two calls a day, each ending in a hang-up. Some hang-ups were immediate, some came after several seconds of silence. Still others came after a couple of words had been growled in his ear, as if some circus lion or tiger had been gifted with the power of speech. Or jackal, he thought.

But the guttural cadence didn't disguise the caller's identity. Nick knew in his gut that it was Linda's brother, Sean, bent on harassing him. Bent on playing mind games in some pathetic attempt to torture him.

Nick's first thought was to get his phone number

changed. But he'd only had this one for a month. And he was unlisted. If Sean could get this number, he could get any other number the phone company would issue just as easily.

The surprising thing was that, so far, no nuisance calls had come in on his cell phone. He supposed he should count his blessings. It was only a matter of time before Sean latched on to that number as well and continued with his program of harassment.

With any luck, Nick promised himself, he'd be able to deal with the bastard before that happened. As far as the word "deal" went, that was open to interpretation. Regular channels weren't going to work. Court injunctions issued to keep Linda's brother a prescribed number of feet away wouldn't mean anything to Dixon. No, the only way to get Dixon to back off was to put the fear of God—or him—into the man.

Still, Nick couldn't help hoping that it wouldn't come to a showdown. He had no desire for a confrontation with Dixon, he just wanted the man to go away. Far away.

Just like he wished that the residue guilt over Linda's suicide would go away. It wasn't his fault that she had taken her life, everyone had said so. In his own mind, he knew that. And yet, he couldn't help blaming himself. He should have never allowed the woman to get close enough to begin fabricating her delusions.

He should have known right from the start that there was something wrong with Linda. Red flags should have immediately shot up like the hands of third-graders eager to answer an easy question. He'd gone out with a hell of a lot of women and not one of them had been a nester like Linda Dixon. Linda had moved in, figuratively, after the very first date. Cooking for him, rearranging things in his apartment. Talking about the future. A future she saw involving them both.

She'd tried to move in literally, as well, but there he'd held his ground. He'd done it to protect her. In hindsight, it wound up protecting him. But that hadn't been his initial intent. He hadn't wanted them living together because of the nature of his work at the Bureau. It was classified as top secret. Public knowledge of the program he was involved in could have very possibly put her life in jeopardy.

He was now paying the price for having been flattered by her attention. In the beginning, a part of him had entertained the idea of settling down and starting a family. He'd wanted to have what his parents had. He still did.

Granted, to the casual observer, the Colonel was a stern man. But Retired Colonel Harlan Brannigan was a fair man and he loved his wife. Had loved her since the very first moment he'd laid eyes on her. Their union was strong, with a great deal of mutual affection. Nick supposed that his envy of that had blinded him to the telltale signs Linda exhibited, until it was too late to do anything about it.

When they were together, three months at most, he tried to attribute Linda's mercurial behavior to the shift in her hormones. Pregnant women were not often known to be the stablest people on the face of the earth, especially in their first trimester. As he recalled, his sister Ashley had been a raving loon for a couple of weeks when she was first pregnant. Mercifully for her husband and the rest of the world, Ashley got it under control relatively quickly.

That was what had ultimately tipped him off about

Linda. Linda couldn't get her moods under control, running the full gamut from laughter to tears. A great many tears. She'd used those like an arsenal. She pressed, pushed, threatened and obsessed. Always obsessed about what she wanted out of life. At thirty, she was older than him and saw life drying up and blowing away right before her eyes. She acted as if Nick was her last chance.

All she wanted to do was get married.

And all he had wanted to do, Nick thought wearily now, was put it all behind him. He'd fully intended to live up to his financial obligations to the baby. He had wanted joint custody, as well, but he'd inherently known that applying for it would be a large mistake. A gut instinct told him that the baby would wind up a pawn for Linda to use against him. It was better if she was granted custody and he had visitation rights.

When he told her as much at the uncomfortably romantic dinner she'd arranged for the two of them, she became hysterical. She wound up throwing the meal she'd labored over, nearly hitting him in the eye. As it was, she managed to bruise his chin while screaming obscenities at him, accusing him of all sorts of things. She'd reviled him with a list of women he was to have cheated on her with, women he didn't even know.

The police had come, called in by a neighbor. It took them exactly thirty seconds to assess the situation. The fact that she came at him with a tenderizing hammer didn't help her cause. But he refused to press charges and the police "escorted" her back to her home. With a policeman on each side, she'd left screaming how he'd used her, how he was going to pay for what he'd done.

A week later, she was dead by her own hand. The note she left behind blamed him for everything.

As did her brother.

He sighed as he glanced out the window. The street-lamp right before his door illuminated the immediate area. No one was around. But that didn't mean there wouldn't be. Tonight. Tomorrow night. Soon.

There was no use trying to ignore his situation. He was going to have to find Dixon and have it out with him before things got completely out of hand. He didn't want to find any more dead animals on his doorstep.

He needed a beer.

Nick made his way to the kitchen. His living arrangement hadn't really improved any. The boxes were still mostly packed and in the way. Maybe on the weekend, he told himself, circumventing a large box that probably contained his winter clothes. He could start unpacking on the weekend.

He'd almost reached the refrigerator when the phone rang again.

Damn it, what did it take to make the Neanderthal stop?

Furious now, Nick doubled back, knocking over a tower comprised of three medium-size boxes. The top two went flying and he kicked the bottom box as he leaned over for the phone.

Grabbing the receiver, Nick brought it to his ear. Seething.

"Look, you jerk—"

"Is that any way for you to talk to your mother?" The voice on the other end of the line was teeming with amusement.

The fury instantly left him, like water running down

an unobstructed drain. "Mom?" Her laugh took away
the last doubt as to her identity.

"Really, Nickolas, what kind of people does the
Bureau have you dealing with out there?"

His family had known about Linda and had mourned
the senseless death of the baby they would never come to
know. But there was no way he was going to tell his mother
that Dixon had materialized on this side of the Rockies and
was leaving gutted calling cards on his doorstep.

"Just some wrong number that keeps calling. Nearly
broke my neck last time, answering it."

There was a silence on the other end of the line that
told him he hadn't fooled her. Not for a moment. He and
his mother were very much alike, which meant their
minds worked along the same paths.

"Wrong number," she repeated slowly. "Is it that
girl's brother? Does he still hold you accountable?"

He didn't want her worrying. "No, just a wrong
number," he insisted. "It happens, Mom. Don't let your
imagination run away with you."

The small sigh on the other end told him she wasn't
buying it. "Nick, is your nose growing?"

"Maybe just a little."

"Nick, if it is him," she instructed in the firm, un-
shakable voice of a colonel's wife, "I want you to go
to the police."

Nick laughed. Unbelievable. He had towered over
her by the time he was twelve and she still insisted on
treating him as if he needed help crossing the street.
"Mom, I'm an FBI agent. The police come to me."

If he meant to make her laugh, he failed. "This is
different."

"No," Nick pointed out patiently, "he's an ex-

criminal and not too bright to boot. I can handle it."
Tactfully, he moved the conversation away from him
and back to her. "So, why did you call?"

"I need an excuse to talk to my son?"

"You usually come up with one as a cover," he
reminded her.

His mother laughed. He missed that sound, Nick
thought. Missed being home. His apartment was more
than decent, but it didn't feel like home, just a place to store
his boxes and his life until he got it together a little more.

"I wanted to know if you were going to be home for
the holidays."

"Holidays," he repeated. "As in Christmas?"

"Yes."

It was his turn to laugh. "Mom, that's more than six
months away."

"I like to plan ahead."

"As long as you don't set the table early," he kidded
her. "Sure, I'll be home. Where else would I be?"

"I have your promise?"

He heard the hint of sadness in her voice. That wasn't
like her. "Why, what's up?"

"Nothing. I just miss you, that's all. You were always
my favorite—" she confided in hushed tones, adding,
"Don't tell the others."

It was a familiar game, one his mother had played
with him as well as Jeff and Ashley since they were old
enough to remember. They knew she had no favorite.
Helen Brannigan's heart was bigger than the Grand
Canyon and she shared it with all of them.

"I won't." Taking a beer out of the refrigerator, Nick
balanced the phone between his shoulder and his ear as
he popped the tab. "So, tell me what's been going on

with you and everyone," he coaxed. Returning to the living room, he sat down on the sofa and leaned back, losing himself in the conversation and the sound of his mother's voice.

For the next half hour, he was back in D.C.

CHAPTER EIGHTEEN

CHARLEY BECAME AWARE of the aroma the moment she walked into the task-force area the next morning. It filled her senses half a heartbeat before she saw that her desk had been turned into a giant bakery display dish.

Files were neatly pushed to one side, the computer monitor angled so that it faced sideways instead of forward. Someone had used the rest of the available space on her desk to deposit a variety of baked goods. There were at least five kinds of cookies with an abundance of each variety, a huge angel food cake frosted in virginal white, and a pie overflowing with cinnamon-spiced apples beneath its crust.

The aroma alone made her stomach plead for attention. And samples.

Where the hell had all this come from and what was it doing on her desk? Looking around for an explanation, Charley found that she didn't have far to look.

Bill Chan came in right behind her. And headed straight toward the goods. She took that as an admission of culpability.

"Your girlfriend have a going-out-of-business sale, Bill?"

Holding up his hand for a time-out, Bill swallowed a mouthful of chocolate-chip cookie. "Don't look at me.

I didn't bring this in." He pointed out the obvious. "If I had, it would have been on my desk, not yours." Taking two more cookies, he retreated to his desk. Several crumbs fell to mark his passage.

"Is this bring-food-to-work day?" Nick asked, walking in. "If it is, nobody told me." Without waiting for an invitation, he snagged a macaroon cookie. "Good," he pronounced, nodding his head as if to underscore his opinion. "Why's it all on your desk?"

Charley spread her hands. "Not a clue."

Over her shoulder Charley saw Sam enter, holding his coffee mug. By the look of him, he'd already been in the task room this morning. Which meant that he might have brought them in. Sam's wife Eva loved to cook and was always sending food into the office.

Charley beckoned him over to her desk. "You responsible for this?"

By the look on his face, Charley realized that this was the first Sam had seen of the display.

"No, but hey, this solves my breakfast dilemma." Setting his mug down on his desk, Sam proceeded to help himself to one of each variety of cookie. He held them against his chest and retreated to his desk to enjoy his booty.

"Hey look," Nick announced loudly, pointing to something partially hidden beneath one of the platters. "A clue." He picked up a small, cream-colored card, embossed with the letter *A*. Inside was a neatly handwritten note. "And it appears to be addressed to you." He held it out to her, a whimsical expression on his face indicating that he might pull the note back as she reached for it.

Charley snatched it away from Nick's hand.

"Charley's got a secret admirer," Bill teased.

"Who really knows his way around a stove," Sam added, polishing off a second cookie.

Charley tuned out the ribbing as she scanned the note. She looked up at the other agents in dismay. Obviously no good deed went unpunished. "This is from Alice."

"Alice made all this?" Bill looked incredulously at the baked goods on her desk. His expression turned sly as he looked back at her. "Maybe someone should tell A.D. Kelly's secretary you don't bat for that team."

"Alice isn't gay," Charley retorted. "She's just needy." Very needy, she added silently. There had to be something she could do to help the woman. The wheels in her head turned and her eyes swept over the three men in the room. "Speaking of which, any of you know someone we could fix her up with?"

"Alice?" Bill asked. "You mean like in go out with?"

She took offense for the woman. There was no doubt in her mind that Alice Sullivan had been a victim of teasing all her life. Everything about her fairly screamed of it. "That's exactly what I mean."

"What about you, Chan?" Sam proposed. "Alice can bake for you. These are even better than your girlfriend makes."

"Baking isn't Abby's only attribute," Bill informed his partner with a smile that had Charley rolling her eyes.

She knew the rookie Jack was married so there was no point in going there. "Seriously, guys, if you could come up with someone, it might go a long way toward building up Alice's self-esteem." She deliberately looked at Nick.

Nick raised his hands, warding off any further suggestions that might come out of Charley's mouth. He backed away at the same time. "Sorry, I'm too busy catching bad guys."

He was right. They were wasting precious time. Charley looked around for an available space to house the desserts.

"Speaking of which," Bill added his two cents, "since we found that link between the first and last victim, I went over the reports on the women I was supposed to review and talked to some of the family members again."

She noted that Bill had deliberately not made any reference to Cris's name or her relationship with her twin. She flashed him a grateful smile as she said, "And?"

Bill seemed particularly satisfied with himself. "Amanda Watley and Donna Baker both had affairs with married men," he said, referring to the two by name.

"Same goes for Carla Sommers and Lilah Gibbs," Jack reported, helping himself to a piece of the pie.

Sam wiped his mouth. Finished for the time being, he tossed the crumpled napkin into the wastebasket beneath his desk. "Mine, too. Lynn Todd and Melissa Winthrop were both having affairs with married men at the time of their deaths."

Charley was stunned. How had that gone undetected before? She and the team had been brought in when the serial killer had murdered his fourth victim and the pattern had established itself. Someone should have noticed before now.

"Why didn't anyone say anything before?" Charley asked in frustration.

"An affair with a married man isn't exactly something you shout from the rooftops, Charley," Sam reminded her. "You know, don't speak ill of the dead, that kind of thing. Whoever knew about the victim's affair must have decided to keep it to themselves. Keep the victim's name unsullied."

"Unsullied?" Bill echoed, looking at his partner. "Who talks like that?"

Sam frowned at him.

She didn't have time for another round of the boys' club. "What about the others?" she asked. "Did they all have affairs with married men?"

"Still trying to track that piece of information down about Sally Forbs, but I got the best friend to finally admit it about Sandra Cummings," Nick told her.

She turned to look at her partner. This was his doing. If Nick hadn't pointed it out, hadn't started digging into her sister's past, they wouldn't be working on this link. He deserved to have that acknowledged, even if it did bother her.

"This could be it," Charley finally said. "This could be our link. Good work."

Nick nodded at the acknowledgment. Jack was still chewing on the significance of what they'd discovered. "So that means, what? Our killer is a deranged minister casting the first stone?"

Sam shrugged. "Whatever message he's trying to get across, it's tied in with the cross he carves on their foreheads."

"Maybe there is no message," Charley said, thinking out loud. The others looked at her. "Maybe what he's doing is just between the killer and his victim."

Nick extrapolated on her theory. "Vengeance?" he guessed, looking at her.

"That," she allowed, and then she took it in another biblical direction. "Or salvation."

"Salvation?" Nick echoed.

She nodded. "After saying the blessing over the deceased, the priest makes the sign of the cross. That's a symbol that the dead person's soul is being commended to God, sent off to heaven, that sort of thing. Maybe the serial killer thinks that by killing these sinners—which is what the Bible calls people committing adultery—he's sending them off to a better life."

"Or maybe he acts on the rage he feels," Sam said.

Nick disagreed. "Rage might be too strong a word here. If there was rage, he'd carve up their faces or their bodies. Or assault them sexually, degrading them. Even if he was impotent, he could use any number of surrogate instruments to achieve penetration. But he doesn't. I think Charley's right. This has to do with saving."

Sam sighed, shaking his head as he reviewed the photographs on the wall. "Only thing I'm interested in is saving the next victim," he commented.

"Amen to that."

They turned to see Alice standing in the doorway. The secretary was staring at the array with a sad expression on her face. As she sensed their attention, her eyes darted from one agent to another before she lowered her gaze to the points of her shoes. She appeared clearly embarrassed at having interrupted them.

"I'm sorry, I didn't mean to butt in."

Charley stepped forward, crossing to her. "You weren't. Um, Alice—" she lowered her voice "—may I speak to you for a moment?"

Nerves seemed to surface as Alice bobbed her head up and down. Her tone matched Charley's. "Of course."

Hooking her arm through Alice's, Charley brought the woman over to the side. Her manner was gentle, kind. Alice shifted nervously from foot to foot.

"It's not that I don't appreciate all this, Alice…" she began "…but well, I'm on a diet and all this is very hard to resist."

"Oh." She looked over her shoulder at the display. She'd probably spent all evening baking, putting her heart into her offerings. Her shoulders seemed to visibly sag. "I'm sorry—"

"There's nothing to apologize for," Charley assured her quickly. She didn't want to offend the woman. Her goal was to make sure she didn't go overboard like this again. "It's all really wonderful. I had no idea you could bake like that."

"Just something I used to do to please my father," she volunteered. "Before he died."

Charley nodded. "I'm sure you succeeded. As a matter of fact, you might even consider this as another profession. But I don't think the A.D. would appreciate one of the desks being turned into a bakery display if he came out and saw all this."

Alice's eyes widened behind her glasses. "A.D. Kelly." The lingering effects of the chewing-out she'd received yesterday were still very much with her. "Do you think he'd get angry?"

"Not angry, but—" Charley stopped abruptly. Music worked to soothe people, so did food. Maybe Alice could use this to her advantage. "Why don't you offer some of these cookies to him? Might be a good way to get on his better side." If such a thing existed at the moment. Pressure to solve the case was being brought down on Kelly, who in turn was leaning on them.

Never harder than she leaned on herself, Charley thought.

Disappointment drizzled down Alice's angular face, although she struggled not to show it as she gathered up her offerings. "If you say so."

"Not everything," Charley interjected, placing her hand over the other woman's to still it. "Leave a little something for us."

Alice smiled at her. "For you," she emphasized, deliberately avoiding looking at the others. The woman took as much as she could carry in one trip and retreated.

Bill exchanged looks with Jack and struggled hard to suppress the grin that wanted to surface. "Definitely batting for the other team," he repeated as he sat down at his desk.

Charley didn't bother coming to the woman's defense again. Her mind was already elsewhere. She was trying to figure out exactly how the link they'd just uncovered was going to help them find the serial killer.

CHAPTER NINETEEN

"WANT TO GO get a drink?"

Charley didn't realize the question was directed at her. She was still lost in thought, trying to figure out what it all meant. Why someone was killing women having affairs with married men.

Or, in their eagerness to find a link between the victims, had they strayed in an unproductive direction?

When the voiced question finally registered, she looked up, convinced that she had imagined the invitation coming from Brannigan. At this point, she was probably on the verge of hallucinating.

It had been another long, hard, fruitless day, filled with endless reports to wade through and frustrating interviews to reconduct. Interviews that led nowhere and yielded nothing new. Even the phone calls from people swearing they knew who the killer was had tapered off.

Charley felt she and the task force were going around in circles. As much as she wanted to solve the case her hope was fading. She felt as if she'd been through all this before. Again and again. Even the new link that Brannigan had uncovered had brought them back to the same old place. The corner of Nowhere and Nothing.

Brannigan.

He was looking at her across their two desks, his expression that of a man waiting for a response. Since there was no one else left in the vicinity, it was safe to assume he was the one to have posed the question to her.

But she sincerely doubted it was what she thought he had said.

They'd been partnered a month now and although there might have been tiny moments when she could have sworn she'd felt some kind of electricity, she chalked it up to a malfunction on her part. A malfunction brought on by too much work and not enough sleep. Even as the spark registered, she convinced herself that it was only in her imagination.

What else could it be? Together a month and in all that time, they had yet to socialize off the job. Going out the door together to head their separate ways had been as close as they'd come.

"Excuse me?" Charley asked.

"A drink," Nick repeated, as if all his energy had left the building. "Would you like to go out and get one?"

Charley stared. Was it her imagination, or was the lighting in the area dimmer with just the two of them here? Was the Bureau economizing on electricity?

The words emerged slowly, teenagers slipping out of the house after curfew. "With you?"

Nick blew out a breath. "No, I'm taking a survey. Of course with me." His eyes seemed to examine her. Probably trying to detect if she had a brain, Charley thought. "Why else would I ask?"

Charley shrugged, stalling for time and wondering why she felt so undecided. If Ben had suggested it, she would have jumped at the chance. And if Bill or Sam had asked, even in the early days, she wouldn't have hesitated for a moment. Why was she hesitating now? What was there about Brannigan that was so different?

"Curiosity," she suggested finally.

His brows drew together. And then his lips quirked in a smile.

"Sorry, Special Agent Dow, but my curiosity tank's on empty." He gestured to the piles of paperwork spread out on his desk. Charts, theories. And mountains of evidence that didn't help a damn. "I used it all up on the job."

Charley laughed. Or at least she thought she did. She was too tired to really be sure.

"Me, too," she agreed. Although she had to admit that she still had a tiny bit of curiosity left and it centered around him.

"So, are you game?"

She almost asked for what, which would have sounded damn coy on her part. Smiling, she shook her head.

"Thanks, but I'm going to have to take a rain check." The soft laugh was directed at herself. "If I go out for a drink now, I might drown in it."

Amusement glittered in his green eyes as they watched her. He rose from his desk and moved closer to hers. "I wasn't planning on buying you that big a drink."

His words caught her by surprise. She hadn't realized that Brannigan's invitation included paying for her drink. Maybe he meant nothing by it, but in her book, if he was paying, that made it something a little more than just two partners grabbing a beer. Exactly what, she was too tired to contemplate.

Maybe it was the hour, or her state of near-exhaustion, but he was standing too close. The air-conditioning in the building had long since shut off and the room was getting decidedly warmer.

She pushed her chair back from her desk—and him.

"Wouldn't take much to drown me right now," she countered.

Nick inclined his head, knowing when not to push. "Okay, then, see you tomorrow."

"Tomorrow," she echoed.

He was gone before she could think of anything else to say.

She would have liked to have had that drink, but if she'd gone in her present state, things might have happened that she wasn't ready for. She'd gotten an inkling of that when he'd stood so close to her.

No use borrowing trouble, and Nick Brannigan was trouble if she ever saw it.

She had to get home. It was a mayday cry from her body. Absently, Charley neatened the converging piles on her desk before they became one huge mass. The scent of Brannigan's aftershave suddenly came to her. Or maybe that was just her imagination.

She shook her head. Definitely overtired.

She couldn't help wondering if her partner was aware of all the looks he garnered from the women in the immediate area whenever he walked by. Probably so used to admiration, it didn't even register.

There was such a thing as being too good-looking, Charley mused. Whoever fell for Brannigan was asking for a heartache. Acquiring a heartache was very, very low on her priority list.

Pressing a series of keys, Charley closed down her computer. Once the light disappeared from the screen and the soft humming noise faded, she locked her desk.

With a sigh, she longed for a magical way to get home just by wishing herself there.

She got up and slipped on the light blue linen jacket that had spent most of the day slung over the back of her chair. The entire day had been hot, but Southern California evenings were surprising sometimes.

Her purse straps slung over her shoulder, Charley made her way to the elevator and then to the front entrance. Exiting, she stood at the top of the stairs for a moment, breathing in the cool air.

Despite the fact that summer had settled in, dusk began to embrace the parking lot. Only a handful of cars were left on the lot. She spent too many hours here. A family of dust mites had probably moved into her lungs a long time ago. There had to be something more to living than this.

But for the life of her, Charley couldn't think of what.

Something dark caught her eye. Staring, trying to accustom her eyes to the limited light, Charley saw a movement near her vehicle.

Someone was lurking around her car.

Tension, her tired state—everything—vanished to be replaced by a rush of adrenaline that surged through her entire system. In less time than it took to think about it, Charley had her weapon in both hands, holding it steady and trained on the shadow in the distance.

"Step away from the car," she ordered in a loud voice. "FBI."

The shadow took on substance and form as it moved from the vehicle, out into the light being cast by the parking-lot lamps.

It was a man and his hands were raised. He spoke as

he drew closer. "I know what you are, Charley. I was there at the graduation ceremony, remember?"

Charley holstered her weapon on the fly. With a whoop comprised of sheer joy, she leaped into her older brother's arms. The bear hug lasted what seemed like several minutes.

Stepping back, she threaded her arms around his neck the way she had when they were younger. "David, why didn't you tell me you were coming?"

"Then I wouldn't have had the thrill of having you point your gun at me," he deadpanned. After giving her a bear hug of his own, he released her. Still beaming at him, she straightened her jacket.

"Besides, I like seeing your face light up when you realize you almost killed a civilian."

She didn't take his bait. Hundreds of questions popped into her head. Questions it would take him all night to answer.

She began at the beginning. "How long are you in town for?" But before he could answer, Charley stepped back and looked him over. "God, you've gotten skinnier. Don't the Marines believe in feeding their people?"

David held his hand up in self-defense, well aware that if he let her, his sister would bury him in questions before he had a chance to answer the first one.

"I've just gotten transferred to Southern California and I'm living on love, not mess-hall cooking." He grinned at her. Since he had her full attention, David dropped his bombshell. "I'm getting married, Charley. I wanted you to be the first to know."

CHAPTER TWENTY

IT TOOK HER a second to recover. Maybe two. And then she grinned. From ear to ear as she hugged him again. David was a good guy. He deserved to be happy.

"I hope you told the bride-to-be before you told me."

David laughed as she released him. "Yeah, well, okay, you're the second to know."

More questions crowded in with the first set. They couldn't just stand here talking in the parking lot. She looked around for his old car and didn't see it. Charley drew her brother over to the passenger side of her vehicle and opened the door.

"C'mon, let's go get a drink and you can fill me in on everything. The first thing I want to know is who is this hussy who's got her claws into my big brother."

David got in and buckled up. "I thought that might be the first question on the list." He leaned back, getting comfortable. As he did, he looked around inside the vehicle. He'd gone with her when she'd bought this, years ago. "Glad you still drive this old heap."

Charley patted the dashboard in the same manner she petted Dakota. "Mind your language. It's sensitive. Besides, four years doesn't exactly qualify as old."

"If the car's anything like you," he informed her, "it's got the hide of a rhino."

Charley took a swat at him without even taking her eyes off the road.

THE LOCAL BAR and grill frequented by the federal agents who worked in the nearby building was filled to capacity at that hour. People came there looking to unwind and to hang up the heavy burden of their responsibilities.

The big, beefy bartender behind the bar moved faster than he looked capable of, mixing and serving drinks at a feverish pace. Two barmaids equipped with damp trays moved between the bar and the tables scattered throughout the room, bringing back the tall glasses of liquid reinforcement.

Smoking had long since been banned in establishments such as Reilly's, but the air was thick with the sound of voices. A jukebox in the corner was stocked with nothing but Elvis songs. If one was playing now, it didn't manage to break through the din.

The press of flesh and warm breath instantly greeted Charley the moment she pushed open the front door. She glanced back at her brother. "Too crowded?"

"Just right," he judged.

She grinned. Seeing two people getting up from a table, Charley immediately plowed through the tangle of bodies in her way, determined to stake a claim. She threw her jacket over one of the seats a heartbeat before another customer reached it. The man scowled at her but backed away.

Only then did she turn around to make sure David was behind her.

Before sitting down, she held up her hand until she caught the eye of one of the barmaids. Nodding, the woman started moving in their direction.

David sat down opposite his sister. He shook his head with a laugh. "Same old Charley."

She knew he was referring to her pushiness. It was a trait she'd developed in the past five years. Because Cris was no longer around to lead the way.

"Ditch the 'old,'" Charley instructed. "Two beers," she told the willowy blonde when the barmaid was close enough to hear. "Whatever's on tap," she added, then glanced at David to see if that met with his approval. He nodded his head.

"So…" Knotting her hands together, Charley leaned forward the moment the barmaid withdrew to get their beers. "Been to see Dad yet?"

The corners of David's smile leveled out ever so slightly and became grim. "No."

She hadn't thought so. Never really a candidate for father of the year, Christopher Dow had had a particularly difficult time relating to his son. Things became more estranged as David grew up. Every frustration their father felt, real or imagined, he'd taken out on David until he had finally had enough. He'd enlisted in the Marines, against his father's wishes. There'd been a few visits—until Cris's murder. After that, David stopped coming around on leave.

She studied her brother's face. "Should I tell him you're here?"

David paused before answering. "Only if he asks." He looked at Charley. "And he won't ask."

Charley nodded, momentarily abiding by his wishes. "What about the wedding? Are you inviting him?"

She knew, being David, he wanted to. But that didn't mean he was going to. You could only have your hand slapped away so often before you stopped extending it.

He shrugged. "He wouldn't come even if I invited him, so why bother?"

More than anything, she wanted peace in the family. She could see how the schism bothered her brother. "David, maybe it's time to bury the hatchet."

"He made it perfectly clear the last time we talked that he wanted nothing to do with me."

Because it was impossible to lower her voice and still be heard, Charley hunched forward even closer to her brother. "He's an unhappy, bitter old man, David—"

David laughed, but there was no humor in the sound. "So far, you're not saying anything to recommend my getting in contact with him." Their father had been far from perfect before the murder. But after Cris was killed, things became that much worse. "Look, Cris's death didn't just happen to him, it happened to all of us. If he'd reached out to Mom when she was sinking into that abyss, maybe she wouldn't be spending her days and nights locked away where we can't reach her."

She knew he wasn't talking about the nursing facility. "You've been to see her."

For just a moment, his expression bordered on bitter. "Yeah, I've been to see her. Thought I'd get that over with before I came to find you."

She knew he didn't mean it the way it sounded. Seeing their mother, a woman who had been beautiful by anyone's standards, a woman who had been lively and happy, reduced to a shell of her former self, was hard on all of them. Especially David, who'd been so close to her.

Banishing the serious moment, David's expression softened as he forced a smile to his lips. He reached across the table and took her hand in his. "I can't wait for you to meet Lisa. You're going to love her."

"As long as she's good to you, I promise I'll adore her. Tell me all about her."

He thought for a moment, as if wondering where to begin. "In a way, I guess she reminds me a little bit of you."

"Love her already." About to pump him for more information, she stopped as another thought occurred to her. "Where are you staying tonight?"

"Lisa isn't due in for a couple of days. I thought I'd get a room at this motel—"

Charley stared at him, stunned. "The hell you will. I've got a fold-out sofa in my living room. I'll take that, you take the bed."

"I can't do that."

The look Charley gave him said it was useless to argue. "You can if I want you to."

"Charley—"

Giving him a smug look, Charley patted her brother's hand. "If you're getting married, Davy-boy, I think you'd better get used to being ordered around by a woman."

David shook his head. "She's not like that."

He might be her older brother and a Marine, but if he believed that, he knew nothing about women. She gave him an amused smile.

"All women are like that, David. We just wait around until we've won you over, then we spring the trap." She leaned back in her chair, looking at him. Remembering when they were children, playing together. Life had been so simple back then. Simple and innocent. "God, married. I can't believe it. When's the big day?"

"A month from this coming Sunday."

Her mouth dropped open. She'd expected him to say something like "in six months," or "next spring." This was so sudden.

"A month?" she echoed. She tried to remember what tradition dictated in their religion. It had been a very long time since she'd attended services. She had stopped going right after Cris's funeral. "Don't you need to post the banns for a month or something like that?"

"The chaplain on my old base knows a priest at the local church here. He put in a good word for me and a few rules were bent."

"Ah." She nodded knowingly. "The ever-popular rule bending." She saw the barmaid finally approaching with their beers. "Just what makes the world go around."

The young woman quickly placed each large mug on a tiny coaster. Charley gave her a twenty. When the barmaid began to make change, Charley waved her on. The barmaid flashed a row of gleaming teeth, then hurried off.

Charley moved her glass in front of her. As she did so, she absently glanced into the crowd. Charley had no idea why her eyes were drawn to the far right.

Recognition was instant.

Standing with his back to the bar, scanning the room, Brannigan had obviously seen her several minutes before she was aware of him. Long enough to observe the exchange between his partner and the tall, good-looking blond-haired man with her.

When she looked in his direction, he raised his mug of beer, as if in a silent toast.

Her heart stopped, as if holding its breath. And then she realized that she was the one holding her breath. Charley forced herself to inhale slowly, then exhale again. For the life of her, she couldn't read the expression on her partner's face. Only that Brannigan's lips seemed to be twisted in what looked like a bemused smirk.

There was absolutely no reason for her to feel guilty. No reason to feel like a kid who'd been discovered with her hand in the cookie jar. No reason at all.

But she did.

"What's the matter?" David asked. He scanned the immediate area to see who had caught his sister's attention. "You look the way you did that time when Mrs. McCann sent you to the principal's office for cheating."

Charley looked back at her brother. "I didn't cheat," she informed him. "Mary Ellen Walters was the one who cheated. She was looking at my test paper, not the other way around. Just took her a while to admit it, that's all." She remembered that Cris had been the one who'd finally made the other girl confess. Cris, pretending to be her. Back then, it had always been Cris who'd been the gutsy one, not her. "I just saw someone I knew," she explained.

"Seeing as how every person here is connected to the FBI in some way, I'd figure it's hard for you *not* to see someone you know."

"Very funny, wise guy."

Maybe she should invite Brannigan over, introduce him to her brother. Deciding that was the way to go, she looked back toward the bar.

But Brannigan was nowhere in sight.

CHAPTER TWENTY-ONE

HE'D BEEN WATCHING her.

Watched her for longer than he could remember watching any of the others. Had begun watching her even before he'd brought the other one to her eternal salvation.

He'd hoped that he was wrong, that there had been some mistake. But there wasn't. She was a sinner. Just like the others.

Just like the very first one.

Learning her routine had been difficult because people were always around her. He'd turned that to his advantage, slipping into the crowd. Hiding in plain sight. He was ever afraid that someone might see him. Actually see him instead of just looking through him. But he'd had nothing to fear. So far, he doubted anyone would have even been aware that he was anywhere in the vicinity.

He was one of those people other people looked right through without realizing that there had been anyone in that spot at all. Whether he wanted it or not, anonymity cloaked him wherever he went.

He'd resented that deeply as a child. He had tried very hard to be noticed, at least by the one person who mattered in his life. His father. The one man he could bond with against his mother. She'd treated them both as if they were dirt beneath her feet, even though his father was a minister.

It made no difference to her.

And he, as her son, had made no difference to her. But he had so badly wanted to make a difference as far as his father was concerned.

Sometimes when he was a child, lying awake at night in his bed, he would fantasize about how his father and he would just run off, leaving his mother far behind. Run off and do anything they wanted to.

His father was his best friend, as well as his first line of defense against his sharp-tongued, hurtful mother. His best friend, that is, until the day he'd discovered his father had betrayed him. Had been betraying him all along.

With her.

The one with the large luminous eyes. Eyes that stared at him in the last few moments of her life, begging for mercy as eloquently as she had. But mercy was something he'd suddenly found that he was devoid of. Because he had been betrayed. By the man he'd worshipped ahead of all others. Even ahead of God.

He knew it was blasphemous, but he would have gone to hell for his father. Instead, hell was where his father and that whore were destined.

"Leave her alone," his father had cried, no, begged when the minister had realized that he was no longer listening.

Even now, he could hear his father's voice in his head. Begging. Except this time, he was begging him to spare Rita Daly.

"Leave her alone, son. You have to leave her alone. Please."

But he knew he couldn't. For her own good.

He looked at the calendar on the kitchen wall. The calendar that helped him track his time. Track his missions. There were so many missions. And he was tired. But he knew what was required of him.

It was almost Sunday.

And on this Sunday Rita Daly would finally be free of the mortal clay that held her to this immoral existence. Sunday she would meet her salvation, he promised himself. He could almost taste it.

He began to move about. There was a great deal to prepare before the big day.

Before Sunday.

CHARLEY HARDLY SLEPT. She and David had stayed up all night, talking. When he finally begged off, it was after two o'clock in the morning. She'd left him sleeping like the proverbial baby. She, on the other hand, was operating on four hours' sleep. Even her morning run with Dakota hadn't managed to wake her up.

She'd come into the office dragging, only to be subjected to a silent once-over by her partner. Then, for the rest of the day, whenever they were in each other's company, they'd conducted themselves like two foreign dignitaries in the UN who had only the smallest understanding of the other's language.

It was beginning to rub her the wrong way. Being a professional, she'd held her tongue during the interviews. But the moment they went back to their vehicle, she hit him full force with her ire.

"Okay," she declared as she buckled up, "what the hell is going on?" When Nick made no answer, she pushed harder, even as she jammed her key into the ignition. "You've had something on your mind all day. Spit it out. What is it?"

Nick kept his face forward as she eased the vehicle into traffic. Whenever he was annoyed, he found it better not to talk until the feeling passed. It hadn't passed yet.

"You're my partner," he told her evenly. "That doesn't mean you're privy to my every thought."

They were heading back to the station. Thank God it was Friday, she thought. This week had had at least three extra days. "No, just the ones that concern me."

Nick slanted a glance at her that fit anyone's definition of icy. "Got a swelled head, Special Agent Dow? Not everything is about you."

If he meant to make her back off with his deep-freeze look, he was in for a surprise. Her father hadn't managed to intimidate her and he was a world-class expert.

Charley took a quick left turn just as the light was turning red. "It is when I catch you looking at me as if you were a rich socialite and I was a leper about to invade your exclusive party." She didn't like being the recipient of dark looks, nor did she care for the silent treatment. "Now, if I've done something—"

"Not a thing." Despite his best efforts, there was sarcasm in his voice. "I just don't appreciate being paired up with someone I can't trust."

She pressed down hard on the accelerator to make the next light. "Excuse me?"

He bit his tongue. The woman drove as if the car was on fire and she was trying to head straight for the lake, obstacles be damned.

"Hearing going, too?"

"My hearing's in a lot better condition than your

brain," she snapped, then regained control over her emotions. In a more even tone, she demanded, "What the hell are you talking about? What have I done to make you think you can't trust me?"

He snorted, as if the answer was self-evident. "You lied."

"I what?" This time, when her temper flared, she just let it go. "Listen, buster, I don't lie. Lies are for people with things to hide. My life isn't anywhere near that complicated."

He almost believed her, she sounded that sincere. But he'd seen what he'd seen and there was no getting around that. "Then why didn't you have the decency to tell me you couldn't go out for a drink yesterday because you were meeting your boyfriend?"

Bringing the vehicle to a screeching stop within the Federal Building parking structure, Charley shifted in her seat to glare at him. She opened her mouth to answer, then shut it, swallowing a scathing retort. She struggled to keep her temper in check.

Brannigan reached for the door handle, but she threw the remote lock on, locking all four of the doors. He looked at her as if she'd lost her mind.

Composing herself, Charley held up first her index finger, then two more, raising the fingers one at a time. Banking down the temptation to hold only one digit up to tell him how she felt.

"Because one, I don't owe you any explanations," she informed him evenly. "Two, I didn't know he was in town and three, David is not my boyfriend, or whatever it is you imagined he was—he's my brother."

The last word seemed to echo within the vehicle's interior. "Brother."

"Brother," she repeated with verve.

Nick studied her for a long moment, telling himself he'd know if she was lying. Gut instincts rather than her protestations told him she wasn't. "That was your brother?"

Was the man deaf as well as dense? "I just said that. Do you need to see his ID? Because I can call David up to bring it over if you like. He's staying at my place until he settles in."

Nick had never felt stupid before. He didn't much care for it. Waving away her offer, he muttered, "No, your word's good enough."

"You're sure?" she pressed sarcastically. "Because back there, for a second, it didn't seem as if my word was worth as much as dirt to you."

When he turned to look at her, her eyes were blazing.

"You are an arrogant son of a bitch, you know that?" Charley spit.

Arrogance had nothing to do with it. He felt relieved. And that bothered him. Just as much as his jealousy last night had bothered him. When he'd first seen her at the bar last night, he'd thought she'd had a change of heart. And then he'd realized that she was with someone. Someone she was talking to and laughing with. Standing at the bar, he'd observed her for several minutes before she'd finally looked his way. Observed the way she placed her hand on the other man's arm, the way her fingertips caressed his wrist.

Observed, too, that a strange displeasure wove through him as he witnessed her behavior with another man. A lover.

The relief he experienced at learning that Charley and the man were siblings was as unexpected as the stab of jealousy he'd felt last night.

He had always kept the lines between work and private

life drawn, if not tightly, at least noticeably. He sensed the dangers that would arise out of mingling the two. But right now, the only thing on his mind was the desire to satisfy his curiosity. There was a volley of sizzling words leaving Charley's mouth. Did that make her lips hot?

He suddenly needed to know.

In a move that surprised them both, he leaned over in the car, threaded his fingers through her hair in order to bring her closer. And kissed her.

Shock vibrated through her. Charley's first reaction was to pull away, to wedge her hands between them and shove this man back as hard as she could. Maybe even as she called him a few choice names. And threatened to put him on report.

She did none of that, said none of that. She was too busy trying to catch her breath as she clung to a runaway roller coaster. Her reaction, this feeling that was zooming through her, surprised the hell out of her.

Especially since she wasn't the type to believe in feelings like this. Until this very moment, she'd been firmly convinced it was all a lie made up by men and women who wanted only to make everyone around them jealous. Jealous as hell over something that really wasn't out there to feel.

Except that it was. Neverland *did* exist. And she'd found a sliver of it within this enigma that the Bureau had pushed into her life.

Charley bit back a moan as she leaned in closer to him. She intended to glide on the winds with Peter Pan for as long as she could manage. It was her first visit here. And undoubtedly her last, she thought with the part of her brain that still functioned.

CHAPTER TWENTY-TWO

FINALLY, ALTHOUGH IT almost hurt to do so, Charley drew back.

As did Nick.

Heat swam through her, casting out long, searing rays. Pulling herself together took effort. She sought refuge in anger. Except she didn't actually feel angry. Just confused.

"What the hell was that?" she demanded, hoping she sounded sufficiently put out.

She watched as a bemused, almost lopsided grin—not a smile, but a grin—slipped over his lips. "I was hoping you could tell me."

She caught herself tossing her hair and stopped mid-motion. Too melodramatic, she upbraided herself silently. Except that she felt melodramatic. She felt a lot of things. Mostly turned inside out.

"I'm not the one who kissed you."

The grin moved slowly along his lips, taking her prisoner. "The hell you didn't, Special Agent Dow. You kissed me just as much as I kissed you."

He was right. To deny it would be doing the very thing she'd said she didn't. It would be lying. She had no choice but to admit it. Kind of.

"Don't let it happen again," she warned. *Because I*

might just kiss you back again. She fervently hoped he couldn't read minds.

Damn, that had been good. If he kissed like that on the spur of the moment, what must the man be like in…

Startled at the direction her mind was going, Charley refused to allow herself to complete the thought.

"I won't." But even as Nick said it, he wasn't sure he could back that up. Because he'd liked what he'd sampled. Liked it more than he should have. And, God help him, he wanted to do it again.

CHARLEY SPENT the weekend trying to catch up on the rest of her life. Catching up with her brother and just fussing over him. More than anything, she enjoyed the feeling of being part of a family again. It was something she had acutely missed when David enlisted.

Although both her parents were still alive, she thought of herself as alone. Especially when her mother began to swiftly deteriorate. Not long after David had gone through basic training, their mother had drifted away.

And her father only thought of Charley as a means to an end. The end being that she would find her sister's murderer and bring him to justice. Or, better yet, hand the man over to her father for vengeance. She and her father had nothing in common except for a last name. He wasn't really family anymore, not in the true sense of the word.

For the most part, Charley thought of the people she worked with as her family. This helped over the bumpier times.

Early Monday morning, over her own protests, Charley drove her brother to a car rental agency. But even as they pulled up in the parking lot, she made a last-ditch attempt at getting him to change his mind. And save money.

"You can take my car," she offered, coming to a stop before a pleasant-looking ground-floor office. The sign above the door proclaimed it to be the leading car rental agency in three counties.

His fingers resting on the door handle, David shook his head. "You need your car."

"One of the agents can pick me up."

But David laughed, turning her down. "Don't try to mother me. Besides, any car I rent is bound to leave me cleaner than yours." He glanced down at his civilian clothing. "Look at all this dog fur."

"A, that's not from my car, it's from my dog, and B, serves you right for roughhousing with Dakota. You know how much she loves you."

He lifted his shoulders in a self-deprecating shrug. "I've always had a fatal charm when it comes to the ladies," he laughed.

Before she could make a comment, her cell phone began to ring. She fished it out of her pocket and answered, putting a finger up for David to hold whatever thought he had until she was off.

"Dow."

"Charlotte? It's Alice."

She stiffened. Since they'd gone out to lunch together, the secretary seemed intent on getting closer to her. Although she felt sorry for the woman, she had no desire for a lasting, long-term friendship. "Alice, can this be quick? I have to—"

"There's been another murder," Alice told her, a smattering of authority infused into her normally timid voice.

Damn.

Thoughts of another chatty, nonsensical conversation vanished. Charley was alert, all business. She'd hoped the killer would just stop. Maybe it wasn't realistic, but things happened to people all the time. Their serial killer could have been involved in a fatal car accident and they would never know. Except that the killings would stop.

"Where?"

Alice recited a Newport Beach address. Vaguely familiar with the location, she knew that it belonged to one of the more exclusive neighborhoods, a gated development with its own guard.

Not even the rich were safe.

"A.D. Kelly wants you and Special Agent Brannigan on-site," Alice told her.

"I'm on my way." Closing the telephone, she looked at her brother. David was still in the car. Charley nodded toward the rental office. "You'll be okay?"

She could see that David was doing his best not to laugh at the question. "Marines made a man out of me, remember?"

Okay, so she was being overprotective. "And you can walk and chew gum at the same time, yes, I know. Sorry. I have a tendency to mother and ordinarily, the only one on the receiving end is Dakota."

David laughed, letting her know that no offense was taken. "Go." He waved her off. "Get the bad guys."

She flashed him a smile. "I only wish."

She hit the road less than a minute later.

David never asked her about her work. Unlike their father, David never asked in his letters if she was close to catching the man who had robbed them of a sister.

She truly didn't know if that was because David knew she couldn't discuss an ongoing investigation, or if her brother had to pretend that the taking of Cris's life hadn't happened.

It was a question to ponder for another day. Right now, she had a fresh murder on her hands.

BRANNIGAN WAS THERE ahead of her. It figured, she thought, disgruntled as she parked near his vehicle. She got out quickly. Ever since the man had kissed her Friday, she felt as if she was running in slow motion, ten paces behind him. Not particularly a good thing, seeing as how she was the lead.

Police milled around, obviously called in to control any crowds that might begin to gather around outside the fashionable house. Crowds drew reporters and the latter would be here soon enough.

She couldn't help being a little awed by the structure as she walked through the entrance. It was a rich neighborhood. The least expensive home in the area went for approximately one point two million dollars.

When she entered the room where the body had been discovered, she saw Brannigan crouching over the woman. He looked up as she approached. They exchanged polite nods.

It wasn't going to get any more personal than that, she promised herself. And as she did, she felt her fingertips tingle, as if telling her she was lying.

"What are we looking at?" Slipping on a pair of plastic gloves, Charley squatted down beside Brannigan and looked at the victim. Like the others, the woman had been posed to lie on her back. As if she was asleep.

"Same guy?" Even as she asked, she gently moved

aside the blond bangs that covered the woman's forehead. The same faint cross was carved on her skin.

Nick went over the M.O. "Manual strangulation from behind. A cross carved on her forehead. No loose, telltale signs. No signs of forced entry." Rising, he shook his head.

"You'd think someone would have noticed him by now," Bill complained, coming forth.

Charley looked over her shoulder at the man. Sam was behind him. She saw Jack passing by the living-room doorway. Apparently, she was the last one to get here. Getting up, Charley left her gloves on. They would be doing a lot of looking around in the next few hours. Not to mention a lot of praying that, for once, they would finally get lucky.

"Maybe it's someone nobody would think of questioning." She was only saying out loud what everyone had to be thinking. "A cop, a delivery man, a public utilities repairman. Maybe the cable guy or someone posing as a mail carrier."

"In other words, someone you wouldn't look at twice," Sam supplied.

"Exactly. He tells the victim there's a package that needs a signature, a leak in the neighborhood that he's tracking to its source, he's collecting for the policemen's ball." She shrugged. "Something that gets him into the house without a problem while keeping him invisible as far as everyone else is concerned."

She sighed, shaking her head. The deceased looked a little like Cris. It brought it all too close again.

Charley threw up her hands. "Hell, all I know is that he's good, he's getting cocky and he's killing more often. The first three murders were exactly a year apart, then they began to escalate." She looked at Sam. "Now, it's, what, a little more than a month? We've got to catch this bastard before he starts making it a weekly event. Or decides that Sundays aren't the only day he wants to kill women."

"I don't think so," Nick ventured slowly. The others looked at him. "I think Sundays mean too much to him, for some reason." He paused for a moment, thinking. When he spoke again, he looked at Charley. "We need to look at newspaper archives."

She wasn't sure she followed him. "For?"

Nick recalled the date the first victim was killed. Her sister. "Something happened to him on March twenty-fourth. Something that made him snap, made him do what he's doing. Maybe there's something in one of the local papers on March twenty-fourth or twenty-fifth, 1998 or maybe even 1999, that can enlighten us."

Bill eyed him incredulously. "Do you have any idea how many local newspapers there are?"

"Since the first murder took place in Orange County, I think it's safe to say that our killer is probably from around here," Nick told him.

"Can't be a hundred-percent certain of that," Charley pointed out.

"No, you're right. If we don't find anything, we widen our scope," Nick answered.

"There's also the possibility that whatever happened didn't make the papers, was only important to our killer," Charley said.

"Gotta start someplace," Sam interjected.

Charley frowned. "It's a long shot."

Nick surprised her by admitting, "I agree. But it's better than no shot at all."

She supposed he had something. She wasn't going to be the one to vote it down. She turned to Sam, Bill and Jack, who'd just walked into the room. "Okay, but in the meantime, why don't you three canvass the area and ask the same old tired questions."

"You got it." Bill gave her a two-finger salute.

Just as they began to leave, Assistant Director Kelly walked in. He saw the crime scene and shook his head. "Do you have any idea who the victim is?" he asked Charley.

"Unlucky number 13," she replied.

Kelly frowned. "She's also Rita Daly, the mayor's niece." He looked from one person to another, including the forensic team. "I want to get this solved yesterday."

Charley's mouth curved in a humorless smile. "If we had the ability for time travel, Assistant Director, the killer would have never had a chance to get his second victim."

Kelly grumbled something inaudible at her back. Charley decided not to ask him to repeat himself.

CHAPTER TWENTY-THREE

"A LITTLE EARLY in the season for a barbecue, isn't it?"

From the very first syllable he uttered, Charley could feel the hairs on the back of her neck stand up as if they'd been exposed to a jolt of electricity. Maybe they had.

She turned around slowly, a margarita in her hand. The sound of children playing, fragments of conversations and Dakota barking joyfully all faded into the background like so many soft whispers. The smile that sprang to her lips was genuine, but she attempted to tone it down.

Charley tried to tell herself that she hadn't been watching for him, wondering if her partner was going to attend the impromptu barbecue Sam had decided to throw. Nick hadn't given her an answer when she'd tossed out the question about his attendance late yesterday afternoon.

Working almost around-the-clock ever since the mayor's niece had been murdered, they all needed a break in the tension. More than anything, they needed an afternoon in which they could forget the gruesome details that haunted their everyday lives. Just for a few hours, they could pretend nothing was more important than consuming well-done hamburgers in the company of a few dozen friends.

In his generosity, Sam had invited the entire task force and their families. That included the A.D. and his secretary, as well as the forensic crew. But when she'd arrived with her dog, who was quickly spirited away by Sam's children, she hadn't see Nick anywhere in the area.

An hour into the barbecue and he still hadn't turned up. Until now.

The smile she offered Nick began at her inner core, even though she told herself she was being foolish. She saw this man every day. They spent over eight hours each day in each other's company. Why should seeing him in jeans and a pullover, miles away from the Federal Building, be any different?

"This is Southern California. We can have a barbecue here anytime." Her smile broadened. "Not like back East." Charley took a sip of her drink. Sam's wife had gone heavy on the tequila again, she thought, looking at Nick's eyes. She hadn't realized just how green they were. Green and smoky. She forced herself to focus. "I hear an unexpected cold front is moving in around D.C. The weatherman said they're expecting unseasonably low temperatures." Talk of weather was about as bland as it could get. Yet she was feeling warm. "Should make you glad to be out here."

Nick felt something humming between them. Again. He'd thought, away from the tension of the job, their attraction might lessen. Instead, it felt even more pronounced.

He shrugged casually in response to her words. "I like the change of seasons."

She combed her fingers through her hair, pushing it away from her face.

"Not me. A variance of about ten degrees is about all I can put up with. And I like having my rain scheduled inside of a season, not falling unexpectedly." She supposed that probably sounded spoiled to him. But she was a California girl, through and through.

He studied her for a moment. Sam's wife passed by, pausing only long enough to slip a can of beer into his hand. "Don't you miss snow?"

She didn't even have to think about her answer. "Can't miss what you've never had." The idea of snow had never really intrigued her. She preferred the white sands of beaches. "And if I feel deprived in any way, I can always drive up to the mountains to visit it."

A boy and a girl of about eight or nine flew by, narrowly missing them both. Instinctively, Nick put his arm around her to move her out of harm's way. Contact brought everything to a momentary standstill as they looked at each other.

Clearing his throat, Nick dropped his arm. "You were born here?"

Maybe the margarita was *too* strong, Charley thought. She deposited the emptied glass on a nearby table, forgoing the idea of having another until she'd had something to eat.

"Down in Newport Beach," she told him. "I'm one of the few natives around." She grinned at Sam, who'd transferred in from Seattle around the time that she joined the Bureau. "Everyone else comes here. And usually likes it." She cocked her head slightly, studying him. Daring him to be negative. "How about you?"

The shrug he offered was not quite as casual as he would have liked. That was because his eyes were on hers. Without his being conscious of it beginning, somehow they were involved in a dance. And he had no idea how it would end up.

He could feel a wave of excitement traveling through his veins, even as he told himself this was ultimately all wrong. But his edict regarding separation of work and pleasure somehow wasn't sticking.

"It has some things to recommend it," he finally allowed.

Charley tried not to shiver. Her response certainly wasn't because the day was cold or even cool. It was one of those days in paradise everyone dreamed about. The temperature a perfect seventy-eight, the sky was a brilliant blue with pristine white clouds creasing the horizon and there was just enough of a breeze stirring to keep things comfortable.

But despite the weather, something electric had scurried across her spine with a light touch. She couldn't remember the last time she'd reacted like that to a man. With or without a margarita.

"Hey, man, glad you could make it." Sam's jovial voice broke through the bubble that had suddenly surrounded them. "What'll it be?"

She was never so grateful to have Sam interrupt in her life. She flashed a smile as she turned toward him, mentally returning to her surroundings out of the nebulous regions she'd just traveled to.

Sex, served hot. The thought shot through Nick's brain in response to Sam's question. He kept it to himself. Without missing a beat, Nick turned to look at his host. Sam had raised his king-size spatula to emphasize his meaning.

"Charcoal, well-done, medium or rare?" Sam asked.

Nick bestowed the briefest of glances in Charley's direction before answering, "Rare."

Oh, wow. Belatedly, Charley realized that she'd stopped breathing. As discreetly as she could, she drew in a breath but couldn't seem to draw her eyes away.

Laughter from a far corner of the wide backyard caught her attention. Grateful, she looked in the direction it came from. Dressed in a shirt that looked as if a Hawaiian garden had exploded all over it, A.D. Kelly was standing at the center of a group, telling a story. Away from the office, the A.D. was a great one for long, involved stories that carried a punch line. Usually a good one.

She glanced at Nick, who seemed amused by Kelly. For once, she could almost read his thoughts.

"Surprised me, too," she admitted. "Away from the office, Kelly's just a regular person." Crossing over to a huge ice chest, she dug out a can of diet soda and popped the top. "Took him a while to come around. Something about maintaining control by keeping his distance." More laughter came from that quarter and Charley smiled. "Luckily, the A.D. has a wife who loves to socialize. Now all Sam has to do is throw a hot dog on a grill and they're here."

"One big happy family," Nick commented.

She couldn't tell if he was being sarcastic, or just talking. The margarita made her feel rosy. She gave him the benefit of the doubt.

"We try. Whenever there's a party, everyone shows up. With a few exceptions every now and then." She added, "I thought you might be one of them."

He had thought about offering his apologies and staying home. But he wasn't a loner by nature. Traveling from base to base had given him the tools to adapt. And staying away from a barbecue when everyone else was attending wasn't the way to fit in.

"Hey, I'm the new guy." Finishing his beer, he tossed the can into one of the garbage pails scattered throughout the yard. "If I stayed away, I'd look as if I felt I was too good for this kind of a get-together. Don't want anyone getting the wrong impression."

She nodded, taking another sip of her soda. "You alone?"

He grinned and she bit her tongue. Why the hell had she asked that? He was getting the wrong idea. *Or maybe the right one.*

"Like I said, I'm the new guy. I haven't had any time to get to know anyone to bring." His gaze seemed to go right through her. "You?"

"Did I bring anyone?" she asked.

He nodded.

Charley gave a half shrug. "I've had too much time to get to know everyone," she countered, then smiled. "The kind of life we lead, it's hard meeting anyone outside the Bureau."

He wasn't about to let her go that easily. Over the past few weeks, she'd pumped him for information he'd never thought of volunteering. It was his turn. "How about inside the Bureau?"

She shook her head, even as something quickened within her. "That kind of thing never works out."

His slow, sexy smile nearly undid her. "I was taught never to say never."

"Cute." To save herself from saying or doing something stupid, she looked away, pretending to scan the area. When she did so in earnest, she frowned.

"Anything wrong?" he asked.

"I don't see Alice."

Nick couldn't make out the woman's gangly form in the crowd either, but her absence came as no surprise. "She doesn't strike me as the type to attend this kind of a group gathering."

Because Alice was such a loner, Charley felt a need to defend the woman. She doubted if anyone actually ever stood up for her. "What makes you say that?"

"She doesn't look comfortable away from her desk."

"She's just very shy and awkward. But she's attended parties before," she added. "Once in a while," she qualified. "She's usually the last to arrive and the first to leave, but she comes."

Readjusting his apron that boldly proclaimed Kiss Me, I'm The Cook, Sam picked up a plate of fresh burgers and began to put them on the grill one at a time.

"I thought for sure she'd be here," Sam said. Then he added, after comically raising and lowering his somewhat shaggy eyebrows, "Especially since she's taken such a shine to our Charley here."

"She didn't 'take a shine to me,'" Charley protested. "I was just being nice to her and she was grateful."

"Speak of the devil," Bill commented, nodding toward the sliding-glass doors that led into the rear of his house.

Alice was tugging the door back into place after having stepped out. As always, she stood out. Not because of her gangly form or height, but because of her clothes. Sam had sent the word out that the barbecue was strictly casual. To Alice, that meant low-heeled pumps, a pleated skirt and a long-sleeved cotton blouse.

Nick shook his head. "I guess you can take the

woman out of the office, but you can't take the office out of the woman."

Maybe if she actively took the woman under her wing, Charley thought. Taught her a few things about dressing for the occasion. And worked on Alice's makeup, she added as an afterthought. All she needed was for God to create a twenty-eight-hour day.

To Charley's relief, she saw Kelly calling the woman over to his circle. For the time being, that took the burden off her.

"You know, you're not responsible for her."

She looked at Nick sharply. "How did you—"

"Body language," he answered, realizing he was watching his partner's body a lot lately. He was going to have to stop that. Unless he was ready to suffer whatever consequences came of going down this road.

"You read minds, too?" she asked.

Nick grinned now. "On occasion."

Charley was extremely glad that her partner was only kidding.

CHAPTER TWENTY-FOUR

THE WARM SCENT of lovemaking lingered along the curves of her body.

Laura Brigham wrapped her arms around her torso, hugging herself. Both her smile and her eyes were dreamy as she pressed the last remnants of euphoria to her.

The spot beside her was still warm. She snuggled against it, reliving every wild, passionate moment she'd just enjoyed. Eventually, the warmth slipped away into the corners of the room like a feline padding softly into the mists. With a sigh, Laura sat up and threw off the covers. She reached for the cream-colored silk robe that lay across the foot of the bed and slipped it on. The delicate material felt good against her naked skin. Sensual.

Her lover had left her bed no more than ten minutes ago. As was her habit, she didn't see him to the door. Didn't watch him walk away from her and back to the shrew of a wife who held on to his purse strings. He'd confided he'd only married Joan to secure a partnership in the lucrative dental office. If he divorced her now, it would ruin everything. But someday soon, his father-in-law was going to retire, leaving the practice to him. And then things would change.

Someday soon.

It couldn't be soon enough for her.

With a sigh, Laura combed her fingers through her hair, then paused to look at herself in the mirror above the bedroom bureau. Her eyes fell on the tiny gold cross that she wore around her neck. The catch had moved forward again. Holding on to the cross, she moved the chain until the catch was at the back of her neck and then smiled at her reflection.

Dennis had given the necklace to her. She thought of it as her secret talisman. No one else in the dental office knew where it had come from, although one of the other hygienists had commented on it. Gina had noticed the first day she'd worn it and asked all sorts of questions. She'd answered none of them.

She'd said it was a gift from someone who meant a lot to her. It was all she could do not to look at Dennis then, so handsome in his white smock. So damn sexy without it.

She giggled then stopped.

The doorbell.

It was ringing. Her heart leaped up into her throat and she fairly flew to the front door, her robe parting and flying out on either side of her like wings. She paused only to tug the ends around her before throwing open the door.

"Back for seconds, lover?"

Disappointment was immediate. It wasn't Dennis at the door. It was one of the people whose teeth she cleaned. Whenever he came, even though his teeth were in perfect condition, she couldn't wait to have him out of her chair. Something about the man gave her the creeps.

She stared at him. "Oh. What are you doing here?"

And then she frowned as she saw the roses he was

holding. The bouquet he now thrust forward. Man, this was awkward. Searching for something to say, she took a step back as the man took a step forward.

Belatedly, she realized her mistake. Now she was going to have trouble getting him out again.

"Really, Mr. Sykes, I told you last week that I make it a rule never to get involved with any of the doctor's patients. It wouldn't be ethical."

Her words froze in her throat as she saw the man's expression change.

"What would you know about ethical?" he asked.

"DAMN, WHAT IS HE, on a marathon?" Charley demanded, frustration drumming through her. "What made him go from once a year to this?"

She felt an ache inside as she looked down at the face of yet another victim. She always saw Cris even as she took in the different details of each new body.

"Bloodlust is my guess," Bill volunteered.

The steady click of the camera continued as one of the crime scene investigators took an abundance of overlapping photographs of everything within the room. Charley tried to ignore it, even though the rhythm seemed to shout: *Dead, dead, dead.*

"Maybe he has a sense of urgency," Nick suggested. The others looked at him. "Who the hell knows? Maybe his doctor told him he has only six months to live and he wants to kill as many women as he can before then."

"Save," Charley corrected. "He wants to save as many women as he can before he dies."

Sam frowned as he surveyed the room, making notes. "You still plucking that one note?"

"Until something better comes along," Charley told him.

She turned her attention to the woman who had called in the homicide. Laura Brigham's housemate had come home from a date that had ended particularly badly. All she'd wanted to do was to grab a container of ice cream from the freezer and curl up in front of the television set. She'd almost walked right on top of Laura's body. Her throat was raw from screaming.

Charley looked at the woman with compassion, remembering how she'd felt six years ago. As if everything was surreal, because she just couldn't be seeing what she thought she was seeing.

"Is there anything missing?" Charley asked gently.

Rachel Fox looked as if she was going to break down again. Her eyes kept darting to the body on the floor and then back again. She wrung her hands helplessly. "I can't—I don't—"

Charley slipped an arm around the woman. Rachel flinched then relaxed, or attempted to.

"Think carefully," Charley said to her, her voice as gentle as if she were speaking to a child. "Take your time. Can you think of anything? Anything at all? You never know what might help us find this guy."

Rachel shook her head, and tears slipped down her cheeks. She stole another glance at the body on the floor, then quickly looked away. But then she forced herself to look again. She pointed toward her housemate. "Her cross," she said hoarsely, wiping away fresh tears.

"You mean the one on her forehead?" Nick asked.

"No, no, the one she wore." Hysteria mounted in the woman's voice. "She had on a tiny cross. Never took it off, not even in the shower." Rachel pressed her lips together. "She was very proud of it. I think her boyfriend gave it to her. Oh God—"

"You're doing fine, Rachel," Nick soothed. Charley stepped back, letting him take over. This wasn't about one-upmanship. It was about getting the serial killer. And Nick seemed to have a calming effect on the woman. "Boyfriend?" he asked.

Rachel nodded numbly and her breathing began to grow erratic. "Yeah."

"Do you have his name?" Nick asked.

But Rachel shook her head. "Laura is—was very secretive about it. I thought I knew who it was, but…" Her voice trailed off.

"Who did you think it was?" Charley asked in a coaxing tone.

Rachel's eyes had grown large, as if the horror was finally sinking in. Her distress seemed to grow by the moment. "Her boss," she said.

Red flags went up. Their killer was staying true to form. Charley exchanged looks with Nick. "This person you suspect," she pressed, "would you happen to know if he is married?"

Rachel nodded her head. The next moment, Nick reached out to catch her as she fainted.

Charley had moved out of the way just in time. "Good hands," she said to her partner.

Holding Rachel in his arms, Nick looked around for somewhere he could safely place the unconscious woman without contaminating the crime scene. The sofa looked like the safest bet and he crossed to it.

"Just knowing the signs." He carefully placed Rachel on the sofa. "My sister looked like that just before she passed out. She was pregnant at the time," he added before Charley could ask for details.

Charley waved the M.E. over. "This one's alive."

"It's been so long, I'm not sure I know what to do with live ones," Dr. Rose Morales cracked.

Charley and Nick got out of the medical examiner's way. "Any more in your family?" Charley asked him, her curiosity stirred by his reference to a sister.

"A brother," he replied absently as they moved back into what had turned out to be the main crime area. Raising his voice, he addressed the group of people methodically combing through the scene. "Anyone find a tiny cross?"

Several of the crew shook their heads. "Found a jewelry box in the bedroom," Jack offered, walking into the living room. He held it open as he rummaged around the small wooden box. "Doesn't look as if there's a cross in here." He held the box out to Charley in case he'd missed the item.

She looked quickly and shook her head. "It's not in here."

"If the victim was never without it she might have lost it in the struggle," Nick ventured.

Charley scanned the room. The crime-scene investigators attempted to go through everything without contaminating the evidence. The living room looked to have been the setting of some sort of intimate party. Two empty champagne glasses stood on the coffee table. "What struggle?"

Bill nodded as he surveyed the area as well. "She's got a point."

"Maybe that's his souvenir," Nick said suddenly. "Every nutcase takes something so that he can relive the moment. So far, nothing's stood out up until now. Maybe our Sunday Killer takes a piece of the victim's jewelry."

The moment her partner said that, something clicked inside of Charley's head. In her mind's eye, she could see her sister. When she'd walked in that awful night, Cris was lying on the floor as if she'd suddenly decided to take a nap. At first she'd thought that Cris was either playing a trick on her or had passed out. Until she realized that her sister wasn't breathing. Not a hair of Cris's head was out of place, she looked that natural.

But the cross their mother had given each of them the first day of elementary school, the cross Cris always wore because she was superstitious, wasn't there. Charley's grief over her loss was so overwhelming it hadn't hit her until just now.

Some Special Agent, Charley mocked herself.

"Not just any piece, a specific piece." Her voice had taken on an edge of excitement. The others turned to her. "A cross. The guy takes a cross. Maybe that's even how he selects his victims. He doesn't just kill someone having an affair with a married man, he kills them for defying God. Because they should have known better. He takes the cross they're wearing and replaces it with one he carves into their skin, symbolically their soul."

"Sounds like you're on to something," Sam agreed.

"Sam, Bill, Jack, go back through the files and see if you can find some mention of the victims missing a cross. If it's not in the reports, maybe you can question their families, their friends," Charley instructed.

"Where does that get us?" Bill wanted to know.

"Hopefully, a step closer to catching our serial killer." Charley turned to several of the other team members. "You know the drill. Canvass the area. See if anyone saw or heard anything. Maybe someone was walking their dog at the right time to spot our killer. We're due for a break." And then she looked at Nick. "C'mon, you and I have a dentist to see."

Nick followed her out of the house. She heard him laughing to himself. "This'll be a first."

She opened the driver's side of her car, motioning for him to get in. "What do you mean?"

He glanced back at the car he'd driven over here. He was going to have to come back for it later, he thought. But maybe that would give him some time to poke around after everyone else was finished.

"I always hated going to see the dentist," he told her, getting in. "This will be the first time a dentist is going to hate seeing me."

CHAPTER TWENTY-FIVE

CHARLEY SHOOK her head. "He's not the one."

She was referring to Laura Brigham's lover. The man on the other side of the one-way mirror. The moment they had walked into Dr. Dennis Washburn's office, identifying themselves, he'd seemed incredibly nervous to them. So much so that they politely suggested he accompany them back to the Bureau's field office.

It wasn't that she thought the man was the Sunday Killer, but there was the outside chance the dentist had used the recurring scenario to his own advantage. To camouflage his getting rid of a mistress who had proved to be too much of a liability. A copycat killing. It wouldn't have been the first time, Charley thought.

But after several hours in which she and Nick had tag-teamed each other, taking turns assaulting Washburn with question after question, she was fairly convinced that all the man was truly guilty of was bad choices.

"I don't think he's our guy, either," Nick agreed. Standing beside her, he studied the man sitting in the next room. Washburn looked like a man on the verge of an anxiety attack. The only thing he was really afraid of was that his wife might find out about his affair. He seemed unconcerned over the death of his mistress. "Washburn's a poor excuse for a human being, but I don't think he killed Laura Brigham." As he slanted a glance at Charley, his mouth quirked. "Still would have liked to have nailed him for principle's sake." Charley raised an eyebrow in silent inquiry and he added, "Never liked dentists."

Charley shoved her hands into her pockets. Trying to deal with her frustration over yet another dead end.

"What makes you say Washburn's a poor excuse for a human being?" She agreed with him a hundred percent, but she wanted to hear his reasons.

"Because he cheats on his wife," Nick said simply. He had no burning desire to commit to anyone, but marriage meant something. It did *not* mean you got to tomcat around. He frowned at the blond-haired man. "He'll probably pad his bills once he gets his hooks into the practice."

Charley allowed her curiosity to take her a little further. "Think he would have married Laura Brigham then?"

Nick laughed shortly. "Not a chance. He would have moved on to another woman by then. The only one the bastard is loyal to is himself."

Charley nodded. "You know, Special Agent Brannigan, you surprise me. I do believe you have some sterling qualities going for you."

He looked at her, mentally taking just a momentary respite from their gruesome business. Damn, but his partner got better looking every day. Even with the onset of an overcast sky, Charley Dow was a beautiful woman.

The smile that graced his lips was an open invitation. "Maybe I could give you a further tour sometime."

Charley heard herself saying, "Maybe," knowing that she sounded as if she was carrying on a mild flirtation. Exercising her sexual muscles with nothing short of smooth nonchalance. Inside, however, was a whole different story. Inside she felt like a garage sale inside of a tornado. She was just grateful the man possessed neither X-ray vision nor the ability to read minds.

Because he'd boasted of being able to read body language, Charley made doubly sure that hers gave nothing away.

Getting back to her first priority, Charley turned to another member of the task force, who had been watching the door for them in order to keep the dentist from suddenly leaving.

"Cut the good doctor loose, Eli. And tell him not to go forth being fruitful and multiplying anymore." She caught the odd look Nick gave her. "The Sunday Killer got two for the price of one this time."

"What do you mean?"

"I just got the M.E.'s preliminary report. According to her, our latest victim was three weeks pregnant. I doubt she even knew." The moment the word *pregnant* was out of her mouth, she remembered what he'd told her weeks ago. "Have any more dead rabbits turned up on your doorstep?"

"No," he replied with a cold finality that closed the subject, if not for good, at least for now.

Nick didn't add that there were irritating calls, hangups mostly now, that continued at a steady pace. Nor did he tell her that it was really starting to get under his skin.

He'd finally broken down and called the phone company to change his unlisted number. Twice. Each time, the caller had gotten it. He still had no idea how he'd managed that. Someone working for the government might have been able to track down the number changes, but Sean Dixon was not the kind of man to be hired by a government office. Not with a prison sentence in his background.

Of course, if he'd stolen someone's identity, that changed everything. He could even be working for the phone company, which gave Dixon access to any new number. He'd debated just leaving the ringer turned off on his phone. But that was not an option since the Bureau might try to get in touch with him via the landline.

For the time being, because most of his hours were taken up by the serial killer investigation, he couldn't look into tracking Dixon down. The guy was smart, Nick thought. Smarter than he would have believed Linda's brother to be. Dixon was obviously paying for everything with cash, eliminating a paper trail. Finding him was going to be a bear.

SHUT OUT by her partner and shut down in her immediate investigation, Charley started to head back to her desk. The plan was to plow through everything for the hundredth time, searching for that elusive something, the one clue that she and the others had overlooked.

Charley had taken exactly two steps when her cell phone begin to ring. Or rather, play "Tara," the theme song from *Gone with the Wind*.

She paused to dig the phone out of her pocket, then placed it against her ear. "Dow."

"Charley, I'm standing in Valentine's Pawnshop," she heard Bill say. She felt her adrenaline accelerate. "I think we just got lucky. Some of the pieces of Rita Daly's jewelry turned up. Including her cross."

"Are you sure?"

"I'm holding the insurance photos right next to them," he confirmed.

Finally, *something*. "Hot damn. Give me the address, Bill."

Beside her, Nick stood silently watching as she scribbled on her notepad.

"'Hot damn?'" he echoed with an air of amusement and incredulity the second she terminated her call. "Who says 'hot damn' anymore?"

"I do," she informed him tersely, slipping both the phone and her pad back into her pocket. "Get your running shoes on, Special Agent Brannigan. We've got ourselves a bona fide potential lead."

He fell into step beside her as they headed for the elevators. "Like all the other so-called leads?"

She didn't blame him for being skeptical. They were getting jaded and burned-out. It was hard keeping up momentum and enthusiasm when everything kept leading them back to the starting point.

"This time I think we've got a little more to work with. Some of the mayor's niece's jewelry has turned up at a pawnshop." She'd saved the best for last. "Including the cross she usually wore."

They got into the elevator. The gunmetal-gray car was empty. She glanced at her partner. Nick looked less than enthusiastic about the news.

"Did you hear what I just said?"

"I heard." Nick pressed for the ground floor and frowned. "Something doesn't smell right," he told her. "A serial killer keeps his trophies, that's the point of them. He wants them around to help him relive his 'greatest hits' list. He wouldn't go and try to pawn them."

"Maybe our serial killer never read the manual." She resented the man raining on her parade. This was the first decent lead they'd had to follow up since she couldn't begin to remember when. "One step at a time, Brannigan. One step at a time will eventually get us there."

"That all depends. If our destination's Japan, the trip will take us ten years. Not to mention we'd need to learn how to walk on water."

She grudgingly admitted that Nick had a point about the cross being a trophy. Maybe the man had accidentally included the necklace in the lot he'd brought to the pawnbroker. She didn't know, but for now, this puzzle piece might give them a clearer picture.

"I'm guessing that in your high-school yearbook, they didn't vote you as most optimistic, did they?"

Humor curved his mouth. "The word realist was bandied about."

Realist had its place. But so did other things. "This job operates on hope, Special Agent Brannigan. Hope and a prayer." The elevator doors opened on the ground floor. "And a damn good forensic unit," she tagged on as she got out. "Let's go."

Nick got off behind her, sidestepping two people who hurried onto the same elevator car. Charley was walking toward the rear of the building in what amounted to double time. For a little thing, she could really move. He lengthened his stride to catch up.

"Lead on, MacDuff."

Heading for the parking lot where she'd left her vehicle this morning, Charley never broke stride. "That's actually 'Lay on, MacDuff.' The rest of the line goes, 'And damn'd be him that first cries, Hold, enough!'"

Nick laughed, shaking his head. "Being with you is a constant education, Charley."

Still ahead by a step, Charley flashed a grin at him over her shoulder. It found an unexpected target in his gut.

Nick chose to ignore it for the time being, because they had work to do. But he promised to do a little exploring the very first opportunity he found.

THE INSIDE of the pawnshop smelled of old memories and dust. Charley wrinkled her nose the moment they walked in. Her allergies were going to be unforgiving, she thought. But it would be worth the suffering if they finally got a break. Any kind of a break.

Bill started filling them in. "I've already asked Mr. Valentine here for the surveillance tape for that day. The items were pawned yesterday afternoon."

Jeremy Valentine appeared to be nervous. There were large sweat stains beneath each armpit, spreading across the light blue material of his shirt. It was not the sweat of an honest man. Charley's guess was that the man probably dealt with stolen goods on a more or less regular basis. But that wasn't of any interest to her right now.

She took out her wallet, holding up her shield. Beside her, Nick followed suit. "Good afternoon, Mr. Valentine. I'm Special Agent Dow, this is my partner, Special Agent Brannigan." The man squinted intently at both IDs, then straightened and nodded. "Do you remember who sold you the items in question?"

In reply, Valentine produced the slip he had already located from a jumble of receipts when Bill had asked him the same question.

Taking the receipt, Charley read the name, then held it up for Nick to see.

"John Smith." She raised her eyes to the pawnshop owner. "Didn't you think this was just a little suspicious?"

Valentine's wide shoulders moved beneath his wrinkled shirt. "Hey, it's a name. I just care if the merchandise is good."

Out of the corner of her eye, she saw Bill shaking his head. When she looked at him, he promised, "It gets better."

Charley frowned. She couldn't say that she really liked the sound of that.

CHAPTER TWENTY-SIX

"A HOMELESS MAN?" Charley cried, looking at the shadowy figure on the surveillance tape. The back room of the pawnshop was an area the size of a Cracker Jack box on steroids and the smell of sweat and onions permeated the small space. Bill was forced to stand outside as she and Nick reviewed the tape with the pawnshop owner.

She turned to Valentine. "You bought jewelry from a homeless man?"

"I didn't know he was homeless," Valentine protested. "He gave me an address."

Charley rolled her eyes. "Yeah. An address that would have put him smack in the middle of the Santa Ana River."

In response, Valentine mutely spread his hands.

Exasperated, Charley crossed to Bill. She took a deep breath as she did so. The air might have been stale in the showroom area, but it was positively stifling in the back room.

"I want the tape taken back to the lab. Have Juarez freeze-frame that photo, blow it up and enhance it as much as possible." She glanced at Nick. "Looks like we're looking for a homeless man." Together they headed for the door.

"Is he the one?" Valentine called out just as they

pushed open the front door. His voice was eager, throb-bing with curiosity. "Is he the serial killer? The guy who kills his victims on Sundays?"

Nick gave the man a cold look. Valentine's interest bordered on ghoulish. He had no patience with people like that.

"You can read all about it in the newspaper," he told the pawnbroker. Without thinking, he placed a hand to the small of Charley's back, ushering her out. "He's probably not the one, you know," he told her once they'd cleared the shop.

Charley walked quickly to the curb where her car was parked. Quicker than she might have under ordinary circumstances. It bothered her that she was so aware of Nick each time he touched her, however inno-cently. She was going to have to deal with that sooner or later. Later sounded like a better option.

She forced herself to focus on Nick's comment. "I know. But maybe 'John Smith' saw something. Or somebody. He had to have been at Rita Daly's house around the same time as the killer." After unlocking her door, she got in. "First order of business is finding the guy," she told Nick as he got in on the passenger side.

LESS THAN TWO HOURS later, the twelve task force members, armed with a fuzzy black-and-white photo of "John Smith," fanned out in and around Rita Daly's neighborhood, as well as the vicinity of the pawnshop. They showed the photograph to everyone who passed by, as well as the residents in the area.

FOR TWO DAYS, the canvass went unrewarded. On the af-ternoon of the third day, a homeless woman known as

Big Betty cackled with glee as she eyed the photograph Nick held in front of her. Of an indiscernible age ranging anywhere from late thirties to early fifties, Betty's grimy face cracked into a series of creases that rallied around a huge grin.

"John Smith my ass," she hooted. "That's Wally."

Catching Charley's eye, Nick beckoned her over from the person she'd just stopped. "Wally?"

"Wally," she said with finality.

Charley joined them in time to hear Betty's answer. "Does Wally have a last name?" she asked.

Betty addressed her answer to Nick to whom she had obviously taken a fancy. "Not that I know of."

"Do you know where we could find him?" Nick pressed.

The woman's bloodshot eyes lit up and her grin widened. It didn't take a mind reader to realize that Betty saw herself as holding a winning lottery ticket. "I might."

Charley began to say something, but Nick held up his hand, stopping her. His eyes never left the homeless woman's face. "What would it take for that 'might' to become a 'yes'?"

Betty's furrowed brow became a veritable map of crisscrossing lines. She pursed her lips as if that would help her think. "Gimme a minute."

Charley exchanged glances with Nick, waiting. Wondering if the woman was a con artist who was playing them.

Finally, offering Nick a smile that lacked several teeth, Big Betty announced her price. The woman did not come cheap. She crossed her arms before her chest as if she was settling in. "Take it or leave it."

"We'll take it," Charley said before Nick could

respond. If the Bureau didn't okay the total sum, she was willing to take the money out of her own pocket. Finding Cris's killer meant everything to her. "But we'll also take you," she told the woman. "You're coming along with us, Betty, and if your information's valid, you'll get your money."

Betty didn't look very pleased about being taken hostage by the woman beside Nick. She tossed her head. Long, stringy hair clumped together with grease and months of dirt barely moved. "Oh, it's correct all right. I never lie."

"Good for you," Nick said, taking her by the arm. "You lead the way."

"Sure, honey," Betty answered, her voice husky. "Anything for you."

Charley had trouble keeping a straight face as she led the way back to the car. The guys back at the office were going to love hearing about Brannigan's new love interest.

WALLY, aka John Smith, was lying inside an old discarded cardboard box once used to transport a refrigerator. Lined with ragged blankets and towels he'd scavenged, he kept his home hidden from view beneath the bridge near the Santa Ana River. When Betty led them to the man whose face matched the surveillance photo, he was happily wrapped in a whisky-laced cocoon. There were two empty bottles lying beside him.

"Pay up," she instructed, her dirty palm up, waiting for the cash.

"We need to requisition the money," Charley began, then stopped as she saw Nick open his wallet. To her surprise, she saw him take out three hundred-dollar bills and give them to Betty, who immediately stuffed them down a bra that had not seen detergent in years.

Betty was gone in a heartbeat, hurrying away before they could change their minds.

"You carry that kind of cash around all the time?"

"I like being prepared."

"Don't let word about that spread," she warned. "Or you'll be the guy everyone'll want to put the touch on."

"Don't worry, I know how to say no," he assured her with a smile, then looked at the prize he had paid for. Wally was snoring. "Not much to look at, is he?"

"I don't care what he looks like, as long as he talks," Charley answered. Bending over, she put her hand on the man's shoulder, first shaking it lightly, then harder. "Wally, wake up. We need to talk to you." The man went on snoring.

"Maybe he's dead," he said.

"Dead people don't snore and there's a whole different smell about them. Dead for him would be an upgrade," she commented. Between the whiskey their man had consumed and the fact that bathing was obviously a low priority, Wally was positively pungent, like a fading romance writer who doesn't know when to quit.

"Wally, wake up." Nick shook him hard.

The man's eyes popped open, then quickly shut again in defense against the light. He moaned loudly.

"C'mon, Wally, you're coming with us," Nick told him. He motioned over the two men they had called in as backup.

"You know, he didn't exactly lie," Charley observed as the two men flanked Wally and each took hold of one of his arms. "This *is* the middle of the Santa Ana River."

"Reassuring," Nick commented.

Charley watched as the task-force members took Wally to the van they had driven. They were in essence holding him up between them. "Well, at least he's not resisting arrest."

"Resisting?" Nick laughed. "I don't think he could even if he wanted to. Every bone in his body looks like it's fluid."

She glanced at the collection of empty bottles that littered the area. "Probably is."

IT TOOK a good amount of patience and several cups of black coffee before they managed to get Wally sober enough to realize the seriousness of his situation. When he finally comprehended where he was and why, his wind-burned face turned several shades paler. Breathing hard, he clutched his chest as if waiting for a heart attack.

Charley sensed the man was not above employing drama, but he did seem genuinely alarmed when she pointed out the wall of victims' photographs, specifically Rita Daly's.

"I didn't do it," he cried, his voice reedy and high-pitched. "I didn't kill nobody." Then, as they watched, he clutched his filthy clothes closer to him and began to rock back and forth in his seat. His eyes glazed over. His voice was deeper but no less frightened, as he said, "Told you not to go in. Told you it was a trap."

Charley looked at Nick. From the sound of it, their suspect was carrying on a conversation with someone other than them. Someone who wasn't in the room. At least, not visibly.

She put her hand on Wally's shoulder, trying to get his attention. "Who are you talking to, Wally?"

The answer came without hesitation. He continued

rocking. "Jonesy. Jonesy always knows what's best. But I don't always listen to him." The rocking increased with his mounting agitation. "Jonesy said I shouldn't go in. But I did."

He was talking about Rita's house, Charley thought. "Do you mean Rita Daly's house, Wally?"

"Sleeping lady's house," was all he said, looking down at his filthy knees.

"Why did you go in, Wally?" she asked softly.

He curled his fingers about his jacket, pressing it to him. Rocking. "Because the door was open. Wide-open. And it was warm. I could tell it was warm in there." He raised his bloodshot eyes to hers. His face looked pathetically innocent. "I was cold."

"So you went in to get warm," Charley coaxed. "And then what happened?"

"And then I saw her. The lady." He pointed toward Rita's photograph. "That one. She was just lying there, asleep. Jonesy told me to get the hell out of there, but I was still cold. I thought maybe there was something around I could, you know, have. Something to help me get warm."

"You took her jewelry box," Nick reminded him. Wally turned to look at him. "How was that going to keep you warm?"

"There was stuff there I could sell," Wally cried, his expression that of a hunted, fearful animal. "Sell to get something to make me warm."

Charley shook her head, her voice gentle, nonthreatening. "You would have been better off buying a coat, not whiskey."

"Coat don't taste good," Wally answered.

MARIE FERRARELLA 213

Nick laughed shortly under his breath. "Can't argue with that."

"Where did you find the cross, Wally?" Charley asked.

"Jonesy found it," Wally corrected her.

Charley drew on her patience. Trying to communicate with her mother had schooled her to have infinite patience. "Where did Jonesy find it?"

Wally became more and more agitated. He looked from one to the other, apparently afraid of being hurt. "On the floor. By the sleeping lady."

"Killer might have dropped it," Nick theorized. Charley nodded. He bent down until his face was level with Wally's. "Wally, did you or Jonesy see anyone?"

"The lady."

Nick took a deep breath. He figured the alcohol had probably reduced the man's mental capacity to that of a five-year-old. "Besides the lady, Wally. Did you see anyone besides the lady?"

"No. Nobody."

Nick rose to his feet, disgusted. They were up against another blank wall. This was getting very, very old.

"Nobody except for that guy."

Charley felt like someone on a roller coaster who thought it had come to a stop, only to have it start again and plunge down a steep incline.

"What guy?" she demanded before Nick could.

Wally looked at her innocently. "The guy who left the door open."

CHAPTER TWENTY-SEVEN

IT TOOK CHARLEY a moment to process what the man had said. She exchanged glances with Nick. They had waited so long for a witness to turn up.

She shifted her position so that Wally couldn't avoid making direct eye contact with her. "Are you sure you saw someone leaving Rita's house?"

The homeless man stared at her blankly, his shaggy eyebrows drawing together as he attempted to concentrate. "Who's Rita?"

"The victim," Nick told him. Hands on her shoulders, he moved Charley to one side and came at Wally. "The lady you saw on the floor," he clarified, using Wally's term for Rita.

"Oh." Wally paused, thinking. And then he looked up at Nick. "Rita." He repeated. "Feels funny when you put a name to them."

Feelings, the man was registering feelings, Charley thought. She pushed a little harder to take advantage of the situation. "Yes, it does. Did you get a look at this guy?"

Wally pressed his lips together. He seemed uncomfortable. Charley realized that he probably thought the person he'd seen had lived in the house. "Sorta."

It was hard banking down her excitement, but she

didn't want to scare Wally. "Could you describe him? Think very carefully now," Charley coaxed. "This is very important, Wally."

Wally got a deer-in-the-headlights expression in his eyes. Nick took over, his voice friendly, engaging. "What you tell us could help us catch a very bad man. You'd be a hero."

That seemed to appeal to Wally. Relaxing, he smiled. "I would?"

Nick nodded his head. "Definitely."

Wally rubbed his stained fingers over the salt-and-pepper stubble that covered his face. "I think I remember."

Nick patted his shoulder. The clothes under his palm felt greasy. "Good man. We'll put you together with a sketch artist."

"Can I get something to eat?" Wally asked hopefully.

"Absolutely," Charley promised. "We'll get you anything you want. You can eat and work with the sketch artist at the same time."

"Okay."

Gingerly taking Wally's arm, being careful not to startle him, Nick helped the smaller man up from the table. "This way." Charley followed behind them.

ONCE THE FOOD that Wally requested had been delivered, they paired the overjoyed man with the Bureau's sketch artist. Ryan William was also their resident software wizard.

Charley was hopeful as she stepped back. At the same time, she was afraid of letting hope in and being disappointed again. She looked at Nick. "Think he really remembers?"

Nick shrugged. "Fifty-fifty chance. Better than nothing."

She crossed her arms before her as she watched Wally talk to the sketch artist. The clicking sound of fingertips hitting keys reverberated through her, echoing in her chest. Shadowing her prayers. "You were very good with him back there."

Nick passed off the compliment. "I just talked to him the way I do to my nephew. Kyle's five."

"Brother's kid?"

"Sister's," Nick corrected. And then he added, "And Ashley's got another one on the way."

Ashley. Charley heard the affection in his voice when he spoke about his sister. He got along with his family, she thought wistfully. "Sounds like you have a nice family."

Nick took his happy family life for granted. Pausing to think about it now, he nodded. "It is." And then he looked at Charley, amused. "Any other questions I can answer?"

A smile played on her lips. "I'll let you know when I think of them."

THEY HAD A VIABLE sketch within the half hour. Dozens of copies were run off. Some were sent to the local newspapers and news stations, while others were handed to the task force special agents who took them to the family and friends of the various victims. Someone had to have seen the man. But so far, there'd been no positive feedback.

There would be, Charley promised herself.

The day she'd put in hadn't been as long as it was hard. And at the end, she still had one more thing to do. Her conscience would give her no peace until she did it. Once she left the Federal Building, she drove to

Tustin. To the house where she had grown up. She needed to talk to her father.

The trip wasn't long. She was parking her car in the driveway beside her father's old Pontiac all too soon. Getting out, she felt a sense of dread. She shouldn't be dreading a visit to her own father. But the fault lay with her father. With the atmosphere that he generated.

But this had to be done.

Charley stood before the single-story house where she had lived as a girl. The house where she'd once had a fairly happy childhood. She and her family had enjoyed an all-too-common lifestyle, nothing different from millions of other middle-class families. They went on vacation once a year. Unshackled from his desk where he worked as senior engineer, her father liked to get behind the wheel of a car two weeks a year and drive as far as he could in a day. They got to see a lot of the country that way.

And she got to spend a lot of time packed in the back seat with her sister and brother for hours on end. Once started, her father didn't like to stop unless it was absolutely necessary. Luckily, the children had gotten along, with one another and with their parents, although it was clearly their mother who created the warm atmosphere. Their father wasn't as approachable, but in his own fashion, he did his best.

All that was in the past.

Now, whenever she approached the house, it was with a sense of reluctance. She had a hard time communicating with her father, a hard time having a conversation with him that didn't turn into a one-sided diatribe delivered by him. Yet she kept coming back. Because he was her father and she fervently hoped things would change and he would finally come around. Finally be grateful for what he had instead of focusing on what he had lost.

After Cris was killed, her father had climbed into his own dark shell. Not unlike her mother. He still walked and talked and functioned, but he became just as unapproachable as his wife.

Charley wanted him back.

She wanted for them to be a family again. Even with Cris gone, there was still so much to be grateful for. If he could only see that, for once see the pluses instead of dwelling exclusively on the huge minus, they might stand a chance to be a family again.

"Not going to get anywhere standing out here, Charley," she told herself. She hated behaving like a coward. That wasn't who she was.

Taking in a deep breath, she went up the front walk and rang the doorbell. There was a key in her pocket that matched the lock, but she never felt comfortable using it. Not since her mother had gone into the hospital. This was her father's house, not hers any longer.

When there was no response from inside, Charley rang the doorbell again. She knew he had to be home, because his car was in the driveway.

Finally the door opened.

Of average height and slightly wider than average build, Christopher Dow possessed a mane of gray hair and piercing blue eyes. His face bore a sour expression, as if he'd just digested food that was past its expiration date.

He stood in the doorway, scowling at her. He was clearly surprised by the visit.

Charley forced a smile to her lips. "Hi, Dad. Mind if I come in?"

He paused, as if thinking it over, then shuffled back, allowing her access. "You got any news?"

Charley went no farther than the foyer. Turning around to face him, she measured her words. "As a matter of fact, I do."

Her father came to life before her eyes. Color entered his cheeks. "You caught the bastard?"

With all her heart, she wished she could have said yes. But she wasn't here because of the case. She was here because of her brother. Not that David had asked her to come, but she knew in her heart that if the schism between him and their father could somehow be resolved, or simply put aside and forgotten, her brother would be happier.

They all would.

"No, it's not about the serial killer, Dad. It's about David." She saw his face fall instantly. The scowl returned. "Your son."

"I know who David is," he snapped. "What about him?"

"David's been transferred back to Southern California. He's stationed at Camp Pendleton." That was only about thirty miles south of where they lived. When her father said nothing, she continued, coming to the heart of the reason behind her visit. "David's getting married."

She watched her father's face for some sort of reaction. There was only impatience. "Yeah?"

"Yeah," she echoed. "The wedding's this Sunday. The reception's going to be at the Hyatt Hotel in Newport Beach."

Her father didn't even blink. "So?"

She tried very hard not to lose her temper. Not to

shout at him and demand to know why he was behaving as if David were a stranger instead of his son.

Forgive me, David. "So, he'd like you to come."

His eyes narrowed. "He doesn't have enough courage to face me himself?"

She knew David would have been annoyed if he knew that she was here on his behalf, but there had to be some way to end this unofficial war. Maybe the wedding could be a new beginning for all of them. "Think of me as the scout that was sent on ahead."

"Well, you can just go back, 'scout,' and tell him I'm busy."

Charley refused to drop the subject. "Doing what?"

"Not attending his wedding. Look, as far as I'm concerned, I don't have a son. The kid and I never had anything in common. He grew up, he's out on his own, Godspeed and leave me alone."

Charley dug in. He wasn't happy being like this. Why couldn't he see that? "Dad, David's family."

Her words had no effect on him. "So?"

"*We're* a family," she insisted. "Isn't it about time we all started acting like one? A lot of people are alone in this world—"

His expression grew even darker. "I *am* alone."

She knew he was thinking of Cris. And perhaps her mother. "No, damn it, you're *not* alone. You have David, you have me." She paused, her voice softening just a little. "You have Mom."

She saw the anger in his eyes. "Who's a vegetable because you can't catch your sister's killer!"

"Don't put this all on me," she shouted back at him. "And Mom's not a vegetable. She's just lost—"

He didn't wait for her to finish. "Maybe you should take a cue."

She knew what he was saying. That he wanted her to leave. Charley drew herself to her full height. Coming here was a mistake. It always was. But she kept on doing it anyway, kept on hoping that one day a miracle would happen and things would turn around.

But not today.

"Okay, I'll go."

If she expected him to say anything to stop her, to change his mind or take back his words, she'd left herself open to disappointment. Again. "Good."

Charley turned on her heel. She stopped just short of the doorway. "You know, Dad, someday you're going to regret throwing away what you have."

He laughed shortly. "I'll let you know when that happens." Not waiting for her to go, he walked away and into the next room.

Swallowing a curse, Charley slammed the door behind her.

CHAPTER TWENTY-EIGHT

CHARLEY MANAGED to keep the tears at bay until she was safely inside her car and had pulled away from the house.

Trying to get a grip, she turned up the radio until it was blasting. Sound filled every inch of space within the car. Normally she'd sing along, but this time she couldn't. The music didn't help, didn't cut through the ache inside her chest.

Why did he have to be that way? Why couldn't her father just be happy for David? Why couldn't he see her career as something other than a means to an end? A means to finding Cris's killer?

Damn it, why couldn't he be the father she needed him to be?

"You're twenty-eight years old, Charley. It's about time you stopped wanting your father's approval," she reproached herself bitterly. "It's just not going to happen."

She'd accomplished a lot in her life and she didn't need her father's approval to function. But it would have been a nice thing to have. A nice thing for David to have, she added silently.

"Sorry, David. I tried," she whispered softly.

She felt the tears coming and cursed her own weakness. Her father could tie her up in knots better than anyone. She supposed that was part of the reason she'd never had a serious relationship, never wanted one. Because what if the man she fell in love with turned out to be an emotional eunuch like her father? Charley was sure that when her mother had married him, she hadn't known her husband would be like this. That he would step away from everyone when they needed him most.

There were plenty of explanations as to why her father was the way he was, but they didn't alter the situation. The bottom line was that he was unavailable emotionally and probably always would be. She was going to have to make her peace with that and move on.

With a sigh, she pulled into her parking space at the apartment complex. After pulling up the hand brake and turning off the ignition, she slowly got out of the car. She felt more drained than she had in a very long time.

When she walked into her apartment, she found Dakota waiting for her behind the door. The dog's greeting was instant and enthusiastic. Within seconds, she'd been leaped on and repeatedly licked.

Charley sank down to her knees. She put her arms around the dog's neck and buried her face against Dakota's back.

"You always know, don't you?" she murmured against the fur.

Dakota barked, as if in reply. And agreement. The German shepherd stood patiently, waiting for her mistress to pull herself together.

"You're better than therapy," she told the dog, getting to her feet. Reaching for the leash that was hung by the door, she took Dakota out for a walk. They both needed it.

When she returned half an hour later, Charley gave some thought to dinner. She didn't feel like cooking and there was nothing in the refrigerator that she could pop into the microwave. She opened the pantry to see if there was anything she could have straight out of a can. Calling for takeout felt like too much of an effort.

Charley was still rummaging when her cell phone rang. For a moment, she gave serious thought to just ignoring it. But she was too well trained and disciplined to indulge herself. The call could be important. Screening would waste precious time.

She had the phone out and against her ear by the third ring. "Dow."

"Charley, it's Nick."

It hit her how friendly that sounded. How personal. She never called him by his first name when she spoke to him. Maybe she should think about removing that barrier. She'd called Ben by his name an hour after they'd been introduced.

"What's up?" she asked. As she spoke, she realized that her voice was still raspy. That's what she got for crying, she upbraided herself, hoping her partner wouldn't notice.

"I had a thought about the case."

She tried to subtly clear her throat. "Go ahead, I'm listening."

But instead of telling her, there was a pause on the other end.

"Charley, am I interrupting something?"

"No. I just got back in. I took Dakota out for a walk." As she talked, she realized her emotions were still in turmoil. Everything had converged at once tonight—the case, her father. She needed more time to pull herself together. "Listen, is this something that can wait until morning? I'm a little bushed." It was only a little past seven o'clock. Too early to be calling it a night.

"Charley, what's wrong?"

"Nothing," she insisted. She had every intention of leaving it at that. But somehow, more words pushed their way forward. "I just went to see my father. I invited him to David's wedding."

"And?"

"And he won't come." Damn it, she could feel the tears clawing up her throat. What was the matter with her, anyway? She knew her father was like this, and she should have been used to it by now. "Look, I've got to go."

Charley hung up without waiting for Nick to respond. She didn't want to be on the phone just in case she started crying again. This was far too personal to share and she had no desire to appear vulnerable.

With a sigh that went clear down to her toes, she tossed the cell phone onto the kitchen table.

"I'm going to have to apologize to him tomorrow," she told Dakota. "Maybe if I'm lucky, Brannigan won't say anything." She looked down at the German shepherd's face. Dakota seemed to take in every word. "Guys don't like to deal with emotions, anyway." Right now, neither did she. Charley pulled out a bag of tortilla chips that was shoved in the back of one of the pantry shelves. "Feel like watching something on TV?"

As if taking a cue, Dakota trotted into the living room and hopped onto the sofa, settling into her favorite corner.

Charley crossed to the set and turned it on. Armed with the remote control, she sat down beside the dog and started flipping through the classic movie channels.

She made a selection based on need, not on interest. She didn't really care what the movie was, as long as it produced the required wall of noise. When she was like this, she didn't like the silence and there was something sad about having just disembodied music fill the air once the sun had gone down.

The flickering images on the TV set kept her company.

Picking up the bag of semi-stale chips and can of diet soda she'd put on the side table, Charley prepared to have her dinner. But not without help. Even before the first crunch, Dakota had raised her head from the arm of the sofa, looking at her and waiting. The dog liked tortilla chips, stale or otherwise, even more than she did.

Charley smiled for the first time since she'd pulled her car up in front of her father's house.

When the doorbell rang twenty minutes later, she decided to ignore it. But whoever was on the other side didn't take the hint and refused to leave. The doorbell rang at regular intervals.

On the fourth go-round, Charley sighed and put the bag of chips on the coffee table. "Keep your nose out of them," she instructed the dog. Dakota had been trained not to eat anything off the table. Hopefully, the pet's training would continue to hold.

Crossing to the door, Charley felt her mood grow a little testy. She didn't want to talk to anyone outside of Dakota. When she looked through the peephole, the words *Go away* were hovering on her lips. They never got the chance to emerge.

Nick was standing on the other side of her door.

Now what?

Yanking it open, she greeted him with, "Maybe your watch is fast, Brannigan, but it's not tomorrow yet."

"I know." Not waiting for an invitation, he walked into the apartment. "This is hot," he told her. "I need someplace to put it down."

He referred to the large rectangular box he was holding. The logo in the center had a short, squat man in a chef's hat grinning as he flipped a pizza over his head.

The pizza's aroma filled the air. Hunger began to nudge at her, reminding her that tortilla chips weren't considered an acceptable dinner. She tried to ignore it. "I didn't order takeout. Or company."

Flipping open the box he'd brought, Nick looked unfazed by her disclaimer. "I figured you needed both." He looked around the kitchen and began opening cupboards until he found where she kept her dishes. "Or at least the latter. I need the former." He took two plates out and put them on the table beside the box. "I haven't had dinner yet."

"Look, I know you mean well, but—"

Nick took a slice of pizza and deposited it on the first plate, then repeated the process before glancing in her direction. "You're my partner, Charley," he told her matter-of-factly. "If something's bothering you, I need to know."

She didn't like being on the receiving end. She was the one who pried, not the other way around. "Why?"

Nick sat down at the table. He didn't answer at first. He was too busy taking his first bite of pizza and evaluating it. The slice wasn't as good as back east, but it would do, he thought. It would definitely do.

"Because it can affect what happens out in the field."

Charley pressed her lips together. If she didn't know better, she would have said the man was being sensitive. But men weren't sensitive. It wasn't the nature of the beast. Except for maybe David. And Ben.

In response to his statement, she shrugged. "Don't worry, you're not going to get shot because I'm having a bad-hair day. I'll have your back."

About to take another bite, he put the slice down and glared at her. "Don't insult my intelligence, Charley. There's something going on with you and you need to unload."

"You mean like you?" she asked sarcastically. "Pulling information out of you is like pulling teeth."

"Point is, you pulled." He plucked two napkins from the holder, one for himself and one for her. "Turnaround is fair play. You wanna tell me about it?"

"No."

"Okay." He seemed willing to let the matter drop, but Charley knew better than to let her guard down. He was up to something. "Then I'll just sit here and eat." He broke off a piece and held it out to Dakota. The dog was by his side in a shot. She daintily separated the pizza from his fingers without touching his skin. He grinned at the dog, then nodded toward the television set. "You like old movies?"

She glanced over her shoulder at the TV. She'd forgotten what was playing. A very blond Barbara Stanwyck was attempting to coax a very young Fred MacMurray into killing her husband for the insurance money. Not one of her favorites, Charley thought.

"Sometimes," she answered. Nick was holding out another piece to Dakota. Her pet eyed her partner adoringly as she took the second offering. Charley frowned. "Dakota shouldn't have too much cheese."

Nick wiped his fingers. "Duly noted."

With a sigh, she sat down opposite him. "You're nicer than I thought you were."

Nick helped himself to a second slice. "I get that all the time."

He made her smile.

CHAPTER TWENTY-NINE

"So," NICK BEGAN after shifting the pizza box so that they could watch the end of *Double Indemnity*. Dakota had shadowed his every move, waiting for another handout. Her partner made himself comfortable on her sofa, as if he'd been dropping over every night instead of never. "Are you planning on telling me what's wrong, or am I going to have to resort to torturing it out of you?"

Charley placed the plates on either side of the box, then sank down on the sofa herself. Dakota was positioned on the floor between them, an unofficial sentry in charge of watching the contents of the pizza box.

Toying with the last of her slice, Charley slanted her eyes toward her partner. The handle she thought she had on the man was fading and that bothered her. "You know, I can't really tell if you're kidding or not."

"You're not supposed to." His smile was enigmatic. "That's one of those things that works in my favor."

She'd finished her slice, he noticed. Leaning over, Nick took another slice from the box and eased it onto her plate before taking one more for himself. He was up to three, she was working on her second.

"Talk," he told her.

Ordinarily she wasn't one to take orders, not from

cohorts and only grudgingly from superiors. But this time, for reasons she couldn't unravel, she did what he said.

Charley looked away. "No big deal, really. I just stopped by to visit my father. He always affects me this way." Even as she said it, she cursed herself for her reaction. What was she, ten?

Nick found it telling that she avoided his eyes. And couldn't help wondering why she'd put herself in that sort of situation in the first place. "Why do you go, then?"

She didn't like have her motives questioned. A little of her desperation surfaced, along with her temper. "Because he's my father. Because I keep hoping he'll change. And because I wanted to tell him that David's stationed here now and is getting married." She sighed. "I invited him to the wedding."

So she had said over the phone. He studied her over his slice. "And he's really not coming?"

"No." Charley caught her lower lip between her teeth, thinking. And then she decided to push ahead and ask, "Are you doing anything Sunday?"

He thought of the boxes that littered his apartment. Somehow, he still hadn't unpacked them. He just kept putting off the task to the weekend. For the last four weekends. They could keep yet another week.

"No, why?"

She knew she was going out on a limb, but suddenly, she wanted a friend there with her. Someone she could talk to, perhaps dance with. Sam and Jack were married and Bill was currently spoken for. That left Nick.

She tried to sound as nonchalant as possible. "Want to go to a wedding?"

He lifted a shoulder carelessly, then let it drop. The

idea of spending an afternoon with her away from the office and the serial-killer data was not without its appeal. "As long as it's not my own."

"Are you a confirmed bachelor or did your last marriage leave a bad taste in your mouth?"

"Neither," he told her simply. "I just haven't found anyone I want to spend the rest of my life with. Marriage is a really serious step."

His declaration took her aback. Whether Brannigan knew it or not, he'd just professed to having old-fashioned values. He really was deeper than she'd given him credit for.

"You actually think that way?" She shook her head in wonder. "Most people these days look at their first marriage the way people used to look at their first house. Like a way to get their feet wet. A starter."

Nick paused to wash down the slice he'd just consumed with a long drag of soda. Lowering it down, he looked at her for a long moment, thinking how beautiful her eyes were.

"I don't subscribe to a throwaway economy," he said.

His gaze unsettled her. Charley did her best to disregard the effect he had on her. "And with that philosophy, no one's run off with you?"

"No." He grinned. The devil at his best couldn't have been sexier, she thought. "Are you thinking of making me an offer?"

It was warm in here, she thought. Very warm. Her skin was heating up at an incredible rate. And all the moisture had left her mouth. Maneuvering her tongue took a bit of doing.

"Yes." And then she smiled, knowing what he was thinking. "The next pizza's on me."

On her.

Nick caught himself squeezing the soda can he was holding a little too tightly. The pressure caused the shape to change. He laughed as he set the can down. Maybe he *had* been without female companionship too long.

"Okay."

When he looked at her like that, she found it hard to form complete sentences. What the hell was going on here? Was she just being emotionally needy because of the scene she'd endured with her father, or was there something else at play?

Charley cleared her throat. "You still really haven't answered my question. Do you want to go to my brother's wedding with me?"

"In place of your father?"

"No. As yourself." As she said it, something told her that she was *really* asking for trouble.

"Sure." Dakota barked, as if to say that she approved of his response. Nick laughed and petted the animal on the head.

Charley watched the way the dog rubbed her head against Nick, forcing him to continue petting her. "I think Dakota approves of you."

He laughed, seeing right through the animal. "I've got a feeling Dakota would approve of anyone who fed her pizza."

"You'd be surprised," Charley told him, running her hand down along the dog's coat. Dakota continued looking at Nick. *Hussy,* Charley thought affectionately. "She'll take food from anyone, but then she'll bark at them once she's finished."

Nick smiled as he debated between taking another

slice or walking away slightly hungry. He had the capacity to consume a great deal and never gain an ounce. "Sounds like some of the women I knew."

Charley leaned back in her corner of the sofa, shifting so that she could study him. "And just how many women did you know?"

There was no way he was answering that one. "The average amount." And then he turned the tables on her, his eyes holding her prisoner. "How many men have been in your life?"

She busied herself with what was on her plate, avoiding his eyes. "If you mean suspects and victims, too many to count."

Crooking his index finger, he slipped it beneath her chin and lifted her head until her eyes met his. "How about the ones you can count?"

She drew back her head. He could have sworn he saw a curtain go down. "Are you asking me about my love life, Special Agent Brannigan?"

"I brought you pizza. I'm entitled to ask you a few questions." His smile was easy. Seductive. "And it's Nick, remember?"

"You can ask as many questions as you want, *Nick*." She deliberately emphasized his given name, as if it was a label for a condition instead of a name. "Doesn't mean I have to answer."

Humor entered his eyes. This was a game now and he wasn't one to give up easily. "But if you were to answer, what would it be?"

She laughed. The man was persistent all right. A good asset for any decent law-enforcement agent. "My job keeps me too busy to notice men I'm not questioning or investigating." She paused, then blew out a breath. Oh, what the hell, it wasn't as if she was ashamed of it. "None."

"None," he repeated, not believing the answer for a minute. But for the sake of the game, he played along. "You mean as in none currently?"

"I mean as in *none*." She enunciated the word with feeling. "I don't have the time to get involved."

"You've never been involved." Even as he said it, he couldn't convince himself that she was telling him the truth. You didn't look like that, with a killer face and a drop-dead gorgeous body and go through life uncoupled. She was putting him on. It was just a matter of getting her to admit it. "How about when you were in college?"

She didn't want to think back to that. Not that the years had been painful, but if she thought of college, she had to think of the way she'd found Cris. And she really didn't want to think about that tonight.

She shrugged. Tucking her feet under her on the sofa, she looked away. "Cris got all the attention. I did the studying for both of us. And the exam taking."

He stared at her, processing what she'd just admitted to. She'd cheated. Not for herself, but for her sister. Somehow, that seemed in keeping with the woman he was getting to know. It was a selfless, risky act. Caught, she would have been expelled along with her sister. She'd been willing to ruin her academic career for someone she loved.

Nick saw her with new eyes. "Why, Special Agent Dow, this is a side of you I wouldn't have guessed existed. I had no idea you were capable of being underhanded."

A protest rose to her lips, but underhanded was as good a label as any. Probably more charitable than most.

"It was Cris," she said softly, aching as the memory of her sister intruded. "No one said no to Cris. She was vivacious, dynamic. Everybody loved her. Including me," she added wistfully.

"Everybody but the person who killed her."

The stark sentence had her shoulders stiffen. The ache inside grew stronger. "Maybe they were after me," she told him. "Cris and I looked so alike that even my mother got us confused sometimes."

She'd advanced this theory before. But that was before they'd known the full extent of the Sunday Killer's M.O. He turned her face until she looked at him. "Hasn't it hit you yet?"

"Hasn't what hit me yet?"

"The serial killer thinks he's bringing redemption when he kills a victim. He only kills women having affairs with married men." He wondered how long she had been letting this eat away at her. Was that why she allowed her father to browbeat her the way he did? Because she felt guilty? Because she thought she deserved it for being alive? "Were you having an affair with a married man?"

"No." Her answer was emphatic.

"Then it was your sister the guy was after, not you." His eyes held hers. "There was no mistake."

Charley sat as still as a statue, hardly breathing. Digesting what Nick had just said to her. The more she thought about it, the more it made sense. An incredible wave of relief washed over her as the words sank in.

Finally she looked at him. "It wasn't a mistake."

Slowly he shook his head. "No."

She wanted to shout it. Instead, the words came out in a whisper. "Cris didn't die in my place."

"No." Nick saw the tears glistening on her lashes and held himself in check, refraining from taking her into his arms. She wouldn't have appreciated that, he thought.

Charley covered her mouth with her fingertips until the sob subsided. And then she breathed a long, soul-cleansing sigh. "You have no idea what kind of a rock was just lifted from my shoulders. All this time, I couldn't shake the feeling that it was me, that the killer had come looking for me that night. Because no one would have wanted to kill Cris."

"It wasn't your fault," he said gently.

Fault.

He'd hit on the right word. She'd always thought that Cris's death was her fault. Except that he'd just shown her that it wasn't.

She blinked again, shedding the tears from her lashes. From her soul.

Charley turned toward him. "Thank you," she cried. "Thank you."

"Nothing to thank me for," he assured her.

But by then impulse had taken over. Charley leaned into him and kissed him. Hard. On the mouth.

CHAPTER THIRTY

WITHOUT THINKING TWICE, Nick took hold of Charley's arms. He wanted to hold her in place in case she was thinking of moving. Of pulling away.

Because he didn't want her to.

Damn, this was a first. His head was spinning. Spinning as if he were a little kid running around in small, tight circles. The sensation was pleasurable. It went along with the pounding of his heart, the surging of blood through his veins like a strong current.

There was chemistry here. A hell of a lot of chemistry. Enough to blow up the forensic lab in the Federal Building's basement. And it just kept growing, getting stronger with each moment he kissed her back. What the hell was she doing to him? Why did he feel so disembodied? This was something new. He didn't like the feeling that things were beyond his control.

But they were. There was no denying it.

Nick pulled her closer to him. With a sound that was remarkably like a protest, Dakota sank down until she was crouching beneath the coffee table. Clearing a path for them.

Nick could feel every breath she took in. It was as if they were fused together in time and space. And all the while, the kiss continued. Weakening him. Annihilating him until he felt as if he began and ended right here, on this gray, worn sofa.

A sense of urgency rose, pushing him forward. Demanding. An equal sense of urgency told him to leave. Now. Before it was too late. For both of them.

He wasn't altogether sure just how he managed, but he broke away. Creating a pocket of air between them that neither of them desired.

Her mouth looked almost swollen. Had he been that ardent? He stole a breath before he spoke, hoping it would steady him. Hoping he wouldn't sound as blown away as he felt.

One look into her eyes told him he wasn't fooling her. "I think maybe I'd better go."

Charley trembled inside. She was surprised that she wasn't actually shaking. It took her a moment before she could focus, before his words sank in.

And then she tried to smile. "Was it something I said?"

Nick laughed, grateful that she had a sense of humor. It helped break whatever sizzled between them. He damn well didn't want to walk away. He just knew he should.

He rose to his feet and discovered that although his legs were shaky, they were still functioning.

Thank heaven for small favors, he thought.

He watched Charley swing her legs down and stand up. Nick found himself wrestling with the desire to pull her into his arms again. He shoved his hands into his pockets instead. Beside him, Dakota danced from foot to foot, as if anticipating something.

You and me, both, dog, he thought. Out loud he asked Charley, "What time should I pick you up on Sunday?"

Wedding. Her brother and Lisa. Sunday. The pieces

slowly pulled themselves together into a whole thought. Charley forced herself not to look at his lips, not to think about tasting them again.

"The wedding's at one," she told him, grateful that she remembered. Details that David had given her swam around in her head like so many ducks racing about in a pond. "At Our Lady Queen of Angels in Newport Beach," she added for good measure, although she doubted he was familiar with the church. She had been. Once, but it had been years since she'd attended any services in that or in any other house of worship. This would be the first time since she'd attended her sister's funeral. "Pick me up at noon."

He nodded. "Noon it is."

Nick made his way to the door, then turned to look at her. Without thinking, he began to draw his hands from his pockets, anticipating the feel of her skin beneath his fingertips even before contact was made. Uttering a silent oath, Nick shoved his hands back deep into his pockets. He had to get out of here. "See you tomorrow, Charley."

"Tomorrow," she echoed.

The moment Nick crossed the threshold, she closed the door quickly behind him, and then not only locked the door but slipped the chain into place.

Not to keep him out, but to keep herself in.

Because for the first time that she could remember, she'd fervently wanted a man to press his advantage.

She'd wanted Nick to stay the night.

NICK DROVE BACK to his place with the air-conditioning set on high. He needed to cool off. He had no idea what had come over him or why Charley got to him the way she did. He found himself progressively more and more attracted to her. Something in her voice had compelled him to go over there tonight. Something that had made him want to protect her.

There was no doubt in his mind that the woman could handle herself with the best of them. But that didn't change the vulnerability he'd witnessed in her voice and her eyes. A vulnerability that had reeled him in as if he were a two-pound mackerel with no fight in him.

Lord knows he'd wanted to stay. To stay and make love with her through the whole damn night.

Heat throbbed along his skin. He turned up the air-conditioning to the last notch.

He'd sensed her willingness. It would have taken very little on his part to make it happen.

But that would have been a mistake.

For both of them.

He kept telling himself that over and over again as he struggled to shake off the effects of what had just happened in her apartment.

She left his body humming.

Nick sighed. Maybe a cold shower would do the trick. A cold shower and some time spent on the case. He'd copied some of the files and brought them home with him in the hopes that something might come to him.

It occurred to him that he'd never told Charley the reason he'd called her in the first place. A theory kicked around in the back of his mind. Something that might have them reexamining the evidence in a different light.

It could keep until morning.

He drove into his apartment complex and made his

way to his space. But just as he began to make the turn, he saw that someone had parked in his spot. An old Mustang, its paint peeling in several places, was sitting beneath the number assigned to him.

Irritated, Nick turned his attention to the guest parking area opposite the covered carports. At first glance, there were no empty spaces, but then he saw one at the end of the row. It was the last one beside the rectangular enclosure that housed a group of four Dumpsters.

Nick parked and got out. It was too late to call and complain to the manager about the other car. With luck, whoever it was in his space would be gone by morning. People who flaunted simple rules annoyed him.

Everything annoyed him tonight, Nick thought. The sooner he got that shower, the better. A scotch and soda wouldn't be out of order either, he mused as he started to walk toward his apartment.

He heard a *clink* just beneath his foot. He'd kicked something. When he looked back on it later, Nick realized that if he hadn't picked that moment to look down on the ground, he would have never seen the shadow there cast by the streetlamp.

Never seen the outline of a lead pipe raised to strike.

Spinning around, Nick moved to the side in one quick motion. And just narrowly avoided having his head bashed in.

His Bureau self-defense training was second nature to him. Although the other man had more than thirty pounds on him, as well as several inches in height, it wasn't a contest. Within less than three minutes, the battle was all over. The man who had tried to attack him was lying writhing in pain on the ground with Nick's foot pressing down on his throat. Nick held the man's hand in both of his and twisted as far as it would go without snapping.

The assailant's bloodcurdling screams brought out several of Nick's neighbors. As they converged, Nick heard the sound of a siren in the distance. It grew steadily louder. Someone must have seen the fight and called 911.

"Hey, man, you need any help?"

The question came from a tall man wearing a ripped T-shirt that barely covered his rippling muscles. It was his next-door neighbor and apparently a bodybuilder.

"No," Nick assured him, "I've got it covered." For the first time, he looked down at his assailant. Recognition was immediate. Linda's brother, Sean.

The man was swearing at him, his voice a croaking sound, his face a beet-red because of the pressure against his throat. His eyes were fiery as he glared up at Nick.

"Let me up, Brannigan," Sean rasped. "Let me up so I can kill you," he cried. "The way you killed Linda."

Some of the neighbors around him looked at Nick warily, as if they weren't a hundred percent sure that the man on the floor was lying.

Swallowing a curse, Nick dug into his back pocket. He pulled out his wallet and held it open above his head, turning it first in one direction, then another so that everyone around him could see.

"I'm an FBI agent," he told them. "This man is dangerous and deranged."

The information seemed to erase the doubts amid some in the crowd.

"Who is he?" someone asked.

"Nobody you need to worry about," Nick answered. By the sound of the siren, the police were almost here.

"Let me up!" Sean demanded.

In response, Nick twisted the man's hand a little harder. Dixon whimpered.

"Not today," Nick told him.

The squad car pulled up a foot away from the cluster of people. Two policemen got out, their guns drawn and aimed at Nick. Nick headed them off quickly, holding up his badge again.

"I'm a federal agent," he told the two officers, "and this man's been stalking me."

And hopefully, he added silently, it's all over.

CHAPTER THIRTY-ONE

"HE'S GETTING MARRIED, Mama."

Charley's words seemed to make no more of an impression on her mother than the warm rays of the sun shining through the window. Claire Dow's expression was vacant, as if no one had spoken. As if she were alone in the small bedroom of the psychiatric hospital, her home for so many years.

A sliver of frustration pricked at Charley. Coming here was like willfully banging her head against the wall. But she couldn't stop. Couldn't just give up the way her father had. Because maybe, just maybe, the next time she did it, there'd be a dent. A breakthrough. A sign of recognition, no matter how small.

Charley took her mother's small, pale hand in hers. There was no quickening grasp. No response at all. Claire Dow ate and slept, sat and walked, all while existing in a shadowy land where no one else could enter.

Suppressing a sigh, Charley pressed her lips together. She'd stopped by the hospital after work even though she would have liked to have gone straight home. The investigation wasn't progressing very well. No one seemed to have seen the man Wally had identified as leaving the victim's house. She was beginning to wonder if perhaps it was just the fabrication of an overactive mind.

But David's wedding was on Sunday, only a couple of days away and she wanted to make sure that her mother was aware of it. She kept hoping that somehow, her mother stored the words in the recesses of her mind, to be accessed at a later date.

That Claire Dow would never be well again never crossed her mind. Just as she believed that someday, she was going to catch her sister's killer.

Charley knelt beside her mother's chair, taking her hand again. Despite the fact that she was sitting in the sun, Claire's hand felt cool. It was as if her mother's entire body was just an empty shell, waiting for her return.

Charley tried to infuse enthusiasm into her voice, to talk to her mother as if they were on the telephone and she'd just called to give an update.

"I met her. The three of us went out to dinner. David, Lisa and me. You'd like her, Mama. She's pretty and smart and she makes David laugh. He needs to laugh after all the things he's been through." She looked at her mother's face. Her pale eyes seemed to stare right through her. She could remember when her mother's eyes were warm, expressive. Was it really only six years ago? Or a lifetime? "We all do.

"Lisa's a captain's daughter. That's how they met. She's about your height, slender, with medium brown hair and brown eyes. I think David said she's twenty-five, I'm not sure. But he's crazy about her." She paused, watching the smooth, impassive face. Her mother had always looked younger than her age.

A lot of good that did her now, Charley thought ruefully.

"I wish you could be there, at the wedding," she added. "So does David." She tried to keep the condemnation out of her voice. "Dad's probably not coming, but then, David didn't really expect him to. Dad was never exactly that much a part of the family, was he?" Charley forced a smile, wondering if her mother even saw it. "Not like you."

Charley sighed. These meetings took a great deal out of her. But she couldn't think of her own discomfort, couldn't give up. Her mother was going to be well again someday. Medicine continued to make great strides, and maybe there'd be a breakthrough that would bring her mother around by this time, next year. Or maybe a spare miracle would somehow find its way down to her mother.

You never know, Charley thought. It was going to turn out all right. As long as she didn't give up on her mother.

Charley rose to her feet, bumping against her mother's chair. There was only the slightest reaction, a bracing of the shoulders. But Claire didn't look her way.

Maybe next time, Charley hoped.

"I've got to get going, Mama. It's been another long day. When I come back, I'll tell you all about the wedding," she promised.

Leaning over, Charley brushed her lips across her mother's cheek. She thought she heard just the slightest sigh escape her mother's lips, but that was probably only her imagination.

"Whenever you're ready to come out," she whispered to her mother, "I'll be here, waiting."

Charley walked out of the room and then hurried down the long hallway, out of the building. She blinked back tears as she went, refusing to allow them to be shed in public.

Federal agents weren't supposed to cry.

WHEN CHARLEY HEARD the knock on her door, she didn't bother pretending to be busy. She yanked it open. Never one to fuss, it had taken her all of fifteen minutes to get dressed and do her hair. She'd been ready for the past forty-five minutes, during which time she'd been desperately trying to occupy herself. Wondering all the while if Nick would come and how she'd feel if he did—or didn't.

"I wasn't sure if you were coming," she confessed.

It took her a second to catch her breath. Not because she'd run to the door, but because Nick had managed to steal it from her. He was wearing a light gray suit, a white shirt and a blue tie. And he looked incredible, as if he'd just stepped out of the pages of a men's fashion magazine. Picture perfect.

For his part, Nick was giving her a long once-over. He hadn't meant to be so obvious, but it was hard not to stare. Her dress was tight. Strapless, aqua, it brushed against her thighs and made his palms itch.

It took him a second to discover where he'd put his voice. "Why? Am I that unreliable?" He grinned, his eyes sweeping over her again. "Man, but you clean up well, Special Agent Dow."

Charley didn't bother playing coy. She allowed the pleased smile to blossom on her lips.

"Thank you." And then, because she wanted to keep this light, to disguise the fact that her pulse was only now settling down, she murmured, "Right back at you."

Most women he knew would have wanted to milk the moment, to draw out a few more compliments. Just when he thought of her as the personification of womanhood, she turned into a guy on him. Always full of surprises, he thought.

Nick held out the crook of his arm to her. "Ready?"

Charley grabbed the clutch purse she'd left on the kitchen table. "Ready," she declared, slipping her arm through his. Outside, she paused to lock her door, then slipped her key into her purse.

Nick escorted her to his car, then held the door open. Flashing a smile at him, she got in.

There were butterflies in her stomach, Charley realized as she buckled up. Butterflies for David, and butterflies for herself. The latter were bigger than the former. That had to do with the fact that Nick was sitting so close to her.

She was being stupid. She and Nick were partners. He rode around with her in one vehicle or another all the time. There was no reason to be entertaining flying insects the size of Learjets inside her stomach just because it was happening again. Maybe he didn't normally look as handsome as he did now, but under no circumstances had he ever had features that could have been rented out to haunt a house.

Maybe a woman, but not a house.

Taking a breath, pretending to settle in as she stared straight ahead, Charley said, "Thanks for doing this for me."

"My pleasure." Backing out of the guest parking space, Nick drove from the lot. She'd given him the location of the ceremony and he'd plotted it out for himself. He didn't particularly want to look like a fool and nothing did that faster than getting lost. "You saved me from unpacking."

She didn't follow him. "Unpacking?"

He nodded, making a right at the corner, beating out another car by a fraction. "My stuff."

Charley still didn't understand. She glanced down at her hands and saw that she was holding on to her clutch purse too tightly. One of her knuckles was turning white. She loosened her grip. "You moved again?"

"No," he said mildly, "the boxes are from the original move."

"That was over a month ago."

He shrugged, coming to a stop as a light started turning red. Out of the corner of his eye, he saw her shift restlessly in her seat. If she'd been at the wheel, he knew they would have flown through the light. "Some things take me more time than others."

"I'll say. There's taking your time," she pointed out, "and then there's utter procrastination." The light turned green. She leaned forward ever so slightly, as if that would give him the momentum to make it through the next light. You missed one, you missed them all, usually. "Need help?" she offered.

"I can manage."

Curiosity nudged at her. "How long does it usually take you to unpack when you move?"

He thought about giving her an answer, then decided to be honest. "I don't know. This is the first time I've made a move without having my family around somewhere." He spared her a glance, telling her before she could ask, "My mother and sister are very good at unpacking."

She smiled. "And you're not."

Nick merely shrugged. "I'm better at other things."

SHE DIDN'T ASK him to specify just what other things he was referring to. Nonetheless, she got her answer some time later. He might not be good at unpacking, but dancing was another story.

During the reception, after the bride and groom had had their customary dance and the floor opened up to everyone, Charley decided to coax Nick out. At first, he'd demurred, but then agreed. She was surprised it had only taken her two requests to get him on the dance floor.

And more surprised once he was there.

Nick blew her away with the way he moved to the beat of the band. As if the music began inside his body. As if he was one with it. She barely kept up.

By the end of the number, she could only stare at him as she tried to get her breath back. "Special Agent Brannigan, you have hidden talents."

He looked at her for a long moment. A slow song began. He took her into his arms, tucking her hand against his chest as he held her close with the other. They began to sway to the melody.

"You'd be surprised," he told her.

His words rippled along her skin, leaving her with a promise of things to come. A promise that had very little to do with their joint venture as partners and everything to do with the woman inside her.

He felt her stiffen ever so slightly and drew back his head. "What?"

"Nothing," she murmured, then decided to tell him. "Did you ever see someone you thought you knew, but you couldn't remember where you had seen them? Or even if you knew them enough to speak to?"

He laughed. "I know exactly what you mean. Why, who do you think you see?"

She looked toward the bar, but the person she thought she saw was gone, and with him, that wispy thread of recognition. "Nobody. Just my imagination, working overtime."

"You need to learn how to relax," he told her.

Not while you're holding me like this. "I'll work on it," she promised.

SHE'D ALMOST SEEN HIM. He was going to have to be more careful.

The tall, willowy waiter picked up a tray, going through the motions he knew were expected of him by anyone looking his way. He'd paused to look at the couple. To look at *her*.

Very slowly, his back to the couple, he began to pick up empty glasses. Behind him, the small reception, attended by mostly Marine personnel, was becoming boisterous. He didn't hear. His mind was on the couple he'd been watching. On the blonde.

His lips all but disappeared as his frown deepened.

He'd thought she was different. Would have bet his life on it. But apparently, he would have lost that bet. Because she wasn't different.

The thought telegraphed itself across his brain with an urgency he couldn't shut away. She was just like the others, but he was going to have to save her. Save her immortal soul before it slipped into the ravages of hell for all eternity. Good thing he'd been watching out for her, for a long time now. Even as he saved the others, he'd always get back to her. To make sure she was all right, that she remained pure.

But she wasn't pure. He could sense it. Smell it. Even from across the room with all those other bodies in the way.

Oh, she wasn't as bad as her sister, but she still needed saving. And he was going to be the one to do it.

Even if it wound up killing them both.

CHAPTER THIRTY-TWO

"YOU'RE A REALLY, really good sport," Charley said as Nick drove her back to her apartment.

The reception had run longer than they'd anticipated. The sun had gone down and evening shadows stretched out before them as they drove north along Bristol. The profusion of lights illuminated buildings that had emptied out hours ago. The shoppers had gone home and the city was preparing to take a little catnap before starting the process all over again.

"I've got to do something to pay you back," Charley told him.

Nick tried very hard to keep a straight face. "Just what did you have in mind?"

She thought of their earlier conversation, the one they'd had while heading toward the church in Newport. "Unpacking."

"Excuse me?" He slowed down for a light, then looked at her. "Is that some kind of euphemism?"

"Don't see how it might be," she answered innocently, then her mouth curved in what he could only describe as a sexy smile, "unless you consider unpacking the boxes in your apartment symbolic of something."

His apartment and its boxes were the furthest things

from his mind as he glanced at her. Exploring her had his attention, front and center.

A deep, appreciative smile curved his mouth. Watching it, Charley could almost feel the smile on her own lips. Feel it against her own lips. Heat flashed through her.

Careful. Charley, don't get carried away. He's going to get the wrong idea. Or maybe the right one.

In either case, she was not about to let Brannigan see what she was thinking. Or how he was affecting her. Most likely, it was just the alcohol, nothing more. They were partners, just partners, that's all. And partners covered each other's backs. He'd covered hers by doing her a favor. A pretty big favor, she had to admit. By coming with her to her brother's wedding today Brannigan had taken away her stigma about being a fifth wheel. Nothing she hated more than standing out for the wrong reasons.

"I don't need help unpacking," he told her. He pulled into a parking space several spaces closer than he'd parked in earlier today. After shutting off the engine, he turned to her. He didn't want the evening to end, not just yet. He'd seen a side to her today that he wanted to investigate. "But you can invite me in for a nightcap."

Not a good idea, her own personal version of Jiminy Cricket whispered in her brain. But she couldn't very well turn him out after he'd come through for her.

"Okay," Charley agreed, getting out. "But just one," she cautioned, then added, "I don't want you on my conscience."

Once he got out, he closed his door, then pressed the security lock, never taking his eyes off her. Making her skin warm. "Meaning?"

"If you get into an accident…" She let her voice trail off, not bothering to finish the sentence. He was bright enough to know where she was headed with this, she thought. It didn't diminish her meaning.

"I can always call a cab if I've had too much to drink," he told her. "Not that I intend to." And then his smile softened. "But thanks for worrying."

"You're my partner," Charley replied, taking out her key. "I'm supposed to worry about you."

His eyes washed over her again. And there was no way that she could guess his thoughts.

"Maybe you should, at that," he allowed.

His voice was low, seductive, creating goose bumps in its wake. She struggled to keep presence of mind. Not easy when her mind was attempting to jump ship.

Charley cleared her throat and tried to sound unaffected as she slipped her key into the lock. "What do you mean?"

Nick didn't bother answering her with words. Most notably because none were forming in his brain. Instead, he tilted her head back ever so slightly and lightly brushed his lips against hers.

A fatal mistake.

Because it didn't end there.

His hands on her shoulders, Nick kissed her again. Harder this time. Longer. Deeper.

Her head spinning, Charley felt as if she was melting right there on her doorstep. She had just gotten the key into the lock. Now she was trying to open the door without the benefit of visual aids. Her eyes were shut, her body otherwise occupied, bordering on liquefying. After what seemed like endless attempts, she finally managed to turn the doorknob and open the door.

Still sealed in a kiss that continued, that drew them closer to each other and into a swirling abyss of heat and promises, they moved inside. Nick removed the key with a snap of his wrist, then pushed the door closed behind them.

They were in her apartment, in the dark.

The moment the door shut, they heard it. A low moaning noise. Nick drew back from her, his body alert, anticipating danger even if it had no form yet.

He heard Charley laugh softly. "Dakota, go to your room."

"Dakota?"

"My dog, remember?" Charley laughed even as the animal trotted obediently into the next room. "Treat me right or she'll rip your heart out, pizza or no pizza," she said, referring to the last time he'd been by.

He drew her back into his arms, unable to think of anything but her. "I'll keep that in mind." He kissed her again. A long, openmouthed kiss that inflamed her.

Charley felt something snap open inside of her. Desire, passion, need all danced around a blazing campfire, demanding attention. Demanding a piece of her. Sanity vanished. Maybe it was her brother's wedding, maybe seeing him so happy and herself alone had been the final straw. She didn't know. But now was not the time to analyze.

Now was the time to seize the moment.

She didn't hang back.

With eager hands Charley began to undo his jacket, pushing it from his shoulders. It hadn't even fallen on the floor before she started on his shirt, pulling buttons free. She could feel the blood pounding in her veins, hear it rushing in her ears as she yanked the shirt from his body. All the while, she could feel Nick's strong hands roaming over her, molding her to him. Making her body sing.

He slid the zipper down her spine, separating the material. Swiftly taking away one barrier after another until all that was left was the slinky garter belt and the stockings they held in place. The garter belt she'd expressly bought for the wedding because she'd wanted to feel like someone other than a federal agent. She wanted to feel like a woman.

Tidal waves of emotions washed over him, causing his head to spin. If it weren't spinning so badly out of control, he might have somehow stopped himself. The edict about not mixing business with pleasure had always been his first commandment. But he no longer wanted to adhere to it.

Not if it meant backing away.

If someone had told him only a short while ago, he would have never believed them, never believed that he could have wanted anyone as much as he wanted this woman. But he did. Wanted her with a fierceness that rattled his teeth, jarred his foundations. He refused to try to understand why. All he wanted to do was act on his desire. He feasted on the sight of her, the taste of her.

He buried his fingers in her hair, holding her to him as he kissed her mouth over and over again, feeling insatiable and wondering if he had lost his mind.

She made him crazy.

Damn, but she was going to regret this in the morning, Charley thought. Maybe even in a few hours, but right now, this was all she wanted. To make love. To feel love, even if it was only the most superficial kind.

She needed to feel alive.

She'd been happy for David, but at the same time, she'd felt so alone. David had his wife now. And she had case files.

And a partner who made her fantasies take flight, a voice whispered in her head, along with her pulse.

Charley gasped as she tried to draw in more air. Her lungs felt the way they had when she'd run that twenty-six-mile marathon. She tingled as she twisted against Nick's hands while they roamed over her body. He touched her as if he knew her body better than she did. His fingers gently strummed along her skin, made her whole body hum.

The places he touched, the way he touched, he expertly brought her from one climax to another, exhausting her even as he filled her with an exhilaration she'd never experienced before.

And his lips—his lips were magnificent. He kissed her eyes, her cheeks, her throat, skimming down lower to the tender skin between her breasts, along her belly. Between her thighs.

Making the ache for him grow.

Determined to give as good as she received, Charley fought her way up from the haze closing in around her brain, the fire consuming her body, and brought her mouth down on his. Ran her long, graceful fingers along his hard body. Tantalizing him the way he had tantalized her. There was no resistance, no reluctance, no shyness. No eleventh-hour thunderbolt of thought to make her stop. There was only a crying need. To touch and be touched. To join with him.

Damp, her skin close to sizzling, Charley arched her body as he entered her. Arched and savored and absorbed. She wrapped her legs around his torso, a silent plea for him to remain where he was. She sealed herself to him. And felt wild bursts of energy inside as he moved with more and more urgency and force.

She matched him, movement for movement, as they raced up to the final plateau.

It took everything she had not to scream when he finally brought her to where she so desperately had wanted to go. She swallowed the sound, not wanting to share the moment with either the neighbors or Dakota. The former might not come to what they believed was her aid, but the latter most definitely would.

HE'D FOLLOWED THEM.

Followed *her*. Shedding the white jacket he'd stolen, identifying him as one of the hotel's employees, and the wig he'd donned, throwing both into the Dumpster, he stood now across the way from her apartment, bathed in shadows.

Cursing her.

There was no light coming from any of the windows. He didn't need light. Didn't need to see. He knew what she was doing.

She was giving herself to him, to that man she was always with. The man who was responsible for the death of the mother of his child. She was using her body as an instrument of temptation. Of evil. Used it just the way that woman had used hers to tempt his father.

The way the others had to tempt and lead faithful husbands astray.

He clenched his hands at his sides, rage growing within him as he remembered. Remembered how that horrible woman had used her wiles to steal his father's affections. Not from his mother, but from him.

His breathing grew more pronounced.

From him. She'd stolen his father from him. He would have done anything for his father. Anything, even killed for him. But his father had turned his back on him. Because of her. He'd picked that whore over him.

And they had both paid.

Just the way that *she* was going to pay. For doing the wrong thing. For making the wrong choice.

CHAPTER THIRTY-THREE

THE EUPHORIA LEFT much too quickly, ushering in uncertainty and doubt in its wake.

Sitting up on the floor, feeling incredibly naked and exposed, Charley reached over and dragged off the fleece throw she kept draped over one end of the sofa. She avoided looking in Nick's direction as she tucked the material around herself. Only when she was covered did she turn her head toward him. He looked mildly amused. And very naked.

The man was built like a rock. She felt her pulse accelerate again.

It took her a second to find her voice. "This was a mistake."

"Why?" Humor curved his mouth, shone in his eyes. "Did I do it wrong?"

Dragging a hand through her hair, she blew out a breath. Looking for words that wouldn't come. Looking for a way to make this clear to herself as well as him. She'd just had the greatest sexual experience of her life, but everything about it spelled disaster.

She cast an accusing glance at him. He could be making this easier on her. "You know what I mean."

"No." Very lightly, he skimmed his fingertips along Charley's exposed spine and then smiled as she shivered. Just touching her made him want to do it all over again. "Enlighten me."

She looked at him, feeling helpless. Feeling drawn. And very, very confused. Her mind was going one way, her body definitely another. "We work together."

His eyes crinkled as the smile grew into a grin. "So that's where I know you from."

She would have thrown up her hands if it wouldn't have caused the light blue throw to sink to her nether regions, leaving the rest of her open to the viewing public. "I'm being serious, Brannigan."

"Maybe that's the problem." Nick took her hand, lacing his fingers through it. He made no effort to draw her into his arms the way he wanted to. But every ounce of his being wanted her back for another round. "Maybe you're being too serious. Not everything is life and death, Charley. Some things are just meant to be enjoyed." His eyes held hers. "To be."

Charley took a breath, trying to steel herself off from him, from the drawing power of his eyes. Of his being. She discovered that she might as well have been tossing an aluminum can in front of an oncoming tank to act as a roadblock.

This was one battle she was losing quickly. "Everything has consequences."

Releasing her hand, Nick wove his fingers through her hair. "No need to draw everything to a quick, logical conclusion." He smiled into her eyes, signaling her undoing. "I never took you for a pragmatist."

Each word felt as if it weighed at least ten pounds on her tongue. It took effort to push them out. "I never took you for a romantic."

"See?" He brought his mouth very close to hers. So close that all she had to do was move a fraction of an inch and it would be hers. Excitement stood on the shoulders of anticipation. Breathing became a tricky business. "We've learned something about each other already." He ran a thumb ever so slowly along her collar bone. Melting her. "Not to mention that I've discovered you've got skin that tastes like vanilla."

She laughed, shaking her head. "I do not."

His eyes told her he knew differently. The words skimmed along her skin. He tugged gently on the fleece throw and suddenly, she was exposed.

"Trust me, I'm in a position to know." As he brought his mouth down on hers, a cell phone started ringing. Releasing her, Nick groaned. As did she. Silently. "Yours or mine?"

The second he asked, a second cell phone rang.

She sighed in response. "Both."

They knew what that meant. Another body had been discovered. The murders were occurring frequently now. For whatever reason, their killer was on an escalated schedule.

Nick looked around for his phone. It was still in the pocket of his trousers. He pulled it over toward him by one leg.

"At least they had the decency to wait until after the wedding," he murmured, fishing his cell phone out.

Charley was silently grateful for that as she retrieved her phone from her clutch purse.

"Dow."

"Brannigan."

Their voices mingled. Their messages didn't. Charley's call came from the assistant director, Nick's from

Bill Chan. The message was the same in both cases. Another body had been found.

LESS THAN HALF AN HOUR LATER, they were on the scene, a single-story building in a development located in Costa Mesa. Bill and Sam were there ahead of them. Sam had on sweats, Bill jeans and a baggy sweater. Both men had obviously been dragged out of bed, grabbing the first thing they could find.

Without thinking, Charley had put on the dress she'd worn to the wedding. Nick had no choice in what he wore. As they came in, Sam and Bill both stopped what they were doing and gave low, appreciative whistles.

"Nobody told me this was formal," Sam commented to Bill. "They tell you it was formal?"

"Nope, not me." Bill grinned for the first time since he'd been summoned. "I feel underdressed."

"Can it, you two. I invited Brannigan to my brother's wedding," she informed them tersely. She saw the two men exchange looks and ignored them. "What have we got?"

The playful mood vanished and they became all business as information was quickly and economically rattled off. Sam was the one who filled her in, lowering his voice so that it wouldn't carry to the devastated-looking man on the side of the room.

"The victim was found by her estranged husband." Sam indicated the man the A.D. was questioning. "So far, the guy's too choked up to give us a very clear statement. He came in half an hour ago to get some of his things, he said, and found her like this."

Bill joined them. "Marcus Froman," he said, giving

them the man's name. "He keeps breaking down, saying he should have been here sooner, the way he'd planned."

Charley eyed the man under discussion. She watched as he spoke to the assistant director, gesturing wildly. He seemed clearly beside himself.

Perhaps a little too much so, she judged.

At her elbow, Sam went on filling them in. She listened to him but continued observing the victim's husband. And chewing her lower lip.

Finished, Sam flipped closed the notepad he'd been reading from.

"Anyone offer to take Mr. Froman to the hospital to have him checked out for shock?" Charley asked.

"I did," Bill volunteered, "but he said no, he was okay. He said he could call someone to come get him, but that he wanted to stay here as long as his wife's body remained."

Charley nodded to herself. "He did, huh?"

"I'm beginning to know that look," Nick told her, moving in closer as the assistant director had someone usher the victim's husband to another room.

Momentarily lost in thought, in evaluation, Charley roused herself at the sound of Nick's voice. She blinked as she eyed him. "What look?"

Nick glanced over her head toward Sam and Bill. Both men nodded in silent agreement before he continued. "The look that says you think something's off."

She did. Big-time. "Don't you?" she asked.

He knew she wasn't referring to what had happened between them earlier. He could tell by her tone she expected him to come to the same conclusion she had.

Nick thought for a moment, staring at the victim, who

was lying on the living-room rug, a look of surprise and disbelief frozen on her face. The crime-scene unit was still taking photographs. Flashes of light went off every few seconds as two people circled the body, then the room, preserving the scene. It was almost hypnotic to watch.

Nick moved closer to the body. "The killer didn't pose her."

Charley nodded. "And she looks surprised. All the other victims looked as if they'd just fallen asleep. Her eyes are wide-open. And," she added with feeling, "she's also the first victim who wasn't single."

"Husband said they were estranged," Sam interjected. "On the verge of getting a divorce."

"He said she was moving on with her life," Bill added. "They both were."

Charley looked from one man to another. They all knew better. "We only have his word for it."

Nick was the first to voice what they were all thinking. "You think he killed her?"

That would have been her first guess, Charley thought. "Best way I can think of to avoid losing half of everything because of the community property law. And with a serial killer loose…"

Bill pointed toward the body as the technicians with the camera finally withdrew. "She has a cross carved into her forehead."

Squatting down, Charley feathered her gloved fingers through the woman's bangs, pushing them back. "Right. Look at it."

Nick leaned over the body and saw what she was referring to. "It's carved in deeply."

"Exactly." Charley rose to her feet. "Now unless our killer has suddenly become heavy-handed, I'd say that somehow that bit about the cross leaked out and what we've got here is a copycat killing."

"You want me to bring the grieving husband in for further questioning?" Sam offered.

Charley shook her head. If this was a copycat killing, it didn't belong with their case file. "Call the local police department. Have someone from there do the honors."

Bill looked back at the body. "What do we do in the meantime?"

She paused. "Cover our bases." She looked at Sam, then Bill, giving them each an immediate assignment. "Find out if Mrs. Froman was having an affair with a married man and if she's missing a cross."

"You got it," Sam told her.

"Got time for me to bounce something off you?" Nick asked as the other two men left the room.

She did her best not to look at him as if they'd just spent the past few hours making love. The last thing she needed was gossip. "Sure, shoot."

"Okay, we know that our killer focuses on women who are having affairs with married men." Nick paused, then added, "Their bosses. Or at least one of them."

"Not Cris." But the moment she said it, Charley remembered something. "That professor was her mentor." The sound of the words as she uttered them almost surprised her. "She was conducting some kind of a study for him."

"In other words, her boss," Nick pointed out. "Did you ever stop to think that our serial killer might be a woman?"

Behind her, the M.E. was placing the late Mrs.

Froman into a black body bag. Charley tried not to listen as the zipper was being drawn. "What?"

"Humor me for a moment," Nick told her. "Maybe the killer is a wife herself. Or was until her husband cheated on her with someone he was working with. Maybe something snapped and she's taking her revenge out on women similar to the one who stole her husband from her."

It had possibilities, but she wasn't completely buying this. "Where does the cross come in?"

Nick shrugged, then as he talked, he began to evolve more of his theory. "She thinks that as Christian women, they should know better?" It was more of a question than an answer.

Charley shook her head. "I don't know. It would have taken an awfully strong woman to strangle them like that."

"There are strong women." He leaned his head in so that no one else could hear what he had to say. "You, for instance."

She knew he was referring to the way she'd wrapped her legs around him while they were making love. She'd always prided herself on her strength. "I suppose it's worth considering," she allowed.

"So is this a step back?" he asked. "If I'm right."

"Big *if*," she emphasized. "Don't forget, we do have that sketch."

"Based on the recollections of a wino," he reminded her. "Not exactly the most reliable source."

"Even winos are right once in a while," she commented, chewing again on her lower lip. The thought nagged at her that they were no further along than they'd been before.

CHAPTER THIRTY-FOUR

"YOU WERE RIGHT," Nick told her as he hung up the telephone. He turned from his desk to look at Charley. "That was a Detective Alberts with the Costa Mesa police department. Froman gave it up as soon as the local police began leaning on him. Got his story all confused and then just broke down."

It had been two days since they'd discovered their so-called latest victim. Two days since he'd made love with Charley and he couldn't get her out of his mind. Or out of his blood. At this point, he wasn't sure if that was a bad thing or a good one.

Nick smiled, nodding. "Nice call."

Looking up from her desk, Charley began to answer, then stopped to sneeze. "You saw it, too."

But she'd been the first to call attention to it, Nick thought. And he'd always believed in giving credit where it was due. Obviously she wasn't the kind who liked to hog the glory. Nice to know, he mused. There were a lot of things he liked about his partner.

He inclined his head. "Generous."

She didn't feel very generous. More like this side of miserable. She sneezed twice more before she could comment.

"Thanks. I do what I can," she quipped. "Which right

now isn't very much." She stared at the screen she'd been looking at now for the past few minutes. Her eyes felt dry. Too bad the rest of her didn't. "I have this awful feeling he's going to strike again. I don't know if it's because he's thumbing his nose at us, or because his need to bring sinners back to the fold has gotten too much for him."

"So we've pretty much thrown out my theory about it being a woman," Nick guessed.

Charley nodded, stifling another sneeze. "Pretty much." She grinned. "Maybe some other time."

Nick picked up a box of tissues from another desk and brought it over to hers. "Cold or allergies?"

Charley pulled out a tissue just in time. "I don't have allergies."

Facing her, Nick rested his hip against the next desk. "Then by process of elimination, it's a cold." That same smile entered his eyes, the one that had been her undoing the other night. He leaned forward, lowering his voice so that only she could hear. "Floor too cold for you the other night?" he asked. And then he smiled. "I didn't notice any lack of heat."

She felt something sting her cheeks and had to concentrate to keep the color from rising. She answered each of his questions. "Yes, maybe and I don't remember—except that there was a rug in the room."

"I stand corrected. But I remember everything else vividly." The humor was only marginally present as he looked at her.

A giant of a butterfly came out of nowhere, insisting on fluttering in the pit of her stomach. Or maybe that was just her reacting to her cold, Charley thought. The next minute, her eyes were squeezing shut as another sneeze all but exploded. Her chest began to ache. Charley grabbed a tissue and put it to use.

"Maybe I do, too," she finally admitted, saying the words so softly he had to stare at her lips even though he was right next to her. Charley took in a deep breath, telling herself she wasn't going to sneeze anymore. Or react to this man beside her.

Taking a breath, she nodded toward the adjacent room, which was barely more than a cubbyhole with phones. "Isn't it your turn to go through the calls and see if there's anything worth looking at twice?"

They all took their turn at that. Per the assistant director's orders, each call that came in with supposed information about the serial killer had to be followed up, no matter how off-the-wall the claim seemed to be. No one wanted to take a chance of having a vital clue fall through the cracks.

Because he'd groaned instead of voicing a denial, she knew she'd guessed right.

"The Bureau better come through with a good vision-care plan," Nick muttered as he withdrew. "My eyes, not to mention my mind, are about to go numb."

As he left, he passed Alice on her way in. The woman barely looked at him as she acknowledged his presence. He wondered how long the secretary was going to bear a grudge. He'd yelled at her when she'd called several weeks ago, thinking that she was Dixon, calling to rattle him again. He'd apologized once he realized his mistake, but the woman looked nervous whenever she was around him now.

She was an odd one, he thought. He knew that Charley had taken it upon herself to try to find someone to go out with Alice. So far, there were no takers. He didn't wonder.

Placing the papers she was holding on Charley's desk, Alice pushed back a strand of her hair. The tall, angular blonde looked visibly distressed. She offered a spasmodic smile and pushed her glasses back up her nose. Neither her hair nor her glasses obeyed. Both slipped forward again.

"Assistant Director Kelly would like you to sign these papers." A clear-nail-polished finger pointed to the top paper.

Looking away from her monitor, her sneezing temporarily on hold, Charley glanced at the heading on the top sheet. She frowned. She thought she'd already signed that one. Her brain was getting muddled. With a sigh, she picked up a pen from her desk and signed in the appropriate places, initialing where Alice instructed.

Finished, she glanced up. Something akin to fear was on the other woman's face. Charley braced herself. She knew she didn't have to say anything. Alice was too timid to begin a conversation on her own. In a minute, the woman would be gone.

But she just couldn't ignore the secretary's expression.

"What's the matter, Alice?"

The woman always looked as if she felt she was intruding, as if she wasn't comfortable in her own skin. Charley felt sorry for her.

"How close are you to catching this monster?" Alice finally managed to ask.

"Not as close as I'd like." And then, because it was Alice, because she could see that the woman was struggling with her fears since she lived alone, Charley added, "But probably closer than he'd like. If you're worried, Alice, you don't have to be." She felt another sneeze coming on. Grabbing a tissue, she waited. "Unless you have a secret lover we don't know about."

Alice's brown eyes widened. "No, I—what do you mean?"

Charley wondered if Alice read the reports she was given to input into the database. This wasn't anything new anymore. Charley specifically remembered entering it into a report she subsequently gave to the A.D. Maybe the woman's fears had blocked out everything else.

In any case, Charley knew she wasn't telling any tales out of school. Cases couldn't be discussed with outsiders, not people who were part of the task force.

"The affairs," she repeated. The sneeze she was waiting for seemed to subside. Charley took a breath, then continued. "Rule one for our killer is that he only kills women who are having affairs with married men. Unless you're doing that, I don't think you have anything to worry about. And even then, he only seems to go after women who were wearing crosses." She looked at the woman's high-necked blouse. She'd never seen Alice wearing any jewelry at all. "And you don't."

Alice surprised her by announcing, "Oh, but I do." Digging into the high collar, she fished out a long chain. On the end of it was a rather large, plain gold cross. "It belonged to my father. It's not delicate like yours, but it's all I have to remember him by."

Charley fingered the small cross, a duplicate of her sister's, at her throat. "You have your memories," Charley pointed out just as an unexpected sneeze got the better of her.

A sad expression washed over Alice's face, lasting only a moment as she attempted to rally. "Memories are

hard to hold in your hand." Alice looked at her pointedly. "Are you taking anything for that?"

Her eyes felt watery, Charley thought as she shook
her head. "It'll pass."

Aside from taking an all-day cold tablet before she
left the apartment, she didn't have time to baby a cold.
There was a serial killer to track down before he killed
again. And it was a he. Despite what Nick had suggested, she was willing to bet her life that the killer was
a man. Granted there seemed to be some feminine over-
tones in the case, such as the gentle way the victims
were all laid out, as if remorse was involved at the last
moment. But if the killer was a woman, there was no
doubt in Charley's mind that the victims would have
been stabbed. Knives were instruments of passion and
women were passionate when they killed.

"STAY BACK," Charley warned Dakota as she walked
into the apartment that evening. She dropped her purse
on the floor by the door, tossing her keys into the
opening. The keys drooped and fell on the floor beside
the purse. "You might catch this cold and believe me,
you *really* don't want it."

Dakota ignored the command and pranced from foot
to foot in front of her mistress, eager for companionship and to be petted. With a sigh, Charley sank down
on a nearby chair.

"You want to go out for a run, don't you? I'm sorry
girl, maybe tomorrow." She thought about taking the
dog for a short walk, then decided to wait. The cold had
definitely gotten the better of her for the moment. "How
are you at boiling tea?" The German shepherd cocked
her head, looking at her. "I didn't think so. I should have

picked up one on the way home." But all she could think about on her way home was *getting* home before her eyes closed. The way they were doing now. "Maybe I'll take just a short nap," she said to the dog. "With any luck, I should be good as new, or some reasonable facsimile of it, after a short nap."

Getting up, she paused only long enough to make sure the dog still had water in her bowl, then pointed herself in the direction of the bedroom. Dakota trotted after her. The animal lost no time in making herself comfortable on the worn comforter that was kept on the floor beside the double bed.

"It was that run in the rain that did it," Charley muttered as she sank down on top of the bed. She closed her eyes. "Remind me never to run in the rain again. And remind me to send a nasty letter to the weather bureau. It's not supposed to rain this time of year." She sighed, willing herself to relax. "I've got it someplace in writing."

The moment she drew the comforter on the bed around her body, chimes echoed in the bedroom.

"I must be worse than I thought," she murmured to the dog. "I'm hearing bells."

Opening her eyes, she saw that Dakota was no longer sprawled out on the floor. Her body was rigid, at attention and her ears were pointed in the direction of the front door.

"Guess I'm not hearing bells after all. Not unless they're loud enough for you to hear, too." She closed her eyes again, deciding to ignore her visitor.

But whoever it was rang the doorbell again. And again.

"Only one way to handle this, I guess." Charley was not in the best of moods as she threw off the comforter and sat up. What she needed, aside from peace and quiet, was another dose of cold tablets. The ones she'd taken at lunch had worn off an hour ago. They usually kept her going for a while.

With a sigh of resignation, Charley dragged herself into an upright position and then got off the bed. Dakota followed suit like a four-legged, furry shadow.

Charley looked through the peephole. If it was someone selling subscriptions or cookies, she was just going to silently move away from the door and return to the bedroom.

But it wasn't someone selling subscriptions or cookies, or anything else for that matter. It was Alice. There was a smile on her face and a large, white Styrofoam container in her hands.

CHAPTER THIRTY-FIVE

PUZZLED, CHARLEY UNLOCKED and opened the door.

"What are you doing here?" Realizing that her question probably sounded rude to Alice, she cleared her throat and started again. "I mean, hi." She offered the woman a smile. "But what are you doing here?"

Alice looked over Charley's shoulder into the apartment. She regarded the dog uneasily. "May I come in?"

"Sure. Sure."

Charley stepped back. Beside her, Dakota remained where she was, guarding her territory. The moment Alice began to enter, a low, guttural sound came from the canine. Sucking in her breath, Alice looked at the animal in alarm. Charley grabbed the dog's collar and pulled her to the side before Dakota could do anything beyond growl.

"Don't mind Dakota. She's not always the friendliest dog."

But even as Charley said the words, she remembered that her pet had reacted differently to Nick right from the start. The animal had sniffed, checked him out and then behaved as if the man had always been coming by the apartment. Maybe it was the pizza. But now that she thought about it, Dakota's reaction to Nick, pizza or no pizza, was unusual. The dog's response to Alice was more in keeping with her general behavior. Maybe the German shepherd had given her seal of approval to Brannigan.

Why not? Charley mused. After all, Dakota was a female.

She gave Alice an encouraging smile as she drew Dakota back a little further. "It takes her time to warm up to strangers."

Alice's eyes never left the canine at Charley's side, even as she moved stiffly into the kitchen, placing the container she'd brought with her on the table.

The woman looked as if she was going to hyperventilate, Charley thought.

Alice ran her tongue along her lips. "Would you mind very much putting her into another room? I was bitten by a dog once and they scare me."

The idea of being afraid of a dog was completely foreign to Charley. But there was a line of perspiration forming along the other woman's brow, sticking her bangs to her forehead. Alice was obviously terrified.

"No problem." Holding on to Dakota's collar, Charley maneuvered the dog back into the bedroom. Unlike Sunday when she'd trotted into the bedroom on command, this time Dakota clearly was not happy about being shut out. "This won't take long, girl," she promised. Closing the door, she crossed back into the living room where Alice stood waiting.

"I brought you some chicken soup," Alice told her, nodding toward the container. "Homemade," she added. "You sounded pretty bad in the office."

"Nothing a few hours' sleep and some cold tablets won't cure," Charley assured her. "I bounce back pretty fast." She noted that Alice seemed crestfallen. Not wanting to hurt the woman's feelings, Charley did what she could to soothe them. "But the chicken soup is certainly welcome." The kitchen was only two steps from where she was standing. Charley reached for the container. "I didn't realize you knew where I lived."

The small smile that graced Alice's thin lips was almost philosophical in nature. "People forget that all the information in the department gets filtered through me in one way or another. I tend to just fade into the walls."

Although agreeing with her, Charley took the diplomatic approach. "I wouldn't go that far."

Prying off the lid, she took a deep whiff of the aroma that came swirling from depths of the container. It did smell good, she thought. She felt Alice watching her every move.

Obligingly, she took a small sip. The soup was still warm, bordering on hot. She had to admit that it did feel good going down.

"But you could dress a little more, um, vividly," Charley suggested, settling on a word she hoped wouldn't offend Alice. Her self-esteem reminded Charley of delicate china, china that would easily crack at the slightest bit of jostling. "Beiges, browns and the color taupe don't exactly stick in anyone's mind. Maybe you could try something brash," Charley suggested, then added with a smile, "like light blue."

She earned a shy smile in return. "Maybe I'll go shopping," Alice told her softly.

The woman needed help. Otherwise, her wardrobe wouldn't have been so dated. These days, almost every fashion had a following. Styles from decades ago had made a comeback. But even with all this going on, Alice still managed to look as if she couldn't fit in anywhere. As if there was no place for her in any decade.

"I'll go with you if you like," Charley offered, making what she felt was the ultimate sacrifice for another woman. Then, in case Alice took that to mean tomorrow, she said, "When I'm feeling better."

Alice stared at her for a long moment. So long that Charley was tempted to ask if anything was wrong. And then the secretary asked, "Would you?"

Charley smiled. She'd never seen Alice socialize with anyone. Even at the company functions she had attended, she always hung back in the shadows. Having someone volunteer for something as simple as accompanying her on a shopping trip was probably a big deal for her.

Charley smiled. "Sure."

"You're not too busy?"

Charley shrugged, taking another sip of the soup. "This case has to break sometime. And even if it doesn't, I still have some time coming to me."

But Alice shook her head. "I meant in your personal life," she explained. When Charley eyed her quizzically, Alice stammered, "You and Special Agent Brannigan…" Unable to finish her statement, her voice trailed off.

Maybe it was the fog in her brain, or maybe Bill and Sam were right when they'd kidded her that Alice had some kind of a female crush on her, but Charley could have sworn she detected a note of accusation in the other woman's voice.

"What about us?" Charley wanted to know.

Alice moved her shoulders in a vague, incomplete shrug. "Well, the way he looks at you sometimes…"

"Nick Brannigan, doesn't look at me any differently than the other members of the team do," Charley said dismissively.

Alice surprised her by not backing down or agreeing. Instead, she laughed softly. "Oh, I don't know. Do you like him?"

"Alice, you're getting very personal here."

Contrition was immediate as it flooded Alice's eyes. Charley felt guilty for having brought it on. "Sorry. It's just that I guess I don't really have a life," Alice confessed. "So I like peeking into other people's lives occasionally."

Wandering through the small living room, avoiding Charley's eyes, Alice looked around at the decor. There was a cluster of framed photographs arranged neatly on a side table. She drifted over in that direction, picking up a framed photograph that was in the center. Holding the frame in both hands, she turned it so that Charley could see which one she'd picked. "Is this your family?"

Charley looked at it for a moment. Remembering. Alice was holding the photograph taken at her graduation. At *their* graduation, she corrected silently. Hers and Cris's. David was home on leave. He and her father flanked the three of them, Cris, their mother, and her. She was standing beside her brother. Miraculously, all of them were smiling. It was a rare shot.

Six months later, Cris was dead.

"Yes." The word felt tight in her throat, Charley thought. This was her family. Had been her family. They weren't like that anymore.

"Your sister looks just like you." Alice raised her eyes. There was a slight flush of embarrassment. "I mean looked."

Charley raised her eyes sharply to the woman's face, then realized that of course Alice would know that Cris was dead. After all, like she had said, as the A.D.'s secretary, she was privy to all the information in and about the task force. Including the fact that Cris had been the first victim.

"We were identical," Charley told her.

Very gently, she took the framed photograph from Alice and looked at it for a moment before returning it to its place.

Alice turned toward her, a wistfulness in her eyes. "Must be nice, having a family."

"Must be," Charley couldn't help echoing. As far as she was concerned, she now had fragments of a family. Fragments that she believed in her heart could only be pulled together by catching this killer.

"You're not drinking your soup," Alice chided softly. Picking up the container, she handed it back to Charley. "It'll get cold."

Because the secretary had gone out of her way, Charley took another sip. The soup's temperature was dropping quickly. Under Alice's watchful eye, she took a second, longer sip.

Behind her, from the bedroom, Charley could hear Dakota scratching on the door, impatient to get out. The dog rarely did that. But then, she remembered that she hadn't taken Dakota out when she came home. Poor thing was probably wondering what was going on.

Alice's eyes darted toward the bedroom. Her entreaty was silent. Charley knew the woman was asking her not to let the dog out. She didn't like confining Dakota this way. It was bad enough that, except for the teenager she paid to take Dakota out around three o'clock, the dog had to stay in all day while she worked.

Jittery, as if filled with an energy that had no channel, no recourse, Alice moved about the living room touching knickknacks, straightening papers on the coffee table, moving the television guide turned sideways on top of the set.

"Can I do anything for you while I'm here?" she offered, glancing at Charley over her shoulder. "Get you anything?"

"No, I'm fine, really. You've already done more than enough. I just—" As she began to beg off, saying she was really tired, the doorbell rang.

Alice looked startled by the sound. "Are you expecting anyone?" she asked.

"No, but then, I wasn't expecting you, either."

Alice moved in front of her, blocking her access to the door. "You don't have to answer," Alice told her softly. "Whoever it is will go away."

Very firmly, Charley sidestepped her. "You didn't," she pointed out. The woman meant well, Charley thought, but she really didn't like the way Alice was trying to take over.

Her hand on the doorknob, Charley looked through the peephole. The person standing on the other side filled it completely.

Nick.

CHAPTER THIRTY-SIX

A SECOND AGO, she'd been tired, a little achy and somewhat irritable. All that faded in the face of the excitement that came rushing out of nowhere. She told herself she was being adolescent and blamed it on her cold and her desire to have Alice leave.

The feeling didn't fade.

Charley yanked open the door. "Hi. What are you doing here?" She purposely worded her greeting to echo the one she'd given Alice, so that the other woman wouldn't feel slighted.

"I stopped by to see how you were doing." Crossing the threshold, Nick saw Alice. Mild surprise passed over his face as he nodded toward her. "Alice." And then he turned back to Charley. "Looks like I'm not the only one checking up on you."

"Alice brought me chicken soup." Charley raised the container she held in her hand.

"Oldest remedies are the best."

From his tone, Charley couldn't tell if he was being serious, or droll. He glanced toward Alice.

The woman offered a spasmodic smile that disappeared from her lips almost as it appeared. She looked awkward again, as if she wasn't sure what to do with her hands, her arms, her torso.

Alice backed away toward the door. "Maybe I'd better be going," she murmured.

This time, Nick's voice was warm as he protested, "Don't leave on my account."

Alice's tongue darted nervously along her lower lip, moistening it before she spoke. "No, really, I just wanted to drop that off." She nodded at the container Charley was holding. "I hope you feel better," she interjected before abruptly turning on her heel.

"Thanks, I—" But her words had no one to receive them. Alice had fled, pulling the door closed behind her. Charley turned toward Nick, an amused expression on her face. "You really frighten her, don't you?" He'd told her about the telephone incident. "Just exactly how much did you yell at her?"

He had the good grace to seem slightly repentant. "It was just a couple of words. Unfortunately, they weren't the kind of words you could find in a Victorian dictionary and our Miss Sullivan seems to be very, very prim and proper." Moving toward the front door, Nick tried the lock to make sure it had taken. Satisfied, he scanned her apartment. "Where's your furry friend?"

A smile teased her mouth, spreading to her eyes. "I thought I was looking at him."

"The dog." The sound of nails urgently scratching against wood underscored his question. Nick looked at her, his brow furrowed. "You locked her up?"

"Not by choice," Charley explained. "She made Alice nervous."

Nick reached the bedroom door first, opening it. Dakota burst out as if she was afraid that the door might be shut again. The animal immediately began to wag her tail and dashed back and forth several times, as if she couldn't decide where to go and how to celebrate both her liberation and the appearance of her rescuer.

Laughing at the unabashed display of affection, Nick ruffled the dog's fur.

"The Pope would make Alice nervous." He glanced toward Charley to see if she agreed. Receiving no argument, he added, "Never saw a woman more skittish than the A.D.'s secretary. It's like that old expression, she seems to be afraid of her own shadow. You'd think working at the Bureau would give her a feeling of security." His mouth quirked into a grin as he said, "I mean, if big, powerful FBI special agents can't protect you, who can?"

She liked having him here. Liked having him pet her dog, fill up her air with his manly scent. Liked watching his mouth as it curved into a sexy smile.

God help her, she wasn't supposed to think like this. Not about her partner. Not about a man who had made a point of saying that they could keep things very casual. What she was feeling right now was anything but casual. She wanted to stop talking and start making love.

Had to be the fever.

Except, she noted ruefully, she didn't have one.

"Been reading our recruitment package again?" she finally managed to ask, hoping her playful tone masked her feelings.

"Memorized every word when I was a kid." Dakota was brushing up against him as if she were a giant cat. Charley cringed when she thought of the amount of dog hair Nick was going to find on his pants once he really looked down. "This was all I ever wanted to be."

Content that he was going to remain, Dakota trotted

off to the sofa, hopped onto it and made herself comfortable in her favorite corner. Laying her head on her paws, she continued watching him until her eyes drooped shut.

"Really? Not me," Charley confessed. She'd toyed with the idea of going into law enforcement, but on a smaller scale. "But then, everything changed after Cris was killed. I decided that being an FBI special agent was the only career choice I *could* make."

He'd seen her dedication, knew how focused she was on bringing in the Sunday Killer. But that only took her to a finite point. "What happens after we catch the guy? If we catch the guy," he qualified.

There was no if. She couldn't allow herself to believe that, to even mildly entertain the possibility that, though more crimes went unsolved than solved, this particular series of crimes would join that group. She wouldn't allow it.

"*When* we catch the guy," Charley corrected. "I don't know. I'll probably continue being a special agent. Where else can you start out with the word "special" attached to your name?" she laughed. And then she grew serious. "I like making a difference and this is the best way I know how. Besides, I've gotten to like the people I work with."

"Like the people?" Nick echoed. Very carefully, he took the half-empty container out of her hand and put it on the table. His eyes never left hers the whole time.

"Yes." She smiled. She was flirting, she thought. She was actually flirting. Wow, this was a first. "Some of them."

His body was only a fraction from hers. Somehow, he had managed to slip his hands to the swell of her waist. Positioning her closer. Charley could feel her blood heating.

"You know," he told her slowly, his eyes still holding hers, "I've been having trouble sleeping since last Sunday."

Me, too.

She measured her words out slowly, so that he wouldn't hear how breathless she'd suddenly become. "They have pills for that."

His eyes were smiling into hers. "Not for this." His arms pulled her in closer than a sigh. The next moment, he lowered his mouth to hers.

Charley could have sworn she heard the strains of the "Hallelujah Chorus" echoing somewhere as she sank into the kiss. The moment that she did, a sense of urgency burst forward. Urgency and hunger. She wrapped her arms around him, raising herself up on her toes.

She'd only been in a holding pattern these past few days, pretending that she was unaffected by what had happened on Sunday. Pretending that it had been just one of those pleasurable things and not to make too much of it.

She'd never been much good at pretending. She knew that all the while she'd been holding her breath, waiting for this to happen again.

But it couldn't. Not now.

With a huge pang of regret, Charley wedged her hands against his chest. When she pushed him back, he looked at her in confusion.

"Nick, you'll catch my cold," she protested.

His laugh was deep and rich, like the first cup of black coffee on a cold winter's morning.

"I'll chance it," he told her. "Besides, that they do have pills for." Nick kissed her again. Over and over, shattering her reluctance while firing up his own desire. "Unless of course you don't feel up to it," he added, after what seemed like a blissful eternity, his breath skimming her lips.

Any noble thoughts of walking away for his sake melted away in the heat of his mouth. If she stopped now, she knew she was in genuine danger of withering away and dying.

Nick felt her grin as it spread out on her lips, touching his.

"Hell of a way to die, Brannigan," she told him, her eyes laughing. And then she sighed. "Can't think of a better one."

Damn but he wanted her. Desire pulsed through his veins, hardening his body and filling his head with improbable thoughts. And all the while, he felt like smiling. Hell of a mess he'd gotten himself into, he thought, enjoying every second of it.

"I'll see what I can do about keeping you alive," he promised.

Alive. That was how he made her feel, Charley suddenly realized. Alive. Completely and utterly alive. Alive the way she hadn't been before. He brought sunshine into her world. Sunshine and hope and a host of emotions she couldn't even begin to identify.

The moment his lips had come down on hers, all she could focus on was making love with him. Of racing to that final moment when all the fireworks went off simultaneously.

And yet she wanted to linger on the path as well.

To savor the way he made every inch of her flower with awareness.

She loved the feel of his hands as they passed over her, touching, claiming. Arousing. She cautioned herself to slow down, but she couldn't.

He made her feel insatiable.

"Your body's hot." His words were thick as he stripped away her clothing.

Twisting and turning against his hands, absorbing every pass, she found she had trouble concentrating as she tried to follow suit and remove his clothing as well.

"You might have something to do with that," she told him.

He stopped and looked at her. There was a note of concern in his voice when he spoke. "Are you sure I'm not pushing you?"

"What I am sure of—" her voice was low, husky, as it struggled past the desire that seemed to fill every single pore "—is that if you don't make love to me, Special Agent Brannigan, there's going to be a dead body found here and it won't be mine."

He laughed then. She felt the sound echoing within her own chest. Tickling her. Stimulating her.

When he smiled, the man was the personification of sin. And sin had never taken on such a tempting, pleasing form or seemed so delicious.

"Your wish," he told her, pressing a lingering kiss to the hollow of her throat, causing her pulse to jump even higher, "is my command."

For the next few hours, Nick made her forget about everything. Forget about her cold, about the serial killer she was so determined to bring down. Forget her very name. He made her forget everything except for the haven he had so unexpectedly and expertly created for her.

A haven where she could pretend she belonged, at least for a little while.

CHAPTER THIRTY-SEVEN

THE INTERIOR of the sedan she was sharing with Nick seemed smaller somehow. More confining than usual. Staring out the window, Charley drummed her fingers on the armrest. The restlessness pervaded her.

This wasn't like her.

She was supposed to be concentrating on the reason why they were sitting parked across the street from a dilapidated apartment building, waiting for the appearance of a man someone had tipped them off about this morning. A man whose face matched the one in the sketch they'd been circulating.

But all her thoughts kept centering on the man beside her. No matter how hard or how many times she tried to refocus them, they would just return to Nick. To the way he'd been the other night when he lit up her sky, not to mention every inch of her body.

Sitting here these past few hours, she'd become aware of every breath Nick took, of the faint scent of his soap, of the shampoo he used. Aware of absolutely everything about him.

It made her very uneasy.

She'd never been in this place before. Never been attracted to anyone so much that everything else, *everything*, took a back seat. Never spent any time before wondering whether or not the night would find them together in each other's arms. Never wasted moments wondering what a man was thinking. Or agonized over whether she was just being a fool or if something good had finally come her way.

What was she, eighteen? But even at eighteen, this hadn't been her. Why was it her now of all times?

It was too much to deal with, given everything else. She didn't have time for this, to feel this unsteady, this ambivalent. The case was supposed to be of paramount importance right now, nothing else. Solving this case meant life or death for the next possible victim. She had to remember that, had to keep her mind on the goal and not on the way Nick's hands felt as they moved along her body.

Her teeth sinking into her lower lip, Charley shifted in her seat. It was too damn hot in this car.

"You're quiet," she heard Nick comment. "You're never quiet. Something wrong, Charley?"

Yes, you've upended my whole damn world and I don't like it. She shrugged, still keeping her attention on the front of the building they were watching. "Just thinking."

Nick touched her face, breaking any concentration she struggled to maintain. When he softly brushed his thumb along her cheek, she had no choice but to look at him. If she hoped to summon a poker face, that hope died a quick death.

"Don't think too hard, Charley," he teased quietly, his mouth curving ever so slightly. "You'll wear your brain out."

His eyes spoke volumes, but she wasn't sure what they were saying. Right now, she was at a crossroads. She didn't actually know what she wanted from him. Or from herself.

SUNDAYS ARE FOR MURDER

And then she saw Nick stiffen. He was looking over her head.

"What?" Was he going to tell her not to get hung up on him? That he was one of those guys who came and went out of a woman's life, leaving an indelible impression but nothing more of himself? She was pretty sure she already knew that.

"Showtime, Special Agent Dow," he announced.

Nick swung his long legs out of the car and she turned to look over her shoulder to see what he saw. The man they'd been getting leg cramps for these past five hours was here and apparently entering his apartment building.

As she hurried out, Charley switched on her walkie-talkie. She needed to alert the others. "Suspect in view. All units converge. Converge," she repeated with urgency.

They came at him from all sides. Men and women, all wearing FBI jackets, swarmed around the tall, thin man, announcing their presence with shouts and warnings.

Clearly confused and frightened, Milton Hines didn't know where to look first. The paper bag with his groceries slipped from his hands and met the cracked concrete beneath his feet with a crash. Broken eggs ran together with the newly liberated mayonnaise, cradled by shards of glass. At the sight of the revolvers all aimed toward him, Milton raised his trembling hands above his head.

"Don't shoot, don't shoot," he begged. "I didn't do anything." He looked right at Charley as he repeated, "I didn't do anything."

Charley sidestepped the oozing mess on the ground, her eyes never leaving his face. "Well, then you won't mind coming with us for a little talk."

Milton lowered a hand to push his glasses up on his nose, then quickly raised it again, afraid of what the special agents around him might do. His breathing became labored and his brown eyes all but bugged out of his head.

Afraid to make eye contract with the woman he'd just spoken to, he looked at the man next to her. "Do I need a lawyer?"

"I don't know," Nick said evenly. "Do you?"

"I didn't do anything." This time, Milton ended his statement with a sob.

Nick turned Milton around and snapped handcuffs on his wrists while reciting his rights to him. Satisfied that the handcuffs were secure after giving them a tug, Nick ushered the man into a waiting vehicle at the curb.

"If you didn't do anything," Nick qualified, "then you won't need a lawyer." Protecting the man's head as he pushed him in all the way, Nick gave him a smile that had no humor behind it. "Just consider this a little joyride."

Charley's heart was pounding. The man in the back seat looked close enough to their sketch to have posed for it.

TEN HOURS LATER, they were forced to let the near-hysterical man go. Nick was the one who came to break the news to her. After interrogating Hines for several hours, Charley was taking a break. She'd just gotten water from the water cooler when Nick found her.

Milton Hines was not their man.

Charley crushed the paper cup in her hand, tossing it into the wastepaper basket with a hiss of disgust. "Looks like we have to replace his eggs and mayo jar." Frustration echoed in her voice. "Damn it, Hines looked just like the guy in the sketch."

Nick was as disappointed as she was. "Yeah, I know. But he has airtight alibis for at least two of the murders. We just finished checking them out. Hines was in Phoenix when Rita Daly was killed and he was involved in a traffic accident in Indio about an hour before the M.E. says the dental hygienist was murdered. Indio's near Palm Springs," he commented. "That's over a hundred and fifty miles from the scene of the crime. Hines would have never been able to make the drive in time."

"I'm a native, I know where Indio is," Charley snapped. Frustration got the better of her and she kicked the bottom of her chair. The next moment, she flushed, embarrassed at the momentary break. "Sorry. It's just that I'm so tired of getting my hopes up and then watching them be dashed again."

She wasn't saying anything the rest of them didn't feel, Nick thought. They were all getting pretty burned-out, putting in time after hours, all hoping that the extra push would yield the desired results. Every one of them felt as if they were on borrowed time. Someone else's borrowed time. And if they didn't find the killer soon, another body was going to turn up. Maybe even this Sunday.

But the other side of it was jumping on someone for the sake of having someone to hang the crimes on. That got them nowhere. And it didn't stop the killer. "Better dashing your hopes than sending an innocent man away."

Her eyes narrowed. The past few hours, her patience had been growing shorter and shorter, in direct contrast to her temper, which became more explosive by the second. "Are you lecturing me?"

"Just pointing out the obvious, Special Agent," Nick told her wearily. He paused, studying her. The added stake she had in this was making her edgier than the rest of them. Mentally, he cut her some slack. "Want to apologize again?"

She frowned, knowing he was right. She had to get a grip on herself, otherwise she was going to unravel. But that didn't change the way she felt right at this moment. Angry at an unfair world. "No."

Nick took her answer in stride. She was burned out. They all were. "It's Friday, Charley. I suggest you go home. Everyone else has."

She knew it was the hour and the situation, but she resented him standing there, telling her what he thought was best for her. "Everyone else's sister wasn't murdered by a serial killer."

"If you expect me to argue with that, I'm going to have to disappoint you. But I am going to say that you should give yourself a break." He nodded at all the files on her desk. It looked as if she was conducting a paper drive. "Go home, Special Agent Dow. You're not going to find anything in all that tonight."

Stubborn to the last breath, Charley dug in. "You never know."

Nick sighed, surrendering. The woman gave new meaning to the word *pigheaded*. But he was too tired to argue and he knew better than to try to haul her away physically. He straightened, moving back from her desk. "Well, I'm going home."

"Fine." Moving her mug to the far corner of her desk, she sat down. "Why don't you try unpacking some-thing when you get there? Maybe stay awhile."

He laughed shortly. He'd already decided to settle in for the long run. She'd made his mind up for him. But he knew better than to say that to her. "I'll give it some thought. G'night."

Charley looked down at the files on her desk. Or pretended to. "G'night."

The sound of his fading footsteps left her with an incredible sense of longing. Of sadness. She felt alone and it wasn't anything he'd said or done. She'd never shake the feeling of being in isolation until she solved this thing. Until she had the killer in her sights and made him confess.

Charley realized that she was clenching her hands. With effort, she forced herself to relax. But inside, the frustration continued.

They were going around in circles. In giant, pointless circles.

The killer had to be out there somewhere. Why hadn't anyone seen him? Why hadn't at least one of those calls panned out?

Her throat felt dry. She picked up her mug, thinking to get a cup of coffee. But as she lifted it, the sheet of paper it had been sitting on caught her eye. She had inadvertently moved the mug onto one of the sketches of the serial killer. The mug had formed a ring where it had made contact. Right over the serial killer's eye. It looked like half of a monocle.

A wave of recognition passed over her, only to be gone the next second. It teased her brain.

That looked like…

Stifling a sudden shiver, telling herself she was out of her mind, Charley grabbed a pen and began to trace the wet ring, giving it substance. Drawing in a small bridge over the man's nose, she made another ring over his other eye, giving him a pair of glasses.

Looking at the results, her heart tightened in her chest.

Quickly, like a woman possessed, she moved the

pen up and down, drawing in longer hair. When she was finished, her mouth was completely dry.

She was looking at a sketch of Alice.

CHAPTER THIRTY-EIGHT

THIS WAS CRAZY.

It had to be some kind of mistake. After all, it was just a rough sketch, nothing more. And the drawing was based on details given to them by a homeless man who regularly conversed with an imaginary man called Jonesy.

Charley picked up the sketch and looked at it intently. How accurate could the drawing really be? And yet she couldn't let this go. What if she was right?

She took out her cell phone, then put it away, squelching her impulse. She wasn't going to call Nick and tell him about this. More than likely, he'd either laugh himself sick or tell her that she needed an extended vacation. In her present mood, she'd be inclined to take his head clean off. If it wasn't Alice, Charley didn't want to embarrass the woman or herself in front of her partner.

Charley stared at the sketch and the changes she'd just made. Damn, but it looked just like Alice. Or someone related to the woman. Could Alice have a brother, a cousin? Could she possibly be protecting that brother or cousin? As the A.D.'s secretary, the woman was privy to information the public didn't have. She was in a position to know the task force's every move. That way, she could help whoever was doing this stay one step ahead of being apprehended.

This was insane. This was Alice. Alice, who was afraid of her own shadow. Alice, who had confided that she feared she'd be the next victim.

And yet…

An even more insane thought hit her.

What if the killer was Alice?

The more she struggled with the sketch, the more Charley knew she was right. Alice Sullivan, with her narrow, gaunt features, had the kind of face that could go either way. And she was always wearing those high-necked blouses and turtleneck sweaters. Even in the summer, Alice always looked formal, was always covered up. In the four years that Alice had been in their department, Charley couldn't remember ever seeing the woman wearing any other style. Was she dressed like that to hide an Adam's apple?

Alice? A man?

It made the hair stand up on the back of her neck.

"You're getting carried away, Charley," she muttered to herself.

But Charley rose to her feet and went for her purse. Only one way to put this to rest. To move on to something else if she was wrong.

She had to confront Alice, or whoever the hell had actually been working in their department these past four years.

ALICE SULLIVAN LIVED on the opposite outskirts of Santa Ana in a house that had been new more than a hundred years ago, when the city was just beginning to grow.

With the shadows of night around it, the elegant building looked as if it had fallen on hard times. The white paint had surrendered its battle against the sun and was buckling and peeling in too many places to count, even by the faint illumination cast by the street-lamp.

Arriving on Alice's street, Charley almost turned around. This was crazy. And if she was right, she could wait until morning. Tomorrow was only Saturday. Sunday would still be a day away.

But something, maybe dogged instincts, maybe the desire to find out that she *was* wrong, drove her on.

Pulling her car up to the curb, she turned off the engine and got out.

The lawn was immaculate, she noticed. Not a single weed or dandelion poked its head up amid the blades of green. It made her wonder why the house wasn't freshly painted. Given Alice's nature, it didn't add up.

Neither did thinking that Alice had something to do with the serial murders, and yet here she was at the woman's home.

Let's get this over with.

Going up the four steps, she paused on the front porch and then pressed the doorbell. She heard nothing. Was it broken? Trying it again, she listened intently and still heard nothing.

She knocked next. Her knuckles had hardly left the wood when the door opened.

Alice had on a long, flowing yellow silk robe, tightly tied at her waist. With one hand, she clutched at her throat, gathering the material closely to her. Utter surprise had her eyes all but bugging out.

"Charlotte, I didn't expect to see you here." Perfectly made-up eyebrows drew together in consternation. "Especially not at this hour. Is anything wrong?"

Looking at Alice, hearing her voice, reinforced all of Charley's doubts. Of course Alice wasn't the one she was looking for. She was too timid, too feminine, too everything. This was all wrong. Her mind had slipped a gear, that was the problem.

But she was here—she might as well stay for a few moments. Maybe look around to lay any last residual doubts to rest.

Charley did her best to appear contrite and tired. And play on Alice's sympathies. "Nothing's wrong, Alice, I just needed to talk to someone."

"And you picked me?" Alice's face lit up, making Charley feel that much more guilty about the thoughts she'd been entertaining. Alice opened the door wide. "Come in, come in, please." She shut the door and then flipped the lock. "It's not a safe neighborhood after dark," she explained, coming away from the door. "I must say, I'm very flattered you came to me. I would have thought you might have turned to Agent Brannigan. Or your ex-partner, Ben."

Charley was startled. How would Alice know about her visits to Ben? But then, she and Ben had been close the years they'd worked together. She supposed guessing that she might want to seek him out wasn't really much of a stretch.

"No," Charley said, "this is girl stuff."

"Ah, girl stuff." Alice smiled. "Would you like some tea?"

Tea didn't even come in last on her top-ten list. It was something she faced only when she was sick, and only as a last resort. But she forced a smile to her lips. "Tea would be very nice."

Alice nodded, gathering together the folds of her

flowing robe in order to move faster. "Wait here. I'll be right back."

"You have a lovely home," Charley told her as Alice left the room.

"Thank you," she responded from the hallway. "I've grown used to it."

What an odd thing to say, Charley thought. The moment Alice was gone, Charley immediately crossed to the only place in the room that might have held anything of interest. Against the far wall Alice had an enclosed oak bookcase. From the looks of it, it was old and had probably once cost a great deal. There were nicks and chips along some of the shelves. An attempt to negate the effects had been made by applying layer upon layer of lemon-scented furniture polish.

Losing no time, Charley opened the glass doors. The shelves were packed with books, arranged by topic and then placed by size. There were drawers beneath the shelves. She tried the center one and found it locked. So were the two that flanked it.

With an impatient hiss, Charley took something out of her pocket and began to pick the center lock. It went against every rule in the book. If she found something, she would have to lie about how she discovered it in court. But that was a step she would cross when she came to it. If she came to it.

Right now, she needed to find evidence that would either put this to rest, or tie Alice to the murders.

Charley's head swam. She felt as if she'd just taken a half-gainer into the deep end of the pool. Holding her breath, she opened the drawer, prepared to be disappointed.

Not prepared to find what she did.

There was a tray inside the drawer. A long, white tray with small compartments separating each item it held from the others.

There were thirteen crosses in the tray. Thirteen, because Rita Daly's cross had been lost.

As her heart thundered in her chest in triple time, Charley's fingers felt icy cold as she picked up the cross in the first compartment. The cross that was an exact duplicate of her own.

She knew what she would find even before she turned it around. Her breath lodged in her throat. The inscription read To Cris. Love, Mom.

The sudden crash nearly made her drop the cross. Her eyes darted to the doorway. Alice had dropped the tray containing the teapot and cups. Her face was a contorted mask of rage and fury.

The image of a harpy flashed across Charley's mind as the woman flew toward her from across the room.

"You shouldn't have done that!" Alice shouted. Her voice had lowered into a rumble of malice. "But then, you're a whore just like they were. Why would I have expected anything different from you?"

Charley quickly drew her gun. Though prepared, she didn't expect Alice to come charging at her. The woman ducked her head and aimed at her legs like a lineman making a game-winning tackle. Charley went down. Her gun flew from her hands.

Alice was on top of her, pinning down her hands and legs with surprising force. Then, unable to hold that position, Alice grabbed her little pinkie and twisted it in the opposite direction until Charley felt as if there were stars circling her head. Pain went shooting up her arm into her shoulder and neck. It took everything not to cry out in anguish.

"You taught me this move, remember?" Alice taunted. "To protect myself against the serial killer." She laughed as she said it.

The next moment, Alice jerked her up to her feet, twisting her arm behind her back. Charley had started to turn when the other woman slammed her head against the wall, knocking the wind out of her. It took everything she had to remain conscious.

Grabbing the handcuffs from Charley's belt, Alice quickly snapped them on her wrists. "Those were all very handy little self-defense tips, Charlotte. I don't know if I ever properly thanked you." Alice smirked as she spun her around to face her.

"You can thank me by letting me go."

"Sorry, not an option." Alice's eyes almost glittered as they looked down at her.

"Didn't think so," Charley murmured, doing her best not to let the woman see that she was really worried. No one knew she was here and she was powerless at the moment. She'd been in better positions. "Then you are behind this? Behind the murders?"

"Behind it, in front of it, any position you like," Alice boasted.

The woman was crazy. Certifiably crazy. "Why?" Charley demanded, anger giving her strength. "Why did you kill them? Why did you kill my sister?"

"Because they were whores. All whores. Whores like that strumpet from Babylon. Whores are supposed to be stoned, eliminated. Killed. You should know that, being a whore," Alice spit in her face.

Charley's mind raced. God, but she wished she'd

called Nick and told him. It wasn't so much that she was afraid for herself as she was afraid that Alice would somehow manage to continue with her spree and go unpunished. Unstopped.

Alice sneered. "What, you don't think I know about you and Nick Brannigan? Don't know about how you tempted him, lay with him and made him forget about all his responsibilities?"

Charley had no idea what she was babbling about. The only thing she knew was that Alice had slipped up. "You made a mistake, Alice. Nick Brannigan is not a married man."

"Yes, he is!" Alice screamed the words into her face. "You don't have to take formal vows to be married. You just need to make a commitment." She brought her face down close to Charley's. "And by planting his seed in that woman, he made a commitment. He was her husband and you came between them."

"The woman is dead," Charley pointed out.

"She has an eternal soul. Souls don't die," Alice insisted.

"How do you even know about all this?" Charley demanded. As far as she knew, Nick hadn't told anyone else about the woman who had killed herself. She'd barely gotten it out of him herself.

Alice's smile was pure malice, and triumph shone in her eyes. "Everything goes through me, one way or another. I've gotten very good at the computer. Agent Brannigan's wife's brother gave a statement to the police on his arrest," she informed her. And then impatience creased her brow. "But all that's beside the point. The point is, you're not fit to live. You break up homes, lead good men astray—"

"Who, Alice, who was led astray?" Charley asked. *Keep her talking. Make her confess everything. The longer she talks, the better the chance that you can figure out a way to get free.* "What set you off on this crusade of yours?"

The triumphant look on Alice's pale face intensified. "Sorry, you're going to go to your grave wondering about that." And then she sneered. "I'm not in the mood to make a clean breast of it to a whore."

After pushing Charley down onto a chair, Alice grabbed a fistful of her hair to hold her in place. Charley saw the knife in Alice's other hand and struggled not to cringe.

"I think I'll carve your cross while you're still alive. The others were dead when I did it. I have to keep you alive until Sunday, but there's no reason I can't make you repent. You disappointed me most of all, Charlotte." Alice began to breathe heavily. "We could have been friends, but you had to ruin everything. Everything!" Alice screamed.

She was looking up into the eyes of a person who was possessed, Charley thought, trying to curb the panic that began to tighten around her heart. She tried to pull back.

Pain flashed through the top of her head as Alice yanked harder.

"Alice, you're going to regret this."

The grin on the gaunt face was nothing short of macabre. "Not nearly as much as you are, Charlotte."

CHAPTER THIRTY-NINE

CHARLEY PULLED against her ropes, but they were too tight. No way was she going to get free. All she could do was stall and hope that she could somehow talk the deranged woman out of torturing her.

She banked down her fear. "Alice, you don't want to do this."

The secretary's eyes seemed to glow with pleasure. Her breathing had grown shallow and quick, as if this torture gave her sexual gratification.

"Yes, I do. Don't you understand? This is the only way you'll be saved? I *have* to do this. Your soul will go to hell if I don't." She surprised Charley by releasing her hair. Alice was focusing on her forehead. It took everything Charley had not to shiver. "Now hold still. If you move, the lines will be wavy." She angled her head, like an artist, searching for just the right light. "You can't get to heaven if the lines are wavy."

Intent on what she was about to do, confident that there would be no further resistance, Alice leaned forward. The second she did, so did Charley. Straining, Charley managed to push herself up on the balls of her feet just enough to bridge the small distance that existed between them. With a bloodcurdling cry, Charley head-butted her would-be emancipator as hard as she could.

Caught off guard, Alice cried out in surprise as pain seared through her. She stumbled backward, almost losing her balance.

"Bitch! Whore!" Alice screamed at her, enraged. "I'm trying to save you!"

"Your saving days are over."

An almost feral, guttural sound escaped her lips as Alice swung around. In an instant, she had a new target. Clutching her knife, she raised it, ready to strike, to slash away at the man who had somehow materialized out of nowhere to challenge her authority.

"Nick!" Charley stared, afraid that terror had somehow made her hallucinate. But Alice was reacting as well. He had to be real. He had to be here.

Her head was spinning, aching from the head butt she'd used to ward off Alice.

Nick had arrived moments ago. Seeing Charley's car parked at the curb, his instincts warned him that if he knocked on the door, it would be too late. So he'd quickly circled the house and found a window in the back that he could jimmy open.

The second he did, he heard Alice cursing and Charley trying to talk to her. His heart froze in his chest. He didn't remember drawing the gun he now had in his hand. The gun he aimed at the willowy figure in the yellow dressing gown.

"What the hell's going on here?" he demanded. He spared a single, quick glance in Charley's direction. If he hadn't come when he did… Nick couldn't control the flash of temper that surfaced. "Don't you know any better than to go after a suspect by yourself?"

Keeping himself as far away from Alice as he could, Nick took a step toward Charley.

"Don't," Alice warned angrily. She pointed her knife at him, ready to run him through at the slightest movement on his part. Her eyes looked red rimmed and maniacal.

And then an expression came over her face that stunned Nick. It appeared almost pathetic.

"Don't touch her, Dad," Alice pleaded. "She's evil. Can't you see Alice is evil? Look what she's made you do already. She's made you commit adultery, sinning in the very church where people come to hear you preach to them every Sunday. To hear you tell them how to be good." A sob tore from her throat. "Why, Dad? Why did you let Alice lead you astray like that? I know what Mom's like, but why wasn't I enough for you? I would have done anything, *anything* for you."

The killer's face turned dark, her eyes malevolent. "But all you wanted was her." She squared her thin shoulders, as if preparing herself for an unseen battle. "And now I have to kill you both. Kill you so that you can be washed clean again. Become pure again." The reedy voice became almost singsong. "God doesn't want you if you're not pure. That's what you said. Over and over again, that's what you told me."

Breathing harder now, Alice pressed her lips together. Her eyes gleamed as a savage cry tore from her throat. Fury radiated from every inch of her body as she raised the knife high and charged at Nick.

It happened so fast, it didn't even seem real. All Charley knew was that she had to deflect Alice's knife before it reached Nick. Using the chair for leverage, Charley threw herself in Alice's direction with all her might. Falling, she managed to just catch the woman's legs, tripping her. Alice, Charley and the chair went down with a hard clatter.

Crashing to the floor, Alice hit her head against the corner of the white stone fireplace. Her wig slid off as she screamed. And then her expression went blank.

Nick, his weapon trained on the fallen figure, quickly circled around to get to Charley. His heart felt permanently lodged in his throat. Was she crazy? He could have shot Alice if it came down to that. There was no need for Charley to take that kind of a risk.

He squatted beside her, his gun trained on the unconscious serial killer. "Are you okay?"

"I've been better," Charley ground out. She hurt in more places than she could count, starting with the roots of her hair. But hurting was good. Hurting meant she was still breathing. "But I'm alive and that'll do for now."

Still holding his gun on Alice, Nick hooked his arm around Charley's waist and brought her and the chair into an upright position. His eyes never leaving the inert form beside the hearth, he undid the ropes around Charley's chest and legs. Unable to do it with one hand the way he would have preferred, he lay the gun at his feet and used both hands.

The room pulsed with tension.

"Any more tricks up your sleeve?" he asked.

"Fresh out."

Alice, the killer, had referred to her father's lover as Alice. Had her personality split, or had she taken on the identity of her first victim?

Her first victim.

Charley's eyes grew wide. "Cris wasn't the first one she killed."

"Apparently not," Nick agreed. The ties gave him trouble. "Where the hell did she learn to make knots like this?" He cursed roundly. "Finally!" he declared, throwing the rope on the floor.

Charley bounced to her feet, nearly tripping over the rope. She wanted to be as far away from the chair as possible. But she was still cuffed.

"The keys to my handcuffs are in my pocket." Holding her hands to the side, Charley presented her left hip to him.

The gun back in his hand, Nick shifted it to his left hand, then slipped his right into Charley's pocket. The fit was tight and he had to wiggle his fingers to get to the bottom and the keys.

"In some areas, this would be considered foreplay," he commented.

"That's what got us in trouble in the first place," she reminded him. "Or at least me."

She felt Nick's fingers along her thigh as he located the keys and drew them out. Charley eagerly held up her iron-clad wrists. They were chafed from where she'd attempted to struggle against the steel bracelets.

"Why the sudden change in M.O.?" Nick wondered out loud as he unlocked her handcuffs.

Charley shook her head. "No change." She saw the protest rise to his lips. She rubbed first one wrist, then the other, relieved to be free again. "Alice, or whoever that is, somehow felt that you were eternally bound to the woman who killed herself. In Alice's mind, you were married. That made me the whore of Babylon." Nick raised his eyebrows at the label. "Her words."

Cautiously Charley crouched down beside the serial killer. She pulled the wig completely aside and found herself staring down at the face of the man in the sketch. "Who the hell is this, anyway?"

Nick came to stand next to her. "Some deranged person whose father was a minister."

Charley rose, backing away. "Dead minister from the sound of it."

Nick nodded. Using the handcuffs he'd just removed from Charley, he crouched down and snapped them on the killer's wrists after positioning them behind the man's back.

The sound of a gun being cocked brought him quickly around.

Charley was standing only a foot away, her own weapon drawn and aimed at the unconscious killer.

"Charley, what are you doing?" Nick asked, his voice low, calm, as he slowly rose to his feet.

"Getting even." Her hands shook slightly as she held the gun in them. It was aimed dead center at the serial killer's head. "He killed Cris, Nick. I found her necklace in the drawer. He took it as a souvenir. He killed my sister and wanted to relive the experience every time he looked at her cross." She blinked away the tears beginning to form. "Damn it, Nick, you can't talk me out of this. I need to kill him."

He never took his eyes off her. As carefully as possible, he approached her, cutting the distance down one inch at a time.

"Charley, we've got him. Dead to rights, we've got him. Don't do this," he begged. "Don't throw away your career and your life just for a momentary lapse."

"It's not a lapse," she insisted, struggling to keep her voice from breaking. "He made my family's life a living hell. My mother's in an institution because of him, my sister's in a grave. My father's done nothing but live and breathe his capture for the last six years. Whoever the hell he is, he has to pay for that."

"He will, Charley, he will." Nick took another step forward. "He's never going to hurt anyone again. And your mother and sister would never have wanted you to do this. This isn't you, Charley," he told her softly. "This cretin takes revenge, you don't. You don't," he repeated. As he did, he slowly removed the weapon from her hand. Once he had it, he put the safety on and tucked it into the waistband of his jeans.

Something broke inside of her. Charley crumpled into his arms and began to cry.

"It's over, honey, it's over," he told her softly again and again as he stroked her hair.

And then he just held her until she had no more tears left. He held her for a long time.

CHAPTER FORTY

"OKAY, I'LL BITE. Just how did you manage to suddenly appear like some knight in shining armor riding to my rescue?"

More than an hour had passed since Nick had handcuffed "Alice Sullivan" and called in the task force. In that entire time, Charley's head had been spinning, processing very little of what happened around her.

She found it hard to believe that the nightmare was finally over. Harder still to believe the killer had been among them almost from the first.

It wasn't until she was in the car with Nick, on their way to rouse a judge in order to get a search warrant, that Charley remembered to ask the question that had first occurred to her when he had appeared in "Alice's" living room.

Nick glanced in Charley's direction. They'd left twenty people behind them, give or take a few, combing the immediate crime scene. "Alice" had finally come around after the paramedics had used common smelling salts to make him regain consciousness. Rather than say anything, the serial killer cried.

Charley had sat beside Nick in silence since she'd buckled up. He'd let her alone, content with the fact that she was alive, and that he'd prevented her from being charged with the serial killer's murder. If Charley wanted her space, to pull herself together or whatever, he was okay with that.

But hearing her voice was a relief to him. He wasn't used to her being so quiet. He'd grown accustomed to the sound of her endless chatter.

"I called you when I got home and you didn't answer. Not your home phone, not your cell. I can't explain it, but I got this uneasy feeling, like maybe something was off, something was wrong." He realized he was pressing down too hard on the accelerator and forced himself to ease back. "I swung by your apartment, but you weren't there, so I went to the office. I figured if you were still working, I was going to drag you home."

He took a deep breath, reliving the feeling in the pit of his stomach when he saw what she'd done to the sketch they'd released.

"That's when I saw the alterations you made to the sketch." They came to a stop at a red light. Nick slanted a glance at her. The main thing that had kept going through his head was why hadn't she called him about this? Why had she gone off on her own? "I believe when I first came to the Santa Ana field office, someone said something to me about always 'sharing with the class' and not riding off like the Lone Ranger." His eyes went soft. "Why didn't you share with the class, Charley? Why didn't you at least call me?"

"Light's green," she pointed out. She heard Nick mutter under his breath and then shift from the brake to the gas. "And say what?" she asked as they began to travel again. "That I thought the A.D.'s secretary, a woman who looked like the personification of a large bird, was really our serial killer? That I thought maybe

'Alice' might actually be a transvestite, or a man in drag committing the murders? If I had said that, you would have had me locked up."

There was no arguing that he would have thought she was hallucinating, but that didn't change what happened. "Instead, you were almost killed, *would* have been killed if I hadn't come in just in time."

"Alice was going to wait for Sunday to kill me." Charley did her best to make light of it and take away the dark edge. "You're going to hold that over me, aren't you?"

He knew better than to push. Very little was gained that way. So he laughed and said, "I figure I can get a little mileage out of that, yes." But then something inside him refused to make a joke out of it. "Oh damn, Charley, that nutcase could have killed you." And if that had happened, he would have never forgiven himself for not second-guessing her. For not being there to save her.

His head reeled from the consequences.

"I know, you already said that." She looked at him. Nick was pulling the car over to the side of the road. Before she could ask him why he'd done that, he'd turned off the engine. And then he unbuckled his seat belt. "What are you doing?"

He didn't answer her. Instead, he reached over and hit the release button for her seat belt, then pulled her into his arms as best he could from that position. Her eyes widened in surprise a beat before his mouth went down over hers.

Nick kissed her with all the feeling, all the emotion that ran rampant through him. And all the while, one thought kept repeating itself in his head.

He could have lost her.

And until this very moment, he hadn't realized just how badly that would have hurt. How devastated he would have been. Not just for an hour or a week, but quite possibly, for the rest of his life.

When he let her go some three minutes later, shaken and not a little dazed, Nick gave her a warning. "Don't ever, *ever* do that to me again, Charley. Do you understand?"

She understood, or thought she did. And what she understood sent tidal waves through her world.

But even so, she clung to humor as if it was a life preserver. Clung to it until she could examine her own feelings.

Charley ran the tip of her tongue along her lips. Whatever happened between them, there was no denying the man was one hell of a kisser.

"Right," she said in a voice that was deliberately light. "No more social calls to serial killers who dress up like women." She raised her right hand as if taking an oath. "I promise."

His eyebrows drew together over the bridge of his nose as he started the car. "Charley." There was a warning note in his voice.

Charley stared at his profile. There was a little nerve winking in and out along his jawline. For the first time since this awful business had gone down tonight, she felt something akin to a smile budding.

It was with no small amount of glee that she came to her conclusion. "You care, don't you?"

Nick kept his eyes straight ahead, fixed on the road they were traveling. "Yeah."

Charley's smile grew.

THE SEARCH WARRANT issued by a bleary-eyed Judge Monroe allowed them to return and methodically sift through the old Victorian house, all in the name of finding clues to "Alice Sullivan's" true identity.

Sam, Bill and Jack looked more than a little surprised to see Charley return. It was taken for granted that Nick would drop her off at her apartment after they'd obtained the search warrant. They all thought she'd been through more than her share tonight.

Sam spoke up first. "What are you doing back?" he asked. His eyes shifted from Charley to Nick. The accusation was unspoken but clear.

Nick spread his hands. "Don't look at me. I wanted to take her home. You guys know better than I do how pigheaded she can be."

"You've got one get-out-of-jail card, Brannigan, and you just used it." She put a pair of latex gloves on. "Got my second wind," Charley told Sam, answering his question. "Besides, I won't be able to sleep tonight anyway. Not until I get a clue about who or what that lowlife is."

"Whoever he is, it's pretty clear he—or she—had a crush on you," Sam said. The observation brought him a swipe at the back of the head from Charley.

Staying out of hitting range, Bill lifted his shoulders in an elaborate shiver. "To think, we worked with her-him-whatever for two years."

"Four," Charley corrected. "You joined the team late," she pointed out. "'Alice' became the A.D.'s secretary when Mrs. MacGuire retired. 'She' was handpicked out of the data-processing pool for 'her' efficiency."

Jack laughed, shaking his head. "Think how he must feel now, knowing the killer was right under his nose all the time. It's got to get to a guy. Even a guy like Kelly."

"Well, there's an upside to that, I guess," Charley observed.

All four men looked at her incredulously.

Bill put it into a single demanding word. "What?"

Charley smiled. "At least his wife'll know that he's not the type to fool around with his secretary."

"Not unless he's got god-awful taste," Bill commented.

Charley made no reply. She was focused on the bookcase in the rear of the room. She went toward it now, intent on retrieving the rectangular box in the center drawer.

She got as far as putting her hand on the drawer before Nick moved in, putting himself in the way. Charley raised her eyes to his in a mute query, confused about what he was up to.

He looked at her meaningfully. "Let me do it," he said quietly.

And then she understood. If he was the one who uncovered the box of souvenirs the killer had collected, there would be no question of prior knowledge. She had gone through the drawer without a warrant. A clever lawyer would get that out of her and have the evidence thrown out of court. Since she hadn't actually told Nick where the souvenirs were kept, he wouldn't be guilty of introducing tainted evidence.

Charley lifted her hand from the drawer and then stepped back.

Nick opened the drawer. Very carefully, he took out

the rectangular white tray. Once he set it on the coffee table, he examined its contents.

Inside the tray, neatly arranged were thirteen crosses, each still on its chain, each inhabiting a tiny cubicle of equal proportions.

Nick shut the box again. "We've got everything we need right here," he told the others. "Even without a confession."

Kneeling before the fireplace, Bill glanced in their direction just before his gloved hands came in contact with something hard and metallic lodged inside the chimney. "I think I've got something," he announced.

Using both hands, he grasped the hidden object and gave it a hard yank. Dirt and debris rained down into the hearth, creating a cloud of dust that took a moment to subside. In the cloud's wake a rectangular metal box came clattering down.

The fall broke the lock and the lid popped open. Photographs and papers came spilling out like so many escapees from a prison.

"Eureka, I believe the man said," Bill muttered in wonder as he stared down at the treasure trove.

CHAPTER FORTY-ONE

CHARLEY DIDN'T WANT to waste any time getting to the photographs within the box. She had Nick drive her to the field office while Jack and Bill drove her car back. A cold chill kept roaming along her back as she viewed captured images from the serial killer's past. There weren't all that many, but enough to give her a feel for the life he had led.

He was a thin, sad-eyed boy. There were photographs of him alone and him with a dour-faced older woman.

Probably his mother, Charley thought. The woman looked as if she might have once been pretty, but the expression on her face negated that. For all intents and purposes, she was a caricature of a strict headmistress out of an old melodrama.

Then there were the half pictures. Photographs with pieces missing where another person might have been standing. Except in one case.

"This was a time bomb, looking to go off," she commented.

When stopped at a light, Nick glanced over. Charley held up the photograph she was looking at. It was of the serial killer as a teenager. He was standing on one side of someone, with the woman who was most probably his mother standing on the other side. The figure in the middle had no head. That piece of the photograph had been ripped away. What remained had sustained multiple holes delivered by most likely a pencil. It looked as if the body had been stabbed repeatedly.

Charley angled the photo, trying to discern as much as she could about the mystery figure in the middle. He was wearing a black suit jacket, black pants and she could just make out something white around the neck region. Maybe a collar?

She had a feeling she was looking at the killer's father. "The guy might have been a minister."

Nick took his foot off the brake. He laughed drily. "Either that, or he was an umpire."

There had been a great deal of anger dispensed on the man's image. "From the looks of it, he certainly struck out with our 'suspect.'"

Charley all but spit out the last word. *Suspect.* That was the technical, noncommittal term they were all supposed to use. There was no way in hell that the man the team had taken into custody was a mere "suspect." With all due respect to their judicial system, she thought darkly, "Alice Sullivan" or "John Doe" as he had now become since he refused to give them his real name, was the inhuman monster who had cut short the lives of fourteen women and had ruined countless other lives as well. Lives that would never be put back together again.

There was no one else out on the road at this time of the evening. Nick slowed so that he could gaze at her for more than half a heartbeat. And then he smiled. "Nice work, Special Agent Dow. You got your man."

For reasons she didn't have the luxury to delve into right now, when Nick uttered the last phrase, her mind focused, however briefly, on him.

The next moment, she managed to tear her thoughts away and back on target. "Thanks," she murmured. "Wouldn't be here without you."

He didn't rub it in, the way she knew he could have. Instead, all Nick said was, "What are partners for?" making her wonder if he was up to something, or if the job had gotten to her and she was being paranoid.

WITHIN TWENTY MINUTES of finding the box of photographs, Charley had the entire task force assembled in the field office in a conference room. The photographs along the back wall bore silent witness to the proceedings. Charley couldn't help glancing at the first photograph in the lineup before addressing the team.

We got him, Cris. We got the bastard.

Turning toward the team members, she dove in. They had a lot to do but, for once, it was with the full knowledge that they had gotten who they were after. And that the women in Southern California didn't have to look at their calendars in fear as Sunday approached.

"Okay, I want copies made of these and distributed." She dropped the box onto her desk. "I want several different photographs released to the press." She picked up two that she had deposited right on top. "Like this one of our killer when he was a teenager, or this one, standing in front of the church. Maybe someone seeing it will remember him and/or the church." She pushed the box toward Bill, who had originally discovered it, and Sam. Her meaning was clear. "I want a photograph taken of our John Doe after someone cleans him up and takes that awful makeup off him." She reached for the box just as Bill was taking it. He looked at her quizzically. "Publish that photograph of the mother, too."

Sam frowned, taking the photograph out. He shuddered in response to the woman's expression. "We sure that's his mother?"

Charley shook her head. "We're not sure of anything, but we will be," she promised. "*Somebody* has to recognize him." She looked around at the faces of the people surrounding her desk. It didn't look like enough for the avalanche that might ensue. "We might need extra people on the phones, but I want every single lead tracked down. Sam—" she turned to the man on her left "—I want his alter ego traced. Maybe there is or was an Alice Sullivan. Use the social security number our human resources department has on file and track down any past income-tax filings. See how far back they go."

She leaned against her desk, exhausted but utterly wired at the same time. "Maybe we can find out what happened to the real Alice Sullivan. Or at least her point of origin. Who knows, she might somehow lead us to whoever is in our holding cell right now."

As the task force members broke up to follow instructions, Nick moved next to her. With his body blocking direct view of her from the others, he lowered his voice and asked, "Don't you think maybe you should get some rest?"

There was a time when she would have taken his suggestion as an insult, a slam against her stamina and capabilities. But instead, something warmed within her. Nick was just watching out for her like any good partner would.

"I appreciate the concern, Brannigan. But this is really a lot better than rest." She smiled. "Besides, I'm so wound up now, if I lay down, I'd probably spin like a top."

"I'd pay to see that."

"Hold on to your money," she advised and then winked. "Maybe next time." She moved away from her desk and opened the bottom drawer to retrieve her purse. "But I do have to go somewhere. I'll be back in an hour."

For a moment, he debated whether or not he should intrude. Concern got the better of diplomacy. "Want me to drive?"

"Thanks, but I need everyone else working on this. I need you to go through 'Alice's' computer, see if there's anything there we can use." She set her mouth grimly. "There might be more bodies we don't even know about. It wasn't as if the Sunday Killer had an ego thing going."

Nick nodded. "I'm on it."

She paused for a second to look first at the row of victims' photographs on the wall, then around the room at the activity that was underway. God, but she felt like cheering.

"We're finally hot, people," she cried. A number of faces turned her way. All seemed relieved that the ordeal was finally coming to an end.

Nick caught her eye just before she walked out. "My thoughts exactly."

There was something in his tone, in his look, that made her feel with a fair amount of certainty that he wasn't talking about the case. A thrill rippled through her. She didn't bother banking it down. She felt too good to even try.

"Yeah," she responded.

As she turned on her heel, the excitement she felt continued to vibrate through her, giving no indication that there was an end in sight.

CHARLEY STOOD on the porch. Shifting, she heard it creak beneath her feet. For the first time in a very long while, she was tempted to use her key. To insert it into the lock, turn the doorknob and just walk into the house where she had grown up. To keep walking until she was inside her father's bedroom. When he woke up to look at her, she'd tell him the news. Tell it to him the way she had envisioned and dreamed of doing all these many years.

In a way, it still felt like a dream.

Except that she knew it was real. Her scalp still hurt where "Alice" had pulled her hair.

Charley took her hand out of her pocket, leaving the key there, and rang the doorbell.

When Christopher Dow finally came to the door, his eyes bleary, his white hair divided into peaks and tufts that bore silent testimony to the fitful way he tossed and turned each night, his mood was far from the best.

"What do you want?" he growled angrily at his daughter, not bothering to open the door any further than it already was.

Some things never changed. He always was a bear when he woke up, Charley thought. "I came to tell you before you read it in the paper."

"Tell me what?" he snapped. And then he stopped and stared at her. His eyes widened. The next words out of his mouth came in a whisper. "You got him."

Everything within Charley smiled except for her lips. "We got him."

"You're sure?" The question was almost timidly uttered.

She knew her father. The man was cautious to the nth degree, never wanting to venture out on the side of optimism unless it was guaranteed. They'd already had one false alarm a number of years ago, when she and the task force had thought they had the right man, only to suffer the disappointment of discovering, a number of days later, that they didn't.

That time had taught her. From then on, she never gave any indication of how the case was going. But now she could. For his sake. "I wouldn't be here if I wasn't."

Her father scrubbed a hand over his face, still afraid to absorb the information. The scratchy sound of flesh meeting stubble whispered between them.

"And he'll pay?"

"He'll pay," she promised.

Only then did her father take a step back, silently inviting her into the house. When she made no move, he asked, "Do you want to come in?"

Charley shook her head. "I can't. There's still a lot to do. I've got to be getting back." She was already moving away from the door. "I just wanted you to know."

Her father nodded and she took that as her cue to turn away. But she'd only taken a few steps toward her vehicle when he called out to her.

"Charlotte."

Charley stopped and turned only her head, looking at her father over her shoulder. "Yes?"

It took him a moment to form the words. There was a sea of emotion in the way and he was a man who refused to display any. But even so, Charley could see tears in his eyes.

"You did good."

Charley smiled for the first time. It burst free from deep within her. "Thanks."

Her smile grew as she hurried back to her vehicle.

CHAPTER FORTY-TWO

"WE'VE GOT A HIT."

It was less than twelve hours later. Twelve hours of exhaustive, nonstop work. The only personal time Charley had allowed herself, other than her visit to her father, was a phone call to David to tell him the good news. Her brother had been overjoyed, displaying all the emotion that their father had not.

But once she'd gotten off the telephone with David, she'd worked along with the other members of the task force, trying to come up with a further lead. And trying, too, to discover how something like this could have happened in the first place.

The answer to that was easy enough once they had "Alice's" computer. Not the one at the Bureau's field office, but the laptop from the house. The person who had been Assistant Director Kelly's secretary for four years was an excellent computer hacker. Forging the necessary documents and background references had been a walk in the park for him.

"I went back ten years," Nick told her. "According to the back taxes filed with the Internal Revenue Service, there was an Alice Sullivan with that social security number living in the Bakersfield area." He checked the notes he'd made. The resourcefulness of the criminally insane never ceased to amaze him. "Ten years ago, the real Alice Sullivan was working as a secretary for a Reverend Sykes in Beaumont, a small town of about three thousand people located right outside of Bakersfield."

Charley's mouth dropped open. A reverend. Like the decapitated figure in the photograph.

They'd been right.

The pieces were all coming together to form a whole.

Charley was on her feet immediately. There were answers that were best gotten firsthand. "You and I are going to Beaumont," she told Nick.

"Funny," he said, following from the room, "I had someplace a little more exotic in mind for our first getaway together."

He was probably kidding, Charley thought, but just in case, she tossed the word "rain check" over her shoulder as she hurried out.

SHE CLEARED the trip with Kelly via cell phone on the way to the airport. Eager to put this behind him, the assistant director gave her no argument about expenses. Charley was counting on that.

The Bakersfield airport was less than forty-five minutes away by plane. Kelly had arranged for a car to be waiting for them as soon as they landed. Gassed and ready, the 2002 navy-blue sedan came equipped with a navigator as well as maps of the area. No one wanted to waste any more time. It was almost a race now to get all their ducks in a row before the media pounced on the latest developments.

The drive to the work address imprinted on Alice Sullivan's W-2 forms took longer than the flight.

Despite the full color GPS unit on the dashboard, Charley missed the building the first time around because it had been abandoned and left in disrepair.

"I'm asking for directions," she announced, looking at Nick. She expected to be confronted with the typical male reticence, since in her experience, men drove, they didn't inquire. Even her brother was like that.

But Nick just waved her on, directing her attention to a group of bicyclists up ahead who might be able to help.

Not your typical male, Charley thought as she honked the car's horn. The bicyclists all pulled over to the side of the road.

Only one of the bicyclists was acquainted with the church she was asking about.

"They've built a new one closer to the center of the town," the woman told her. "There's talk of tearing the old one down, but nobody can get the minister's wife to move."

Charley exchanged looks with Nick. "The minister's wife still lives there?"

The young blonde bobbed her head. "Mrs. Sykes. The church committee felt sorry for her. Her husband disappeared and her son ran off somewhere, oh, maybe five, six years now. It's straight back down the road you came. Can't miss it."

"Want to bet?" Nick murmured under his breath.

"You didn't see it, either," Charley pointed out as she turned the car around again.

"Got me there," he admitted.

Charley pulled the sedan up a weed-encrusted driveway, parking the car before a run-down building that looked as if it had come straight out of some second-rate horror movie. It was badly in need of paint and several pairs of loving hands to replace loose boards and missing shingles.

She realized she was looking at the same church that had been in the photograph.

"I think I saw this one in *The Amityville Horror*," Nick commented, leading the way up the cracked walk. "The first sign of a spinning head and we're out of here."

"That was in *The Exorcist*. I think you're mixing your horror movies," she told him. What kind of a person lived in a place like this? she wondered.

A person who raised a serial killer.

The bell was broken, so she knocked. And then Nick tried when there was no response. Finally, someone approached the door.

An older version of the woman in the photographs Bill had discovered opened the door. She stood barring the way with her heavyset body, her eyes cold and assessing as she looked first at her, then at Nick.

Her breath was stale, like lost years, when she spoke. "If you're here to sell me something, I don't have any money. If you're here to rob me, you're going to be disappointed."

"Mrs. Sykes, I'm Special Agent Dow, this is Special Agent Brannigan—"

"I didn't ask for any agents, special or otherwise," she said, slamming the door in their faces.

"Not exactly the last word in friendly," Nick commented.

"We can come back with a warrant, Mrs. Sykes." Charley addressed her warning to the door, raising her voice. After a beat, it opened again. Edith Sykes shifted her piercing, disapproving blue eyes from one face to the other and then back again.

And then she surprised them by sighing and shaking her head. It was as if all the fight had suddenly and inexplicably drained out of her.

"You're finally here," she said with both anger and resignation in her voice. "I've been waiting for you for six years." As if consulting with her own inner voice, she stood undecided before them, and then stepped back. "Come in."

It was a cold house. Charley felt it instantly. The house was filled with shadows and the ghosts of unhappy hours that had somehow knit themselves into a sorrowful lifetime. A house where love was not even an invited guest or an occasional intruder.

Mrs. Sykes closed the door softly behind them. "You're here about Ronald, aren't you?"

Charley and Nick exchanged glances. It was Nick who asked, "Ronald?"

"My son." The words came out as if she was uttering a curse in mixed company. "I always wanted a daughter. But I got Ronald. A male. Just like his father." Her mouth was pinched. The condemnation said it all. The woman raised her chin with an air of superiority that her parishioners must always have resented. "Robert got what he deserved, you know. Nothing short of that. Ministers are supposed to be good, not weak."

"And what is it that your husband deserved?" Nick asked the woman.

There was malice in the blue eyes. "To burn in hell with his whore for all eternity."

"Did you kill them?" Charley asked in the same voice she might have used to ask the woman if she had received the morning newspaper.

Mrs. Sykes glanced at her in surprise. And perhaps

a little sadness. "Me? No. I wanted to, but no, I left that to God and he used his instrument." There was something incredibly chilling about the smile on the woman's face. Seeing it, Charley had to concentrate in order not to shiver. "He used Ronald."

"And what did Ronald do?" Charley asked.

"What he had to do," Edith snapped. "What needed to be done," she said a little more softly. "Oh, he babbled about saving them after it was over. About having no choice because their souls would be lost otherwise, but I knew better. They had no souls." She enunciated each word with the same amount of emphasis. "They were just evil and evil should never see the light of day."

She continued ranting, her voice and zeal growing until she looked and sounded almost possessed. Charley remained silent, giving the woman center stage, letting her talk until they had what they needed. Edith Sykes did not disappointment them.

The story emerged in full regalia. Her "pathetic" son, as she referred to him, had adored his father and tried in every manner to cull the reverend's favor. For all of Ronald's efforts, Robert Sykes barely noticed his son.

"He did, however, notice his slut of a secretary," Edith said, her mouth turning down. "When Ronald found the two of them having sex in the back of the church early one Sunday morning like two dogs in heat, he killed them both. I found him there, standing over their bodies, crying like the weakling he was. He was talking to his father as if Robert was still alive. As if he could explain his behavior."

"Why didn't you call the police?" Nick asked.

SUNDAYS ARE FOR MURDER

Edith eyed him. "And have them cause a scandal for me as their last act of defiance? Not very likely."

"What did you do with the bodies?" Charley asked matter-of-factly.

"I had Ronald get rid of them."

"Where?" Nick pressed.

There was hostility in her voice at his tone. "In the basement. Robert was to pour a new floor for me. There was some cement left over. He and his whore are under it now," she informed them smugly.

"How did you explain that your husband was missing?" Charley asked.

"I told people that the Reverend had been called away, transferred to another parish back east and that I didn't want to leave. I was born near here, you know," she said with an air of someone who expected her every movement to be observed and preserved. And then she shrugged. "Ronald took off not long after that. Not so much as a Christmas card from him in all these years." Everything in her manner condemned the child she'd given birth to. "Just like his father," she repeated.

They let her talk longer, but she had little to add. For the most part, she repeated what she had already said. With each pass, she sounded more incoherent, more fanatical.

When Mrs. Sykes finished, Charley put in a call to the local police to have the woman arrested as an accessory after the fact. Given her mental state and her rage, Charley felt fairly confident that the late Reverend Sykes's wife had earned herself a padded cell.

"IT'S ALMOST ANTICLIMACTIC," Nick commented as they disembarked from their plane at John Wayne

Airport. It was a good five hours after they had boarded it for Bakersfield.

He took the words right out of her head, Charley thought. Walking through the noisy terminal, she glanced at him and smiled.

"I know, after all this time, waiting, trying to find just a shred of evidence, suddenly it all comes tumbling together. Kind of takes your breath away."

"My breath's more stable than that," he commented. And then he looked at her. "It takes more than that to take mine away."

She had no explanation, or excuse, for the little thrill that shimmied up and down her spine. "Like what?"

He stopped just past the electronic doors that let them out to the parking lots. "Like you."

Because the notion of what was behind the words un-settled her, Charley tried to shrug it off. "You're punchier than I am."

"Doesn't change the facts," he said softly.

If he kept talking like that, she was going to jump him, right there, right now, with a terminal full of people as witnesses.

"Look, why don't you pack it in?" she suggested as a last-ditch attempt to save herself. "You've earned it, doing the knight-in-shining-armor bit, coming to my rescue and all."

"What about you?"

The Robert Frost poem about having miles to go before he slept raced through her brain. "I've got one more stop to make."

"The office?" he guessed.

"No, they've got everything they need right now." She approached the car. They'd come here in hers, so she was going to have to drop him off before she went where she needed to go. "This is personal."

"So are car accidents." He positioned himself on the driver's side. "You navigate, I'll drive."

Her eyebrows narrowed. "You saying I'm too tired to drive?"

If she was spoiling for a battle, she was going to have to fight it alone. "That's exactly what I'm saying."

She gave it thought—exactly five seconds—and then opened the passenger door. "If I wasn't so tired, I'd argue with that."

"Good, get in the car." Sliding in himself, Nick watched as she buckled up. "Where to?"

She gave him the address to the psychiatric hospital that had been her mother's address for the past five years. Nick made no comment as he nodded and pulled out of the lot.

CHAPTER FORTY-THREE

CHARLEY DID HER BEST, under the circumstances, to talk him out of coming into the hospital with her. Admittedly, she was too drained to put up a decent fight.

She said as much when he pulled the car up into a parking space. "This isn't fair, you know. You're taking advantage of the fact that I'm having trouble thinking straight."

He shrugged carelessly. "I use what I can."

So she gave in even though her pride told her that she should have stood her ground. Because this was so very personal, so very private.

But because it *was* so personal, there was this need inside of her to hold on to something. To hold on to someone.

Even so, she had her doubts as she walked in through the front entrance of the squat, two-story building that did its best to put on a cheery face and pretend that all was well within.

It wasn't and everyone knew.

Charley never felt more naked than when she came to visit her mother. She could feel every one of her emotions exposed for all to see. But because she was Charley, she gave it one more shot. Nick was as tenacious as she was, a disturbing thought if ever there was one.

"I don't see why you won't stay in the car. I won't be long," she promised, her words almost echoing down the long, winding corridor as she led the way to the room where her mother existed. She couldn't truthfully refer to it as the room her mother lived in because her mother wasn't really living. Claire Dow was in a place somewhere in between the living and the dead, a limbo created for the soul that hadn't quite left the body yet.

Nick noticed that she had picked up her pace. He matched it.

"I don't like sitting in cars," he told her. "It's too much like a stakeout. Besides," he added after a momentary internal debate about the wisdom of giving voice to his concern, "you look like you might need the moral support."

Charley slowed down. She didn't know whether to feel touched or invaded. "This is my mother, not my father. She never uttered a harsh word to anyone, least of all to me."

"That's why I figure you might need the support. Because it hurts to see her like this."

Charley did her best to hide the effect his words had on her. She'd never had anyone care like that before. She'd even shut her old partner out on this level. But there was no shutting out Nick.

"Wow, one course in Bureau profiling and you think you can read everyone."

"Two courses." He held up two fingers. "And not everyone. Just you, Special Agent Dow. Just you."

The way he looked at her, she could almost believe him. Her mouth felt dry. "Lucky me."

They'd reached her mother's door and Charley hesitated before it, the way she always did. Not because she wanted to turn on her heel and run, but because she was bracing herself.

And then she glanced at Nick, about to make one last appeal for him to remain outside. Or better yet, to say she'd decided to come back tomorrow because she was too tired for this.

"If you're going to say you've changed your mind, I'm not buying it." Leaning over her, Nick knocked once, then turned the knob and opened the door.

Sunlight streamed into the room, bathing everything it touched in shades of gold. Claire Dow sat by the window. Her face was turned toward the sun, but she seemed to be in the shade. It was as if the rays couldn't quite penetrate the shield of sorrow that surrounded her like an invisible veil.

Charley approached quietly, on the balls of her feet, as if any undue noise would disturb the silent woman in the armchair.

"I brought someone with me, Mama." Her voice was so soft Nick had to concentrate to hear her. Moving so that she could be in her mother's line of vision if the woman turned her head, Charley introduced him. "This is my partner, Special Agent Nick Brannigan."

"I'm very pleased to meet you, Mrs. Dow." He moved forward, just to the left of Charley, and took the woman's hand in his. He kissed it, then gently placed it back in her lap.

Charley thought she saw something flicker in her mother's eyes but knew it was just wishful thinking on her part.

"Your daughter's a very good FBI agent, Mrs. Dow," Nick said to her mother. "She keeps me on my toes constantly."

Claire continued looking out the window.

Charley pressed her lips together, wondering if any of the words she was about to say would get through to her mother, or if, like every other time, they would float aimlessly through the air. She knew in her heart that if this news had come five years earlier, it might have meant all the difference in the world. It might have saved her mother from this living tomb.

"We got him, Mama. We got the man who killed Cristine. And it wasn't a mistake." Charley dropped down to her knees beside her mother's armchair, the way she used to when she was a little girl. She placed her hand over her mother's, trying desperately to reach her, to somehow bridge the gap that only seemed to grow wider each time she came here. "It wasn't me he was trying to kill. It's not my fault that she's gone, Mama. It's not."

It was a plea, a plea for her mother's forgiveness. A plea to her mother to have her return.

And then Charley felt hands coming around her. Felt Nick carefully raising her to her feet. As she allowed herself to be helped, she realized there were tears on her cheeks.

Realized it at the same time that Nick saw them. Before she could brush the tears away, he had tilted her head toward him. Very gently, using his thumb and knuckles, he did away with the evidence.

"C'mon," he whispered softly, urging her to move toward the door. "Give your mother a little time to absorb what you just told her."

If only, she thought. If only it was just a matter of time and nothing more.

Charley shook her head, struggling to keep fresh

tears from seeping through. "I don't even know if she heard me."

Nick checked the older woman's profile. "She heard." Something within his gut told him that he was right.

But Charley wasn't sure. "I wish I could believe that."

Taking her hand, Nick looked at her. His eyes held hers. "She heard, Charley," he repeated. "She heard."

Charley clutched the thought to her.

They were almost at the door, about to open it, when the words "not your fault" seemed to softly float through the air.

Charley's heart stopped. She looked at Nick, her eyes wide. He was as surprised as she was, and then he simply looked pleased. Like someone whose faith had been rewarded. He nodded, confirming what she was afraid to ask.

Charley looked past his shoulder toward her mother. "Mama?"

But the woman at the window continued looking out. A sliver of sunshine seemed to slip along her form, drawing it out of the dark.

"Did you hear it?" Charley asked once they were at the car. "Or was I just hallucinating?" Because at this point, she was ready to believe almost anything.

Nick grinned at her as he got into the car, commandeering the driver's side again. She realized that she had let him hang on to the keys. "I heard."

She eyed him, trying to make a decision as she slipped on her seat belt. "You're not just humoring me."

He laughed softly, starting up the car. "Humoring you is not one of the things on my list, Charley. I heard what you heard. Your mother spoke." He backed the car out of the space. "And when she's ready, she'll come back to you."

He guided the car onto the road. Charley stared at his profile. "Since when did you become such an optimist?"

He slanted a glance toward her. "Must be the company I keep. It rubs off no matter how hard I try to stay out of the way." He realized that he hadn't a destination. "Now can I take you home?"

She leaned back in the seat. The day had been forty-eight hours long. "Now."

There were only a few cars on the road. He relaxed a little. Perhaps for the first time in a very long time. Glancing at her profile, Nick gauged his words carefully, trying to keep them casual. At least in tone.

"You know, my family's coming out here for the holidays. At first they wanted me to come there, but they decided maybe they'd like to see what a Christmas with temperatures above freezing is like." He paused, then said the only sentence that counted. "I'd like you to meet them when they come."

"Sure, why not?" But even though her tone was almost flippant, something inside her was cheering. This could be the beginning of something meaningful. "You met my mother. Kind of."

Nick spared her a look as he took another turn. "It's going to be all right, Charley."

"Yeah, it is." And for the first time in six years, she believed it was a distinct possibility.

* * * * *

Be sure to read Marie Ferrarella's next novel, HUSBANDS AND OTHER STRANGERS, *available February 2006 from Silhouette Special Edition.*

Everything you love about romance...
and more!

*Please turn the page for Signature
Select™ Bonus Features.*

Sundays Are
For Murder

Alternate Ending

Sundays Are for Murder
by
Marie Ferrarella

*After reading Sundays Are for Murder, did you
wonder how the story would have ended if there
had been an alternate last chapter? If so, read on
and find out what could have been....*

ALTERNATE LAST CHAPTER

CHARLEY DID HER BEST to talk him out of coming with her to the hospital. Admittedly, she was too drained to put up a decent fight.

She said as much when he pulled the car into a parking space. "This isn't fair, you know. You're taking advantage of the fact that I'm having trouble thinking straight."

He shrugged carelessly. "I use what I can."

So she gave in even though her pride told her that she should have stood her ground. Because this was so very personal, so very private. But because it *was* so personal, there was this need inside her to hold on to something. To hold on to someone.

Even so, she had her doubts as she walked through the front entrance of the squat, two-story building.

Charley never felt more naked than when she came to visit her mother. She could feel every one of her emotions being exposed for all to see.

But because she was Charley, she gave it one more shot, even though she knew it was hopeless. Nick was as tenacious as she was. A disturbing thought if ever there was one.

"I don't see why you won't stay in the car. I won't be long," she promised, her words almost echoing down the long, winding corridor as she led the way to the room where her mother existed.

Nick noticed that she had picked up her pace. He matched it.

"I don't like sitting in cars," he told her. "It's too much like a stakeout. Besides," he added after a momentary internal debate about the wisdom of giving voice to his concern, "you look like you might need the moral support."

Charley slowed down and looked at him. She didn't know whether to feel touched or invaded. "This is my mother, not my father. She never uttered a harsh word to anyone, least of all to me."

"That's why I figure you might need the support. Because it hurts to see her like this."

Charley did her best to hide the effect his words had on her. She'd never had anyone care like that before. She'd even shut her old part-ner out on this level. But there was no shutting out Nick.

"Wow, one course in Bureau profiling and you think you can read everyone."

"Two courses." He held up two fingers. "And not everyone. Just you, Special Agent Dow. Just you."

The way he looked at her, she could almost believe him. Her mouth felt dry. "Lucky me."

They'd reached her mother's door and Charley hesitated before it, the way she always did. Not because she wanted to turn on her heel and run, but because she was bracing herself. And then she glanced at Nick, about to make one last appeal for him to remain outside. Or better yet, to say she'd decided to come back tomorrow because she was too tired for this.

"If you're going to say you've changed your mind, I'm not buying it." Leaning over her, Nick knocked once, then turned the knob and opened the door.

Sunlight streamed into the room, bathing everything it touched in shades of gold. Claire Dow sat by the window, where the attendants had placed her this morning. Her face was turned toward the sun, but she seemed to be in the shade.

Charley approached quietly, on the balls of her feet, as if any undue noise would disturb the silent woman in the armchair.

"I brought someone with me, Mama." Her voice was so soft, Nick had to concentrate to hear her. Moving so that she could be in her mother's line of vision if the woman turned her head, Charley introduced him. "This is my partner, Special Agent Nick Brannigan."

"I'm very pleased to meet you, Mrs. Dow." He moved forward, just to the left of Charley, and took the woman's hand in his. He kissed it, then gently placed it back in her lap.

Charley thought she saw something flicker in her mother's eyes, but knew it was just wishful thinking on her part.

8

"Your daughter's a very good FBI agent, Mrs. Dow," Nick said to her mother. "She keeps me on my toes constantly."

Claire continued looking out the window.

Charley pressed her lips together, wondering if any of the words she was about to say would get through to her mother, or if, like every other time, they would somehow float through the air without finding a target. She knew in her heart that if this news had come five years earlier, it might have meant all the difference in the world. It might have saved her mother from this living tomb.

"We got him, Mama. We got the man who killed Cristine. And it wasn't a mistake." Charley dropped to her knees beside her mother's armchair, the way she used to when she was a little girl. She placed her hand over her mother's, trying desperately to reach her, to somehow bridge the gap that seemed only to grow wider each time she came here. "It wasn't me he was trying kill. It's not my fault that she's gone, Mama. It's not."

It was a plea, a plea for her mother's forgiveness. A plea to her mother to have her return.

And then Charley felt hands coming around her. Felt Nick carefully raising her to her feet. As she allowed herself to be helped, she realized there were tears on her cheeks.

Realized it at the same time that Nick saw them. Before she could brush the tears away, he had tilted her head toward him. Very gently, using his thumb and knuckles, he did away with the evidence.

"C'mon," he whispered softly, urging her to move toward the door. "Give your mother a little time to absorb what you just told her."

If only, she thought. If only it was just a matter of time and nothing more.

Charley shook her head, struggling to keep fresh tears from seeping through. "I don't even know if she heard me."

Nick glanced at the older woman's profile. "She heard." Something within his gut told him that he was right.

BONUS FEATURE

"I wish I could believe that."

Taking her hand, Nick looked at her. His eyes held hers. "She heard, Charley," he repeated. "She heard."

Charley clutched the thought to her.

They were almost at the door, about to open it, when the words "Not your fault" seemed to softly float through the air.

Charley's heart almost stopped. She looked at Nick, her eyes wide. He was as surprised as she was, and then he simply looked pleased. Like someone whose faith had been rewarded. He nodded, confirming what she was afraid to ask.

Charley looked past his shoulder toward her mother. "Mama?"

But the woman at the window continued looking out. A sliver of sunshine seemed to slip along her form, drawing it out of the dark.

"DID YOU HEAR IT?" Charley asked once they were at the car. "Or was I just hallucinating?" Because at this point, she was ready to believe almost anything.

Nick grinned at her as he got into the car, commandeering the driver's side again. She realized that she had let him hang on to the keys. "I heard."

She eyed him, trying to make a decision as she slipped on her seat belt. "You're not just humoring me."

He laughed softly, starting up the car. "Humoring you is not one of the things on my list, Charley. I heard what you heard. Your mother spoke." He backed the car out of the space. "And when she's ready, she'll come back to you."

He guided the car onto the road. Charley stared at his profile. "Since when did you become such an optimist?"

He slanted a glance toward her. "Must be the company I keep. It rubs off no matter how hard I try to stay out of the way." He realized that he hadn't a destination. "Now can I take you home?"

She leaned back in the seat. The day had been forty-eight hours long. "Now."

There were only a few cars on the road. He relaxed a little. Perhaps for the first time in a very long time. Glancing at her profile, Nick gauged his words carefully, trying to keep them casual. At least in tone.

"You know, my family's coming out here for the holidays. At first they wanted me to come there, but they decided maybe they'd like to see what a Christmas with temperatures above freezing is like." He paused, then said the only sentence that counted. "I'd like you to meet them when they come."

"Sure, why not?" But even though her tone was almost flippant, something inside her was cheering. This could be the beginning of some-thing meaningful. "You met my mother. Kind of."

Nick spared her a look as he took another turn. "It's going to be all right, Charley."

"Yeah, it is." And for the first time in five years she believed it was a distinct possibility.

"You know," he continued in his casual tone, "you've got a lot on your shoulders. Most burdens are easier when you share them."

She glanced at him. Where was this headed? "You volunteering to adopt my mother?"

He laughed. "No, I was thinking more along the lines of marriage."

Charley shifted in her seat. The seat belt bit into her shoulder. "You want to marry my mother?"

"Someone a little younger, with a smart mouth." He glanced at her. Okay, so she was going to need the whole nine yards. He could go the distance. She deserved it. "You, Charley, you. I want to marry you."

This had to be some trick. Her hearing was going. Or her mind. "Why?"

He blew out a breath. Was she trying to make him jump through hoops? Was that what a woman wanted when the most important question of their collective lives was on the table? "Why do you think?"

She ran a hand over her forehead. "I've done enough thinking these last few days, Special Agent Brannigan. I don't want to think." And then she grinned. "I want to be spoon-fed the information."

Spoon-feeding it was. He told her the truth. All of it. "Because I love you. I've tried to talk myself out of it, but I'm not listening. I've never felt about a woman the way I do about you. You make me think of forever instead of one day at a time. I like that. I like the idea of you in my forever." He paused, collecting himself. Hearing silence. He glanced at her, worried. "You're not saying anything."

No, she wasn't. She was thinking and wondering how she'd gotten so lucky all at once. The case solved, her mother speaking and a man who made her feel as if the Fourth of July was exploding inside her was proposing. "For once, I'm listening."

"And?" The air in his lungs needed to be moved out by conscious thought, then replaced.

"I like what I'm hearing."

BONUS FEATURE

She still hadn't said yes. "And?"

"Forever sounds pretty good to me. Scary," she told him honestly, "but good."

If Mohammed wouldn't come to the mountain, the mountain was going to have to make the trip to him. "So is that a yes?"

She laughed, enjoying herself. "If you have to ask, then you're not as special an agent as I thought you were."

"Wait until we get to your place, and I'll have you reevaluate that statement," he promised meaningfully. And then, because he was concerned about her, he added, "Unless you're too tired."

"I just suddenly got my second wind." It took everything she had not to throw her arms around him. "Oh, and by the way, I love you, too."

Nick grinned. Having her say the words out loud didn't change anything, but he had to admit it was really nice to hear.

Impulsively he pulled over to the side of the road. It wasn't every day a man proposed to the woman he was meant to be with. It deserved to be sealed with a kiss.

Being Nick, he didn't put it off.

THE END

The Spy Who Loved Her
by Marie Ferrarella

CHAPTER ONE

"NO, I DON'T WANT TO MEET him," Marla O'Connor told her best friend for the third time as the elevator doors of the St. Charles Hotel closed. Miraculously, given the number of people staying at the San Francisco hotel, the car was empty. With luck, she'd reach the twelfth floor in a minimum of time, with a minimum of words from Barbara. Barbara and her fiancé, Stewart, were staying on eleven. "I don't want to meet anyone. This is a teachers' convention, Barbara, not one big singles bar. I came here to learn, not date."

A pert brunette, half a head shorter than her friend, Barbara frowned. "The two are not mutually exclusive, you know. All I'm saying is that you have to keep your eyes and options open."

It was an old tug-of-war, one Marla engaged in with not only Barbara but, it seemed, every female relative in her family tree, including her three very-much-married sisters.

"I'll take care of my own options, thank you very much. And as for my eyes, they're going to be open on this book." She held up the hardback she'd purchased in the hotel gift shop.

"I'd say something here, but it would be X-rated." Barbara glanced at the title. *Mystery at Midnight.* "Honestly, Marla, you're an English teacher. That's pure pulp."

Not to me, Marla thought. To her it was pure escape. She shrugged, tucking the book back under her arm. "So I'm letting my mind go slumming. There's nothing like a good mystery to get you stimulated."

Barbara's smile was positively wicked. "I can think of something else—to get you stimulated."

Marla stopped her before she could elaborate. "I'd rather curl up with a good book than a bad man."

Barbara's smile widened. "That all depends on your definition of bad."

"Does the word *lemon* mean anything to you?"

"Let's see." Barbara pretended to think as the floors slowly passed. "Lemonade sipped slowly at poolside while some gorgeous hunk of a man is gently rubbing suntan lotion on my warm body."

Marla could only sigh, shaking her head. "You are hopeless."

BONUS FEATURE

"No, ever hopeful." Barbara grasped Marla's arm imploringly. "Marla, we're in the big city here. This is our chance to kick up our heels."

"You kick, I'll read."

Barbara sighed in defeat. "Then you won't meet Stewart's friend?"

"Not tonight I won't." Marla had all the excitement she wanted between the covers of the new mystery. "I'm just going to take a nice hot shower, call room service and crack open this book."

"You're passing up the chance of cracking open champagne instead."

Barbara, never one to give up easily, had already elaborated her dinner plans with Stewart and his friend at length.

"Afraid so."

The elevator stopped on eight to pick up two people. Marla moved to the side. "Sometimes I don't know why we're still friends," Barbara whispered to her. "If you're not careful, you're going to turn into Mrs. Everett."

The name from their mutual past pulled up no fond memories. "I promise that before I turn into a dour old assistant principal I'll go out with Stewart's friend."

Barbara looked at her reprovingly. "Dour old assistant principals are made, not born."

The door opened for Barbara's floor. The other two people got off. "Go." Marla all but shooed

18

Barbara out. "Have fun. I hope you have a great dinner. I'll be perfectly happy alone in my hotel room. After listening to all those long-winded seminars I could use a little diversion."

Barbara held the door open with her hand. "My point exactly."

"A diversion that didn't try to get into my bed at the end of the evening just because I absently smiled at it over dinner."

Barbara shook her head. "You really don't know what you're missing."

"Then write me a note about it—fifty words or less. Remember, spelling counts."

"Yes, Miss O'Connor." Barbara released the door and it closed.

Marla laughed to herself as she stepped off the elevator on her floor. Barbara meant well, but she just didn't understand. Barbara found it easy to meet men, to strike up conversations and be vivacious. She, on the other hand, became instantly tongue-tied when confronted with a prospective date. It was only when she was living vicariously, imagining herself the heroine of a wonderful novel, that she knew just what to say, that her conversation was pithy instead of pathetic. She positively shone in the English literature class she taught at Bedford High. But her light was extinguished when it came to face-to-face encounters, especially with good-looking men.

Maybe someday, she mused, someone like Rick Arrowsmith would come into her life. The blurb about the hero in the suspense-thriller she'd picked up made him sound like everything she wanted in a man. Tall, dark, handsome and mysterious, with a lethally sexy mouth and piercing eyes that radiated heat and desire. All that and a mind that was razor sharp.

What a combination. If she ever found a man like Rick Arrowsmith... With a sigh, Marla put her card into the slot of her hotel door and slid it down, then turned the latch.

The lights were on inside the room. Funny, she didn't remember leaving them on. Maybe housekeeping had come in. But there was no reason for them to do that, she thought. This was her first day here—she hadn't even unpacked, much less rumpled her bed. There'd only been time to throw her suitcase into the closet before dashing off to the first lecture.

Bemused, she stepped out of her shoes and tossed her new book on the bed. She could have sworn she heard a shower running. Had to be in the room next to hers.

You'd think an elegant hotel like the St. Charles would have walls that were thicker than that, she thought.

Marla debated calling room service immediately, but then decided against it. She didn't want the waiter arriving while she was in the shower, and she planned to be in there for a very long time. There was something incredibly soothing about having hot water cascade all over your body.

Like a man's hands, gently gliding along your skin.

She pulled herself out of her reverie before she sank in too deeply. Unbuttoning her blouse, she pulled it out of the waistband of her slender dark skirt and walked to the bathroom.

The sound of running water grew louder. She supposed the bathrooms were positioned back-to-back to save on plumbing fixtures.

Opening the door, she felt the mist first. It surrounded her like a veil that then slowly lifted.

A second later she saw the outline of a naked male body on the other side of the translucent glass.

CHAPTER TWO

THE SCREAM FROZE in her throat like a solid piece of ice refusing to melt. Marla took a shaky step back on rubbery legs, feeling for the doorknob. Sneaking into her vision peripherally, the scattered clothes on the floor registered.

22   Male clothes. To go along with the very male body in her shower.

His form was visible through the translucent glass. Specific details might be blotted out, but she could definitely make out the essence of the man. And his essence was nothing short of powerful.

Marla swallowed. The solid block of ice remained lodged where it was.

She was in the wrong room.

The thought desperately tattooed itself through her brain. That had to be it. She was in the wrong room. All the rooms looked alike. That would explain why the lights had been on.

But not, she realized almost instantly, how she'd managed to gain entry into the hotel room—with her card key. With all the different combinations being constantly scrambled, that would mean that the entry codes on her card had to have somehow come out matching the ones to the room she was in.

It was a hell of a coincidence, defying astronomical odds. Odds she wasn't up to calculating at the present moment.

The moment melted away as the man behind the glass suddenly became aware of her presence and grabbed for something that looked as if it was perched on a ledge above the showerhead. The next second, as her heart rate accelerated to a number that surpassed any records known to science, the glass door was pushed back and she found herself looking at the barrel of a gun. A gun that was pointed right at her chest. The gun barrel was almost as sleek as the wet, dark-haired man pointing it.

The frozen scream melted, emerging as a loud gasp by the time it passed Marla's lips. She wasn't sure if the gasp was a reaction to the weapon or the man. Both looked equally lethal from where she was standing.

Sharp blue eyes swiftly scrutinized every inch of the room before returning to her. "What are you doing here?"

She was trying very hard not to give in to a growing sense of panic. "I—I thought this was my room. Twelve-twenty." Even as she said it, the hope that she was in the wrong room evaporated. She specifically remembered seeing the numbers on the door before inserting the entry card into the lock.

Not a muscle on the angular face moved. "Twelve-twenty's supposed to be empty."

"It's not." Her throat had become utterly dry. She found herself longing for the lump of ice she'd imagined there several hundred heartbeats ago. "There was a mix-up at the front desk and the hotel gave me this one." Her mind searched for an explanation. The room had been a last-minute switch. Maybe it hadn't been properly recorded and that was why he was here now. With a gun. Naked.

"I can—I can go," she offered, taking another step back. She froze when she heard the safety being released.

"Stay where you are."

"Okay." Her voice sounded almost normal to her ears, an incredible feat since within her chest her heart was shifting to and fro erratically like a runner trying to avoid a sniper bullet—which at the moment seemed chillingly appropriate to her. "But could you please, um…"

Unable to put her request into a complete sentence, Marla lowered her eyes to his torso, but only for the briefest of seconds. Her meaning, she hoped, was clear, if unspoken.

Raising her eyes again, she saw it.

The smile.

Actually, it was only a glimmer of one. But to her it was even more unsettling than the weapon and his unclad, stone-hard body with its sheen of droplets slowly making their way to his feet.

Somewhere within the confines of a museum in Europe, Michelangelo's David was stepping down off his pedestal, hanging his head in defeat at being usurped.

Maybe it was a dream.

Maybe she'd fallen asleep while reading her book and was even now lying on the bed. It was a silly thought, but it sustained her for all of half a minute until the fogged mirror sent part of her reflection back at her, dashing the desperate thought. She wasn't on the bed—she was here, in the bathroom, trying not to look at the best built man God had ever created.

"Sorry," he apologized in a voice that, at least for the moment, sounded far less threatening. "I forgot I was naked."

He'd be the only one who forgot, although if she were honest he was also the only one who was sorry. She tried to draw oxygen into her lungs as her gaze darted anywhere but at her cleansed intruder while he reached for a towel.

Quickly he secured the towel around his waist, moving so fast that his weapon seemed to remain trained on her almost the entire time.

And then it came to her. With the realization, Marla straightened the backbone that had been in serious jeopardy of melting. This had to be a put-on, she decided, a put-on cashing in on her single-minded romance with mystery novels. "Barbara put you up to this, didn't she?"

"Barbara?" he repeated in a puzzled tone of voice.

Empowered by her theory and managing to ignore the contours of the glistening man less than three feet away from her, Marla felt on solid ground. "Very good—act confused." The pieces came to her in a rush. "You've got to be Stewart's friend. The one she was talking about in the elevator. I don't know how you managed to get into my room, but my answer's still the same. I don't like blind dates."

Although in light of what she'd seen she had to admit that the scale was seriously beginning to tip in the direction of this particular blind date.

"Neither do I." He cocked his head as if straining to listen to something in the other room. "Are you alone?"

A sinking sensation took hold of her stomach. This wasn't her would-be blind date. He was exactly what he seemed—a man with a gun. Panic produced her next answer. "No, I'm here with people, lots of people."

He motioned her out of the bathroom. There was no one in her room and no sign that there had been. Humor curved his mouth. "Are they tiny people?"

"No, they just stepped out. To get ice," she tacked on, her mind working in fits and starts.

"Who stepped out?" He moved around the room like smoke, infiltrating everything, assuring himself that they really were alone. "Husband, lover?"

"Yes." The answer was breathless.

Bending, he quickly checked under the bed. "Which is it? Husband or lover?"

Stupid, she upbraided herself. "Both. He's my husband and my lover."

He looked at her face then and she could feel his eyes touching her. "I'd say he was a lucky man. And an understanding one to let you go out on blind dates." Marla closed her eyes, feeling like an idiot.

"You're alone, aren't you?"

Her eyes flew open, alert. "Yes, but I can scream."

"I wouldn't advise it." At the window he drew the curtain back and looked down at the street. "Damn." Letting the curtain drop again, he looked at her. She thought he was deciding on something. She hoped it wasn't whether or not to kill her. "What's your name?"

"Marla O'Connor." Maybe Barbara would come to drag her to dinner, she prayed, all the while watching the man's every move.

"Well, Marla O'Connor, it looks like I'm going to need your help."

His weapon remained pointed at her.

CHAPTER THREE

PANIC CLAWED AT HER THROAT. It took Marla a second before she found her tongue, another second before she could use it. "Exactly why do you need my help?" Many things suggested themselves to her, none of them good. "And just who are you?"

28

He took a step toward her, admiring the way she held her ground despite the fear in her eyes. He wished he could be completely honest with her, but he'd learned that honesty had its price and it was one he couldn't afford to pay right now.

"Who I am is unimportant. As to why I need you…" His eyes slowly washed over her. "At another time or place, my answer would be completely different. But for the moment my situation supersedes any notions of wining and dining a beautiful woman and spending the night getting lost in her ample charms."

The many bad things Marla had been worrying about temporarily faded into the background. "Beautiful woman?" No one had ever called her that before—if she didn't count her father, who'd been obligated to say that to his ugly duckling of a daughter.

A sexy smile lifted a corner of his mouth. He really would have liked to linger with her, to entertain both of them in the variety of ways he'd learned to pleasure a woman. But even now they were closing in on him, and there was little time left. Perhaps none.

"As beautiful as twilight along a Tahitian shore, but this is no time to hunt for a compliment, Marla O'Connor." He got down to business. "I need your charge card."

The roller-coaster ride she was on came to an abrupt halt, nearly throwing her from the lead car. Anger usurped common sense. "A robbery? This is a robbery? Aren't you a little underdressed for a robber?"

He supposed it probably sounded that way, but he didn't have the time, or the freedom, for elaborate explanations. "No, this is a crisis and I'm underdressed because everything I was wearing was a potential tracking device."

He'd wet his clothes and his shoes down in an attempt to short-circuit the devices. Technology being what it was, he had no idea where the tracking device might have been hidden or if there was more than one.

"Tracking device?" Horror and confusion danced together through her. The only tracking device she could think of was the kind given to people under house arrest. "Are you a criminal?"

There were times when the line that separated one side from the other was finer than he liked, but saying so would only frighten her. "No, I'm one of the good guys." He held out his hand. "Now, the charge card, please."

Marla wasn't sure exactly what possessed her, but she raised her chin. "I know tae kwon do."

He doubted it, but he humored her. "Of course you do. And I know seven ways to kill a man, none of which requires noise."

She swallowed. "Seven?"

30

"Seven." He took another step toward her, cutting the distance between them to almost zero. "The card, please."

She struggled not to tremble. There had to be ground rules of some sort. "No."

He was doing her a favor, asking. In his place, Wallace would have ransacked the room until he found her purse, but he preferred hanging on to the notion that he was civilized. At least, whenever possible.

His voice was dangerous. "No?"

Her escape was blocked by the bed and her knees almost buckled when she backed into it. "No, not until you tell me your name and what's going on."

He shook his head, random drops of water falling from his black hair. "You're either very brave or very stupid, Marla O'Connor. I'm hoping it's very brave. It might come in handy."

He paused, whether to debate or create, she didn't know. And then he answered her. In part. "My name is Erik Carter. I can't tell you what this is about, but if I don't show up tomorrow at precisely two o'clock on the Golden Gate Bridge to meet a certain person, some very bad things are going to happen to some very nice people." This time he raised his weapon, cocking it. "The card, please."

She had no choice.

MARLA COULD FEEL her pulse throbbing wildly in her head. It felt as if her entire body was clenched, waiting for the knock on the door. Erik Carter, or whoever he really was, had ordered clothing from the hotel's men's store.

At least she'd be able to describe him to the police, right down to his shoe size. If she made it through this alive. She'd heard Erik give the clerk his exact measurements. His mistake, she thought with a flash of triumph.

Her fingers closed over the tiny square of tissue she held in her palm. Marla fervently hoped that the dampness wouldn't dissolve the message she'd written using her eyebrow pencil. It was her only hope.

When the knock came, she jumped, her eyes darting toward Erik as her heart slammed against her rib cage. His whole torso was rigid, poised for action. Something inside her began turning to room-temperature Jell-O.

He nodded at her and she asked in a quavering voice, "Who is it?"

The voice on the other side of the door answered, "Renee Russell's."

The clothier. "Showtime, Marla." Weapon at the ready, Erik motioned her to the door, then positioned himself so that he would be behind it when it opened. Just as she reached for the doorknob, he stopped her. "Oh, one more thing."

If her heart pounded any harder, she was certain it was going to break out of her chest. "What?"

32

His eyes indicated her other hand. "Give me the note in your hand," he whispered. "The one you wrote on toilet paper in the bathroom."

Her mouth went dry. "I don't—"

"Don't insult me, Marla."

"How—how did you know?"

"I've been at this for a while." With his free hand, he beckoned for the note. "Time is of the essence." A frustrated hiss escaped her lips as she surrendered the note. Quickly Erik perused the scrap of paper. "Help, I'm being held prisoner." Shredding it, he shook his head. "Really, Marla, a teacher should have done better than that. The deliveryman would have thought it was a joke. Now open the door."

Signing for the packages, Marla silently tried to convey her dilemma to the man from Renee Russell's and succeeded, she knew, only in making the clerk think she was trying to flirt with him. There was no other reason for him to point to his wedding ring with a sad smile on his face as he left.

The instant she closed the door, Erik took the packages from her and began ripping them open. "Sorry your little pantomime didn't work."

She stared at him. Was the man clairvoyant on top of everything else? "How did you—"

"One step ahead, Marla. I've always got to stay one step ahead." His mouth quirked as he dropped the towel and began getting dressed. "Besides, it helps to have a mirror on the opposite wall."

Startled by his casualness, Marla barely had time to avert her eyes before the towel hit the floor. She could feel her face burning. The burn intensified as she heard Erik laugh softly under his breath.

"Modesty. Not something I often encounter these days. Nice to know it still exists. There, you can turn around now."

She did, desperately reaching for anger and trying to cloak herself in it. It wasn't easy being angry at a man who was devastatingly handsome and looking at her with eyes that had sin written all over them.

Marla wet her lips. "Well, you've got what you wanted. Now will you please leave?"

"I fully intend to." He scooped up his old clothes and deposited them in the Renee Russell boxes, then pushed them into the closet. With luck, if the monitoring device did happen to still work, this would buy him some time. Closing the door, he looked at her. "Take whatever you think you might need."

That sinking feeling was beginning to burrow its way through her stomach again. "Why?"

Erik was already taking her hand in his. "Because you're coming with me."

CHAPTER FOUR

MARLA'S MOUTH DROPPED open. "I'm what?"

"Coming with me." Crossing to the closet, Erik pushed open the door and found what he was looking for on the floor beside her suitcase. A purse that doubled as a backpack. Unceremoniously dumping its contents on the bed, he quickly began refilling it with still-damp objects from the pockets of his wet clothing. "As in now."

"Oh, no, I'm not." She grabbed a lipstick that was about to roll off the bed, then glared at him in exasperation. "What are you doing?"

"Getting prepared."

Though his expression hadn't changed, he said the words so grimly Marla felt she was being placed on notice. Awful things were about to happen.

She grabbed his arm, her words tumbling out one after the other. "Look, you can intimidate me into giving you my charge card, because that's only money. But this is my life we're talking about and I've only got one, so no, thank you very much. I'm staying right here." Finished, she dragged in a deep breath.

He glanced into the backpack to make sure he hadn't forgotten anything. The high-priced, innocuous toys deposited inside had saved his skin more than once. Erik spared her a look that said he wasn't about to brook an argument. "It's your life I'm trying to save."

Yeah, right. Stubbornly she folded her arms. "And just how are you going to do that by taking me with you?"

"Because if I leave you here and the men who are after me find you, they'll think you're with me. More important, they'll think you know—" He broke off and shrugged. "You don't want that to happen." Quickly he stuffed her book into the backpack and caught the incredulous look on her face. "In case you want to read later."

The man was insane. In one breath he was talking about her imminent death; in the next he was packing reading matter for her. Following him to the door, she clung to the obvious. "But I don't know anything."

He paused by the door. It'd be easier to just leave her behind, but despite his years of service he still had a conscience. And he knew what his opponents were capable of. Things a woman like Marla O'Connor couldn't begin to fathom. "They won't believe you, and when they're through with you, you won't believe you."

Marla raised her chin, hoping her voice wouldn't give her away. "You're just trying to scare me."

"How am I doing?" Cracking open the door, he looked down the hall, then quickly pulled it shut again. Damn, he'd seen two of them on the far end of the floor.

Marla jumped when he grabbed her wrist and pulled her away from the door. "Congratulations, you've just succeeded in scaring me half to death."

"Just as long as I manage to keep the other half of you alive, I'll be glad." His mind racing, he came up with their only way out. He hoped she was as athletic as she looked. Erik glanced at her feet. "Maybe you'd better put on something without a heel."

"I don't own anything without a heel."

He blew out a breath. "It figures."

Marla's nerves began begetting nerves. He crossed to the sliding glass doors leading to the balcony, dragging her with him. She did not like whatever he was planning. "I thought you said we were leaving."

"We are."

"The door's that way." She used her free hand to point.

"I know." Dropping the backpack to the floor, he pushed open the glass door with one hand, still holding her with the other. "We're going out this way."

BONUS FEATURE

She saw him take something out of the backpack that looked like a small remote control. When he aimed it at the railing, a metal hook shot out and wrapped itself around the bar. Some sort of thin cord followed in its wake.

This wasn't happening. "Are you crazy? We're twelve stories up."

He was more than aware just how far they could fall. But they weren't going to. He hadn't completed what he'd been sent out to do, and he was a firm believer in living up to his commitments. It was as simple as that. "They make the balconies strong."

"But my knees are weak," she protested, even as he pushed her out onto the balcony. She eyed the gun that he'd shoved into the waistband of his slacks and wondered if she could risk trying to grab it.

But if she did, he might push her off the balcony. She had absolutely no idea what he was capable of.

Mechanically he tested the cord. He knew the line was strong enough to support two agile elephants if it came to that. "Just follow my lead. This'll be over before you know it."

"That's what I'm afraid of."

"Sideways or down?" When she looked at him in confusion, he indicated the two ways they could go—down one floor or across to the next building.

Each seemed equally inaccessible to her unless she suddenly sprouted wings. "Now you decide to be gallant." He looked at her expectantly. "Down."

38

Marla wet her lips as her stomach lurched. "I hope that's not a prophecy."

"Not today," he promised her.

She hung on to that, the promise made to her by a madman, though there was no earthly reason she should. But it helped still her trembling fingers.

He went ahead of her, shimmying down the thin line like an Olympic gold-medal winner at his event. "Now you," he called up to her.

For a second she contemplated staying right where she was. Then she heard someone try the knob on the locked door of her hotel room, followed by the sound of a large object crashing against it. Someone was trying to break in. She swung her leg over the railing.

"Maybe this is just a bad dream," she muttered under her breath. "Maybe I'll wake up in a minute."

"This is real, Marla," Erik shouted. "Hurry." He raised his hands to her. "Don't worry, I'll catch you. Just remember, don't look down."

Too late. Panic was scrambling through her with long, jagged fingernails. The line bit into her palms as she lowered herself. "Why do they always say that?"

The breeze from the ocean picked up, billowing her skirt out like a saucy red mushroom as she began her rapid descent. Just as she was afraid her strength would give out she felt his hands gliding up along her legs as he caught hold of her. A flash of heat went barreling through her like a runaway freight. It only intensified as her body slid against his. An eternity later her feet touched the balcony floor.

Her breath froze where it was.

His face inches away from hers, Erik searched it for signs that she was about to break down. He saw none. The woman was gutsier than she thought. "You all right?"

Marla swallowed, hoping she wouldn't squeak when she opened her mouth. "I will be, as soon as I catch my breath." No chance of that happening any time soon, she added silently.

He grinned at her. "You were great." The backpack was already slung over one shoulder. Erik caught hold of her hand. "Let's go."

40

"Go?" She looked around the suite as he pulled her through it, her heart sinking as she realized that there was no one here. No one to rescue her from this man claiming to be rescuing her. "Just exactly where is it we're going?" How far did he intend to drag her? "People do know I'm here. They're going to come looking for me."

Very slowly Erik cracked open the door and looked out. This time there was no one in sight. He took a chance. Hand to the small of her back, he ushered her out and to the stairwell.

"Frankly, at the moment I am less than paralyzed at the thought of a group of teachers hunting me down. And to answer your question, we are going in search of a crowd to get lost in." He smiled at her as he pulled open the stairwell door. "There's safety in numbers."

She sincerely hoped so.

THERE WERE TWO restaurants on the premises, a well-lit establishment that catered to families and a sophisticated bar that echoed of dark blue lights and enticing music. To her surprise, he chose the latter.

Signaling the hostess, he held up two fingers. A moment later the woman was leading them into the heart of the place.

"I thought you wanted a crowd to get lost in," Marla whispered.

"There are people here," he pointed out, keeping a firm hold of her hand. "And enough shadows for us not to stand out."

She tried to make out faces as they followed the hostess. Why was it that everyone had taken on a sinister cast? "So we'll be safe?"

He'd come to know that was only a relative term. "As safe as is possible."

Her stomach tightened another notch. Desperately she tried to be logical.

Marla waited until they were alone in the small booth. "You know, I only have your word for it that there's someone after you. How do I know any of this is true?"

BONUS FEATURE

He'd wondered when she'd get around to interrogating him. "For the moment, in the interests of staying alive, you're going to have to take that on faith." He knew he was asking a lot. "Besides, why would I climb down a balcony if someone wasn't after me?"

She had no answers, only questions. "I don't know. Maybe you're a frustrated Sherpa guide, or—"

The rest of her sentence was abruptly stopped. Sliding closer to her in the tiny booth than her own dress, Erik framed her face with his hands and covered her lips with his own.

She stopped breathing again.

CHAPTER FIVE

HE WAS KISSING HER.

One minute she was talking, the next he was kissing. Kissing her as if they'd been together before the first stars had ever been struck in the sky.

When dazed surprise gave way to realization, Marla had every intention of pushing him away. But it was hard to push with arms that had gone as limp as overcooked spaghetti.

To the best of her knowledge, she'd never been present at a meltdown before. She would have remembered. She was present at one now. Her own.

Erik considered himself a consummate professional. Someone who could keep his head in any given situation, even one that threatened to separate that same head from his shoulders. But for just the tiniest particle of a second he lost track of the tall, distinguished-looking dangerous men he had seen entering the restaurant and focused only on the incredible impact several inches of pliant skin was having on him.

BONUS FEATURE

It took every bit of his intense, rigorous training to distance himself from the kiss and home back in on his situation. Their situation.

Their lips finally separated, Marla waited until the raging inferno within her settled down into a manageable forest fire. It took that long for air to return to her lungs.

"What—what was that?" She was trying for indignation. She managed a squeak.

Pretty damn hot stuff, was the first answer that came into his head, but he replied, "Camouflage."

Marla stared at him, wondering when the pounding of her heart would cease breaking the sound barrier. "Excuse me?"

44

He leaned in close to her, so close that his breath was singeing her skin. "The men who broke in to your room just walked into the restaurant. I didn't want them to see my face."

"So you buried it in mine?"

"Seemed like the thing to do at the time."

She automatically began to turn around to see if she could spot the men he was talking about. The next thing she knew, Erik had her hand again and was bringing her to her feet. "Now what?"

His eyes indicated the small, discreet band playing soft music to fall in love by. "Now we dance."

This was getting stranger and stranger. "And then what? If we dance well enough, they'll go away and leave us alone?"

"No." Deftly he picked up the backpack, slipping it onto the crook of her arm. She had a feeling they weren't coming back to their table or to the food her empty stomach was anticipating. "If we dance well enough, we'll be able to make it to the kitchen before anyone notices what we're doing."

They were on the small dance floor now, mingling with several other couples. Pressing her hand to his chest, Erik slipped his other hand against the small of her back. She felt something hit her hip. Her eyes widened as a warm flush rose from her core and worked its way up to her cheeks.

It was all well and good to fantasize about being whisked away by a secret agent like the one in the book she'd bought, but this wasn't fantasy—this was real. She couldn't make up her mind if she was scared or excited. Or both. All she knew was that her heart was still beating wildly.

A languid, sexy smile slipped across his lips. He knew what she was thinking. Very slowly he moved his head from side to side. "That's your purse getting familiar with you, not me." His smile deepened. "If we get out of this alive, we can see about getting familiar without the purse."

She was still fighting off the effects of his kiss. Contact had very nearly short-circuited her brain and she still couldn't think all that clearly. "If we get out of this alive," she heard herself saying, "I'm finding the nearest policeman and having you arrested."

He smiled into her eyes, resisting the urge to kiss her again. This was not the time. But he wished like hell it was. "Whatever turns you on, Marla."

This wasn't real, not the conversation, not any of it. It couldn't be. And yet…

She found herself getting lost in wondering what turned him on, and then gave herself a mental shake. She opened her mouth to say something cool and cutting. "You dance well, but then I guess that's required of a secret agent."

Darn, she was too aware of being held in his arms to be cool and cutting.

With one eye on his destination, he began directing their steps. The less she knew, the better for both of them. Especially if the two men who were after him succeeded in catching up to them. He glanced back to see if they were watching.

They blended in well. Two suave-looking businessmen of slender build. They could have been brothers. The other side picked their operatives well, Erik thought.

"I'm not a secret agent."

She could feel his body heat. Some very erotic things were happening to her. She was on the brink of meltdown again with a man she knew nothing about except that in another life she would have been willing to spend all of hers with him. "Then what are you?"

"Just a public servant."

He had to think she was an idiot. "Public servants are sanitation engineers and councilmen, not men who play Tarzan off balconies."

He pressed his cheek against her hair. Her perfume curled through his veins, taking a shade of the sharpness from his finely honed edge. "Have it your way."

Frustration burrowed in between some very insensible thoughts that included silk sheets and naked torsos. "Don't humor me."

The phrase *adorable when mad* played across his mind as he looked at her. Up to his neck in danger, he had the sudden urge to nibble on her earlobe. "Then what?"

"Answer me. Tell me one thing that's going on."

His eyes partially closed, he slanted his gaze toward the men again. They were looking in his direction. Erik's hand tightened on hers. "Can't. Now very slowly, we're going in that direction."

She could see out of the corner of her eye. "That's the bar."

"Kitchen's just beyond," he assured her. Once there, they could make a run for it.

She still didn't see it. "How do you know that?"

He continued to steer them slowly across the floor. The inches were painful, but any faster would attract attention. "Easy. I never go into a place I don't know how to get out of."

"Spy by-rules?"

He laughed softly, sending a major shiver down her spine. "Actually, that's something Robert De Niro said in a movie once. Sounded like good advice. Now," he whispered against her ear. The next moment she felt herself being pushed urgently toward the far end of the bar, passing several people seated against it.

One looked up. And gaped. "Oh, my God, Marla, what are you doing here—wow!" The question ended in an exclamation framed in wonder.

48

Marla craned her neck and saw Barbara on the end stool. Her friend was staring at Erik with deep appreciation. Hope sprang up.

"Barbara," Marla called, trying to break free of Erik's grasp. She might as well have tried to bend bare steel in her hands. "I need help."

Barbara smiled at her in sincere envy. "Believe me, if I wasn't engaged, I wouldn't hesitate for a second." She lifted her glass in a toast. "Have a great time, you sly devil. Good for you!" she called after Marla as the latter disappeared through the swinging kitchen doors.

"Who was that?" Erik demanded.

He'd broken into a run. She had no choice but to follow. Kitchen workers and waitstaff yelled at them as they passed. "My best friend up until a second ago." Ducking her head, she narrowly avoided plowing into a waiter carrying a large tray filled wish dishes and wineglasses. "Why are we running?"

"Because your little exchange attracted the very people I was trying to avoid." He looked over his shoulder and saw two men in gray designer suits enter the kitchen. "Damn. Go, go, go!" Not waiting for her to obey the order, Erik took the lead, dragging her in his wake.

Just as they made it into the alley, something whizzed by her head. The noise repeated.

She tried to twist around to see what was going on. Erik wouldn't let her. "What the—"

"Bullets, Marla." He picked up speed. There was a car just up ahead. He had to reach it in time. "They call them bullets. In plain English, the bad guys are shooting at us. Now run, damn it, run!"

CHAPTER SIX

ERIK FELT THE HEAT as a bullet whizzed past his left ear. He silently blessed the shooters' poor aim or luck, whichever was responsible. The next moment, he saw Marla stumble and fall just a foot short of the convertible.

50

In a swift, fluid movement that was as instinctive as breathing, Erik placed his body between her and the men pursuing them. Grabbing her arm, he yanked Marla to her feet while pulling open the passenger door. Pain exploded in his shoulder, then radiated out, infiltrating all parts of him.

Surprised, he loosened his fingers on her arm, then tightened them again. With superhuman effort he tried to hold on to not only her but to consciousness, as well. Erik willed himself to breathe evenly.

The pain began to blend in with everything else. He focused on what he had to do. Get them out of there.

As he'd pushed her into the passenger's side of

the Mustang, Marla had felt Erik stagger behind her, grunting something unintelligible under his breath. It was more like a growl than real words. "What?"

He didn't answer. Erik was already on the other side, throwing himself into the driver's seat. Twisting around, she saw men running in their direction as he began doing something with the wires beneath the dashboard. Wearing suits that seemed in direct contradiction to the activity they were engaged in, the men looked as if they were fresh out of a boardroom meeting. Except for the guns in their hands. Marla had a sick feeling in the pit of her stomach.

She twisted toward Erik again. "This isn't your car, is it?"

His head was pounding and he was struggling to keep from seeing double. It complicated the procedure. "Now isn't the time to worry about legal ownership."

"We can't just steal a car."

"We're borrowing it," he corrected. Sweat was popping out on his brow, between his shoulders, creating tiny rivulets down his back. He felt cold and hot at the same time. "And the alternative isn't pretty." The car started. He would have cheered if he'd had the strength. It was all he could do to straighten up and grab the wheel. Gunfire echoed in his head as he pulled out. "Duck." It was an order.

"Duck?"

"Duck!" he repeated, pushing her head down with his right hand. "You wouldn't look good with a bullet in your forehead. Doesn't go with the outfit." Gritting his teeth against a fresh onslaught of pain, he looked in the rearview mirror. The shooters must have hot-wired a car, as well. A maroon SUV was gaining on them. "Hang on. This is going to be bumpy."

He wasn't kidding.

Fifteen minutes later, after taking more twists and turns along the hilly streets than a wayward tornado, he finally felt confident enough to slow down. "I think we lost them."

52

She wasn't going to throw up. She wasn't. Marla pressed her hand to her midsection. "Along with my stomach." Composure was something that had been lost on the first steep street. She was more angry than frightened. "Can I please go now?"

He didn't want her getting killed because he'd entered the wrong hotel room. He wasn't letting Marla out of his sight until he was sure she would be safe—like on a plane back home. He refused to consider why the thought depressed him. "Not until I'm sure the men following us have given up."

Taking on the tone she used with unruly students, Marla drew herself up. "No more games. We need to go to the police. Those people mean—"

Her eyes widened as she saw the blood on his hand and followed the path up along his sleeve. "My God, you're hurt."

He was twelve degrees past hurt and solidly entrenched in agony. His head felt vaguely hollow. "Deeply, if you keep on arguing with me."

This was serious. "I mean you're bleeding. A lot."

He kept driving, looking for a place that was safe. The streets were blurring. "Just a scratch."

He was being incredibly stubborn. "Only if you're nine foot eleven. We have to get you to a hospital."

He tried to shake his head, and found doing so threatened blacking out. "Not possible."

"But you need to have your injury taken care of."

A smile curved his mouth as he looked at her. "Marla, I'm touched."

"Obviously more than a little." Determined, she looked along the streets they were passing. At least the scenery was no longer whizzing by. "If you won't go to the emergency room, maybe we can find a drugstore."

"I can't exactly go in like this."

The car was beginning to slow down. Was he going to be sensible after all? "I was thinking of me."

"Sorry, I can't…"

She turned her head in time to see his eyes slide shut. "Oh, God." Marla grabbed the wheel. Without knowing how, she guided the Mustang to the curb without a mishap. Heart hammering, she pulled up the hand brake. "Erik?" Half-afraid, she touched his throat, feeling for his pulse. He was alive, but unconscious.

Marla let her hand drop.

It was now or never. Marla seized her opportunity.

Getting out of the car, she quickly walked halfway down the block before her footsteps slowed, then stopped. As she turned around she caught her reflection in a store window and shook her head in disbelief.

"You are an idiot, Marla O'Connor. A first-class idiot."

Frowning, she walked back to the car.

54

THE PAIN CUT THROUGH layers of anesthetizing haze, growing sharper, dragging him up to the surface. Erik started, his hand reaching to his waistband before he even opened his eyes.

"It's not there. I thought you'd be more comfortable without a gun jabbing you in the gut."

Marla. The sound of her voice comforted him like the feel of a blanket on a cold, crisp day. It almost, just for a heartbeat, made him feel safe. It was an odd sensation, given his line of work and the circumstances.

She was the kind of woman his mother would have picked out for him. He could almost hear her voice now. *You need a good woman in your life.* That was Marla. A good woman.

He needed to keep her a good, live woman.

With effort, he focused. First on Marla, then on his surroundings. He was lying on a sagging bed whose sheets hadn't been changed since the Bush administration's first term. The room was small and smelled of cheap liquor and cheaper perfume.

Propping a stiff elbow under him, he managed to sit up. "Where the hell are we?"

Sitting down on the edge of the bed, Marla tried to push him back. It wasn't as easy as she'd expected. The man had amazing stamina. Something inside her vaguely wondered if that extended to all things physical.

"In the seediest motel I could find. This way, the guy at the front desk doesn't ask questions."

A smile formed. She saw it in his eyes before it filtered to his mouth. "Smart thinking." Erik looked down at his shoulder. It still felt as if it were on fire. It was also bandaged. "Who—?"

"Me." She'd found a pharmacy in the area and bought supplies.

Very slowly he eased himself into a sitting position. The room moved only slightly. He'd been worse. "Where did you learn how to patch people up like this?"

"School yard." She liked the surprised look on his face, liked not being completely predictable to him. It was her turn to smile. "First neighborhood I taught in was pretty rough."

A more important question occurred to him. "Why didn't you run when you had the chance?"

She shrugged, swallowing the answer that came immediately. *Because I couldn't.*

"You could have abandoned me at any time, but you didn't."

Her smile softened, her fear fading. There was something about a hero… "If you hadn't stopped to help me when I fell, you wouldn't have gotten shot. I figured I owed you one. Maybe two."

Embarrassed by the way he was looking at her and feeling decidedly warmer than the room would have warranted, she nodded at his shoulder. "You were lucky. The bullet went clean through. But you did lose a lot of blood."

Erik looked out the window. It was dark. "How long have I been out?"

"Long enough for me to patch you up and get some takeout." Rising, she went to the bureau against the wall. A large white paper bag dominated the surface. "How do you feel about Chinese food?"

"We're near Chinatown?"

She nodded. "On the outskirts."

That meant she'd gotten them clear across town. Admiration lifted the corners of his mouth. "You are full of surprises, Marla O'Connor."

She was beginning to think so, too. It was a nice thing to find out about herself.

He was reaching for his shirt. Marla crossed back to him. "What are you doing?"

"I'm getting up." He was uneasy. They had to get moving. There was no telling if she'd been spotted.

Marla frowned. "You need to rest."

"I rested."

"You passed out."

"Same thing." He paused to look at her, amused. "If I didn't know any better, I'd say you cared." His eyes touched her face, lingering on her mouth. Remembering. "And I'm not so dumb. I hooked up with you, didn't I?"

She had no comeback for that. Just a very warm, unsettled feeling unfurling in the pit of her stomach. Especially when he looked at her like that.

The next minute, the feeling was pushed to the background. She heard a noise and turned toward the door of their room. To her disbelief and horror, the doorknob was being turned once again. What was it about her and hotel rooms? She knew she'd locked it after she'd returned with the Chinese takeout.

Marla glanced at Erik, who was stone-faced, and then back to the door and realized she was holding her breath.

"We know you're in there," a deep voice growled from the other side. "If you give us what we want, we won't kill you—or the girl. If you make this difficult…"

Marla did not like the significant pause.

"The girl is going to suffer. A lot."

CHAPTER SEVEN

Marla stared at Erik. The only way out was through the front door—she had checked out any possible escape routes after she'd made sure Erik would live. She was beginning to think like him. She wasn't sure if she liked that.

On the other side of the door were two men who were planning to do unspeakable things to her. She gulped. She did know that she trusted Erik. He grabbed the backpack, making certain that it was zipped shut, then motioned to Marla.

"When I nod my head," he whispered, "open the door."

She was putting her life in the hands of a crazy man. Marla could almost see Erik mentally counting to three, then he nodded his head. Terrified, she flipped the lock and yanked open the door.

Prepared to use force, the first man stumbled in, followed by the second one. Erik swung the backpack like a weapon, felling the first. Marla stuck out

BONUS FEATURE

her leg and tripped the second man, who landed on top of the first goon.

Grabbing Marla's hand, Erik pulled her out of the room and slammed the door shut in his wake. "Nice work."

She didn't know why the compliment had her glowing inside. She had to be going crazy herself. The glow continued.

The lot in front was empty. "Where's the car?"

"I parked it in the back." It had seemed like the thing to do.

He liked how she was beginning to think like him. "Perfect." They ran for the Mustang. "Marla, we'll make a recruit out of you yet."

She opened her mouth to say, "Over my dead body," then realized she really didn't mean that. It startled her to realize that as frightening as this was, it was also exhilarating. As exhilarating as the man holding her hand. Instead, she shot back, "You couldn't afford me."

Reaching the car, he jumped in. Hands on the steering wheel, he was backing out the moment her thigh hit the passenger's side. But he took a split second to look at her. "Give me a price."

Why, in the center of an explosive situation, a situation that could end in death at any moment, did she suddenly feel heat throbbing through her body because he'd given her a penetrating look?

"We'll talk," she breathed.

His smile went clear down to her bones. "Count on it."

She had a feeling he didn't have talking in mind. Marla grew hotter.

They were barreling down the street, careening from one lane to another as Erik jockeyed for distance. Marla forgot to be hot and bothered and concentrated on not falling over in her seat. "Do all spies have a death wish?"

He spared her a look, turning down a street. A glance at the signpost told him where he was. "I'm not a spy. Just a courier." That was his story and he was sticking to it. For her sake.

Right, and she was a hummingbird. Marla sighed. "Okay, whatever you are, answer the question. Do you have a death wish?"

"No more than most people." The silence in the car ate into the darkness. Maybe he owed her something more than a flippant answer, he thought. A little truth wouldn't hurt. He opened a crack into his past. "I was a history teacher."

She turned her head to look at him. She had her doubts. He wasn't like any history teacher she'd ever met. "And what—you wanted to make it, not teach it?"

Her naiveté was almost refreshing. Had he ever seen things that simply? He couldn't remember. "Something like that."

Marla looked out. Nothing looked familiar. They hadn't gone this way before. Was he driving away, or driving to? She settled in, knowing she'd find out when she found out. "So how does a history teacher learn how to scale the sides of tall buildings and hot-wire cars?"

He distanced himself from the memory. "I've been at this for a while. You pick up things."

Marla glanced in the rearview mirror, hoping not to see the police. "Like stolen cars?"

That was the least of his concerns. "It's just borrowed, remember?"

"Shouldn't we 'unborrow' it before some patrol car runs the plates and stops us?"

62

He laughed softly. "I'm impressed."

She didn't know if he was laughing at her or not. "*NYPD Blue,*" she murmured.

"We all have to get our education somewhere." Making a right, he drove into a strip mall. "All right, we'll lose the Mustang. This looks like a good place to ditch it."

They pulled up into a space. She looked out. "A McDonald's?"

He exited the car as if he hadn't a care in the world. She scrambled after him. "A lot of through traffic here. Still hungry?"

She'd had dinner twice within her grasp, only to have to flee without taking a bite. "That is an understatement. I'm starving."

"Then we'll eat." Taking her hand, he led her inside.

The place was packed. There was hardly enough room to walk unobstructed. "Crowded enough for you?" she asked.

He merely smiled in reply. They got in line and ordered, then undertook the ordeal of finding a table. Erik nodded toward one that had just been vacated. "Looks like our luck's changed."

She sincerely hoped so. Sitting down, she made short work of the paper wrapper around the hamburger. Her stomach growled as she bit into the bun. "You really know how to show a girl a good time." She hesitated, then pushed ahead. "I've got a question for you."

There was a dab of ketchup on her chin. Leaning over, he wiped it away with his thumb and felt something stir inside him. Maybe it was the way she looked at him, with large, smoky eyes filled with emotion. With a sincerity that surprised him, he wished there was time to explore that emotion. "Shoot."

For all her hunger, Marla found she was having trouble swallowing. He was looking at her that way again. It curled her toes and made her ache for a warm fireplace and a long, endless night. "Why did you stop to help me up when we were running for the car?"

Did she think he was heartless? he wondered. "I couldn't just leave you."

Marla could still feel her pulse doing tricks. You'd think she'd never had a man touch her before. But she hadn't. Not the way he did. Even wiping away ketchup felt like an erotic activity. "I thought all secret agents were taught to be hard-hearted."

He shrugged and instantly regretted it. Pain scissored through him. "I cut class that day."

"Lucky for me." She took another bite. The door opened and her eyes darted toward it. But it was only a group of teenagers. "How do you suppose they found us at the motel?"

He'd been working on that. "Either blind luck or—" It suddenly occurred to him. "How did you pay for the room?"

"With my charge card. Why?"

An easy mistake. "There's your answer. They tracked you down by the card activity."

Marla laid the hamburger down. She'd thought that happened only in the movies. "What kind of people are you up against?"

"The shrewd, intelligent, ruthless kind. People who take good things and turn them into bad. People who would make those kids in the tough neighborhood you were talking about look like Good Samaritans." He'd dealt with their kind for so long, he'd forgotten there were any other type around. It had taken her to make him remember.

Wouldn't it be nice if he could keep her around? Coming from nowhere, the thought almost succeeded in unsettling him.

She shivered. "Comforting thought."

"Wasn't meant to be." Having finished his fries, he crushed the container. "It was meant to keep you on your toes."

"For how long? I get nosebleeds easily."

"Just until morning. Once I turn the 'product' over, our friends are in a new ball game."

She wished he'd tell her more. "And that makes them harmless?"

"Not harmless, but they won't come after you." And in the past few hours, that had become important to him, he realized. Very important.

"What about you?"

There was nothing but ice chips left in his drink. He stirred them with his straw. "I knew the risks when I signed on."

She wondered about that—and about him. "Is there a Mrs. Spy somewhere? Does she know the risks?" She wondered why the answer was so important to her.

"No, there's no Mrs. Spy." Their eyes held for a long moment. "I wouldn't have kissed you like that if there was."

"Ah, an honorable spy." She'd tried to make a joke of it, but fell short of her goal.

BONUS FEATURE

"I'd try to be—if I were one." Humor entered his voice. "I thought I told you I'm not a spy." A movement caught his eye. The door was opening. Damn. The designer agents had found them. "Here we go again."

She didn't even bother to look as he grabbed her hand and pulled her up with him. Marla caught a handful of fries with her other hand and then they plowed through the crowd, making their way around the counter.

"Hey, you can't go there!" an adolescent food server protested as they hurried through the kitchen, heading for the back door.

Marla pulled herself up short, barely avoiding crashing into one of the help. Her fries flew out of her hand. She sighed in resignation. "You know, I've seen an awful lot of kitchens for someone with an almost empty stomach."

He pushed open the back door. "A full stomach won't do you any good if you're dead."

"Good point."

CHAPTER EIGHT

THEY USED THE CAR one more time, driving into the heart of Chinatown before finally abandoning the Mustang on one of the side streets. As they wove their way from one store to another, Marla noticed that revelers were everywhere. "What is all this?" she finally asked, slightly breathless.

"Chinese New Year."

There were gaily dressed people, bright lights and enough noise to deafen half a city. Marla had to lean in close just to hear what Erik had said. The fact that doing so put him as close to her as her own clothing and that it delighted her was a revelation to her.

She'd always kept both men and feelings at arm's length, afraid that reality was not nearly as satisfying as the fantasies that evolved in her mind, seeded by stories that existed between the pages of books.

But this was outmatching any fantasy she'd ever come up with. And she found herself really getting into it at moments.

BONUS FEATURE

The moments were growing longer.

Who was this man she'd been forced to throw in her lot with? Was he really on the right side, or was she being an unwitting dupe?

Looking into his eyes, she thought not. She knew at least ten people who would have called her a fool for abandoning all logical reasoning and leading with her instincts, but there it was. She was going with her gut. Or, more to the point, with her heart.

Because her heart was definitely going for a ride tonight. And she was loving it.

"Try to blend in."

His words were breathed against her face, and she was more aware of him than what he was saying. She shook her head, inclining it even closer to his mouth. She felt his breath on her temple, and goose bumps rose to attention. "What?"

Erik indicated the throng all around them. "Try to blend in," he repeated.

This was Chinatown, and they were surrounded by its citizens and the relatives of those citizens. She stood out like a red flag on a snowbank.

"In case you haven't noticed, I'm not Chinese."

He smiled at her then. A smile that went clear down to the bone and took up residence within places that, a scant fifty years ago, weren't mentioned in polite society. "Oh, I noticed, all right. I noticed a great deal about you, Marla O'Connor."

He was using her full name again, as if he was mocking her. She frowned as they continued moving with the celebrants. "I wish you'd stop saying my name that way. You make it sound like I'm some backwoods foundling who never graduated third grade."

He laughed at the interpretation. "No offense intended, Marla. I just like the sound of your name." He liked more than that. He liked the whole neat, surprising package that was Marla O'Connor. Erik slipped his arm around her shoulders, bringing her even closer to him. He could almost feel her innocence. It made him remember what this was supposed to be all about and why he'd originally dealt himself into the game. Mom, apple pie and baseball. She made him think of all those things. She also made him think of long, lazy kisses and excitement that was barely contained. The woman merited a great deal of closer examination. "Would you think I was completely crazy if I told you that in a strange way, I'm enjoying myself?"

She stared at him, trying not to notice that when she turned her head, her mouth was less than a heartbeat away from his. The crowd faded. "Getting chased out of a four-star hotel, a fleabag motel, a McDonald's, run down and shot at, yes, I have to say that 'crazy' seems to fit the situation." What was crazier was that she was enjoying it, too. "Is this a typical day for you?"

It was anything but. "No, I don't usually have guardian angels with swirling dark hair and a light touch coming to my aid. Usually I wing it alone."

A chill went through her that had nothing to do with the weather. The press of bodies made it almost warm. "That has a very lonely sound to it."

"At times," he allowed. "At others, I'm too busy to be lonely."

Marla scanned the crowd, wondering how he could seem that complacent. They were out there somewhere, those distinguished-looking men in their designer suits with their guns and their complete disregard for life. Why wasn't he more worried? Her stomach growled, reminding her that she was still hungry. "Do you think there might be something to eat around all these celebrating people?"

"Ask and you shall receive." He surprised her by producing a paper boat filled with tiny blackened chicken wings.

They'd passed a vender a second ago. Was Erik light-fingered as well as everything else? "You didn't steal that, did you?"

Even amid all this, she was a straight arrow. He found he rather liked that. It kept him grounded. He began to wonder about her, about the life she'd led before today. If there was someone special in it. And if there was room for him.

The thought had just snuck up, surprising the hell out of him. Despite the situation, he began to toy with it in earnest. "Would you refuse to eat it if I did?"

She was already biting into a wing. "No, but I'd feel guilty."

He laughed, pleased at the gusto he saw. "Don't. I took it from a vendor, but I left him more money than it cost." He'd found a five in his pocket, money he'd transferred when he'd changed. He'd forgotten about it.

Marla swallowed, her mouth curving. "I guess maybe you are honorable, at that."

Erik inclined his head. Honorable. He liked thinking of himself in those terms. Liked having her think of him in those terms.

They were still moving, carried along by the crowd. He remained alert. "Whenever it doesn't interfere with my living another day."

The wings were gone. Crushing the container, she tossed it into a basket on the corner. An uneasy question had been haunting her. "Have you killed anyone, Erik?"

Reality found him, dissolving more pleasant thoughts. The less she knew, the better for her. His face hardened. "Much to my mother's dismay, I stopped going to confession a long time ago."

Despite the roar of the crowd, she heard only his voice. "You have a mother?"

Humor returned, curving his lips. "Yes, I have a mother. Most people do at some stage of their lives."

Embarrassment dotted her cheeks. "Sorry, I just don't think of spies as having parents."

"Just springing up, full grown, like Athena out of Zeus's head, eh?"

"You know mythology."

He found her surprise amusing rather than insulting. He wondered about that. Had to be the woman. "I know lots of things that don't include bullets and car chases."

"Tell me about your parents. Are they still alive?"

This was where he should cut her off. That he didn't was another revelation. "Yes."

"Do they know? What you do, I mean?"

The smile became a little remote. "At times, I don't know what I do."

"They still think you're a history teacher, don't they?"

Yes, they did. But he didn't want to talk about himself anymore. This was far more personal than he'd been in years. "What about you?"

She took the question for what it was, a signal that they were no longer talking about him. "Well, my parents just celebrated their thirtieth anniversary last month. I've got three older sisters, all gorgeous, all married, and I still go to confession."

He smiled at that. Drawing her over to the curb, he curled a wayward strand of her hair around his finger and looked into her eyes. Carving out a small, private niche for them amid the swirling noise. "I'm curious. What is it that someone like you has to confess?"

His eyes were touching her, reducing her to a semiliquid state "Not much. I don't go that often."

He could have eaten her up right then and there. And he wished they were somewhere private so he could act on some of the feelings ambushing him. "Would you like something to confess next time? Something to keep the old padre from falling asleep?"

His mouth was so close to hers she could taste it. If she didn't say something quickly, he was going to kiss her and she wasn't sure she could handle that right now. Not without dissolving.

Marla took a step back. "Um, is there someplace around here where I, um, could…?"

He drew back, amused at her expression and somewhat taken aback at his own reaction. There had been a moment there that he'd felt like someone else. Like the person he could have been if life had gone a little differently than the way it had. "Are you trying to say you're looking for a restroom?"

Embarrassed, she nodded.

"I think we passed a Chinese restaurant the last block. You can go there."

She wanted to sit down before her knees deserted her. "Could we maybe eat there, too?"

He was acquainted with the place. The food was good. "We'll order to go."

She had a weakness for Chinese food and felt her mouth watering. "Sounds like heaven."

Holding her arm, he created the appearance that they were two tourists, out for a good time. "No, giving you something to confess sounds like heaven. Food is only a basic necessity of life."

Walking into the Red Dragon, Erik bowed to the man behind the counter. The man returned the greeting. Then, in what Marla assumed was one of the many Chinese dialects, Erik asked the owner something. The man pointed behind him.

"The restroom's past the bar," Erik told her. "Go ahead. I'll wait for you here."

She hurried toward the rear of the restaurant, marveling at the growing list of Erik's talents.

74

The ladies' room was small and neat and she was quick, pausing only long enough to fix her makeup before leaving again. Vanity, she thought with a shake of her head. But she wanted to look nice. For Erik.

The moment she opened the door, someone grabbed her from the side, covering her mouth.

CHAPTER NINE

MARLA FELT SHARP PAIN stabbing her scalp. Whoever had grabbed her had twisted her hair around their hand and was close to yanking it out by the roots, half pushing, half dragging her out through a back door of the restaurant.

The pain made her heart race. Terror encompassed her.

Releasing her hair, a man twisted her right arm behind her back, almost snapping it in half. "Well, at least we have her," he snarled to his companion.

Her captor was so average looking, she could have tripped over him and not noticed him at all. Except for his eyes. A cold, almost clear blue, they seemed to slice into her, carving her into little brittle pieces.

There were two of them. Only two. Were there others around? She couldn't focus. The pain was making her eyes well up.

"What good does that do us?" the second man asked. "We still don't have him, and he's the one with the microchip."

"We'll have him soon enough." Her captor twisted Marla around, studying her. "I don't know how you figure into this, Ms. O'Connor, but you obviously mean a lot to our fair-haired boy. I could be wrong, but I think he might even be willing to agree to a little trade just to get you back—in one piece." He laughed quietly, the sound sending salvos of panic through her. "Give us back what's ours for what's his."

His hand still covering her mouth, he began to shove her into a car that was parked in the alley. She knew her chances of getting out alive would evaporate. One look at the man's eyes told her he had no intention of trading her. She was just bait.

And Erik was the fish.

Marla bit down on the fleshy part of the man's hand, simultaneously driving her high heel into his shin.

Squealing in surprise and pain, he stumbled back, pulling his hand away. Marla spun around on her heel and shoved him into the other man. They toppled like well-dressed dominoes and she ran back into the restaurant.

When she flew past Erik, it took him less than a beat to fall in behind her. "Sorry," he called to the owner, who was emerging with their order.

In another beat, Erik was abreast, grabbing her hand. He didn't have to ask what was wrong—he knew. He silently cursed himself for not standing guard at the ladies' room door. What if something had happened to her because of him? What if they'd hurt her?

The image of Marla—hurt or dead—was like a physical blow.

It shocked him. He had always been able to detach himself, to emotionlessly see things from all angles. That was what made him a good operative.

"This way." He pointed.

His target was the long, colorful dragon, comprised of fabric, human participants and imagination, making its way down the street beneath a canopy of fireworks. Pulling Marla in before him, Erik ducked under the sparkling green-and-yellow material that was the dragon's side.

They found themselves between two confused-looking Asian men in their late thirties. A barrage of words flew at them from all directions. Marla understood nothing. Erik responded and the raised voices lowered, and stopped. The men nodded, smiled and returned to the task, moving the dragon forward.

"What did you tell them?" she asked.

"I asked for their help. I said that I'd stolen you from your husband and he was chasing us." Catching the eye of the man in front, he nodded his head. "They're nice guys."

The man in front of Marla smiled, repeating the words *nice guys*.

They were safe. For the moment. As far as she knew, the dragon was weaving its way down streets filled with revelers, but all Marla could see were feet.

She felt the press of Erik's body behind her as they moved. Heat became her companion, as well. "So how long do we hide under here?"

He was acquainted with the route. "The parade winds all the way from the financial district to the end of Chinatown. I think we'd better stay in the dragon's belly for about half an hour or so."

It sounded like a plan to her.

MARLA TRIED TO MAKE OUT the numbers on her watch. They'd dropped out of the parade after what seemed like miles. "I'm so tired, I'm going to drop where I'm standing."

They hurried through the streets. The crowds were beginning to thin out. They needed to find shelter, and soon. It wouldn't be safe to be out. His shoulder was beginning to ache again. "Please don't. I'm not in any condition to carry you."

"We could get a room someplace." She realized her words could be interpreted as a proposition, but she was too tired to care.

His sentiments exactly. "No charge cards. That's how they found us the last time."

"A hotel isn't going to let us stay out of the goodness of their hearts," she pointed out.

"Do you have any money?"

Aside from a few dollars, her pockets were empty. "No."

He saw a bank on the corner. Even at this hour, there was someone making a withdrawal at the ATM window. That was the answer. "Give me your ATM card."

Confused, she looked at him. "What ATM card? I don't have one."

"That's un-American." He blew out a breath. For the moment, he was out of ideas.

Opening her purse, she rummaged through the various items Erik had tossed in, until she found her wallet. "But I've got a Huntly's card."

The name was vaguely familiar. And then he remembered. "A supermarket card?" He laughed shortly. "I don't think you'd find those shelves all that comfortable to sleep on. Too narrow."

Excited now, her fatigue temporarily gone, she began pulling him in the direction of the supermarket. "No, but I can get money that way."

It proved easier to show him than to explain it. Once in the supermarket, she bought a six-pack of cola and a bag of doughnuts. Running her card through the scanner, she punched in her code number and then requested change. A hundred dollars.

Satisfied, she held the money up to him as they walked out. "Now we can get a room somewhere."

He kissed her, taking the money and pocketing it. "That's my girl."

It took a while for her heart to stop racing.

They got a room in the Chandler Hotel. Marla noted that they had made it full circle, back to a four-star hotel. It was after two o'clock in the morning. They had less than twelve hours to go before Erik made his delivery.

Entering, Marla made a beeline for the bed, sinking onto it. After a moment he joined her. They exhaled together, then laughed.

"I'm exhausted. I've never packed so much into one evening in my life." Turning her head to look at him, she realized suddenly how close he was. It took a second to locate her tongue. "Do you think they'll find us here?"

He was thinking that for a woman who was tired, she looked incredibly alluring. He was aware how close they were to each other. "Not with luck." They'd covered their trail pretty well, and it was time they earned a small respite. "They haven't shown up in the last hour."

She wasn't nearly as optimistic as usual. Still, there was nothing they could do right now except get some sleep. Marla propped herself up on her elbow. "I guess you should get the bed. You're wounded."

"Why can't we both get the bed?"

She caught her lower lip between her teeth. "Because—"

THE SPY WHO LOVED HER

His smile was slow, sexy and lethal as hell. She was almost on fire. "Don't trust yourself with me?"

She tried for dignity, but settled for coherence. "I wasn't thinking of me."

He reached over and touched her cheek, sliding his finger down slowly. "I make it a practice never to do anything the lady doesn't want to do." Suddenly he desperately wanted to spend the night with her in the very fullest sense of the word.

She pressed her lips together. "Shouldn't one of us stand guard?"

He laughed. "This isn't Fort Apache. Besides—" he pointed "—I rigged the doorknob."

Squinting, she looked intently at it. It looked untouched. "Where? I don't see anything."

"That's the point." He sensed her uneasiness. This wasn't the way he wanted it to be. Erik sat up. "If it makes you feel better, I'll take the sofa."

Sitting up, Marla looked at it and then at him. It was smaller than a love seat. "The only way you could sleep on that is if you were a Smurf." She debated her options. By tomorrow, he would be gone from her life. And with him the one opportunity she had to live the way the heroines lived in all the books she loved. "It's all right," she said softly. "You can share the bed with me."

"I thought you'd never ask." Because he couldn't resist, Erik took her into his arms, pressing a kiss softly to her neck. Her sigh nearly drove him over the edge. But he held himself in check.

They had until dawn together.

CHAPTER TEN

AS SHE KISSED ERIK, a feeling of panic lunged forward, elbowing sensuality aside. What if this was a huge mistake? What if she was being carried away by the moment, the danger and a man as sexy as sin? Before she'd met Erik, she'd always been levelheaded, but now she was in over her head and going down.

Erik could feel her wrestling with herself, and he drew back. His smile widened. Marla looked rather adorable and flustered. He realized she looked rather adorable no matter what the situation. "Relax, Marla. You've nothing to fear from me."

She wasn't afraid of him. It was herself she feared—feared losing her heart to a man who wouldn't remember her name by this time next week. "Oh, I don't know about that. Sexy men are a danger all their own."

He looked into her eyes and knew she wanted the same things he did. At least for tonight. Softly he caressed the curve of her cheek. "Only if they presume things."

His touch was hypnotic. It took effort to form words. They floated from her lips slowly. "What sort of things?"

He wanted to touch her. Touch her in ways no other man ever had. To make her remember him—always. "Some men presume that being slightly better looking than average entitles them to hold any woman they want." He tightened his embrace just a little. "Like this. Or kiss that woman. Like this." He pressed another kiss to her throat and felt her pulse jump. He looked at her. "Do I make you nervous, Marla?"

Very slowly, her eyes on his, she shook her head. "No, I make me nervous."

There was humor in his eyes. "Why?"

"Because." Breathe, damn it, Marla, breathe, she ordered herself.

Hopelessly lost in her eyes, Erik lowered his mouth to hers.

The kiss gained a speed all its own. Her lungs lost breath. Her body attained the consistency of over-cooked pudding, turning to liquid. Her head spun and her pulse did things that defied description within the known parameters of the AMA.

"That," she finally managed to say. "Because of that."

He combed his fingers through her hair, framing her face, bringing it closer again. "One should always make a point of facing one's fears."

"Show me," she murmured.

"I'm very good in a hands-on situation," he promised her.

"I never doubted it," she whispered before words became obsolete and her lips were otherwise occupied.

A GLIMMER OF SUNLIGHT nudged at her consciousness. Her eyes still shut, savoring the last of this euphoric half dream, Marla reached for him. The place beside her was empty.

The warm haze froze and broke apart into tiny pieces. She opened her eyes in panic to see Erik across the room, tucking his shirt into his pants. He was looking at her.

"Time to go," he said.

How long had she slept? She struggled with the fog around her brain. Erik hadn't left her, but their adventure was coming to an end. "Is it two o'clock already?"

"No, but we have to keep moving. A rolling stone attracts no bullets." Gathering up the clothes he'd slowly removed from her last night, he placed them on the bed beside her. "By my calculations, we've probably used up all the luck allotted to us."

He could have watched her sleep all night. Curled up innocently against his side, her cheek nestled on his arm. She'd made him feel things he'd forgotten he could feel. Some emotions he couldn't remember ever feeling before.

It was dangerous for a man in his line of work to feel anything at all, he reminded himself.

But feelings—his desire to defend what was good—had been what had pulled him into this world with its shades of gray in the first place. The consequences of what he sometimes had to do had meant that he'd shut down emotionally. And now, after a decade on ice, these feelings and wants were flowing back. Because of Marla.

Sitting up, she forgot about the sheet and it drooped. Marla made a grab for it, but not before his eyes claimed her. She felt herself growing warm again. What had happened in the wee hours of this morning was not something she was going to forget any time soon. "Is there time for a shower?"

The question awakened erotic thoughts. "I only wish." But he shook his head.

With the sheet arranged around her like a Roman toga, she rose, the clothes in her arms. "All right. It'll only take me a minute to get ready."

She surprised him by how fast she could get dressed. He wasn't accustomed to women who moved fast, only fast women.

They left by the back stairs, rousing Marla's conscience.

"Is it really necessary to sneak out like thieves?"

He'd sent money in a sealed envelope addressed to the management down the hotel mail chute. The room had been paid for. "Necessary and highly advisable."

She was beginning to recognize his tones. That one left no room for argument.

MINGLING WITH CROWDS of tourists and natives, they boarded the public transit. A bus to the financial district, a trolley to the outskirts of Fisherman's Wharf, the BART through the center of the city. By noon, Marla estimated they'd put in over a hundred miles in a city that spanned forty-nine.

"Are you sure you're not lost?" she finally asked him. "Maybe if we asked directions—"

"I know where I'm going," he assured her, his hand holding hers. "Always."

Her gaze met his. Did he know he was also holding her heart? "Are you sure?"

His silent debate was unexpected. And over within a second. He made up his mind. Taking a detour from his route, he brought her to the park across the street: an open area close to the Presidio.

There, away from people who might overhear, away from everything but pigeons, Erik departed from the straight and narrow line he'd followed for so long. He wanted her to know everything about him.

"I'm guarding a chemical compound that, under the right temperature, becomes self-replicating at an incredible speed. The scientist who made the discovery was killed. We've been playing tag with the compound, and at the moment I'm it."

He saw the question in her eyes and said it simply. "I have the only known quantity. Applied correctly, it can be used to produce microscopic quantum computers capable of doing calculations at a phenomenal speed. Something that currently takes years can be done in a matter of hours. Whatever country owns the secret of this compound will leap forward in all kinds of technology. In the wrong hands, this could mean global enslavement or mass destruction."

88

She grasped the ramifications of what he was saying—but not why. "Why are you telling me this?"

"Because you have a right to know. Because in that hotel room this morning you became more than just a shadow that fell across my life." The corners of his mouth rose. "I guess that sounds pretty sappy, coming from a CIA agent, doesn't it?"

Moved by his words, she turned to him, touching his face. "No, I think it sounds pretty wonderful. It makes you real."

He arched an eyebrow. "And last night I wasn't real?"

She struggled with a blush. "Realer," she corrected.

He glanced at his watch. "Time to make this 'realer' still."

Still holding her hand, Erik picked up his pace. All the while, he remained alert, watching for the men they had thus far managed to elude.

He and Marla arrived at Fort Point, just beyond the Presidio, at the foot of the Golden Gate Bridge at one forty-five precisely. The designer agents, as he'd dubbed them, arrived at one forty-six.

"Time for hide-and-seek again," he hissed against her ear, hurrying her into the building.

She tried to look behind, but Erik blocked her way. Protecting her again. "Are they—?"

He didn't have to look. "They are."

There was an elderly man standing just shy of the entrance, reading a plaque dedicated to the brave soldiers who had spent the duration of the Civil War guarding the bridge from possible seizure by the Confederates. From a distance, the man looked like an elegant Santa Claus.

Marla inclined her head to Erik. "Is that your man?"

"No, that's their man." The agent seemed to be alone. An illusion. But that was all right—their side had illusions, too. "Ours is the one over there."

She saw no one but a man in blue livery, sweeping. "The janitor?"

"Waste management engineer." He held out his hand. She had the backpack. "Give me your book."

BONUS FEATURE

"My book?" Even before she took *Mystery at Midnight* out of her purse, it hit her. No wonder he'd insisted on bringing it along. "It was in here all the time?"

He nodded. "Embedded in a paste compound inside the back flyleaf." One arm threaded through hers, he casually walked by the refuse container beside the janitor. As he passed it, he tossed the book in. The janitor didn't even bother looking in their direction. He continued sweeping, depositing his refuse in the trash can and then moving the can along with him.

If Marla hadn't known what was going on, she wouldn't have realized the agent had been waiting for a delivery.

She heard running footsteps behind her and turned to see two men—the same men who'd been chasing them—taking off after the janitor. But before she could say anything Erik had tackled one of them, and another man, whom she'd thought was a student, had a gun pointed at the second.

Marla held her breath. This was even more exciting than her suspense novels.

Erik handed his guy over to the agent and came back to her. "Is that it?" she asked.

"It is."

She let out a breath. It seemed that they were finally safe. And finished. Disappointment hovered, taking possession. "And that's it?" she repeated.

"That's it." He'd done what he'd been sent to do. Now it was someone else's turn. "Want some breakfast?"

"I want to know what happens next."

He took her arm. "I'll see if I can get them to serve that as a side order."

They sat at an outdoor café. This beautiful San Francisco afternoon was perfect for lovers to share. Marla toyed with her juice, wondering when he would get around to saying goodbye. She stalled for some time, knowing there was none left. "So now what?"

He'd been studying her quietly. And coming to terms with things. "That depends on you."

"On me? How?"

He didn't answer directly. Instead, he asked, "Is it everything you thought it was cracked up to be? Those spy adventures you like to read. Is living one as exciting as you thought?"

Her eyes met his. "More." And she meant it. Both as a response and a request. She wanted more. Wanted to experience more. Most of all, she wanted more of him in her life. "Where do I sign up?"

"Sign up?" he echoed with confusion.

"Yes. You signed up—I want to do the same. Where do I do it?"

He considered the idea of her as an operative. No one would ever suspect. Then his protective nature kicked it. "It isn't that simple."

"I don't mind complicated." She reached over and touched his hand. What she'd meant to say was written in her eyes.

He began to smile. Just a little. "I could help you train."

"I was hoping you might."

She was, as his grandfather liked to say, a pistol. And he wanted to be the only one handling the firing pin. "First step is to take you home to meet my mother."

"Your mother?" Marla blinked. "She's with the CIA?"

"No, she's with me." His mouth softened. "The way I'd like you to be."

92

She knew what he was saying without needing all the words. "So this would be a package deal." He wasn't walking away—he was staying. Her heart felt like singing. "The CIA and you."

His smile grew wider. "In a way." He wanted her with him. Always. The other part they'd work out.

"I've always liked packages."

"Me, too. I like opening them. Slowly."

He was making her warm again. Very warm. She pushed the juice aside and leaned closer. There was no one to hear them. "If I join up, do I get my own gun?"

"Only if you don't use it on me."

Her eyes were smiling. "I've got other things I want to use on you."

He rose, taking her hand in his. "No time like the present to get started."

Marla O'Connor, the girl who had wanted adventure, had found it, and she couldn't have agreed with Erik more.

Originally published as an online read at www.eHarlequin.com.

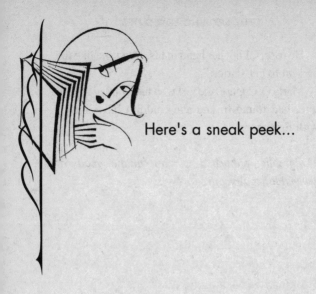

Here's a sneak peek...

Husbands and
Other Strangers
by
Marie Ferrarella

CHAPTER ONE

His hands were gentle, so incredibly gentle. They passed over her body slowly, like a warm spring breeze. The hands of a lover. Caressing her. Stroking her. Making her yearn.

She knew, instinctively knew without explanation, that they were powerful hands. Hands that could just as easily have snapped a neck in two if unrestrained anger had flashed through his veins.

Which made it all the more wondrous that he could touch her this way. As if he were worshiping her. As if he were making love to her with just his hands, just his fingertips.

He *was* making love to her.

A moan slipped from her lips, as if the pleasure that filled her was just too much to contain, to keep captive within the vessel of her body. It overflowed from every pore.

Drenching her.

Drenching him.

And then his hands were no longer there, no longer blazing a trail along her skin. His lips were there instead, anointing her body. She could feel herself trembling as his mouth ever so lightly skimmed along her flesh, following the same path that his fingers had traced just a moment ago.

A century ago, when time began.

She couldn't see him.

Why couldn't she see him? Why, when every fiber of her being felt him, knew him, wanted him, couldn't she see his face?

But no matter how she tried, how she turned, she couldn't see him. His identity remained hidden from her view.

Her eyes opened, but she couldn't see. She could only feel, could only sense him. It was as if something inside her prevented her from seeing him.

He wasn't a stranger. How could he be? She knew who he was, at least in her soul. Somehow she had always known, deep within the secret recesses of her mind, that he would be coming for her. Coming *to* her. Whoever he was, he was her soul mate, her intended, the one she had always been destined for since the very moment that destiny began.

Destined to love until the last grain of the sands of time blew away into the dark abyss of eternity.

So why, if her soul knew him so well, couldn't she see him?

Gayle Conway strained, trying to turn her head, aching for a chance to get a better view. Any view. Aching to see.

But something held her back. Restrained her movement. A weight, a heavy weight, was pressing down on her. And exhaustion consumed her; she couldn't breathe. Still, with the last ounce of strength left within her, she struggled against the iron bands on her arms.

A sense of overwhelming loss edged out the pleasure within her, like a blot of ink absorbing every square inch of the bright, colorful material it had been spilled on, obliterating it.

He was gone.

Gone as if he were nothing more than smoke. As if he hadn't existed at all. But she knew he had. He had been as real as she. But now he was gone and only she was left. Left alone, shackled to a hard bed of loneliness.

The moan that came from her lips this time was devoid of pleasure. It was a keening sound, a noise filled with the sorrow of bereavement and loss.

And then something else cut into it. Another sound, another voice.

Something…someone…

Someone was calling to her. Calling her name. Calling her from this oppressive, weighted darkness she was lost in.

The heaviness began to lift. There were hands on her again. But this time they were not gentle hands. Rough hands, trying to snatch at her consciousness. Trying to bring her back around. She could feel hands rubbing her arms, her legs, coaxing the color, the strength back into them. Back into her.

98

Gayle tried to listen, to hear. To recognize.

But the voice calling her name belonged to someone she didn't know.

A stranger's voice.

"Gayle, please wake up. Honey, please, just open your eyes. Just look at me. Please."

Fingers. Gentle fingers, not running along her body but lacing her fingers with them. More words.

Supplications? Prayers?

Gayle opened her eyes again. She *had* to find who had been loving her. Had to find the man who had so abruptly left her side.

The man she couldn't see.

Slowly, mercifully, she could feel herself rising from the depths, the almost life-threatening heaviness leaving her. A moment longer and it would be all right. She would be out of this lonely, stark world and reunited with the man whose passion had set her on fire.

Already she could feel her body warming again. Warming, as if touched by sunlight.

Sunlight.

It was the sun she felt on her face. On her body. The sun. Nothing more, just the sun.

The realization underlined the emptiness in her soul.

Something moist slid from her lashes and slithered in a zigzag pattern along both cheeks. Gayle opened her eyes and looked up at the concerned ring of faces that were hovering over her.

It took her a moment before she could focus on them. Sam. Jake. The emptiness within her shifted a little as she recognized the familiar faces of her two older brothers.

And then she saw someone else. A man who claimed to be her husband.

BONUS FEATURE

...NOT THE END...

Look for the continuation of this story in Husbands and Other Strangers *by Marie Ferrarella, available in February 2006 from Special Edition.*

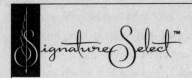

A breathtaking novel of
reunion and romance…

THE
F RTUNES
OF TEXAS:™
Reunion

Once a Rebel

by Sheri WhiteFeather

Returning home to Red Rock after many
years, psychologist Susan Fortune is reunited
with Ethan Eldridge, a man she hasn't gotten
over in seventeen years. When tragedy and grief
overtake the family, Susan leans on Ethan to
overcome her feelings—and soon realizes that
her life can't be complete without him.

Coming in February

Silhouette®
Where love comes alive™

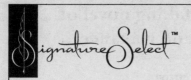

COMING NEXT MONTH

Signature Select Spotlight
THE PLEASURE TRIP by Joanne Rock
Working as a seamstress on a cruise ship called the *Venus*, Rita Frazer hasn't been feeling very goddesslike lately. But when the ship hosts a fashion show, Rita figures she has a chance at being a designer until she finds *herself* on the runway, instead of her designs. But Rita's found her muse....

Signature Select Collection
AND THE ENVELOPE, PLEASE...
by Barbara Bretton, Emilie Rose, Isabel Sharpe
Three couples find romance on the red carpet at the glamorous Reel New York Awards—where the A-list rules and passion and egos collide!

Signature Select Saga
DEAD WRONG by Janice Kay Johnson
Six years ago, prosecutor Will Patton's girlfriend stormed out on him. That night, she was brutally raped and murdered. Wrapped up in his own guilt and anger, Will developed a powerful thirst for justice...and was determined that no criminal would ever walk free again. Now he's returned to his hometown, but his return is greeted by a gruesome discovery. In order to track down this serial killer, Will teams up with detective Trina Giallombardo, only to realize that if he falls for her, she'll be next....

Signature Select Miniseries
FIREFLY GLEN by Kathleen O'Brien
Featuring the first two novels in her acclaimed miniseries *Four Seasons in Firefly Glen*. Two couples, each trying to avoid romance, find exactly that in this small peaceful town in the Adirondacks.

The Fortunes of Texas: Reunion Book #9
ONCE A REBEL by Sheri WhiteFeather
Returning home to Red Rock after many years, psychologist Susan Fortune is reunited with Ethan Eldridge, a man she hasn't gotten over in seventeen years. When tragedy and grief overtake the family, Susan leans on Ethan to overcome her feelings—and soon realizes that her life can't be complete without him.

SIGCNM0106